MAN ON FIRE ☀

Books by the same author

MARSHAL NEY: A DUAL LIFE

ALEXANDRIANA

SHOUT FREEDOM! (*an outdoor drama*)

BOLD GALILEAN

WILLIAM HENRY BELK:
  MERCHANT OF THE SOUTH

A TEAR FOR JUDAS

MIRACLE IN THE HILLS
  (*with Mary Martin Sloop, M.D.*)

VOICE IN THE WILDERNESS (*an outdoor drama*)

JAMES W. DAVIS: NORTH CAROLINA SURGEON

THE CROWN TREE

YES, MA'AM, MISS GEE (*with Mary Wilson Gee*)

GIFT FROM THE HILLS (*with Lucy Morgan*)

CALL DOWN THE STORM

THOMAS WOLFE AND HIS FAMILY
  (*with Mabel Wolfe Wheaton*)

HEAR ME, PILATE!

HORNETS' NEST: THE STORY OF
  CHARLOTTE AND MECKLENBURG COUNTY
  (*with Charles R. Brockmann*)

ECHO IN MY SOUL (*with Septima P. Clark*)

MOUNTAIN DOCTOR

MAN ON FIRE

✝

MAN
ON
FIRE

A novel of the life of St. Paul by
LeGETTE BLYTHE

FUNK & WAGNALLS COMPANY, INC.
NEW YORK

Another to Esther ✸

Author's note

Among world figures of all time the Apostle Paul usually is listed second in importance only to Jesus of Nazareth. Surely Paul was the architect of the formal structure of the Christian Church and the pioneer in formulating the doctrines and ethical implications of the gospel of Jesus.

In this novel I have sought to avoid doing violence to the known facts of his life and teachings. I maintain that no historical novel should bend history to accommodate fiction. Some readers may feel that I have violated this principle in showing Paul a widower and father. Many Pauline scholars, however, point to Paul's membership on the Sanhedrin (according to Jewish law a man had to be a husband and father to sit on that highest court) and insist logically that in his early career as rabbi in Tarsus, Paul had lost by death both wife and child.

The characters in this novel are in three categories: the historical, including such persons as the four emperors of that period and their wives, Pontius Pilate, Legate Vitellius, Proconsul Petronius, Paul, the Apostle Peter, Luke, Timothy, the various Herods; the legendary, notably Claudia and Longinus; and the fabricated. The legendary and the invented find their places among the historical characters; never do the real people of the novel yield position in character or chronology to the invented persons and situations.

To sharpen the reader's feeling of living in that significant era, of participating in the action of the story, I have spelled certain place names as they were anciently spelled, among them Capreae rather than Capri, Salernum instead of Salerno, Italia for Italy. Inconsistently, but thinking it might aid the reader, I have used Rome, Gaul, Spain, and several other modern place names rather than the Latin equivalents of Paul's time. The tribal Yahweh of the Chosen People, rather than the Christian Jehovah, likewise seems to me not only to express more nearly correctly ancient Israel's feeling of her special relationship to God but also serves to help set the reader down among those amazing characters in that tremendous period twenty centuries ago.

LeG. B.

TARSUS

Rabbi Saul stood on a hillside above Tarsus and looked south-ward toward the Great Sea. On other days from this spot he had seen the glint of sunlight on swelling sails as grain ships from Alexandria or swift Roman triremes turned to enter the mouth of the Cydnus River for their ascent to the broad bay, which had been dredged from the sweltering swamplands to provide Tarsus a protected inland harbor.

But now the ships and the sea itself, even the last miles of the river, sluggish and yellow-muddy in its slow crossing of the coastal plain, were shrouded by an early morning fog that clung to the great city's jumble of flat-roofed houses squatting like listless waterfowl drowsing on both sides of the Cydnus. The nearer channel of the river he could trace clearly, even though his ordinarily weak eyes had been weakened further by a siege of fevers that had taken off his wife and their young son. Along this channel the cold waters of the Cydnus came surging down from the Cilician Gates pass in the towering, snow-capped Taurus mountains behind him to race through the city and dissipate their force in the impounded lagoon from which they drained torpidly through miasmal warm marshes and sandbars into the Great Sea.

Saul could even distinguish vessels tied up at the river docks below, for though the larger ships ventured no farther than the bay, light galleys and narrow freight barges pushed upward into the heart of the city. It was down there in the river's channel that Queen Cleopatra of Egypt three-quarters of a century ago had received Mark Antony. As a child Saul had been shown the place in the river at which the Egyptian had anchored her gaily caparisoned galley. The elder citizen of Tarsus who pointed it out to him had been in the press of Tarsians flocking to the water's edge the day of the vessel's arrival. Antony had sent a message to Cleopatra ordering her to come to Tarsus for trial before him. He contended that she had aided with money and soldiers Antony's rival, Gaius Cassius.

The queen had indeed come to Tarsus. She had floated majestically up the river in an ornate barge with gilded stern, propelled by purple sails and uniformed sailors rowing with silver oars to the rhythm of flutes and harps. Cleopatra herself, seductively attired in gossamer silks—so the old man had told the boy Saul—was reclining beneath a cloth of gold canopy while her maids, dressed as sea nymphs, stirred the humid, warm air above her couch with feathered fans.

Antony, seated pompously on a throne set up in the city's principal square, was awaiting her. But the queen had not gone to him. Instead, she had invited him to come to her, and with his retinue he had followed the curious multitude to the riverside. With Oriental hospitality she had welcomed them aboard; quickly Antony succumbed to her charms and soon to marriage with her and death in her arms.

But Rabbi Saul had heard other stories of the famous Roman general. Often, when in reminiscent mood, Saul's grandfather, his father's father, had recounted to the youthful Saul and his sister, two years older, his recollections of visits Mark Antony had made to the mansion, on Esquiline Hill in Rome, of his master, a senator of the illustrious Aemilian clan. Antony had died, of his own dagger thrust, when Saul's grandfather was a young man, years before he had left Rome to settle in the ancestral home at Gischala in northern Galilee; and Saul's grandfather had died while Saul was studying in Jerusalem as a pupil of Rabban Gamaliel.

His grandfather's recounting of those years in Rome had aroused in the young Saul an intense longing, an impelling determination, to visit the great capital of the vast pagan empire that held sway over far-stretching lands and countless peoples. He wanted to see for himself its palatial residences and public edifices, which, his grandfather had declared, were unrivaled by anything in all Jerusalem except the Temple and perhaps old Herod's sprawling palace; he wished to walk its narrow, crowded ways, to stroll through the fabled Forum and its basilicas, and, despite his strict upbringing in the doctrines and ceremonies of the Pharisees, to venture into the temples of the pagan deities. Sometimes he even dared to wonder what it would be like to sit high in the stands of the Circus Maximus and watch the chariot races and, Yahweh forgive, join the screaming mobs of blood-crazed spectators looking down upon gladiators killing one another on the sanded floor of the arena. Someday, the determination held firm in him through his growing years, he would see Imperial Rome.

But this morning, as he gazed southward across fog-shrouded Tarsus toward the Great Sea, his thoughts were not of Rome and the regions of the west; his musings now were of a land eastward across the stretch of blue waters and another city upon hills, the ancient and troubled home of his forefathers, Israel and her wall-encircled stronghold of the Chosen, Jerusalem.

Tied up at one of the wharfs alongside the harbor at Tarsus, the Egyptian grain ship *Memphis* was taking on a cargo of merchandise for delivery at the various port cities along the eastern rim of the Great Sea. A week ago she had come in from Rome after having delivered to the port of Ostia a great quantity of grain and other foodstuffs from Egypt and textiles and products in glass from the manufactories near Tyre in Phoenicia. The bales and boxes consigned for Tarsus had been unloaded, and today the vessel would complete the loading of Tarsian goods for shipment to Antioch and other eastern sea-ports. Early tomorrow the *Memphis* would sail down the Cydnus River and set its great sails for Antioch's port city of Seleucia.

Rabbi Saul, unless something should develop suddenly to thwart his plans, would be aboard. Already he had obtained passage as far as the Palestinian port of Joppa. From there he would journey eastward to Jerusalem.

Ever since his return from the years of study in Jerusalem at the feet of the beloved Gamaliel, grandson of the revered Rabban Hillel, Saul had been looking hopefully to the time that he would go back to the ancient capital to live out his allotted days in the shadow of the glorious Temple of the Most High God of Israel among his fellow elect of God's Chosen. He was indeed a native of Tarsus, born within a Sabbath Day's journey of the Cydnus, and proud of his city as one of the world's great centers of culture and learning, a metropolis whose philosophers and scholars and teachers yielded nothing of fame and reputation to those of Rome and Athens and Alexandria and Antioch. Saul was a citizen of Tarsus, he would proclaim without reservation to any who might question him, and Tarsus was no mean city.

But Tarsus was pagan. Though the Jews had been settled at Tarsus two centuries before in a reconstruction of the city by Antiochus Epiphanes and were now a considerable colony, they remained an island in a sea of idolatry. In all the years of their living in the Cilician capital they had neither amalgamated their blood with the other peoples nor sought to spread their one-god religion among them. Those Tarsians who professed to have any gods shared many. Their religion was an admixture of the legends and philosophies and beliefs of the various races and nationalities that populated the great cosmopolitan city. And Saul, who had listened eagerly to the lectures of the savants at the university, though his loyalty to the God of his fathers was never in jeopardy, perhaps had a clearer comprehension of these idolatries than most of those Tarsians who outwardly at least embraced them. Saul recognized that in this amalgamation of pagan beliefs and practices some elements of Divine truth and goodness had survived. But in them, too, he reasoned that there had been a proportion of evil inherent from their beginnings; and in their mixings, with the conglomerating of the population itself, Saul traced a steady degeneration until little remained but abomination. And it sickened him. He had been longing to escape from this putrescent atmosphere surrounding the worship of Baal-Tarz, Lord of Tarsus, and the other pagan deities, into the uplifting, pure, and ennobling fellowship of those who worshiped the one and only God, Yahweh of the Hebrews. He had been longing for this with greater urgency even than he had longed to flee the miasmal humid marshes of the Tarsus region to the haven of the bracing thinner atmosphere of Jerusalem's hills.

Family responsibilities, however, had held Saul at Tarsus. During much of their married life his wife had been ailing, and she was reluctant to face the long sea voyage to Palestine or the even more hazardous journey by land around the northeastern segment of the coast and the stretch southward from Antioch. His mother also had importuned him to remain in Tarsus.

But now his family was gone, taken from him by the chills and fevers borne to them, he was convinced, by the vapors arising out of the lowlands of this narrow strip of Cilicia between the sea and the upthrust mighty range of the Taurus. Nor was his mother alive now to protest his plans; she had died a few months before his wife and son. Only Saul's father remained of his near relatives; Saul's sister, the only other child in the family, already was living in Jerusalem. And his father, though he was entering his elderly years, was still determined and able to earn his living as a weaver of cloth from goats' hair, an occupation he had taught his son even though he was confident that Saul was destined to wear the mantle and the prayer-shawl of the scholar and rabbi. He would not be content to leave his home at Tarsus to find a new life even within the sacred walls of Jerusalem; he had lived all his adult days in the Cilician capital and his friends were there, both those of the fellowship of the synagogue and of the Gentile population who professed faith in the pagan gods and goddesses or ignored them. Saul's father had lived continuously at Tarsus for almost four decades, since his flight with his father to Cilicia from Galilee during the frightful turmoil of insurrection following the death of King Herod.

In the period since the entombment of his lost beloved ones Rabbi Saul had spent the most of many a long night prone on his face on the cold stones of his bedchamber floor in earnest searching through prayer and in travail of soul for assurance of the Most High's direction of the remaining years or days of his life. Out of this prayer and communion and much thought, there had been coming to him, clearer and clearer and with mounting emphasis, the conviction that it was the will of the God of Israel that he should journey to Jerusalem and there, among the elect and faithful of His Own choosing, establish himself in a new life of praise and service of the one true God in the precincts of His holy Temple. And then as though in confirmation of his conviction had come to him the message from Jerusalem that he had been named to membership in the great Sanhedrin as one of the representatives of the Jews of the Dispersion.

So with the arrival at Tarsus of the returning *Memphis* he had acted upon this newly buttressed conviction and purchased passage to Joppa.

Now as he gazed over the rooftops toward the fog-hidden Great Sea that shortly he would be venturing upon, a patch of warming sunlight burst through a rift in the murk, so that he blinked his fever-weakened eyes. And was not the breaking through of the sunshine, coming at the moment of his reviewing his searching and his decision, a further sign of Divine approval of the course he had set for himself?

Quickly, Rabbi Saul faced about, away from the sun's rays that pricked at his eyeballs. Solemnly he regarded the great rounded wheel of the stone two paces in front of him, oblivious of the sunshine warm on his back. Tears welled in his eyes and, unrestrained, rolled down his wan face.

The time was come now. Resolutely, Saul of Tarsus turned his back upon the stone that sealed away in the hillside tomb chiseled from eternal rock the bodies of his mother, his wife, and his child. Then, lifting his robe to the calves of his bowed but well-muscled legs, he began to pick his way down the slope along the pathway by which he had climbed.

2

Leaning over the port rail, Saul studied on the boiling waters off the stern the great square sail's shadow that pursued relentlessly the *Memphis*, escaping now into the Great Sea from the muddied yellow waters clearing at the spread mouth of the River Cydnus.

Behind him the sunshine was pleasant on his shoulders. Already it had lifted the early morning fog from the river's channel and the swamplands and harbor and city above it, and now it danced and glinted from the walls and rooftops of Tarsus and the gaunt rocks of the slope beyond.

Saul raised his eyes from the sail's shadow doggedly racing the vessel but never coming even with it, and, squinting, he sought to focus them upon a point on that distant hillside toward which in recent months he had often gazed disconsolately from his bedchamber window. Yesterday he had stood at that spot and peered southward above the city toward the fog-obscured blue water over which now the *Memphis* was beginning the turn to set its course eastward. Soon the grain ship would be passing sand dunes that would obliterate the view of Tarsus and the hills beyond the city, and Saul wondered if ever again he would see even from a distance such as this the tomb of his beloved ones. In all probability he would continue many years to reside at Jerusalem; his duties as a member of the Sanhedrin would be demanding. And though he still hoped some day to visit Rome and Athens and other great centers of Western culture and commerce, he reasoned that even if he should be able to make such a journey, he would likely sail

from one of the Palestinian ports that would take him westward
by a more direct route south of Cyprus, so that Tarsus and the
coasts of Cilicia would be far to the northward.

But what can anyone accomplish by visiting the last resting
place of his dearest ones? How much better, reasoned Saul,
to look ahead in faith to that glad day of reunion in the after-
life of God's redeemed ones. Saul in humility thanked the God
of Israel that he was a Pharisee and the son of Pharisees and
possessed of the Pharisees' belief in life after death, in the
immortality of the soul. Humbly he thanked his God that he
was not a Sadducee without hope of seeing again in joyous
reunion his beloved ones gone ahead. So of what moment was
it if indeed he should never come this way again?

The *Memphis* was taking sail; the sand dunes appeared to
be slipping silently westward to obscure Tarsus and the hills
beyond the flat of the metropolis itself. But in the far distance
behind the lost hills, the majestic range of the Taurus, thrusting
its snow-crowned peaks into the clouds, was still visible above
the crouching dunes.

Once again Saul lowered his eyes to watch the jouncing
shadow of the ship's sail sweeping the churning waters in the
vessel's wake. In that instant two elongated narrow shadows
fell across the rail beside him and plunged downward and
across the surface of the sea to thrust themselves into a sudden
merging with the shadow of the great square sail.

Saul turned about quickly. Two uniformed Roman soldiers
were crossing the deck toward him.

"Peace be with you, tribunes." He bowed.

"With you be peace," the soldiers said, almost in unison, as
they lifted their hands in quick salute.

"Sirs, I perceive that you are acquainted with the Hebrews'
manner of response to greeting." Saul's smile was warm, his
tone cordial. "Have you spent some time—a tour of duty perhaps—in Palestine? And would you be returning there after a
leave in Rome?"

"And you appear to be acquainted with the Roman military,"
one of the soldiers observed pleasantly. "You knew our rank,

and that we customarily serve tours of duty and sometimes"—
his smile was wry—"are given leaves home. Yes, both of us
have had considerable experience in Palestine. We were called
to Rome to receive instructions, and now we are returning for
further duty at Caesarea. Would you too be journeying to
Palestine?"

"I am, for Joppa and then Jerusalem. I am called Saul. I
come from Tarsus." He looked inquiringly at the soldier who
had been speaking.

The tribune with a quick motion of his head indicated his
companion. "He is Longinus, Tribune Lucius Cassius Longinus," he said. "I'm Paulus, Lucius Aemilius Paulus. We both
live in Rome."

"Paulus!" Saul's amazement was evident. "Lucius Aemilius
Paulus! That is my father's name. And mine's little different—
Julius Aemilius Paulus. You are the first of the Aemilian clan
I have ever met, tribune." With blinking eyes he studied the
Roman.

Tribune Paulus showed his astonishment. "But aren't you
a—a Jew?"

Saul smiled. "Yes, of an ancient house of Israel unmixed
with Gentile blood. But likewise of the house of Aemilius for
the last century, and proud of that also. And a Roman citizen,
too." He pointed with thumb and closed fist. "Let's sit on the
bench. It's more comfortable." Suddenly, his countenance was
questioning. "If you care to hear about it, and have the time."

The Romans nodded; the three sat down. "Almost a hundred
years ago your General Pompey made conquest of our land and
carried back to Rome (I'm speaking of the land of Israel, of
course) a host of captives, many of whom were sold into
slavery. One of these was my sixteen-year-old great-grandfather.
He was bought by a descendant of the General Paulus who
died about two hundred years ago——"

"Lucius Aemilius Paulus Macedonicus, who was given the
last cognomen after he conquered Macedonia."

"Yes, I believe my grandfather told me that. He related to
us many stories of the years in Rome. My great-grandfather

married an Israelite girl who, with her family, was also among those carried off by Pompey, and soon after their marriage his owner, Senator Aemilius, gave him his freedom. When their son was born, who would be my grandfather, his father out of gratitude named him for the senator, so that his Roman name was Julius Aemilius Paulus. Of course he likewise had a Jewish name. And my father, in accordance with Roman custom, named me for his father.

"But my grandfather and father had come back to my great-grandfather's original home in northern Galilee, and a few years before I was born were forced to flee from there to Tarsus, where I was born. After they left Rome, little mention was made of their Roman names, or mine. At Tarsus and in Jerusalem, where several years ago I studied under one of the great teachers in Israel, I am known only as Saul. But I am likewise Paulus"—his eyes held steady as he looked from one soldier to the other—"and proud that I am a citizen of Rome!"

Tribune Paulus turned sideways on the bench to clap a hand on the Israelite's shoulder. "Indeed, Aemilius Paulus, it's good thus to come upon an unheralded eastern cousin! Tribune, we should urge him to stop for a visit with us at Caesarea." He had twisted about to face his Roman friend, but now he turned back to confront Saul. "Must you continue on to Joppa?"

"I am most anxious to get to Jerusalem before the beginning of the Passover. And from Joppa it is nearer to Jerusalem than it is from Caesarea. I fear that if I were to leave the vessel at Caesarea your hospitality would be so delightful that I would be late in reaching Jerusalem."

"But shortly after our arrival at Caesarea we'll be leaving for Jerusalem. The procurator sends a large detachment of the legionaries to Jerusalem every Passover. You can go with us."

"Your invitation tempts me, tribune. I've been wondering how I would get from Joppa to Jerusalem and whether I would have to journey on foot."

"Then you'll leave the *Memphis* at Caesarea with us, and from there accompany us to Jerusalem, which we should reach several days before the beginning of the Passover season." He eyed the bulging great sail above them. "If this breeze keeps up we should reach Seleucia before sunset. And if the stopovers at Antioch and Tyre aren't too long, we'll likely sail into the harbor at Caesarea in another four or five days."

Tribune Longinus shrugged. "I'll be glad when we get there."

"Even though you'll be back in Palestine?" Tribune Paulus laughed. "Forgive me," he said to Saul, "I meant no offense. But most Roman military men, officers and legionaries, consider it a dreary assignment. What I think, though, makes no difference; I've been reassigned to Caesarea."

"But as commander of the post there," Longinus interjected. "He was promoted while on leave at Rome."

"So was he," said Paulus. "We were centurions when we left for Rome."

"Then your only superior at Caesarea will be the procurator himself?" Saul asked.

"You really are familiar with the Roman military system." Paulus left Saul's question unanswered. "Are you, by any chance, acquainted with the Procurator Pilate?"

"No, I had completed my studies in Jerusalem and had returned to Tarsus before he was sent out to rule Judaea. I saw him only once, during the Passover season three years ago. He and his retinue were entering the Fortress Antonia. It was from a considerable distance, too. I was on my way up to the Temple."

"Three years ago?" For an instant Paulus' forehead crinkled. "Then you must have been in the throng at the Praetorium when the Galilean carpenter was tried before Pilate and sent to the cross?"

"The Galilean carpenter?" Saul was puzzled.

"Yes, the Messiah of the Jews, the son of your Yahweh, the One looked for——"

"The Messiah of Israel! Crucified!"

"Yes, tried before Pilate at the insistence of the high priest Caiaphas and the Temple leadership and crucified on the Hill of the Skull. And you heard nothing of it?"

"Nothing." Saul shook his head. "When was this man crucified? I left Jerusalem early in the morning of the day following the Sabbath."

"The day before the Jewish Sabbath. The trial and crucifixion provoked much excitement in Jerusalem. The man was widely known throughout Judaea and Galilee. It's strange you heard nothing of it."

"A carpenter, you say? What was his name?"

"A carpenter and a teacher of the Jewish law, a learned rabbi," Tribune Longinus spoke up. "His name was Jesus." He had been following the dialogue of the other two intently. "He came from a small place in Galilee called Nazareth."

"I know the place," Saul said. "It's not far from the locality in which my father's people lived. But I don't recall hearing about such a man. He isn't the first pretended Messiah, of course. Through the years since Rome first conquered us we've had, one after another, a number of half-mad fanatics declare themselves the Messiah of Israel and attempt insurrections against Rome. Like this one you speak of, they too have ended up by being killed in battle or on a Roman cross."

"But this one did not end up on a Roman cross. The morning you left Jerusalem he came to life. He walked out of the tomb in which he had been sealed away."

"But, tribune, your friend here said the man was crucified," Saul protested. "If later he walked from his tomb, then he could not have been dead when they took him down from the cross. He must have been in a coma from which he regained consciousness and was rescued."

Longinus shook his head. "No, he was not rescued. He came forth alone and without help. Nor was he taken down from the cross before he was dead." Calmly he looked Saul in the eyes. "He called himself back to life."

Saul looked from Longinus to Paulus and then again toward Longinus, his amazement evident. "Surely, tribune, you are not speaking seriously. Surely you must know that no person actually dead has ever returned to life."

"I was never more serious." The flicker of a smile crossed

Longinus' face. "I know the man was dead. I know that the
third day after he was placed in the tomb, and its mouth sealed,
the tomb was empty, and that no one entered it to bring him
out."

"But how, tribune, do you *know* that he was dead? How do
you know that if he *was* dead, his body was not stolen from
the tomb?" Intently the rabbi from Tarsus studied the face of
the Roman officer.

Longinus was not perturbed. "I know he was dead," he said
calmly, "because I commanded the quaternion that crucified
him. *I* killed him. To put an end to his agony, I drove the
point of my spear deep into his side underneath his heart. I
saw him put into the tomb, dead. And I was charged with
guarding the tomb the morning he arose. My men were stationed about it. No person could have got to the tomb without
being discovered. One moment I was looking at the sealed
tomb's mouth; in the next instant the heavy stone had been
rolled up its trough. And when a moment later I searched the
tomb, the body was gone. Nobody, I repeat"—he looked Saul
full in the eyes—"had ventured to approach that tomb. Nobody!"

"It's an amazing story, tribune—all the more amazing because a Roman officer would give credence to it. There must
be, of course, some simple explanation for the disappearance
of the body." The hint of a smile softened Saul's expression.
"What became of this Galilean after he arose from the dead?
And did you yourself see him?"

"No, Saul, I never saw him alive after he was crucified. But
many others in Jerusalem and even in Galilee have testified to
seeing him and hearing him speak. You will doubtless hear
much of him when you reach Jerusalem. Very likely his fellowship has grown to number many hundreds, perhaps thousands,
who do not doubt that as Israel's Messiah he actually did rise
from the dead. It is strange that no report of him has carried
to Tarsus."

"Had the report of such a pretender reached Cilicia it would
hardly have been noted by those of our synagogue. We give

little heed to addled messengers bringing foolish doctrines. As I said, down through the years in Israel certain ones have risen up to call themselves the Messiah of the Chosen—some in a selfish zeal for authority and riches, some in the sincere, if deluded, belief that they had been called to restore Israel's ancient might. But they have been false leaders, and they have led many to ruin. Their following, too, has always dwindled and died away completely with their own deaths." He narrowed his eyes in searching the tribune's face. "But you say, tribune, that, though it is three years since this carpenter's crucifixion, there is a lively fellowship whose members hold that the fellow was indeed Israel's Messiah? Can it be that in the very citadel of the Chosen People there are Israelites who understand not that our scriptures declare that 'he that is hanged is accursed of God'?" Saul's voice was betraying a rising tenseness.

"I know little of the religious writings of the Hebrew people or of their knowledge of them," Longinus replied, "but I do know that his followers since his crucifixion have increased, and rapidly, rather than diminished. Nor are they all Jews. There are among them even Romans and Greeks who believe that the Galilean is a god. And Romans in high places, too. Nor is the sect confined to Jerusalem; it has spread in many places in Judaea and Galilee, and there are even some of its members as far away as Rome."

"I can understand the spread of such superstition among the Gentiles, who have many gods but generally give strong allegiance to none. But for a son of Israel to sink to such depravity, I cannot comprehend it! Can it be, tribune, that the high priest Caiaphas and the Temple officers have closed their eyes and ears to this idolatry? Or have they lacked the courage to stamp it out as one would extinguish the flames in a field of flax?"

"It was the high priest and his Temple lackeys who forced the Galilean's crucifixion, and Caiaphas has employed all his wiles to destroy the growing fellowship. But he has had little success, and many in Israel worship this Jesus as the son of their one-god, undaunted by the high priest's opposition."

Saul sensed in the tribune's tone a hint of challenge. But it served only to sharpen his words. "Tribune, I cannot accept this amazing story as the truth. I do not question, understand me, your veracity. But you yourself said you never saw this Galilean alive after you saw him dead. You have simply been deceived, tribune, and I can understand how a Roman, brought up to believe in many gods, would not have his credulity greatly strained to believe in one more. Yet——"

"It may surprise you, Rabbi Saul, to learn that few modern Romans of the senatorial or equestrian classes have been brought up to believe in any gods at all. Whatever religion the young Romans profess is but a traditional and ceremonial aspect of Roman life and culture. But this Galilean that I crucified, rabbi, has no resemblance to any pale Roman or Greek god I've ever heard of or"—his eyes held unwavering—"any other man I have ever encountered. Whatever he is, whether god or man or god-man, he is unique. And right now in Jerusalem and various other regions of Israel, there are hundreds, maybe thousands, who would insist if they were not afraid of the high priest and the ruling Temple crowd—that he is indeed a god."

"What you believe, tribune, is of little concern to us of the ancient Hebrew faith. We care not how many gods you Gentiles worship, including this crucified carpenter from Galilee. But it is of great concern to us leaders in Israel what the people of Israel believe. So if it be true that Israelites have fallen into idolatry and follow after this false Messiah, then what is required at Jerusalem is someone to stand up with courage and steadfastness for the God of Israel and fight them, someone who will not be afraid to lay the lash to their backs!" Saul rose to his feet and his countenance was dark with wrath. "They must be driven forth from the camp of Israel!" The Tarsian seemed suddenly to have forgotten the presence of the Roman soldiers. "They must be pruned like the evil growth they are from the body of the Chosen! Blasphemers! Heretics! Abomination! Cursed forever be the brazen idolaters!"

ANTIOCH

3

Steady winds drove the *Memphis* southeastward to dock in the port of Seleucia an hour before sunset. Quickly the few passengers and little freight were put ashore, and the master ordered the vessel held at the wharf for early sailing on the morrow to Antioch.

The capital of Syria, the third greatest city—after Rome and Alexandria—in the empire, sat inland from the Great Sea, like Tarsus, on the banks of a navigable wide stream. Usually, it consumed the greater part of a day to sail up the Orontes from the river's spread mouth to the wharfs at Antioch. But most vessels did not enter the river directly from the sea; they sailed first into the port of Seleucia a short way up the coast from the point at which the Orontes emptied and then along a canal into that river. During seasons favorable for sea travel the movement along the stream was heavy, and vessels of many types and sizes ascended and descended the turgid waters, which bore down to the sea the pollution of this great trading crossroads of the Eastern world.

But the pollution of the river was hardly comparable to the pollution along its banks, which, downward from the city to the stream's juncture with the canal into Seleucia, were swarming day and night with drunken and lustful men and women of all ages, races, and classes who in professed worship of their many gods were abandoning themselves to lust and debauchery. Every day and late into every evening river craft of many types poured hordes of wanton Antiochenes into pagan temples and lush gardens and pleasure houses for revelings in the name of worship. Women of wealth and professed culture glided down the Orontes in gorgeously caparisoned barges or had themselves drawn in carriages or borne on lavish sedan chairs to the temples in the Grove of Daphne and prostituted themselves to the enjoyment of lust-crazed pilgrims for filthy coins handed over to the licentious priests serving the idols. Perverted men gave the use of their bodies to other unnatural men, and even children hardly arrived at the age of puberty unblushingly dispossessed themselves of their virginity. And not infrequently some frenzied youth, lost in the madness of abandon and debauchery, whipped a gleaming knife from his belt and in sacrifice to the wanton goddess Astarte divested himself forever of his masculinity.

Antioch was a metropolis of many races and polyglot tongues. Though preponderantly Syrian, it housed large segments of other races and many nationalities. These were mainly Greeks, Romans, and Hebrews, some of them immigrants from their native lands, others born there. Since the city's establishment some three centuries before by Seleucus, the Jews had been granted full citizenship, and a century earlier Pompey had constituted it a free city, the capital of the province of Syria. Because it was the capital and therefore the home of the Imperial Roman legate, numerous minor Roman officials and their families lived in Antioch, along with business venturers, professional men, and tradespeople. From Antioch, Rome kept an alert eye upon the sprawling Eastern Great Sea lands, and the Roman influence in the region of the city was far greater than the proportion of the Roman population.

Rabbi Saul had visited Antioch several times in journeying between Tarsus and Jerusalem on the Passover holidays, and he had friends and acquaintances among the Jewish population. He was well acquainted, too, with the profligacy of the Antiochenes and the carnal appetites and practices of those countless thousands who professed devotion to the cults of the many and vying rapacious and degenerate gods and goddesses. But being a strict Pharisee, the rabbi had scrupulously avoided setting foot upon the polluted soil of the groves alongside the river or even casting an eye in their direction. Although he had envisioned with considerable pleasure visits some day to the great temples and basilicas at Rome, he had never been tempted to join the mad throngs in the Grove of Daphne or to witness the abominations in and about the shrines and temples. Rome's religion was indeed pagan and idolatrous and her many gods and goddesses but figments of heathen men crying out for communication with their Creator, but that worship was ceremonially clean and morally uplifting and her array of divinities generally were more admirable than despicable. Antioch's religion, if the practice of any particular form of bestiality and abomination could be termed the religion of Antioch, was not only pagan and idolatrous but was also senseless and utterly depraved, and her gods and goddesses the conjurings of evil and disordered mentalities. Rabbi Saul shrank from seeing any of his fellow creatures, made in the image of God, thus in the embrace of death and eternal damnation, condemning themselves to the lowest pits of hell. He would not befoul his eyes with the sight of the abominations along the banks of the Orontes.

So, as the *Memphis* emerged from the waters of the canal into the current of the river and trimmed her sails for Antioch, Saul did not join the other passengers who from both sides of the vessel strained to see all they could of the lascivious revelings and obscene pageantry.

In the throng of passengers at the vessel's rails were the two Roman tribunes. They had come on deck as the *Memphis* was emerging from the canal into the channel of the river. They were standing on the starboard side near the bow. Longinus looked along the rail.

"I don't see your Hebrew cousin from Tarsus," he observed. "Maybe he's over on the port side."

"I think not." Paulus shook his head. "He's a strait-laced Pharisee. He wouldn't dare contaminate himself by looking upon, even from the ship, any of those abominations over there"—he nodded toward the temple in the thicket of small trees and flowering plants that the *Memphis* was passing—"as I am sure he would describe them."

"I agree. That Jew is as inflexible as Caiaphas or even old Annas, I have no doubt."

"As inflexible perhaps, but an honorable man he appears to be."

"Honorable, yes. But intolerant, too, as evidenced by his violent denunciation of the crucified Galilean, whom he admitted he had never even heard of, and all those Jews who believe him to be their Messiah."

"He was bitter, wasn't he? A result, no doubt, of his strict upbringing as a Pharisee. But you'll have to say for him that he wasn't afraid to speak his mind, even to us strangers. But tell me, tribune"—Paulus changed his tone—"what is likely to be the outcome of your meeting with the legate? Do you think he might order Pilate back to Rome to stand trial before the emperor Tiberius?"

"Not immediately. But, unless the situation in Palestine improves greatly, perhaps within a year or two. And I don't foresee Pilate's changing, do you? But maybe we'd better not. . . ." He paused, for several passengers were edging nearer along the rail.

"I understand." Paulus nodded. The *Memphis* was sliding around a slight bending in the channel. They could now see a long way up the yellow stream. Paulus pointed. "That structure—see, the one with the roof tiles showing above the trees—isn't that the Temple of Apollo?"

"I believe so." Longinus grinned. "But like your Hebrew cousin from Tarsus, I know little about this region alongside the river."

They did not see Saul again until midafternoon, when the *Memphis* was nearing the walls of the city. The two were standing again at the starboard rail when Saul joined them. He greeted the tribunes pleasantly. "We'll soon be drawing up to the docks at Antioch," he observed. "Will you be going ashore for the night? The ship's master informed me that we would not be able to leave Antioch, because of the heavy freight unloading and loading, until midday tomorrow."

"So we heard," Longinus said. "I have business there. And you, Paulus, you'll want to have a look at the city—and stretch your legs, won't you?"

"Yes, and get a night's sleep on a bed that isn't rocking, and a change of food perhaps. And you, Rabbi Saul, will you be disembarking too?"

Saul laughed. "Yes, I'll spend the night at the home of a friend who lately emigrated from Tarsus. He lives in the Hebrew community not far from the great synagogue."

"But if you don't find him, if he has moved to another——"

"I have other friends in Antioch," Saul assured Tribune Paulus. "I'll find lodging. But you, tribune, are you well acquainted with the city? And you, Tribune Longinus?"

"Longinus is, but this is my first visit."

"Then let me urge you to be cautious, tribune. Guard yourself well. You agree, Tribune Longinus? Antioch is a great city, and filled with desperately wicked and depraved men. Great harm could befall you, particularly after darkness has descended."

"Harm to my morals, perhaps?" Paulus smiled.

"To your morals, your purse, and your person, tribune."

The *Memphis* was moving along now on a course closely paralleling the river's south bank, and heavy foliage and tall trees effectively screened from passengers on the starboard rail any view of the distant countryside. But as the vessel veered to the left and moved into the middle of the channel and past the luxuriant growth, the passengers saw straight ahead the docks and the stir and commotion of shipping about them.

"Antioch," Saul said. "Proud, beautiful, wicked harlot of the East! Grandly conceived and lavishly built by kings and emperors, filled with splendid edifices and untold treasures of art, prosperous, pleasure-mad, cynical, pagan—like a gorgeously arrayed whore happily and unrepentantly going her evil way, great Antioch is a stench in the nostrils of the Most High, and one day woe will descend upon her utterly!"

A moment Saul was silent, and then quickly the heavy scowl was gone, and smiling again, he pointed off toward the right. "Mount Silphius," he announced calmly. "The mount sits at the northern end of the Lebanon range. The Orontes flows northward east of that range and breaks through the mountains here at Antioch where the Taurus range, which crosses above Tarsus, comes eastward to join the Lebanons. So the city is a gateway into the countries of the East. But"— he shrugged—"what traveled Romans like yourselves aren't familiar with this entire region?"

They disembarked at a pier near the bridge gate where the roads from Tarsus and Seleucia converged to enter the city, and they walked eastward along a heavily traveled way until they came into a broad street intersecting it. They turned left and began walking northward along it.

"This," said Saul as he gestured with outflung arm, "is called the Street of the Colonnades. It was added by Antiochus Epiphanes. It runs roughly parallel with the river. It is the main way in Antioch, as you doubtless know."

"It is amazing." Paulus had been studying the great colonnaded broad way. "Huge carved pillars, trees and flowers, and statues everywhere. How many are there, do you suppose, and how far does this great street extend?"

"All the way through the city," Saul answered. "And I don't know how many scores of statues there are; there must be hundreds, erected to kings and emperors, gods and goddesses uncounted. Even old Herod of Israel, father of Tetrarch Antipas, added statues and buildings and innumerable other gifts to the Antiochenes out of the sweat and blood of his own people." He paused as they came abreast of a narrow way entering the Street of the Colonnades from the right. "The region of the city where many of the Hebrews live." He inclined his head in the direction. "I must leave you here, tribunes, to go to the house of my friend from Tarsus. Tribune Longinus, you know the way, of course, to the legate's palace." He pointed straight ahead. "Continue along this way until you come to the circular plaza with the column in the center bearing the statue of the emperor. There you can cross the plaza and walk northward until you come to the wide way that leads westward across the bend in the river. You remember that the island is formed by the splitting of the stream. When you step onto the island, you will then be at the palace gates." He turned to enter the narrow cobbled street leading off through a maze of sculptured figures and, looking back, raised his arm in salute. "May the Most High preserve us to return in health tomorrow to the *Memphis*," he said. "And remember, Tribune Paulus, be on your guard, even here in the shade of these pillars."

The tribunes returned Saul's salute and then resumed their walking along the colonnaded broad way. In a short while they reached the round plaza, where they paused to study the statue of Tiberius scowling down upon them from high on the slender marble column. "I wonder how long the old man will remain up there after his grandson or Caligula takes his place on the throne," Longinus observed.

"Not long if it's Caligula," Paulus predicted. "The old man's head will come off and the new emperor's will go on; you can be sure of that." He shrugged. "Do you want to turn left here or go on along this way to the next wide crossing?"

"As you wish," Longinus replied. "Are you going with me?"

"No, I have no business with the legate. I'll stroll on to the end of this street and I'll meet you after you have finished your meeting with the legate."

"Then I'll walk on with you as far as the way leading to the river and the palace main gate."

Soon they reached the intersecting street. "Here we are," Paulus said. "Where shall we meet when the legate has dismissed you?"

Longinus thought a moment. "Why don't you come to the palace after you have walked about the city a while? It might be that the legate will invite us to stay the night with him. If he doesn't, we can go to a tavern. Either will be better than another night aboard the *Memphis*."

Paulus nodded, and Longinus turned to cross the esplanade. But when he had taken a few steps to the left, he looked back.

"Tribune," he said, grinning, "remember to guard well your person, your purse, and your virtue."

4

"I have been anxiously awaiting your arrival, Tribune Longinus," Legate Vitellius revealed, after he had inquired of the health of the tribune, his parents, the prefect Marco, and the emperor Tiberius. "A message from the prefect arrived several days ago disclosing that you were bearing important instructions from the emperor. It was brought to Antioch by a courier who sailed aboard a government trireme that paused here on a hurried voyage to Alexandria. That is all the message said, and the courier declared he knew nothing of the nature of the instructions that you would be bringing. So I have been somewhat apprehensive. I trust, tribune"—the legate's expression became perceptibly more taut—"that you are fetching no disquieting information or orders."

Longinus assured Vitellius that the orders he was bringing from the capital should cause him no great concern. "They were considered, however, excellency, highly confidential, so much so that the prefect decided not to write them out. He instructed me instead to bring them by word of mouth, so that there would be no written message that through possible misadventure might get into other hands."

Officially, the tribune further revealed, the orders were being sent to the legate by Tiberius himself rather than by the prefect. Longinus in the company of Marco had visited the palace at Capreae for a brief audience with Tiberius. After the emperor and the prefect had discussed the situation in the Province of

Syria, with particular attention being given to conditions in Judaea, Galilee, and Samaria, Tiberius had instructed Marco to prepare the orders and have them delivered to the legate at Antioch.

"So the prefect returned to Rome and prepared them in accordance with the emperor's instructions," Longinus added. "He actually wrote them out and I have brought them." He withdrew from his toga a sealed packet and laid it on the desk before the legate. "But, excellency, these are not the orders to which the prefect, in his message to you by courier, and I a moment ago were referring. These are perfunctory instructions dealing with certain administrative problems and are not to be interpreted as censuring in any way your administration of the province. The prefect prepared this copy and I deliver it to you in order that no charge could be sustained that he did not carry out the orders of Tiberius. But, excellency"—he leaned forward, lowered his voice, hesitated, as his eyes surveyed the legate's private chamber—"these orders——"

"No other ears can hear what is being said, tribune," Vitellius, interrupting, assured him.

Longinus nodded. "These orders are not the important ones. These could well have been brought by the courier. The important orders come from the prefect alone, and he wanted none of them put on paper so that they might conceivably be used someday against him. In the same way, it could never be established against you that you had received them." He smiled. "And once I have delivered them, excellency, I trust that you will conveniently forget how they came to you."

"I promise, tribune. Let us say that you stopped off in Antioch to bear the legate Vitellius greetings from his beloved friend of many years, Senator Gaius Cassius Longinus, and to bring a packet bearing routine orders from the emperor."

"That is good. Actually your old friend my father did send you his warmest regards, excellency, and so did my mother." Longinus had sat back in his chair. Now he leaned forward again. "Indeed, sir, the orders aren't so much orders as they are instructions concerning the policies of the government at Rome as administered in reality by the prefect, and information concerning the situation at the capital to enable you the more effectively to direct affairs in Syria in accordance with the government's policies. Prefect Marco realizes that because you have been out of Rome a good part of the time in recent years, excellency, you may not have been able to keep abreast of political movements—or, to say it more accurately, intrigue and conniving—in the capital. And he feels that for your protection, as well as his own, you should be told what is happening in Rome and what could happen in the early future."

"Yes, I agree." Vitellius nodded gravely. "I can see how nothing could be more important to me. I hope you will speak freely, and frankly. I presume quite a number of persons in high places are involved?"

"Yes, excellency, including the emperor particularly. Have you had any contact with him, sir, in recent years?"

"None, tribune. What communication we've had has been by couriers sent out from the office of the prefect."

Longinus sat back in his chair. "Our Emperor Tiberius, excellency, is an old man, as you know. But in the last year he has become quite senile and crotchety. He was greatly disturbed at the revelation of Sejanus' treachery. So Prefect Marco isn't certain how much confidence Tiberius places in him, and naturally he wishes to do nothing that might offend the emperor. Now that one powerful prefect has been strangled, reasons Marco, it might be less difficult for Tiberius to permit—or order—the strangling of another. So he is determined to follow a course that will continue him in the good graces of the emperor."

Vitellius nodded. "That is understandable. I follow you, tribune."

"But, excellency"—Longinus sat straight in his chair and with his forefinger tapped the desk, as he looked the legate in the eyes—"Prefect Marco at the same time does not wish to be regarded in the senate and the powerful circles of Rome, and especially among the Praetorian Guardsmen, as the tool and lackey of Tiberius. The prefect would not be greatly surprised, Legate Vitellius"—his eyes were on the heavy door again and instinctively he lowered his voice—"if some grave misfortune befell the emperor, and——"

"Assassination?"

Longinus nodded. "He has accumulated many determined enemies and every day new stories are circulated, many of them doubtless untrue, of his indulging himself in unnatural vice with painted and pampered boys at Capreae, as well as young girls, of his unjustly ordering friends of Sejanus slain simply because they were friends of his once great favorite, and of countless other ill deeds. There has been a renewal of charges, I heard when I was home, that the emperor Tiberius had allowed his wife Julia to starve on the rocks of Pandateria—she's been dead almost twenty years—after her father Augustus banished her because of her lascivious conduct, and also that he banished without adequate reason her daughter Agrippina two years ago. In fact, the senate has been a hotbed of censuring the old man—and for things he has done that the senators themselves approved at the time he did them."

"But, tribune, surely opposition has not developed to the point that assassination might be attempted."

"If you had been in Rome in recent months, excellency, you perhaps would not be surprised at anything that might occur."

"But should such a calamity befall the empire—I say this as the emperor's legate in Syria—then who, tribune, is foreseen as the successor of Tiberius?"

"I have no powers of divination, sir. Nor does the prefect. And that is why he has sent me to you—that is the principal reason—to say that the situation in Rome calls for the exercise of great care even in the administration of the affairs of a province greatly remote from the capital. The prefect suggests that for the next several months, so long as the situation continues as it is in fact, none of us show any especial enthusiasm either for the emperor or for any possible successor to the throne." Longinus was silent a long moment, his forehead crinkled, and the legate waited quietly. "I can tell you though, excellency, as a partial answer to your question"—he resumed speaking—"the talk in Rome at the moment is that Tiberius will name his grandson, young Tiberius, as his heir. But there are many who would wager that Gaius, the son of Tiberius' nephew General Germanicus and his stepdaughter Agrippina, will be the next emperor. But if Tiberius were to be assassinated by his enemies—and few Romans would be surprised should it be attempted—perhaps neither of the two young kinsmen would be acceptable to the conspirators. They might even, the gods forbid, put on the throne some nonentity like the emperor's nephew, bumbling old Claudius, who would be easily controlled, no doubt."

"It was the emperor's letter to the senate two years ago recommending Gaius as his successor, was it not, that precipitated formation by Sejanus of the plot to kill Tiberius?"

"So I understand, excellency."

The legate sat back in his chair. "I haven't seen Gaius since he's grown up, but I knew him as a little boy. He was born while Agrippina was accompanying Germanicus on a campaign in the north. I knew their other son, Nero, too. Agrippina was scheming for him to succeed Tiberius." He shook his head, his mood suddenly meditative. "The gods have dealt severely with the family of Germanicus. A great soldier, too, a noble Roman. And dead in his early thirties . . . poisoned, it was widely rumored, upon the orders of. . . . But you have heard the stories, tribune; we need not go into that. And now Nero dead by his own hand, and Agrippina, exiled to Pandateria where she is, they say, grieving herself to a slow death. Yes, I knew them, Germanicus and his family, in a better day. And now Gaius has a chance at succeeding his great-uncle. Tribune"— he seemed suddenly aroused from revery—"what of Gaius, what sort of young man does he appear to be, this—this—what did the soldiers of his father's command call him? Caligula? Yes, Little Boot. What do they say of him?"

"That he is a worthless rake, a spoiled, pleasure-mad profligate."

"Wouldn't it be a travesty if such a son of such a father

should become emperor?" He held up his hand, smiling. "I am saying this only to you, tribune, understand. I shall be discreet. But didn't Germanicus and Agrippina have several other children?"

"Yes, a son Drusus, I believe, and two or three daughters, one of whom, three or four years younger than Caligula, is Agrippina. They say she is very much like Caligula, though cleverer. No doubt Rome will be hearing more of her, particularly if Caligula should become emperor. And that reminds me, excellency, of another phase of the situation that the prefect spoke about that is of considerable concern to you, since it involves this eastern region of the empire."

The legate leaned forward, attentive. "Yes? What is that, tribune?"

"It is concerned with the friendship of Caligula for Herod Agrippa."

"The brother-in-law of King Herod Antipas, isn't he?"

"Yes, and also his nephew. And likewise his enemy."

"That does make it pertinent to Palestine, doesn't it?"

"Indeed so. And the legate should be familiar with the situation in its ramifications and its possibilities, the prefect pointed out. I wonder, excellency, do you know the story of Agrippa?"

"Only in a general way. I have heard stories of his spendthrift ways and that he is always in trouble with creditors, and that he and King Herod are usually at odds because of Agrippa's profligacy. I know virtually nothing of his conduct in Rome, however, or his reputation there. I understand that he spent most of his early life in the capital."

"Yes, he was sent there after old Herod his grandfather ordered the execution of his son Aristobulus, Agrippa's father, and was brought up in the emperor's palace. He is more Roman than Jewish actually. It's a strange friendship. Agrippa must be twice as old as Caligula; he's perhaps in his middle forties and Caligula in his early twenties. But the disparity in ages is compensated for by their similarities in temperament, tastes, appetites, and conduct, it appears. Agrippa is said also to have some

influence with the emperor, and possibly could help in weight-
ing the scales in Agrippa's favor. And should Caligula become emperor, since Agrippa is so hostile toward his sister
Herodias and his brother-in-law and uncle Antipas——"

"Then the prefect deems it unwise for the emperor's legate
in Syria to be looked upon as the strong partisan of King
Herod Antipas of Galilee and Peraea." He was thoughtful a
moment, his lips pursed. "I believe, Longinus, that I'm beginning to understand Prefect Marco's instructions. They are, in
substance, to be vigilant, to avoid committing himself or the
government to any course, or person or persons, later likely to
fall into disfavor in Rome."

"Exactly so, sir. I think he wishes you to be always in position to move in whatever direction the course of empire is taking."

"A good position, yes." Then suddenly his expression again
was questioning. "But, tribune, what of the procurator of
Judaea, Pontius Pilate? Do you bring no instructions concerning
the procurator? And his wife?"

"Indeed, excellency. I was coming to Pilate and Claudia.
The prefect gave more attention to the problem of the procurator and his wife than to Antipas and Herodias, or any other
single problem, in fact. And you understand, sir, of course that
in everything I say about them I am merely relaying the prefect's instructions?"

"Yes, tribune, I understand, and I appreciate your position.
And what you say to me will not be repeated by me to anyone."

"Thank you, sir. While I'm in Palestine, as you know, he's
my superior officer. Well"—he gestured with hands outflung,
leaned forward, lowered his voice—"Prefect Marco has a very
poor opinion of Pontius Pilate. Were it not for the fact that he
was afraid such action would offend Tiberius, he would already have removed him from office. And if Pilate's administration of Palestinian affairs does not improve—certainly if it continues to deteriorate—he may risk the wrath of Tiberius and
order him to Rome for trial anyway." He paused, and his

forehead crinkled. "Perhaps, sir, you wonder why the prefect thinks removing Pontius Pilate would offend Tiberius?"

"I do. Was not Pilate sent out to Palestine by Sejanus? And with the fall of Sejanus, it seems that the procurator's loyalty, too, would have been questioned."

"But Tiberius was led to believe that he named the procurator to that post. And as Prefect Marco understands it—and I believe myself that is true—Pilate was sent out here, and is kept in the post, because of his wife. Do you know the story of Claudia, excellency?"

"Only that she is related in some way to the emperor."

Longinus nodded. "Yes, she is his stepdaughter. She is the daughter of his wife Julia, the lively daughter of the emperor Augustus, you know, who was banished to Pandateria by Augustus after she became so notoriously profligate. The emperor Augustus, you may recall, after the death of Julia's husband, General Agrippa, made his stepson Tiberius divorce the wife he loved, Vipsania, and marry the widowed Julia, whose amours were beginning to scandalize Rome. But neither Tiberius nor Julia was pleased with Augustus' matchmaking. Julia continued to scandalize Rome and disgrace her father and new husband, and Tiberius retired to Rhodes, disgusted with Augustus, Julia, and her children by Agrippa."

"Then Claudia is the daughter of General Agrippa, who was one of the empire's greatest men."

"No. And that makes all the clearer the situation with respect to her and Pilate. Claudia is the illegitimate daughter, it is generally understood in senatorial circles in Rome, of Julia and a son of Mark Antony and Cleopatra, whom Augustus summarily had executed when he exiled Julia."

The legate, listening intently, drummed the polished desk top with his fingers. "Then Claudia is possessed of an abundance of royal blood, even though its various components may not be altogether compatible." The trace of a smile momentarily lighted his face. "But go on, tribune. It promises to be an intriguing story."

"It is indeed, excellency. And the prefect thinks it important for you to know it. Claudia, you see, is in a unique position; she might well have considerable influence in setting the course of the empire's affairs after the death or removal of Tiberius, even though at the moment she is virtually an exile from Rome. Claudia, you remember, sir, as half-sister of the elder Agrippina, is also a half-aunt of Caligula."

"So that if I should proceed against her husband Pilate, then I might incur her enmity and through her influence with Caligula, the enmity of the possible future emperor?"

"I believe, Legate Vitellius, the *probable* future emperor. But, no, I believe that Claudia would be glad for you to take action against Pilate, particularly if that should help her get back to Rome and divorce him." He sat up to the desk again, and lowered his voice. "You see, she never has loved him, and for the last three years, because of the part he played in an incident in Jerusalem, she has considered him actually repulsive. She was forced by Tiberius to marry Pilate and come out with him to this distant province. Because she was the granddaughter of Augustus and a woman of brains and beauty, the emperor, so I have been told, was afraid she might become involved in a conspiracy to force him from the throne. About that time Prefect Sejanus had been promoting his own interests by sending his protégé, Pilate, to Palestine, to keep the taxes flowing into the imperial coffers, which were controlled, of course, by the wily prefect himself. He felt that Pilate's tenure of the procuratorship would be assured through marriage with Claudia. So while Pilate was in Rome on leave about two years after he first came out here, Sejanus with Tiberius arranged for Claudia to marry Pilate and return with him to Palestine."

The legate shook his head. "It is a complicated situation, isn't it?" His expression betrayed perplexity. "One complicating factor, of course, has been removed—Sejanus himself." He smiled grimly. "And now Pilate's wife is determined to return to Rome and be free of her husband, but were the proposal put to Tiberius, he would disapprove. And Prefect Marco would do nothing to offend the emperor." He shrugged. "Then, tribune, for the moment, what is there for me to do?"

"Nothing, excellency, except to be ready for any developments in Rome."

"Of course. But you spoke of an incident in Jerusalem three years ago, I believe, that has caused Claudia to abhor Pilate. What was that, Longinus? Or was it a personal matter with which I am not concerned?"

"On the contrary, excellency, nothing could have been more publicly done, and it very much concerns you. It happened during the Passover festival when thousands of Jews from every part of the empire had swarmed into Jerusalem, and it was done in the sight of an immense throng. Afterward it occasioned much talk; in fact, talk of it has not yet ceased, and it never will, in my opinion."

"Then it was something done by Pilate?"

"Yes, and it offended many of the Jews. And me, likewise. And it did great damage to Rome's reputation for dealing even-handed justice to all peoples."

"Indeed! By great Jupiter, tribune, what did he do?"

"He did the worst thing, in my opinion, Legate Vitellius, that a Roman official could do. He crucified a good man, an innocent man he *knew* was innocent, a young rabbi loved by the people but hated by the high priest Caiaphas and the Temple clique. He made a mockery of Roman judicial procedure. And in doing so, he earned the enmity of a growing fellowship who believe in the rabbi, and because of his yielding to fear and expediency lost whatever respect the high priest's faction had had for him before the trial."

"A growing fellowship, you say, Longinus, who *believe* in the rabbi. Who *did* believe in him, you mean, don't you? Didn't you say that Pilate sent him to the cross?"

"Yes, excellency, but there are many among the Jews who held him to be their Messiah and who believe that after his death on the cross he returned to life. There are some, too, other than Jews who believe that he was resurrected"—he looked the legate in the eyes and extended his forefinger for emphasis—"including Claudia."

"But surely Claudia does not believe that a crucified man came to life." He leaned forward, his expression intent. "Perhaps he was not actually dead, tribune; maybe he was taken down from the cross and revived."

"No, your doubt is but natural, excellency. It is unbelievable. But the man was dead, I know, because I crucified him, I saw him taken down, and I saw him laid in the tomb. He was dead. And I had charge of the guard at his tomb, which I had helped seal, and saw that no one approached it. Yet the stone closing the mouth was mysteriously rolled up and the body gone."

"Tribune, do you believe the man arose from death?"

"It's an enigma. I know, sir, only what I saw. But Claudia believes he did. She had become interested in the man, a Galilean, before he was brought before Pilate. She even sent Pilate a message warning him to have nothing to do with the rabbi. But he ignored her warning. When she learned that he had condemned the Galilean to the cross, she was furious. Since then she has held him in utter contempt."

"Claudia has told *you* this?"

"Yes, excellency. We have been friends since our childhood days in Rome." Longinus paused, but went on to explain. "That, of course, was in the last years of the reign of Augustus. As a child she was brought up in the palace of her grandfather after he had banished Julia."

"And have you seen her frequently during the years she and Pilate have been in Palestine?" The legate's eyes narrowed perceptibly.

"Often, yes, excellency. During the greater part of my service out here I have been stationed at Caesarea directly under Pilate's command or have journeyed with him when he has visited other regions in the province, as, for example, to be the guest of Antipas at Tiberias and to attend the Passover festival at Jerusalem. Naturally, Claudia and I have been in each other's company on many occasions. But, sir, I'm sure that my report to you concerning her and Pilate has been entirely objective."

"Of course, tribune. I had no other thought. And I appreciate the prefect's report sent through you and your elaboration of it. Both will be most helpful to me; certainly I shall be governed by what you have reported." He paused momentarily and pursed his lips. "As a matter of fact, Longinus, much of what you have told me, with the exception of Claudia's determination to rid herself of Pilate, I knew already. Pilate's obstinacy, his amazing propensity, it appears to me, to provoke the Jews both to hate him and, worse, to hold him in contempt, his failure to administer properly the government in Judaea— none of this has escaped me. I am informed of various incidents when he seems to have gone out of his way to offend the Jews, including his marching into Jerusalem with the unfurled standards bearing the emperor's image, his later blustering at Caesarea and then yielding to the protesting Jews, his revelation of his intention to use funds from the Temple treasury in Jerusalem to build an aqueduct into the city and his orders to his soldiers to silence the Jews' outraged protests by bludgeoning the protesters—I know about all those inexcusable blunders. Yes, and others. I have had complete reports on his trial of the Galilean mystic you referred to, and I had already come to the conclusion that Pilate, because of fear of the high priest Caiaphas or out of desire to please him—either of which positions is of course indefensible—condemned to death a Jew who was guilty certainly of nothing more than the violation of some of the laws relating to the worship of the Jews' Yahweh." The legate leaned forward and a scowl clouded his countenance. "All these actions of Pilate have clearly violated the edict of Emperor Augustus granting the Jews full rights to engage unmolested in the practice of their religious ceremonials and have greatly damaged the image of Rome in the eyes of these eastern subjects of the empire. And the worst thing about Pilate, tribune, isn't that he's a knave; it's that he is such a fool. And I fear he will not improve; he is more likely to become such a burden upon Rome that we will be forced to re-

move him from office"—he paused, and his forehead crinkled
into a troubled, heavy frown—"in spite of the possible reluc-
tance of Tiberius to have him deposed."

Legate Vitellius paused, as if for a comment by his guest,
but Longinus only nodded, and the legate raised his arm to
stab his extended forefinger toward the tribune. "So, tribune,
I have a request to make of you. In fact, it is an order delivered directly to you. Pilate—and no one else—should ever even
suspect that the order was given." He paused again, his questioning countenance unsmiling.

This time Longinus spoke as he nodded. "I understand, sir. I
shall tell no one. What is the order?"

"Nor will I tell anyone, Longinus. I shall protect you. It will
be a matter entirely between you and me." He looked Longinus
full in the face a long moment. Then, his tone and manner, as
he continued speaking, were reassuring. "I will find ways of
communicating with you that will excite no one's suspicions.
Tribune, I want you to keep me continuously informed, by
whatever means you find practicable, of Pontius Pilate's policies and actions, particularly any that may further arouse the
ire of his subject peoples in his administration of the government in Judaea and Samaria. If the situation there continues to
deteriorate and Rome is brought further into disrepute through
the ineptness and perhaps corruption of the procurator, then
I may be forced to take positive action against him. It may develop, too, that I will wish to send you back to Rome to discuss my views about Pilate and my probable plans with Prefect
Marco, or even the emperor. But we won't cross that stream,
tribune, until we reach it. In the meantime, though, it will be
your first and foremost duty, regardless of the assignment you
may have at the moment in the army, to keep your eyes and
ears alert to what is happening at the procurator's palace. And
in so doing, Longinus"—a faint smile lightened for an instant
his serious expression—"it might be helpful for you to keep
closely in touch with Claudia."

CAESAREA

5

In early afternoon the next day, the *Memphis* eased from its dock into the channel of the Orontes, and the current, helped by a stiff breeze, bore the ship steadily toward the Great Sea. After anchoring for the night in the port at Seleucia, where some merchandise and several passengers were put aboard, the vessel at midmorning cleared the harbor and turned southward to sail a course roughly paralleling the coast.

The winds continued favorable, so that two hours before sunset, on the third day out of Seleucia, the *Memphis* slipped through the opening in the mole protecting the harbor at Tyre and tied up at a wharf fronting on a long, sprawling warehouse. On the wharf scores of sweating slaves, clad only in bright-colored loincloths and spurred on by the shouted imprecations and the whips of cursing overseers, struggled with boxes and bales of merchandise being unloaded from other recently arrived vessels or loaded upon them from warehouses and the adjacent docks.

At Tyre the *Memphis* discharged a few passengers and unloaded a small quantity of freight taken on at Rome, Tarsus, and Seleucia. It also took on some passengers and several shipments of merchandise, principally boxes of glassware and bales of textiles manufactured at the nearby plants, for delivery to Caesarea, Joppa, Alexandria, and even Rome. The exchange was completed early the following day, and the *Memphis* sailed past the breakwater into the open sea and turned southward again.

Long before nightfall, before even the sun had disappeared

into the Great Sea, the vessel, running ahead of a moderately steady wind, arrived off Caesarea, and the master ordered her sails trimmed for entering the harbor. An hour later she tied up at the dock and Rabbi Saul and the two Romans, who had met but a few times for brief moments on the deck since their debarking at Antioch, went ashore.

They left their baggage at the dock. "I'll send some of the legionaries to fetch it," Tribune Paulus said to Saul. He noticed that the rabbi's attention had settled for the moment on one of the tall towers atop the massive mole of huge granite blocks almost encircling the harbor to provide protection from the wind and waves. "Welcome, eastern cousin, to Rome-in-Palestine." He waved his arm in a half-circle that embraced the city before them. "You've been to Caesarea before, of course, and know the city's story?"

"Only in journeying between Jerusalem and Tarsus," Saul answered. "But I have heard that old Herod, the father of Herod Antipas, almost starved his Israelite people in order to build this city as well as others after the manner of the Romans."

"Caesarea, indeed, is more Roman than Hebrew," Paulus agreed. He pointed toward a great ornate structure, whose upper masonry could be seen from the docks area, that sat on a slight eminence several furlongs back from the water's edge. "That temple, for example, and many others, and the amphitheater and the stadium, the marketplace, forum, the statues everywhere"—he paused. "It's surely more like Rome than Jerusalem. But there are synagogues here, too, Saul, as you must know. In fact, one of our military comrades, a wealthy centurion, contributed heavily to the building of a synagogue. His friends even chide him, and, I suspect, not without good reason, of being a convert to your one-god religion."

Walking abreast, the three crossed the stone wharf and entered the cobbled way that led up the slope to the portside entrance gate in the wall surrounding the sprawling Roman military post. At the gateway, where a sentry saluted the tribunes, Paulus pointed through the arched opening. "That way."

They crossed the grassed level area to the commander's quarters near the legionaries' barracks. As they neared the squat stone structure, the tribune, with a thrust of his thumb, indicated an imposing edifice on another slight elevation beyond the farther wall of the military compound. "The procurator's palace." He glanced toward Longinus and smiled. "Tribune, you will be reporting to the procurator and his wife tonight?"

"When I've bathed and dressed and had something to eat, yes." He was smiling too. "I must bear to the procurator Prefect Marco's regards, you know."

"Yes. And bearing them from Rome hasn't been burdensome, I suspect."

Saul's expression for the instant was questioning, but he said nothing. And a moment later they entered the quarters. Had they arrived at Caesarea even one day later, they soon learned, they would have been too late to start on the journey with the detachment of legionaries accompanying Pilate to Jerusalem for the annual Passover festival.

"They are setting forth early on the morrow," one of the household servants revealed. "Preparations have been completed; everything is in readiness."

"Then I must report at once to the procurator," Paulus declared, "and get my orders. He may yet want me to go to Jerusalem. And perhaps you, too, tribune. So when we've bathed and put on fresh clothes and had our supper, we'd do well to visit Pilate." When Longinus nodded, Paulus turned to Saul. "Perhaps, Rabbi Saul, you might wish to rest here after you have dined with us until our return from the procurator's palace, when we will be in a better position to make our plans for the journey to Jerusalem."

"You are kind, tribune, and I thank you. But I believe instead that I should walk down into the city and visit one of the synagogues in the hope of coming upon old friends with whom I was associated in Jerusalem when I was a pupil of Rabban Gamaliel. I'll return here later in the evening and discover what plans you have agreed upon for our beginning the journey."

When a few minutes later Saul withdrew, Paulus observed with a wry smile that the rabbi was an unbending Pharisee indeed. "He's unwilling to contaminate himself by sitting down to table with Roman pagans, as he calls us."

Afterward the tribunes went up to the palace, where Pilate greeted them pleasantly, though it was immediately apparent to them that his mood was not jovial. And in the next moments he himself revealed why he appeared somewhat depressed.

"I'm glad you have returned from your leave," he assured them. "Recently in an official packet received from Rome I was notified of your promotions by Prefect Marco and instructed that Tribune Paulus would command the cohort here as my chief subordinate. So, Tribune Paulus, it is fortunate for me that you have reached Caesarea in time to lead the troops I am taking to Jerusalem tomorrow for another of these Passover saturnalias. I'll be able to spend virtually all my time in Herod's palace or in my quarters in the Tower of Antonia out of sight and sound of noisy, pestiferous, troublesome Jews— and smelling distance of them." A heavy scowl darkened his florid round face, which, the tribunes had noticed, was now beginning to sag at the cheeks, and the wrinkles in his forehead ridged upward into perceptibly thinning closely cropped hair. "The longer I stay in this abandoned outpost of civilization, tribunes, the more impatient I am becoming with the members of this obstinate, contemptuous breed. And if I were the emperor I would forbid henceforth the holding of these Passover festivals. They accomplish nothing but trouble for us and arouse in them even more revolutionary spirit." He centered his gaze on Longinus and suddenly his expression was equivocal. "Tribune, you remember what a tumult they raised during the Passover season three years ago, don't you?"

"When you sent the Galilean teacher to the cross?"

"Yes, the one you crucified."

But the procurator did not pursue the discussion. Instead, he asked Tribune Paulus to accompany him to cohort headquarters to arrange for the tribune's participation in the legionaries' assignment of keeping order in the Hebrew capital.

"It shouldn't require much time or effort to accomplish it," Pilate said to Longinus, "and it will not need your presence at headquarters. So, tribune, I suggest that you remain here, until I return, and entertain Claudia with an account of your visit to Rome. You two have so many friends—and interests—in common. And she has been away from the capital a long time. She would appreciate being told about the changes that have taken place during her absence and how her friends have been faring since the death of Prefect Sejanus"—Longinus fancied he caught the trace of a smile on the procurator's heavy face—"and the accession to authority of Prefect Marco, as well as the state of health of her beloved step-father, the emperor."

Now Longinus was certain that Pilate was smiling, though there was little warmth or humor in it. Pilate clapped his palms together and a servant came quickly from the shadows of an ornate column. "Summon my sedan chair," he commanded. "Tribune Paulus, you will accompany me to cohort head-quarters."

6

"This time of evening, sitting here looking down to the harbor, above the basilicas, marketplaces, theaters, forums"—Longinus swept his hand in a wide arc—"I have the feeling that I'm on the terrace before the peristylium at home. From up on the Esquiline the view of the forums, Circus Maximus, the Emporium, and the vast jumble of temples and palaces on the Capitoline and Palatine hills down to the Tiber is very much like that of Caesarea from here, don't you think, Claudia?"

"Yes, it is, though I've been exiled in this dreary outpost so long that sometimes I wonder how things look now in Rome." The procurator's wife smiled wryly. But quickly in the deepening twilight even the trace of smile vanished and her expression and tone of voice hinted desperation. "Oh, Longinus, isn't there something you can do, some way you can rescue me from this gods-forsaken province—and Pilate? Surely the new prefect isn't inclined to further the personal schemes of dead Sejanus, is he? You explained to Marco why Sejanus and Tiberius sent me out here after marrying me off to Pilate, didn't you?"

"Yes, he understands fully. And so does Legate Vitellius." He related the details of his conversation with the legate at Antioch. "But both Marco and Vitellius are fearful that if they do anything for you at this time it would be premature. They fear it might offend the emperor. Marco thinks that were he even to mention to Tiberius that you wanted to divorce Pilate, he would suspect that someone, maybe even the prefect himself, might be plotting with you to have him supplanted on the throne. He even envisions the emperor's having him strangled as he had Sejanus." He smiled humorously. "And it wouldn't surprise me if he did."

"But, oh, Longinus, do take me away from this horrible place!" She seemed not to have been listening. "Can't you arrange some way to free me from Pilate and Palestine before I completely lose my wits?"

He reached across and patted the back of her hand outstretched on her knee. "Something may happen soon to change the situation. Tiberius is an old man and not well; he might die and that——"

"Be assassinated, may the gods grant it!"

"Maybe." He craned his neck to peer behind him toward the door through which they had come out upon the terrace.

"You needn't be alarmed. There are no ears near enough to hear us, unless they're Chloe's. And you know Chloe never repeats anything she hears." She gestured with a quick outflinging of her hands. "And I'm almost past caring who hears.

Everybody in the palace, anyway, knows how I loathe my husband, including him. But, when I interrupted you, you were saying that my beloved stepfather soon might conveniently die—by somebody's sword or a cup of poison, I would hope —and that then. . . . what were you going to say?"

"That then the Legate Vitellius or Prefect Marco might suspend Pilate from the procuratorship and order him to Rome for trial on the charge of malfeasance, and perhaps banish him to some land even more remote from Rome than this one. I discussed such a possibility with the prefect and also the other day in Antioch with Legate Vitellius. Both suggested, as a matter of fact, that should Pilate's administration continue to deteriorate, he might be ordered to Rome even before the emperor dies. What of it, Claudia? Is he doing better?"

"Indeed, no. Since you left for Rome, he has done worse. The government steadily deteriorates. You remember that three years ago he offended the followers of the Galilean rabbi, and infuriated me, by yielding to the high priest Caiaphas and his Temple party and condemning an innocent man to the cross. Now, of course, Caiaphas and old Annas, the former high priest, scorn him because they were able to browbeat him into yielding to them. But the Samaritans, too, are likewise incensed against him; they say he does not hold their religious laws and traditions in proper respect, that he rages against them and threatens to destroy them and their temples if they don't yield without question to his every arbitrary edict."

"Then Pilate himself may resolve your situation before the next emperor has the chance to do it."

"Certainly I hope it's resolved soon—one way or the other. But who will the next emperor be, Longinus? Was there much talk of it in Rome?"

"Much whispering. And a great deal of conjecturing in many a mansion on the hills, and perhaps down in the Subura's tenements likewise. It seems quite likely that Tiberius hasn't yet decided whether to propose as his successor his grandson Tiberius or your nephew Caligula."

"By *Bona Dea*, Longinus, that silly, unprincipled, spoiled

brat! Surely not Gaius. Beside him even old Tiberius is an Augustus. That young rake the emperor of Rome! The gods preserve the empire, Longinus, if Gaius becomes emperor!"

"But if he should become emperor, Claudia, what would his feelings be toward his aunt?"

"Half-aunt, remember. But half-aunt, aunt, mother, sister, brother—what difference would blood kinship make to that worthless rake? Let me see"—she paused, thoughtful—"Gaius must have been seventeen or eighteen when I came out here; he's twenty-one now, but from what I hear he's still an immature, unconscionable wastrel, and rascal. What would his feelings be toward me, you ask? Only the gods know, Longinus. He might order my head off." She laughed derisively. "Surely he would if his great friend Herod Agrippa should suggest it—and Agrippa probably would because I've been friendly with his sister, the tetrarchess Herodias."

"When have you seen Herodias? Have you visited her and the tetrarch at Tiberias since I left for Rome?"

"Yes, once. And I saw her and Antipas last year at the Passover festival in Jerusalem. Doubtless I'll see them this time, too. They both pretend, when the Jews are watching them, to be devout followers of the God of Israel. But Herodias is no more faithful to her Hebrew one-god than I am to our Roman gods and goddesses, and neither is Antipas when the eyes of the Jews aren't upon him." She shrugged her shoulders and gestured with nervous hands. "Herodias and I do have much in common. Each of us loathes her husband, and each is eager to escape from this dismal province." She leaned toward him. "Oh, Longinus, I do so want to get away." Her tone was pleadingly insistent. "Must we do nothing but wait for Tiberius to die, and hope that his successor will be our friend? Cannot the legate arrange it for us before then? Does he know about us? Does he know that we were about to be married when Tiberius and Sejanus, though they didn't know they were doing it, dashed our plans? Did you tell him? Or the prefect?"

"No, I didn't tell either of them about us. I was afraid that if I did so I might prejudice them against us and perhaps cause

them to look upon Pilate's administration with more tolerance."
In the thickening twilight he caught her hand and held it.
"For the moment, my dear, we can do little more than we have
been doing, I fear. If we should attempt some drastic solu-
tion, we would only be courting disaster. We might escape together to Alexandria or Athens or Antioch or even into Gaul
or Germania. But how long would a tribune in the Roman
army, the son of a leading senator, deserting with a procurator's
wife—and that wife the stepdaughter of the emperor himself
—be able to escape the dire vengeance of the emperor whose
personal orders they were so violently flouting? No, Claudia,
we may be forced to wait months, or even years, the gods forbid"—he shook his head somberly—"though, on the other
hand, you may be free of Pilate before next year's Passover
season arrives."

"*Bona Dea* grant it," she observed solemnly. "Yes, Longinus,
we cannot afford to make some move that would inflame Tiberius against us. For if we should escape the headman's ax
until Tiberius died, we might never be permitted to return to
Rome to live. And how could we exist in exile? My poor
mother could have enlightened us on the terrors of exile—or
my half-sister Agrippina could tell us! But surely there is something that we can do," she added hopefully, "to hasten the day
of Pilate's removal, some scheme that we may devise——"

"Yes," he agreed, "there is, and it has already been arranged.
And in carrying it out we shall have the help of both Prefect
Marco and Legate Vitellius to the extent that expediency will
permit. Both of them would like to see Pilate deposed as procurator and sent off into exile or to a small assignment in a distant province such as Gaul or Germania or even Britannia, and
they'll——"

"Then you have talked with them about him," she interrupted.

"About him, yes. But not about us—you and me. And I'm
confident they will proceed to oust him as soon as they believe they can do so without raising Tiberius' ire or suspicion

—certainly as soon as he is dead. Pilate's having got himself into such disrepute among the Jews and their continual protesting to Antioch and Rome have become increasingly annoying and troublesome, I discovered, and if the reports of his conduct of the government out here do not improve——"

"And you will see to it that they don't."

"Yes," he said, "and you will help me. Beginning with the journey to Jerusalem. At the Passover festival he will no doubt succeed in offending the Jews again, as he invariably does when he's there, and will probably offend Antipas and Herodias. And you must remember, and report, everything you see and hear." He paused. "Vitellius instructed me that he wanted to be kept informed about Pilate's actions. So when we assemble a new sheaf of damaging information, I'll return with it to Antioch. By the way, Claudia, does Pilate ever speak of the Galilean he condemned to the cross during the Passover season three years ago? Before I left for Rome you said he was still troubled, you thought, because he had yielded to the high priest's demands and ignored your warning."

"He continues to be troubled, though he never refers to the Galilean. But sometimes, even of late, I've heard him in his chamber crying out in his sleep, so loudly that it awakened me, moaning out his protestations that he was washing his hands of the guilt of shedding the blood of an innocent man. And sometimes in his sleep I also hear him lashing out angrily at the high priest. In his dreaming he seems to possess a courage he cannot command when he's awake. Yes, Longinus, the Galilean haunts him."

"What of the Galilean's following, Claudia? Does the fellowship continue to grow?"

"Yes. And not only in Jerusalem and the villages roundabout. It has spread to more distant regions, I hear—even to Antioch."

"I heard that the other day when we stopped over."

"And here in Caesarea there are quite a number of them. Some of the servants in the palace belong to the group. It is through them—they pass the information to Chloe—that I hear about their movements. And I'll be in touch with several of the Galilean's band in all probability after we get to Jerusalem."

"But have you heard anything about *him*, Claudia?"

"No one has claimed to have seen him while you've been away. Certainly I've heard of no such report. But his followers expect him to reappear any day, I understand, though they've stopped selling their houses and other property in the expectation that they will need them no longer because he will return soon to the earth."

"Claudia"—he looked her full in the face, though in the now fast-descending darkness, he could hardly distinguish one feature from another—"do you really believe the Galilean was a god—is a god—and arose from death to walk forth from that tomb?"

"You told me yourself, Longinus, that he did. Should I doubt you?"

"I know he was dead. I killed him. I saw his body put into the tomb and the mouth sealed with the great circular stone. And though I guarded the tomb carefully and saw that no one came near it—and though I was out at the tomb with the guards early on the morning of the third day after we put him in the tomb and only a moment before had seen that the seal hadn't been tampered with—when I happened to look again toward the tomb I was amazed to see the stone rolled up the trough and the mouth wide open. And his body had disappeared, I discovered, when I rushed inside, though the grave-clothes apparently hadn't been disturbed but lay on the bier as though the body suddenly had dissolved into something ethereal. . . ." He paused, shaking his head. "But of course all this I've told you many times. And others, too."

"Yes, but I've never tired of hearing it. It's an amazing story."

He was still shaking his head in perplexity. "It couldn't have happened, Claudia. A dead man come to life and walk out of his tomb! And he was dead. I know he was dead! But I know, too, that nobody *on the outside* moved that stone! Nobody! And I know I found no dead man in the tomb."

"Truly a mystery, Longinus. Truly a strange being, whether man or god—or both."

"Even during his trial and impaled to the cross he acted like no other man I've ever seen."

"He didn't teach like any man I ever heard in Rome, as I have said to you before, too. When that day out of curiosity I disguised myself as a servant girl and went with Chloe to the Temple court and listened while he talked to the motley crowd gathered there, I realized he was no ordinary person. I knew he was different. And I still feel that way about him, Longinus. Don't you?"

"He was no ordinary mortal, I agree. That day, at the Hill of the Skull, I told the others that the carpenter, as his followers insisted, was indeed the son of their one-god, though I hardly know what I meant by that. Then the morning I discovered the tomb empty and later began to hear stories that he had been seen after that walking about and talking and eating . . . well, I was convinced myself that he was more than an ordinary man and more even than the gods that the Romans and Greeks envisioned back in the days when they really did believe in supernatural beings——"

"Supernatural beings," she repeated his designation, interrupting him. "Do you believe then that there are no supernatural beings—spirits, gods, whatever you may wish to term them?" She paused, but before he could answer, spoke again. "Of course, I'm not talking of our silly, juvenile, jealous-minded, even wicked gods and goddesses that surely no modern person of reasonably sound mind can swallow. I'm speaking of such a supernatural being as the Jews believe their Yahweh to be—an all-powerful ruling spirit, a just, wise, good being, above the natural world. Can you envision such a supernatural being as possibly existing, ruling——"

"I'll confess it's hard for me to envision a supposition so unreasonable."

"So unreasonable to you, yes. But is it really unreasonable, or is it just that our reasoning faculties are so prescribed? And is it necessary to reason one's way to the discovery of truth?

Can't one know something without knowing why he knows it?" She laughed lightly. "Don't they say that women arrive at the truth of something through intuition rather than by logic? But they know when they know. So, Longinus, must you dismiss something as being impossible simply because you cannot reason your way to believing it possible?"

"Claudia, you remind me of my old Greek tutor," he said. "He was always lecturing me on what he called the things of the spirit. The only real things, the truly enduring, imperishable things, he used to din into me, were the intangible things.

"'These grand edifices of stone,' he would say, as he pointed to one of the basilicas in Rome, 'will endure many centuries, no doubt, but one day they will perish and be thrown to the earth and even the stones themselves will have crumbled into the primeval dirt. But, hark, my son'—I can see the old man's eyes dancing as he said it—'the principles upon which these structures were raised, the mathematical principles of weight and stress, the form principles of straight lines and curves, of elaboration and ornamentation—in a word, of pleasing appearance, of what we call beauty—will never perish. That temple up there, Longinus'—he would point to one of the structures on Capitoline—'is a combining of imperishable truth, goodness, and beauty with marble, tile, and metal to form a temporary edifice, a structure that for a thousand years or ten thousand, perhaps, will endure in tangible, measurable, visible form. Then, with the perishing of the material part of the structure, the touchable, see-able element, men will say that it has passed into oblivion. But the truth, the essence of that temple, the intangible reality, will never perish.'"

Longinus was thoughtful a moment, and Claudia did not venture an observation that would intrude upon his reverie. "Old Crito's gods were the trinity of truth, goodness, and beauty," he went on. "They were his realities. I remember once we were walking along Via Sacra. My father had sent him on an errand to his banker's. We were passing a jeweler's shop. We had been talking—he had been talking and I had been listening, rather—about the imperishable nature of certain intangible things like beauty and goodness. Suddenly he handed me a coin.

"'Longinus,' he said, and he pointed to the shop, 'it is said that virtue is a woman's most precious jewel. Go, purchase for me a carat's weight of virtue.'

"'But, Crito, there is no such stone as virtue——'"

"'Go!' he ignored my protest. 'Fetch me a carat's weight.'"

"Did you go into the shop?"—Claudia interrupted the recital. "And did you fetch him the right weight?" she added, amused.

"I went into the shop, looked about for a moment, and then returned to him, held out my hands, empty except for the coin he had given me.

"'But you have brought me nothing. Did the jeweler have no virtue, or was the coin not sufficient to purchase a carat's weight? What did he tell you, Longinus?'

"'I did not ask for it,' I confessed. 'I did not wish him to think me foolish.'

"'But would he have thought you foolish had you asked to see an emerald of that weight, my son?'

"'But an emerald is a real thing,' I protested. 'You can look at it, pick it up and hold it in your hand, and have it set into a ring for your finger.'

"'Yes, but not as real as virtue, my boy, and not as enduring. You can take a hammer and beat an emerald to powder—but can you destroy virtue with a hammer or a sword, or fire, or water? No, Longinus, an emerald only seems to be real, for a time, but virtue is eternally indestructible; it is of the things that have always existed and that shall always exist, it is of the intangible things of the spirit, the everlasting things.'"

Longinus sat silent a long moment, musing. "It's strange, isn't it, that after all these years I can remember so clearly almost his exact words and expressions, and beliefs, as he revealed them to his young pupil? You know, Claudia, old Crito's religion—if you can call it that—must have been very close to being the one-god religion of the Jews. Certainly he was an amazing teacher, no ordinary philosopher, no ordinary man."

"Yes, and hearing you recalling him, I have the feeling that he and the Galilean expressed very similar philosophies. Each apparently was more concerned with things of the spirit"— she smiled, though in the darkening twilight it was hardly discernible—"the world of the supernatural, perhaps? But we've wandered rather far afield from your tale of the Galilean's disappearance from the tomb. You said that one moment the tomb was sealed and that when you looked a moment later the stone had been rolled aside and the body was gone. You said, Longinus, that you were positive that nobody outside the tomb had moved that stone. Then obviously it was removed from within. But, obviously again, a dead man could not move the sealing stone. So"—she gesticulated with hands flung outward, palms up—"the dead man resumed living and, exercising supernatural power, rolled up the stone and emerged from the tomb."

"And so the mystery is solved, the inexplicable is made clear."

"You need not be sarcastic. How else——"

"Forgive me, my dear." He sat up in his chair, and his expression and his tone were serious. "On my trip here I infuriated a Jewish rabbi—a devout Pharisee, I took him to be —who came aboard our ship at Tarsus, by telling him that story and giving him to believe that I had no doubt of the Galilean's resurrection. But, Claudia, even if it did happen that way"—his words now had a tone of pleading—"how do you explain it? How can one reason his way to such an astounding conclusion?"

"I have no idea," she said blandly. "Nor am I concerned with establishing *how* something happened. And in the case of the Galilean, it seems to me that the only reasonable conclusion anybody could reach, given the facts of your personal knowledge, as you say you know them to have been, would be that the man did return to life. And since mortal men do not come to life after they have been dead, it is only reasonable to believe, is it not, that this Jesus of Nazareth was more than mortal man?"

"Indeed, Claudia, I agree. Your logic is unassailable. And I have the feeling that your interest in him is more than academic." But he did not pursue his observation. "When we get to Jerusalem we can talk further of the Galilean though, and perhaps find out from some of his friends from Galilee if they have had any new information about him. But now I must be going." He stood up. "Doubtless Pilate has already let Paulus out at the cohort commander's headquarters and he'll likely be here any moment. The procurator of Judaea probably wouldn't be pleased to find me still at the palace with his wife—and in the darkness." He reached down, caught her hand, and helped her to her feet.

"Pilate wouldn't be concerned enough to come out to the terrace looking for me," she said. "But even if he should discover me out here with you he wouldn't care a fig's worth whether I was with you or anyone else, or whether I was on the dark terrace or in the lighted atrium. And even if he *should* care, he wouldn't have the courage to show that he did." She tossed her head defiantly. "Nor do I care whether he cares or doesn't!"

"Nor do I, as long as you don't!"

He pulled her gently to him in close embrace and, bending down to her eager lips turned up to his, kissed her long and ardently. And when he let go of her lips to kiss her closed eyes, he was aware of her tears.

"Don't despair, my dear," he said gently, as he lifted his face from hers. "You have faith in the Galilean, I know it. Have faith in our future." Turning, he led her toward the square of light on the terrace pavement before the opened doors to the peristylium. "Rest well, and pleasant dreaming; the journey to Jerusalem is likely to be long and tiring."

JERUSALEM

7

When the legionaries escorting Procurator Pontius Pilate paused in late afternoon at the market square outside Joppa Gate, Saul sought out his new-found clansman Tribune Paulus and thanked him for his hospitality. "I hope to see you again soon, tribune," he said, "perhaps here in Jerusalem before the ending of the Passover. But if not, then somewhere else in the empire, maybe even at your father's mansion in Rome."

"My father would indeed welcome you," the tribune assured him, "and I trust that once more our paths will converge. Meanwhile, eastern cousin"—his military mien relaxed in a quick smile—"may all the gods and goddesses guard you in your travels."

"May the one and only God, Yahweh the Most High, keep you safe, tribune."

"Then you pray the blessings of the God of the Israelites on a pagan Gentile?"

"Yes," replied the rabbi from Tarsus. "Upon a Gentile brother."

Saul walked through the great gateway in the city's western wall, and among the stir of people and beasts of burden on the narrow way, he paused to look up to the battlemented parapets of the three towers erected by long dead old King Herod to the memories of a friend, a brother, and a wife. Of the wife it was said he had loved her most but that he had, in a fit of jealousy, slain her; and it was believed that it was her death that had driven the despot to madness. Farther along the worn cobblestones, with hardly a glance to his right, Saul trudged past the frowning stone pile still called Herod's palace, though the Herods no longer possessed authority in Judaea. Here Pilate and his wife Claudia and their entourage of legionaries and servants customarily were quartered during their stays in Jerusalem, although the procurator had quarters also in the Fortress of Antonia, the Roman military headquarters in Israel's capital.

Saul of Tarsus was hoping to obtain lodging at a small hostel on the eastern slope of Mount Zion, as he had done at other Passover festivals in the years since he had completed his rabbinical studies at the House of Interpretation. This tavern sat near the end of the viaduct that spanned the Tyropoeon Valley and provided easy passage between the Zion area and Mount Moriah, on whose summit was the resplendent white-marbled mass of the Temple, the very heart and core of Israel. He murmured a prayer, as he hurried eastward on his hard-muscled but gnarled and bowed short legs, that the inn would not be already overrun with Passover pilgrims.

Saul was well acquainted with this section of Jerusalem. Southward, a little way from this hostel along the rim of Mount Zion, clinging to the descending slope and set upon a series of leveled terraces, was the building of the Synagogue of the Asians and the Cilicians. In this synagogue Saul customarily worshiped when he was visiting Jerusalem, except on those more formal occasions when he went to up to the Temple of the Most High to join in sacrifices and prayers with Israelites gathered from all the lands bordering upon the Great Sea. But sometimes, during the years spent in training at the rabbinical college under Rabban Gamaliel, he went with his beloved friend Joseph bar Nabas, a fellow pupil of the rabban, to other temples in Jerusalem whose congregants in large measure were Jews who had only lately come to settle for the remainder of their lives in the ancient capital of the Chosen. Sometimes Joseph and he joined in the worship at the Synagogue of the Alexandrians; sometimes they paid visits to the temple whose membership in the main was made up of former residents of Cyrene and Libya. But more often, when Saul was not attending the Synagogue of the Asians and the Cilicians, he and Joseph were in the throng worshiping at the Synagogue of Antioch. Joseph, having come with his widowed cousin from the island of Cyprus, was acquainted with several Cypriot families who congregated there. But in the days of their rabbinical training both he and Joseph had felt more at home with the congregants at the Synagogue of the Asians and the Cilicians.

As Saul trudged on wearying legs along the begrimed, unyielding cobbles he wondered if Joseph might still be living in the hospitable home of Mary of Cyprus on the southern descent of Mount Zion.

He remembered the house well; he had been there many times with his friend Joseph, even occasionally to spend a night, though not since his years of study in the rabbinical college. Chafing in the oppressive warmth of the congested narrow street, Saul envisioned Mary's house settled comfortably within the low whitewashed stone walls that enclosed a courtyard surrounded by a small vegetable garden, an orchard and vineyard, and grass plots with trees, a fountain, and many flowers. From the flat roof of the house, reached by an outside stone stairway, he and Joseph in the cool of summer evenings had often watched lights flickering on like fireflies in windows descending the terraced slope in close ranks and in the farther distance the ever-burning slow fires and spiraling smoke of the refuse dumps beyond Jerusalem's south wall in the frightful Vale of Hinnom. As he plodded through the steaming canyon of sun-baked stone houses and acrid shops of the butchers and the tanners, Saul remembered how he and Joseph, lying on their mats in the large upper chamber opening on the roof, had always enjoyed, even on warmest nights, cooling breezes.

How fortunate he would be, Saul suddenly was struck with the thought, if he could arrange with Mary to have his lodging in her upper chamber, even perhaps to share it with her cousin. How pleasant it would be to resume his companionship with Joseph.

But in all probability Joseph bar Nabas had long been married and a father—this was an entirely new thought that was crossing Saul's mind. In recalling their association he had not for the moment stopped to think that more than a decade had passed since they had last attended lectures at the House of Interpretation. Maybe Joseph no longer even lived in Jerusalem.

Saul determined nevertheless that he would seek a good night's rest at the hostel, if a mat remained for him, and early on the morrow he would visit Mary's house and inquire into the possibility of obtaining permanent lodging there. No place in all Jerusalem would offer more pleasurable living, he was convinced. And at the house of Mary of Cyprus he would always be in the company of loyal Israelites, faithful worshipers of Israel's God and upholders of His law.

From Mary's house he would go up to the Temple to report to Caiaphas, the high priest, and make his preparations for the Passover sacrifices. He might come upon his friend Joseph at one place or the other; surely he would at least learn where Joseph was living if by chance he had removed from Jerusalem.

"And if I do find Joseph," he said to himself as he emerged into a crossing of two ways and saw to his right the sprawling Xystus, the Roman-style gymnasium built by King Herod, "I'll learn from him the truth of the preposterous story concerning that crucified Galilean."

8

But Saul did not find Joseph when he went the next morning to the house of Mary of Cyprus.

"They have not returned to Jerusalem, Saul," she revealed, after she had greeted her cousin's friend warmly. "He went to Cyprus for me on a business mission, and my son John Mark accompanied him. You remember John Mark, don't you? We still have some properties on the island. I've been expecting them any moment. Surely they'll be in Jerusalem for the Passover."

"Yes, I remember your son, though he has doubtless grown up to manhood since I saw him last. In fact, it has been a long time since I last saw Joseph. Illness has prevented my attending several Passover festivals. Does he still live with you, or does he have a family?"

"He's married and has two sons, Saul. He married soon after you returned to Tarsus. His house is nearby on Mount Zion. And often he and his family come here to take part in the common meals and the service of worship. We would be happy to have you join us, Saul."

"The common meals and the worship?"

She saw that Saul did not understand. "The brotherhood of Jesus," she explained. "Surely, Saul, you have heard of the Galilean who was crucified——"

"On the vessel from Tarsus two Roman officers whom I chanced upon told me of a Galilean who claimed to be the Messiah. One of the Romans even told me that he was in charge of the fellow's crucifixion."

"That was the Centurion Longinus. He, too, is a believer in Jesus, I understand, though he has made no public avowal." She was hesitant a moment. "And there are other Romans, Saul, who have faith in our Lord Messiah, some in high places. They say that even the wife of Pontius Pilate is a secret follower; certainly she tried to save His life during His trial before her husband. But what did Longinus tell you, Saul?"

Saul's scowl was dark. "He told me that the Galilean was dead when he was taken down from the cross. He declared, in fact, that he himself had thrust the man through with his spear. But he likewise told me the incredible story that the Galilean came to life and escaped from the tomb." He studied Mary intently. "But surely devout Israelites like you and Joseph bar Nabas cannot believe such superstition——"

"It is not superstition," Mary maintained quietly. "He was dead, but He came to life. Many here in Jerusalem will tell you so, as will others in Galilee." She pointed her thumb over her shoulder. "There in the upper room, where He and His friends ate the Passover together the night before He was crucified, He appeared to them *after* His death and talked with them."

"Then where is this Galilean now?" Saul's cold smile was almost a leer.

"He has ascended to the Most High, His Father," Saul's old friend answered calmly. "But He promised to return, and any day He may reappear."

"And Joseph likewise believes this?"

"Indeed. And he is but one in thousands in Jerusalem and other regions of Israel who so believe."

The rabbi from Tarsus shook his head sadly. "How could such error come to have lodgment in the soul of one heretofore so undefiled as my beloved friend Joseph bar Nabas? I would have sworn there was not one in Israel more loyal to our Most High God."

"There is none, Saul."

He answered in a tone plainly edged with anger. "Then how can he, and how can you, Mary, profess faith in a false Messiah who pretended, according to the Roman tribune Longinus, to be possessed of a divine nature and power? Can you worship two gods?"

"I do not understand that in worshiping the risen Messiah I am worshiping two gods," Mary replied simply. "He called Himself the Son of God, and we believe Him to be an emanation of God, sent by the Most High to the earth to reconcile sinful man to Himself, to show man a new way, a way higher than and above the ancient law of Israel——"

"Above the law of Israel!" Saul exclaimed wrathfully. "Mary, how can you utter such blasphemy!"

"But I am not blaspheming," Mary protested. "Nor did the Lord blaspheme——"

"You speak of this crucified carpenter as your *Lord,* your *Messiah?*" His smile was scornful.

"Yes, I do." The woman flung out her hands in frustration. "Saul, I am not wise in the devious twistings and turnings of interpretations of the law by you learned rabbis. But this I do know"—she looked him in the eyes and her own were defiant —Jesus *is* our long-awaited Messiah, the hope of Israel!" Then her tone softened. "Oh, Saul, it may be that Joseph when he comes can make you see. Or Simon, when he arrives from Capernaum. He will be here, staying at my house, for the Passover and perhaps longer. Come, and let Simon teach you——"

"Simon?" Saul interrupted. "Who is Simon? Is he a learned new teacher in Israel?"

"He is a Galilean fisherman. Unlike you and Joseph, he never sat at the feet of Rabban Gamaliel or others learned in the law. But for several years he went about Galilee and Judaea with Jesus, which was far more enlightening—walking the hills and valleys with Him and crossing the mountains and sailing the little sea."

"A fisherman instructed in the laws and the prophets by a carpenter." His smile was derisive, his tone contemptuous. "You would have me, a disciple of the great Rabban Gamaliel, a rabbi in Israel, a member of the Sanhedrin, sit at the feet of a Galilean fisherman?"

"I think, Saul," she answered evenly, "that even you, were you of a mind to, might learn much from the first of our Lord Messiah's apostles. And one day—of this I have no doubt—you yourself will seek Him out."

Saul did not linger at the house of Mary of Cyprus. "I must be taking my leave, Mary," he said, as he turned toward the gate in the wall. "When Joseph returns, convey to him my greetings—and also my sorrow at his turning about from the teachings of our rabban."

"I shall, Saul, but I am not convinced that Joseph has gone astray even now from the teachings of Rabban Gamaliel. There are some who believe that even the rabban is secretly a follower of our Lord. Certainly he has counseled his fellows of the Sanhedrin to withhold the raising of their hands against Simon and the other apostles lest their work be of God. Go then and seek the counsel of your rabban. He, you agree, is neither an illiterate fisherman nor a wandering carpenter."

But Saul did not accept the further challenge. Bowing coldly, he turned and retraced his steps down to the gate in the wall guarding the house of Mary of Cyprus from the intrusion of passers-by along the cobbled way. As the gate closed behind him, Saul turned and spat upon the gatepost.

9

Rabbi Saul returned straightway to the Inn of the Red Heifer and prostrated himself upon the cold stones of his small chamber's floor. In sorrow and pain he pressed his face against the stones and clenched his browned fists until the skin above the knuckles was white.

"O God of Israel, do Thou strengthen Thy servant's arm and steel his heart to smite Thine enemies even though they number my most beloved brother," he prayed. "Imbue me with will and might to punish with all severity those who dishonor Thy Holy Name and flout even the jot and tittle of Thy law. Empower me, O God of Israel, to smite them hip and thigh until the last remembrance of the false Messiah has vanished from the earth!"

Long minutes, Saul lay on the cold stones and prayed for courage and strength sufficient to deal crushing blows to the enemies of the Most High, particularly to those adherents of the crucified Nazarene. In an ecstasy of fervor for the God of Israel, he beat his fists upon the stones, and after a while, as had happened in Tarsus at other moments of great emotional stress, foam issued forth through his grinding teeth, and his eyes, even the nearly sightless one, became fixed and staring; and his small frame, twisted grotesquely, threshed and flailed and in time lay still.

Afterward, how long after Saul never knew, he arose and stripped himself and bathed from the water in the pitcher on the shelf. Then he dressed in fresh linen, and wrapping about himself a clean mantle and donning his sandals, he went into the public room and partook of a simple evening meal, served by Bidkar the tavernkeeper. When he finished eating, he returned to his small chamber, refreshed in body and relaxed, but still impatient to begin the destruction of those idolatrous enemies whose blaspheming lips were speaking in reverence and devotion the name of Jesus of Galilee. So in this mood he sat for a while at his window and watched the shadows deepen along the slope of Mount Zion and the flickering lights spring up in windows sown thick and tumbled in the fetid confusion of Ophel's hovels.

But in the growing gloom of his unlighted warm chamber Saul's thoughts were not upon the lighted windows down in Ophel or the forlorn folk packed together in that sweltering jungle of stone and mortar inhabited in large measure by the more destitute and desolate of Jerusalem's burgeoning population. His countenance, too, like his small room, was dark and his forehead was furrowed like a plowed field laid off in rows. On the morrow, he had determined, he would eat the Passover feast in the home of a friend lately from Tarsus who attended the Synagogue of the Asians and the Cilicians, and with the ending of the holy festival he would seek out Caiaphas.

For in the fecund brain of the rabbi from Tarsus a plan was taking shape.

The implementation of this plan, though, he warned himself as he sat by the window and watched the darkness swallowing all of Ophel but the flickering feeble lights, would have to be pursued with caution and not in too great haste. He had no doubt that he himself, as the avenging, unswerving arm punishing the idolatrous enemies of the God of Israel, would be able to accomplish it.

Saul arose from the bench at the window, threw off his mantle, and curled himself on the mat in the corner.

10

High Priest Joseph Caiaphas had gained no flesh in the years since Saul had last seen him; he appeared to the Tarsian even thinner and taller and of more ascetic mien, though his eyes were sharp and coldly calculating. His father-in-law Annas, the former high priest, seated near him, was in appearance and, Saul had been told, in disposition the antithesis. Where Caiaphas' skin seemed stretched over his bony frame, Annas' enfolded loosely his flabby corpulence like the wrapping of a bale of soft Sidonian textiles carelessly packed for quick shipment.

Their manners, too, were as much in contrast as their physiques. Caiaphas possessed the bearing of an anchorite, stern, dedicated, dictatorial, quick to show resentment at any challenging of his authority or judgment, unbending and humorless. But old Annas, who because of official position or resulting weight of influence had ruled long in Israel, seemed the embodiment of a natural good nature faithfully cultivated. His obesity alone testified to a life spent in the enjoyment of rich food and excellent wines, and his unruffled good humor gave indication that not often or for long had his relishing of the good life been interrupted. In deportment Annas was as smooth and oiled as were the gray hairs of his beard that fell in ornately interwoven braids almost to his bulging middle.

But from what Saul had known of old Annas over many years, and from observing him closely as the three sat today in the high priest's private chamber, he was not misled by Annas' manner into believing that the brain of Annas had become as indolent and fat-ridden as his bloated body. Saul knew, on the contrary, that of the two men, Annas was the more designing, mentally the more agile, and the more courageous.

He had sought the audience with Caiaphas out of a consuming zeal to defend the God of Israel from His enemies by driving forth from Israel's household those faithless ones who were befouling the true worship of God through giving allegiance to the false Messiah, the Nazarene carpenter deservedly done to his death on a Roman cross. Saul had spoken with proper respect to Caiaphas and to Annas, but nevertheless with an excess of passion and determination.

"Israel must be purged of this abomination!" the rabbi from Tarsus had exclaimed. "The perpetrators of this great iniquity in Israel must be cast forth, these marauding wolves in the sheepfold of the God of the Chosen must be utterly destroyed!" He had then proposed that under the authority and direction of the Temple leadership a vigorous movement be initiated to ferret out the leaders of the idolatrous sect, especially those Galileans spoken of as the apostles of the pretended Messiah. These men should be forced to recant their apostasy and pray the forgiveness of God. "And if they refuse," he declared, his good eye ablaze, "they must be dealt with severely. Even in the more flagrant cases, such as that of one Simon of Capernaum, they must be condemned by the Sanhedrin and suffer death by stoning!"

"Brother Saul, it is good to know that there are still young men in Israel who with warmth of feeling show their zeal for the preservation inviolate of the ancient laws and traditions of the fathers and for the worship in all of its purity of the God of Israel," Caiaphas declared, when Saul paused in his impassioned plea. "And it is fortunate that we have coming into the membership of the Sanhedrin a new member fired with zeal for Israel and Israel's God and inflamed against those idolaters who profess allegiance to the false Messiah. But my young brother"—Caiaphas leaned forward and his dark eyes narrowed and he lowered his voice as though some unwelcome ears might be trying to hear—"we must not allow enthusiasm for any cause, even though it be a most righteous one, to lead us into taking action that might jeopardize our ultimate success." Then turning to Annas, he said, "Is it not so, O high priest? Perhaps you have clearer words with which to advise our brother of the situation——"

"You have spoken well, Joseph," Annas agreed, before Caiaphas had finished. "It is indeed inspiring to us older ones who through the years have carried the battle of Israel's Most High to witness such zeal as our younger brother shows." Annas laced ringed fat fingers together above the rounded mound of his stomach as he studied Saul. "But zeal must never be permitted to overreach calm judgment. Fortunately, however, there is a way by which our young brother's love for God and veneration of Israel's laws and traditions can be translated into accomplishing action. It is our task to find that way."

"Yes, our task and our opportunity," said Caiaphas. "But when we have found that plan, we must pursue it with caution, lest we accomplish more harm than good for the cause of our God of Israel."

"But not with such excess of caution and trepidation that it dulls enthusiasm and prevents determined action." With pudgy fingers Annas stroked his elegantly plaited flaring beard, and his bright eyes, alert under the heavy tangle of unrestrained eyebrows, studied the Sanhedrin's newest member.

"Is there not only one way to destroy any evil plant, whether it be tree or vine"—Saul's eyes were bright, too, with the mounting madness of utter dedication to his mission—"and that is to lay the ax to its trunk?"

"And have a forest of new shoots spring up from its roots?" Again Annas crossed his plump hands over his middle and studied his visitor. "No, Saul," he observed after a moment, "I do not think that is the way. This evil growth, I believe, must be killed by stripping it of its leaves, pruning off its twigs, its branches, its smaller limbs, and then its greater limbs. And when this is done, will not the trunk itself die, even to the end of its smallest roots, so that nothing remains from which new shoots can come forth?" He grasped the arms of the carved heavy chair and leaned forward to look Saul in the eyes. "We dare not proceed ruthlessly, Saul, against those Galileans who as the immediate companions and followers of the false Messiah have already in Jerusalem, and the region roundabout, gained a large following themselves. It is already being contended that these men have been given power by this dead carpenter"—he paused and his expression was derisive—"to work wonders of healing in his name, even to raising the dead to life. These simple folk, of course, suffer from a mass-madness, but their faith in these men and their devotion to them is incredible. Were we to offer them hurt, particularly to the most notorious of them all, that fellow Simon, it would be casting oil upon flames to quench them." He turned to Caiaphas. "Is it not so, Joseph?"

"I fear you are right." Joseph Caiaphas nodded solemnly. "To kill or molest Simon or any of the other leaders or to proceed against them as the Great Sanhedrin of Israel would only give support to the cause of the apostate carpenter and bring hundreds of other Israelites flocking into the idolatrous fellowship."

"But surely, O high priest, the Temple leadership is not afraid to defend our God of Israel and the ancient teachings and traditions of His Chosen People against a handful of illiterate Galilean fishermen and those misguided folk who profess to follow them?" Color was rising in Saul's tanned face and tension was raising his voice. "Surely the leaders of Israel have faith that in waging war for the God of Israel they will be protected by His strong arm! Surely"—Saul paused, for he was about to fling bitter words into the faces of that leadership, but proceeded—"you the high priest and you, Annas, have no fear of these Galileans!"

But neither Caiaphas nor Annas evidenced anger or resentment.

"We had no fear of the carpenter himself," said Caiaphas quietly. "We accomplished his death."

"And boldness and courage without reflection can sometimes be foolhardiness." Annas hurried to the support of Caiaphas. "In this matter we must look to the ultimate achievement. And if we are to stamp out this blaze that could spring into flames of disastrous proportions, we must plan carefully our method of proceeding. And when once it is undertaken"—Annas held up his right hand, palm toward Saul and spread wide in warning—"there must be no appearance to the multitude that it was instigated by us of the Sanhedrin. On the contrary, we must be judges and not prosecutors"—his round face relaxed into a bitter smile—"as far as the multitude understands, of course."

"But O sir, should not water be put at once to this spreading blaze?" Saul's tone was still tense and his scowl dark. "Cannot the plan be made and quickly implemented, and cannot I serve the God of Israel by helping carry it out?"

"Indeed, Saul, there is a way and you are the man to carry forward the plan." Annas looked toward Caiaphas, and the high priest nodded. "But you must not molest the so-called apostles of the Nazarene, particularly Simon. Let your ire fall upon others not so closely related to that false Messiah. There is one man"—Annas' black eyes lighted malevolently in the shadows of his beetling brows—"who works day and night to extend the idolatrous faith. And though he is of the Chosen People, he has come lately to Jerusalem, perhaps from Alexandria or Cyrene or even some other region upon the Great Sea. Perhaps you already have heard of one Stephen, the goldsmith who has a shop in the Street of the Metalworkers?"

"No." Saul shook his head. "Nor do I know of his shop."

"It is not far distant from the house of Mary of Cyprus." A cynical smile lifted the corners of his heavy lips. "He is among those, in fact, who frequent that house. Lately, I have learned, he is one of seven chosen to administer the affairs of the idolatrous flock that congregates there for communal meals. But do not offer"—Annas held up his hand in warning—"to challenge Stephen there. Wait rather to accost him when he is talking in one of the Hellenist synagogues. He speaks often, we have been informed, in the Synagogue of the Alexandrians and that one attended by former Cyrenians and Libyans, and likewise the Synagogue of the Asians and Cilicians. In each of these synagogues there are many Jews loyal to the God of Israel who do not hold with Stephen's idolatrous preachments. Doubtless a man of your zeal, Saul, might inflame them against him. And once he is defeated, you may be sure, the strength of the nefarious fellowship will begin to ebb, and presently it will shrivel and die."

The former high priest's eyes glittered evilly. "Could you go, Saul, to hear this Stephen lift his voice in the Hellenist synagogues and with your learning and power of reasoning so oppose him that his hearers would turn upon him?" Annas shrugged his thick shoulders, gestured with upflung palms, but said no more. Joseph Caiaphas nodded solemnly.

"I will seek him out," Saul promised.

11

As Stephen the goldsmith spoke, his words sped like flame-tipped arrows straight to the hearts of many of his hearers. Some swayed from side to side in gentle rhythm to the impassioned roll and surge of his preaching; others rocked forward and backward and moaned low in a composed ecstasy of faith and hope. But among the worshipers this day in the Synagogue of the Asians and the Cilicians, there were also numerous ones who were hearing with mounting pain and anger the goldsmith's frenzied claims of the crucified Nazarene's divinity and denunciation of those who even in the smallest way had shared in sending him to the cross.

Yet Stephen was declaring, and attempting to prove through recital of the writings of the ancient prophets of Israel concerning the nature of the Messiah who would come to earth, that this crucified carpenter from Galilee was indeed that promised Messiah and that it had been ordained of God that he would be sacrificed as a propitiation for man's great sinning. And Stephen was contending, here in the House of God and before this throng, that this false Messiah had returned to life after three days in the tomb and the cold embrace of death as he had promised he would.

In the rear of the synagogue Rabbi Saul, though in his every fiber hostile to the goldsmith and his preachments, sought to comprehend Stephen's words and his reasoning. But to the orderly mind of the rabbi there was no reason in the man's argument. If the omnipotent God of Israel had ordained that the Lord Messiah be a suffering rather than a conquering Messiah and that he be sacrificed as a recompense for man's sinning, how could a righteous and reasonable God hold responsible those of His children by whom the required sacrifice was accomplished? An omnipotent and omniscient and good God—so Saul assured himself—would neither require nor permit the crucifixion of the Messiah of Israel; but in the inconceivable event that He should, He surely would not hold guilty of sinning against Him those whom He had ordained to carry out this strange working of His will.

The unreasonableness of Stephen's argument, Saul assured himself, testified clearly to the fact of Stephen's instability and proneness to error and also to the fact that the crucified carpenter, if indeed he had claimed to be the Messiah of Israel, was no more than a masquerading and doubtless mentally unbalanced wanderer who perhaps actually believed himself the Messiah.

But what of the Galilean's claim that he could destroy the Temple in Jerusalem and in the space of three days rebuild it? Surely if he had made such a statement, and since his return to Jerusalem, Saul had received several reports that the Galilean had thus spoken, such unexampled boasting was a further proof that the man was dispossessed of his wits, that he was a simple, unhinged visionary, doubtless with an attractive personality, a facile tongue——

"Answer us this, goldsmith!"

Saul was startled out of his reflection. At the front of the synagogue, not many paces from Stephen, a man was challenging the speaker. He was a corpulent fellow, elegantly robed, with his great head of black hair and his long double-spiked beard curled and oiled, and when he had gestured with outflung arms in shouting to Stephen, Saul saw the flashing of many rings. The man, he thought in that instant, reminded him of Annas. Though likely a Hellenist Jew, he was in all probability one of the Temple leaders.

But Stephen had interrupted his discourse and nodded to his challenger to ask his question.

"Your rabbi, it has been often reported"—the corpulent one paused, arm upraised and fat forefinger pointed toward Stephen, to run the tip of his red tongue around the flattened circle of his thick lips, so that his dewlaps swung gently— "declared that he would tear down the House of God and in three days rebuild it. What say you to that, goldsmith?"

"I have heard it said that He so declared. But I think He was speaking not of our beautiful Temple on Mount Moriah, or of this synagogue, or of any other edifice in which our God of Israel is worshiped. Of a certainty He did not destroy the Temple. I believe that He was speaking rather of the temple of His own flesh that housed the spirit——"

"You say that he did not destroy our holy Temple." The ponderous one stabbed an angry arm in Stephen's direction. "Thereby you imply, do you not, that your rabbi could have destroyed it had he so willed?" He shook an extended forefinger menacingly. "Do not try to evade, goldsmith! What then do you say? Could your rabbi, had he wished it, have torn down our holy House of God, block by block, and then within the space of three days rebuilt it as it was before he so destroyed it?" He rubbed away with the palm of his hand the beads of sweat on his furrowed forehead, but all the while his furious eyes held riveted to Stephen's calm countenance. "Answer us, goldsmith! Answer us!"

"I implied nothing." Stephen's tone was even. "I know not the will of my Lord Messiah, nor can I conceive of the extent of His power. I only know that the house of His body was destroyed at the instigation"—now color flamed suddenly in his face and the intensity of his voice rose sharply—"of the high priest and his Temple minions, and that after three days *He* restored it. And I believe——"

He paused, for over the assemblage, hisses through gritting teeth were threatening to swell into menacing volume. But then he faced them fearlessly and raised his voice. "I believe that, had He so willed, my Lord Messiah in the twinkling of an eye could have ground into dust our splendrous Temple on Mount Moriah, and then in the fluttering of a bird's wing could have restored it, stone upon stone, cedar beam upon cedar beam. Verily, O you sons of Israel"—color was surging to the goldsmith's perspiring face—"is not the Most High God all-powerful? And my Lord Messiah, Jesus the Christ, is not *He* one with God!"

"Blasphemy!"

"Blasphemy!"

"Away with this idolater! Cast him from the House of the Most High!" The denunciation was swelling into an angry roar. "To the stoning ground with the blasphemer! Kill him! Kill him!"

But Stephen stood unshaken by the turmoil about him and the fringes of his prayer shawl hung even and undisturbed. And when it appeared that the enraged throng would rush upon him and seize him to drag him to his death, one of the Hellenists darted forward and took his stand between Stephen and the menacing multitude.

"Back! Stand away from him!" he shouted, as he thrust forward warning palms. "Would you commit murder in the House of God and on the Sabbath day! Get you back! And calm yourselves, sons of Israel."

His assertion of authority began to prove itself with the angry congregants, and the uproar lessened quickly into murmured epithets and hisses and fist-shakings. But one irate Hellenist was not so easily to be calmed. "Why say you it would be murder to slay the idolator?" he demanded. "Does not our law command that the blasphemer be stoned to death? How say you then that killing this blasphemer would be murder? Is it not a violation of the law of Moses if we allow him to live?"

"But not in the House of the God of Israel and on the holy Sabbath," another man declared.

"Nor can he be stoned until he has been tried by the Sanhedrin and delivered up for death," observed another. "The Sanhedrin must examine the witnesses to this man's blaspheming the Most High. That is the law of Moses. And when the Sanhedrin has passed judgment of death, now that we are under the heel of the Romans, the procurator must likewise decree death. But you have all heard the goldsmith's words this day. When we arraign him before the Sanhedrin, after the Sabbath has passed, there need be no dearth of witnesses to testify to his heinous blaspheming."

"We are witnesses! We have seen and we have heard!" exclaimed a long-necked hawk-nosed Israelite whom Saul remembered having seen the evening before in the public room of the Inn of the Red Heifer. "And so shall we swear before the Sanhedrin!"

"Indeed!" another called out. "I shall not fear to testify to this goldsmith's damnable preachment, his yoking of the false Messiah as one with the Most High. On the morrow when we drag him before the Sanhedrin, I shall relate his blasphemous utterance this day. And from amongst us there will come forth others so to testify."

"One other will be sufficient," declared a man from the rear of the synagogue. "Two witnesses, says the law, shall establish it."

So Stephen the goldsmith walked forth unharmed from the Synagogue of the Asians and the Cilicians. He walked forth boldly, with no fear in his eyes and no recanting on his lips.

And Rabbi Saul returned to his small chamber in the Inn of the Red Heifer. When the Sabbath sun had dropped low over Jerusalem's western wall to mark the end of the holy day, Saul went into the public room and dined sparingly on a round wheaten loaf, a bit of cheese and some ripened olives, a small dried fig and a cup of goat's milk. When he had finished the meal, he returned to his chamber, and as the deepening shadows enveloped it, he fell upon his knees on his mat in the corner. "O God of Israel," he prayed, "O Most High, One and Eternal, Omnipotent and Omniscient, toughen me to the task. Embolden me against them Thy enemies, against *him*, O God. Suffer me not to waver or fall by the wayside in my determination to destroy them utterly, to seek out and uproot and cast into the consuming flames these tares that threaten to impoverish the true plantings in the garden of Israel."

But even as Saul prayed he could not dispel the vision of Stephen the goldsmith standing fearlessly before the congregation of Hellenist Israelites and discoursing in eloquent and flaming words about the crucified Galilean. What facility of tongue the man had, and what power. With what evident sincerity and conviction he presented his cause, even though it was a false and idolatrous one. How tragic that such a man would not defend, rather than seek to destroy, the true worship of the one and only God of Israel.

12

The Temple guardsman sent by Annas found Rabbi Saul at the Inn of the Red Heifer.

"Annas and the high priest Caiaphas wish you, as a member of the Sanhedrin, to sit with the council of that court at the trial of Stephen the goldsmith," the guardsman revealed. "The council awaits you at the house of Annas."

"But why is it sitting there rather than in the Chamber of Hewn Stones at the Temple? Is not that the meeting place of the Sanhedrin?"

"It is, Rabbi Saul. But to assemble the full membership of the Sanhedrin is a difficult task requiring much time," the guardsman answered. "And they wish a quick trial of the goldsmith, conducted with as little public notice as possible, because of the likely reaction a meeting at the Temple would have among members of the sect of the Galilean. So they have called together the council, whose membership is small and drawn almost entirely from the family of Annas and Caiaphas. It is easily assembled."

"What charge are they bringing against the goldsmith?"

"Blasphemy, I believe. It is concerned with a declaration they say he made while speaking in one of the Hellenist synagogues that his Messiah, the Galilean who was crucified, could return and destroy the Temple. At any rate, he so violently offended many among his hearers on that occasion that this day they have laid hands on him and dragged him before Caiaphas and demanded that he be stoned to death."

When Saul with the guardsman arrived at the house of

Annas, the council of the Sanhedrin was ready to proceed with the trial of Stephen. Annas and Caiaphas nodded to him as he entered the chamber, and Caiaphas, without waste of words, presented the new member of Israel's highest court to the others and motioned him to his seat among them.

"Bring in the accused!" Caiaphas commanded.

Two guardsmen stepped through the doorway of an adjoining chamber and in a moment returned with Stephen the goldsmith between them. From the group of irate Hellenists who had surged into Annas' house behind the men who had rushed Stephen into the former high priest's presence, perhaps at his instigation, arose a hissing that Caiaphas stopped instantly with an angry gesture.

"There will be order and proper decorum or you will be forced from this chamber!" he declared, scowling darkly. Then, his anger ameliorating, he turned to the knot of Temple adherents surrounding Stephen. "What is the accusation you bring against this man and where are the witnesses?"

"I, O high priest, am one of the witnesses. I am Hamor. I am but one of many of the Synagogue of the Alexandrians who were witnesses to this man's blaspheming."

"Two witnesses are sufficient to establish it," declared a man back in the throng.

Old Annas nodded; he sat with fat hands folded across his spreading girth. "Two are sufficient, two whose testimony is in agreement, if they speak the truth."

"Yes," agreed Caiaphas. "Proceed then, Hamor. Give these members of the Sanhedrin your testimony."

Hamor cleared his throat, swallowed. "This one," he pointed with shaking forefinger toward Stephen, standing calmly with arms folded across his chest, "who is called Stephen the goldsmith came into the synagogue, and when he was called upon to speak, he did stand up and declare that one Jesus of Nazareth in Galilee, whom he held to be the Messiah of Israel, will destroy our holy Temple stone by stone, abrogate the laws of our father Moses, and himself establish a new kingdom under the rule of a new law."

"Hamor speaks the truth!" shouted a tall, thin Israelite who had been following avidly the witness' testimony. He twisted his thin face from side to side on the stem of his long neck. "Is it not so, brothers? Did not you yourselves hear the blasphemy uttered?"

"Indeed!" screamed one of those near him. "We heard it; we are witnesses likewise!"

"Yes! Yes! Hamor speaks the truth!" exclaimed another. And over the chamber a chorus of shouts affirmed the truthfulness of the testimony offered by Hamor. "We too are witnesses of the blasphemy! Inquire of us, O high priest. We saw, and heard, and we remember!"

When Caiaphas had heard Hamor out, he called forth another witness, who testified likewise that Stephen had said that his rabbi, the crucified carpenter, whom he declared to be the long-awaited Messiah of Israel, could pull down the resplendent House of the Most High stone by stone until it was ground into dust and then in three days rebuild it, and that he would set aside the laws of the fathers and establish new laws and a new kingdom, and these things he would accomplish because he was one with the omnipotent God of Israel.

When the witness had uttered these words a new storm of hisses and curses upon Stephen and his Messiah was threatening to burst furiously upon the chamber, but once more Caiaphas stilled it before it could build strength. Then he turned to confront Stephen, who all the while had been listening calmly to the testimony of the venomous witnesses.

"You have heard the words of the witnesses. Are these things true?"

Stephen remained calm, and when he spoke his voice was even-toned. But he did not directly answer Caiaphas' question. "O high priest, much you have heard said of late of the House of God." Then he raised his eyes and swept the semicircle of the council seats. "Brethren and fathers, hear me. The God of Glory appeared to our father Abraham, when he was in Mesopotamia, before he lived in Haran, and said to him, 'Depart from your land and your kindred and go into the land that I will show you,' " Stephen began.

And then, for a man seriously accused, Stephen did a strange thing. He reviewed the story of Israel through Isaac, Jacob, Joseph, and Moses, to whom He appeared in the burning bush, and God's dealings with His children of ancient times; until Solomon built one for Him, Stephen declared, the Most High possessed no house.

The crowd, hardly sensing the direction his discourse was taking, was growing restive. But again Caiaphas quieted the mutterings. "Let him proceed," the high priest commanded.

"But the goldsmith evades, O high priest," one of the council members, seated beside Rabbi Saul, protested. "He has given no answer to the question you propounded. He has neither affirmed nor denied the charge of the witnesses that *his* Messiah declared that in three days he would tear down our holy Temple and raise it up again stone upon stone. Nor has he said whether *he* believes that his Messiah *could* do so. Let him, O high priest, speak to the question!"

"Must the Most High possess a *house?*" His eyes blazing, Stephen confronted the Sanhedrinist. "Know you not that the Most High does not dwell in houses made with hands? Do you not comprehend that, as our ancient prophet Isaiah declared, *Thus saith the Lord, The heaven is my throne, and the earth is my footstool: where is the house that ye build unto me? and where is the place of my rest?*

"Think you then that God will be destroyed in His Temple if it be thrown down, stone upon stone! Think you God will *die* with the perishing of His house!"

"He blasphemes the House of God! He blasphemes against the God of Israel Himself!" An enraged Hellenist, one whom Saul recognized as one of the congregants of the Synagogue of the Asians and the Cilicians, was waving both arms frantically. "You have heard his words, elders of Israel! Must we listen longer to this abomination!" Flecks of spittle foaming on the man's lips sprayed his neighbors in front of him, and his red-

dened eyeballs rolled in their sockets as quickly he twisted his
head from side to side in his apparent attempt to discover if his
fellow Hellenists were in accord with him. "Is it not so, brothers in Israel? Do you not agree!"

"Yes! Yes! Indeed, Achbor, we agree!"

"Hear him, fathers in Israel! He speaks the truth! Away with
this blasphemer!"

"To the stoning pit with him, lest his blaspheming be held
against us! Kill the blasphemer!"

"Kill him! Kill him!"

Throughout the chamber, knotted fists were uplifted against
the goldsmith as the denunciation grew into a storm of angry
shouts demanding his death. But Stephen stood calmly, arms
folded across his chest, the passion of a moment before spent,
as once again Caiaphas demanded order. Then, as the screams
and hissings subsided to a sullen silence, Stephen's eyes swept
the throng about him, a new flame climbed the stem of his
neck and suffused his cheeks, and suddenly he thrust out both
arms and swung about in a half-circle that embraced both the
angry accusers and the coldly hating Sanhedrinists.

"You stiff-necked people, uncircumcised in heart and
ears, you always resist the Holy Spirit!" he screamed, as his
right hand doubled into a fist that he shook angrily in their
faces. "Which of the prophets did not your fathers persecute?
And they killed those who announced beforehand the coming of the Righteous One, whom *you* have now betrayed and
murdered, *you* who received the law as delivered by angels
and did not keep it!"

"Uncircumcised, he calls us! He would place us in the ranks
of the pagans! He would make of us Gentiles!"

"Kill him! Enough of this abomination! To the stoning
ground!"

All about the chamber the enraged Hellenists stamped their
feet and ground their teeth together and shouted for Stephen's
death, but the high priest's commands, supported by the Temple guardsmen and their upraised menacing cudgels, quieted

them momentarily, though they continued to glare at their traducer, their eyes bright with hate.

And suddenly Stephen's countenance and demeanor were changed. The flame of his indignation against the enemies of his Lord Messiah had drained from his face and down his neck like water from an overturned pitcher. No longer did he appear to be taking notice of them or of the council of the Sanhedrin. His eyes were lifted above them to the topmost opening of the window in the opposite wall. A new light flooded his now calm features, ecstatic, as of a joy perfected. He raised an arm and pointed, and his voice trembled on the edge of a vast excitement. "Behold!" Stephen exclaimed. "I see the heavens opened, and the Son of Man standing at the right hand of God!"

"Blasphemer! Idolater!"

"Stone him! Kill the apostate!"

Screaming their rage, insensate with hate, the Hellenists surged upon Stephen. The handful of Temple guardsmen, had they been of a mind to attempt it, were powerless to protect him. Caiaphas was shouting to them to desist, but this time even those who heard his words refused to obey. And looking down upon the tumult in front of him, Saul felt no pity for the victim of the throng's rage. His feeling, rather, was one of exultation that the apostate Stephen, worshiper of the false Messiah, was about to have visited upon himself the judgment and wrath of the true God of Israel whom he had been, so deliberately and flagrantly, flouting and blaspheming.

"You yourself, O high priest," he called out to Caiaphas, "are a witness to his blaspheming! Seek no longer, O sir, to hold back from his head the just vengeance of our outraged God of Israel!"

"But sentence has not been pronounced!" shouted Caiaphas above the maddened cries of the throng. "Would you commit murder! There has been no verdict of the council, and no sentence! Nor has the approval of the procurator been sought!"

But already they had seized Stephen and were dragging

him, while others spat upon him and belabored him with their fists, across the chamber floor and out through the doorway.

In the soul of Saul of Tarsus a kindling flame leapt into blazing and his frame trembled in an ecstasy of desire to strike down and destroy utterly all those enemies of the Most High God of Israel who would dishonor His Temple, flout His laws, and blaspheme His Glorious Name. And in that instant Saul sprang from his chair, and lifting high his robe to free his knobby legs, ran after the howling mob that was dragging the buffeted and bleeding Stephen down the slope of Mount Zion toward the stoning pit.

13

As the frenzied, blood-scenting mob reached the square in front of Dung Gate and surged through that portal, it caught up idlers lounging before the shops and bore them onward like flies settled upon a beef's carcass being carted to the marketplace. What crime the bruised, hardly conscious and almost naked prisoner of this screaming horde had committed was of no concern to these laggards; they had been aroused from their lethargy at the prospect of being able to witness a man being done to horrible death.

Nor did the vagrants have far to go or long to wait. Some two hundred paces beyond the deep declivity of the Brook Kidron, just beyond the city's eastern wall and along the dust-thick road passing the Garden of Gethsemane, the throng turned aside to cross a rock-strewn stubble field. Beside a slight, rounded depression at a corner of the field where two stone fences came together, it stopped. And strangely, as if for the first time aware of the enormity of the deed it was bent upon doing, the mob of a sudden ceased its uproar.

But only for an instant.

"Strip the blasphemer, and into the pit with him!"

The strident voice of a hawk-nosed Israelite, across the rim of the hollowed circle from the slumped figure of Stephen, shattered the unnatural calm, and signaled a renewal of the savage outburst.

"Kill him! Stone the idolater! Death to the worshiper of the false Messiah!"

Two men jerked Stephen upright and held him on his bleeding feet, for his sandals had been dragged off and his heels mangled by the cobblestones, while another snatched away his torn and bedraggled loincloth, the only clothing that had remained on his beaten body. The fellow held it high, as though he had captured a trophy, and cackled foolishly, as the first two, each seizing Stephen by an arm and leg, swung him out and downward into the pit.

Saul, who had pushed through the shrieking, crazed Hellenists to the edge of the pit, saw the white body of the goldsmith sail through the air; as it plunged downward, the mutilated heels, moving faster, swept around in a bloody arc, and it landed with a heavy thud, spread-eagled on the stones at the bottom of the shallow bowl.

A long moment the naked bleeding white body lay still. But then Saul's eyes, fixed upon the shattered form of Stephen, saw it move; slowly the goldsmith drew his legs and arms beneath himself and pushed upward until with great effort he sat back upon his lacerated heels.

"Quick! Grab stones and hurl them upon him!" yelled the man who a moment before had ended the tense silence with his command to cast the goldsmith into the pit. "Cover the blasphemer in avenging stones!" He bent down to clutch in his two hands a jagged heavy rock.

"Hold! Stand back! Would you commit murder!" Saul, on the rim of the pit, was gesticulating furiously. "Hold your stones!"

"But you sat among the council members! You yourself heard this apostate blaspheming our holy Temple, even the God of Israel Himself!" protested the Israelite whose command Saul had challenged.

"Yes! And you declared yourself to the high priest Caiaphas that Stephen had blasphemed! You declared that Caiaphas should not withhold from this fellow's head the vengeance of the Most High! And now at the sight of blood you lose your courage to lift your hand against the apostate, you refuse to wreak vengeance——"

"No! No!" Saul screamed, his anger rising. "I have lost no courage! I do not cringe at the sight of bloodletting! But I would commit no murder, even in avenging the Most High. Hear me, men! This man must be stoned. His life must be required in payment for his blaspheming our Most High God. But know you not that unless vengeance is wreaked in the name of God and in the manner the commandment prescribes, it is murder!"

"Then tell us, O rabbi, lest we violate the commandment, how——"

"You must know, brothers in Israel, that the Scriptures declare: *The hands of the witnesses shall be first upon him to put him to death, and afterward the hands of all the people. So thou shalt put the evil away from among you.*" Saul turned toward two men who happened to be standing near him, their faces flushed with exertion and their fury against Stephen. "Hamor! Achbor! It was you who first testified before the council to this man's blaspheming. Let you then cast the first stones upon him, and after you, we all."

The witness nearer Saul without a word bent down to pick up a heavy stone at his feet. But the stone was incrusted with soil, and when the man's mantle fell against it, he straightened again and removed the garment.

"Here, Hamor; let me hold it." Seeing that the man had no place to lay the mantle except on the trampled ground, Saul extended his hand and took it. Immediately Achbor handed it to the rabbi from Tarsus.

Now Saul's eyes returned to the man in the pit. Stephen was still crouched back on his heels, but his shoulders were hunched forward and his head hung low, with his chin pressed into his chest and his beard splayed wide. As Saul looked, a rounded, heavy stone arched over the rim of the depression and crashed down upon the naked white body; it only grazed a shoulder though, and Stephen appeared unaware that the missile had touched him.

But before the stone came to rest, another struck him. It was smaller than the other, and with irregular, rough edges. The blow, too, was glancing, but it split a gaping furrow in his scalp just above the hairline at his forehead, and blood gushed forth and poured down his face as suddenly he lifted his head and looked directly toward Saul.

But there was no pain on the countenance of the goldsmith, the rabbi saw. As though the stone against the skull had roused him from rapturous dreaming, he opened his eyes wide, and raising one arm as he braced himself with the other, pointed toward the serene sky, and ecstasy sat like a flame upon his bruised and bloodied face. "Behold!" he exclaimed, his voice resonant and triumphant. "I see the heavens opened, and the Son of Man standing at the right hand of God!" Stephen extended the other fingers of his pointing hand as if to grasp one outstretched to him. "He is beckoning to me! He is reaching forth His hand——"

A stone flung from behind him struck Stephen between the shoulder blades and flattened him on his face, arms outflung. From the rim of the pit, stones and denunciation rained down upon the inert man, as the shrieking, snarling Hellenists, their madness renewed and unleashed in the exercise of their own cowardly violence, hurled their hate with their missiles.

But, miraculously, life had not yet departed the horribly punished body. As Saul watched, his eyes by a terrible fascination fixed upon the broken and bloody pulp below, he saw Stephen move. The arms pulled slowly inward to the body, and with great effort Stephen twisted upon his side and pushed his head and shoulders upward until he could look into the leering faces of his assailants on one segment of the pit's edge. He blinked his eyes, as if to clear his vision of the smeared blood, and as they opened wide and comprehending upon Saul of Tarsus, the ecstasy of the moment before sat triumphant upon his tortured countenance.

"O Lord Jesus, forgive them"—Saul heard the words coming, clear and solemn, as a benediction, through the swelling, bruised lips—"for they understand not what they do." The eyes and the rapturous smile held steady. "O my Lord Messiah, forgive——"

A hurled rough stone smashed against the side of Stephen's head. He pitched forward on his face, one arm crumpled beneath his chest; the other, outstretched, jerked convulsively a moment and lay still, the palm of the hand open wide to the silent sky.

The Hellenists, silent again, their venom suddenly spilled out, began to disperse. Some, talking quietly, retraced their way across the stony field to the road that led down the slope to Dung Gate. Others, likely not wishing to be seen in the group returning to the city, lingered behind and then slunk off like wild dogs gorged on a lamb lost from its flock and set upon and killed.

Saul, having returned their mantles to the witnesses, stood at his place on the rim of the stoning pit looking down upon the mangled body, half-buried in blood-spotted stones. "Thus perish all those apostates"—he said the words aloud—"who give allegiance to the false Messiah, who flout the laws and the Person of our Most High God!"

But as he looked, Saul saw only a rapturous countenance turned upward to him and reflecting an inner ecstasy and an intrenched faith impervious to all threats, imprecations, and cruel stones. And he fancied he was hearing again Stephen's pleading: "O Lord Jesus forgive them . . . forgive . . . forgive . . ."

But the vision and the voice were gone and only the pitiful, broken body lay under the rain of stones. In the depths of

Saul of Tarsus, pity drove out hate of the man Stephen, pity for a potentially good man, potentially a worthy son of Israel and faithful supporter of Israel's God and His laws, but in his weakness of character, led by a false Messiah and the blandishments of his evil apostles into idolatry, apostasy, death, and everlasting hell.

So now a new hate grew in the innermost soul of Saul and possessed him, stronger, fiercer, more implacable, against all those who would seek to spread the teachings of the false Messiah and faith in him and in so doing consign sons of Israel to eternal damnation. He turned away from the stoning pit and lifted his countenance, darkly scowling, to the vaulted blue of the calm Judaean sky. "Strengthen my heart and my arm against them, O Most High. Grant me no rest or peace until every vestige of the apostate Galilean has been utterly destroyed, until every son of the Chosen who has taken upon himself the name of the false one has recanted and returned to the worship of the One God or perished from the earth. Strengthen my arm to lay the lash to their backs until their blood runs red, stop my ears against their pleadings and their groanings. Make even my name among them a loathing and an abomination."

14

In the days and weeks following the death of Stephen the goldsmith, Rabbi Saul went no more to the home of Mary of Cyprus, nor in any of the streets or public houses of the city or the courts of the Temple did he come upon his once dearly beloved friend Joseph bar Nabas.

Saul was thankful that he had not encountered the Cypriote. He feared that when he confronted Bar Nabas, he would allow his feelings of affection to overpower him and he would lack the courage to punish Bar Nabas with the same severity with which he had been dealing with scores of other apostates of that nefarious fellowship already being alluded to in Jerusalem as the Way.

But daily in his chamber in the Inn of the Red Heifer or lying prostrate upon his face on the stones of the Temple courts, Saul besought in utter earnestness of the God of Israel that He would embolden his spirit and strengthen his arm to wreak vengeance in the name of the Most High upon all His enemies, even Joseph bar Nabas. During the daylight hours Saul thus entreated the God of Israel; but in the evenings he and the Temple guardsmen provided by the high priest Caiaphas burst with fury upon workers who had returned to their hovels in noisome Ophel, for most of those of the Way had been drawn into the fellowship from the unfortunate and destitute of Jerusalem and its environs, and with whips and copper-ringed staves the guardsmen beat them oftentimes into insensibility. Some, it was whispered among the terrorized victims and even in a house here and there on Mount Zion, had died from the merciless beatings.

For the man of Tarsus had not relented. Instead, as his rigorous oppression of the faithful had spread over the regions of the city in which the poorer people had their precarious existence, he had grown more implacable in his determination to see excised from the living body of Israel this evil growth that if left to burgeon unmolested might choke out and destroy the body itself. And the name Saul of Tarsus, as that day on the rim of the stoning pit he had prayed it might, had become an anathema and a hissing among the communicants of the Way.

But those of the fellowship were not being persecuted because they were professed followers of the false Messiah, it was claimed. Old Annas and the high priest Caiaphas had agreed that it was not a violation of Israel's law for a son of

Israel to believe that the carpenter of Galilee was indeed the true Messiah of God, that he had been sacrificed on the cross in propitiation for man's sinning, and that he had arisen from the tomb.

"Such an Israelite, however, must obey scrupulously the commandments and laws of Israel," Caiaphas had declared, "And his membership in this wicked company does not permit him to evade punishment for the transgressing of a single law of Israel, nor does it excuse him for failure to perform every duty required to be performed. But even if the law did permit such laxity, it would not be expedient"—he looked toward Annas as if for confirmation of his statement—"for us to proceed against them on the grounds that they belong to this fellowship."

"But it happens that a great many of those who do in one way and another violate the commandments and heed not the ancient statutes in their entirety," observed Annas with a sly smile, "are Hellenists who profess allegiance to this Galilean. Could not our brother Saul, then, in punishing offenders against the laws of Israel discover such offenders among those professing belief in this false Messiah? But, Rabbi Saul, you must be scrupulously careful not to bring against them charges, that if established, would demand exaction of the death penalty." Annas held up his hand, palm outward. "As you know, only the procurator himself can pronounce the sentence of death. The matter, therefore, would have to be taken before Pilate in Caesarea, and a great clamor might arise. And perhaps the charge could not be sustained. We hear that Pilate has been disturbed since pronouncing the sentence of crucifixion against the Galilean. His wife, it was rumored, and doubtless with considerable truth, was outraged when he sent the miscreant to his death; there are some who say that she herself is actually a member of the seditious fellowship. It is fortunate for us, no doubt, that Pilate and his wife were in Caesarea when Stephen was stoned." Out of long habit in plottings and secret dealings, Annas lowered his voice. "So, my brother Saul," he said, leaning forward and rubbing his fat hands together, "bring against them only such charges that will merit the laying of the lash upon their backs. Proceed with cunning. But smite them, O Saul, smite them hip and thigh, until they have become so fearful that they will fall away from Simon and the other leaders and leave the vine of this wickedness to perish because of the pruning from it of the twigs and the small branches."

So under Saul's direction and with himself usually personally leading it, the persecution of the faithful of the Way had been so merciless and so thorough that it seemed that soon, if it had not already become so, the sect of the crucified Galilean would be extinct within Jerusalem and the region immediately roundabout.

Particularly was this true among the Hellenist Jews. Because Saul knew them, and knew many of them to be members of the nefarious fellowship, they were early singled out for his wrath. And finding the punishable offense to serve as a pretext for beating a Hellenist Jew who followed the Way was all too easy for the impassioned Saul. Because the Hellenist Jew had lived so much of his life in a province remote from Jerusalem, before coming to the ancient citadel of Israel, he had not always been brought up to observe punctiliously the strict Hebrew ritual and law, although his reverence for the God of Israel and devotion to Him and to His people was just as strong as that of any dweller in Jerusalem. The Hellenist Jews lived and worshiped in the spirit of the law, but they were frequently remiss about following all the minutiae of observance. Consequently, those among them who were of the Way were quick to feel upon their backs the whips and staves of the rabbi from Tarsus.

There came a day when Saul went again to the high priest Joseph Caiaphas. "The twigs and the branches have been cut away from the iniquitous vine, O high priest," he declared, "so that in the Holy City of Israel the vine itself soon will be fit only to be dug up and cast into the fire. But word has come to us that in other places remote from Jerusalem shoots of the poisonous vine have sprung up and in those areas are threatening to choke out the growth of the true grape of Israel. Those evil plantings must be torn up by the roots and utterly destroyed!" Saul's good eye and the one half-hidden behind the drooping lid were blazing, and his words were impassioned. His whole being, Caiaphas saw, was aflame with devotion to the God of Israel and driven by a determination to defend against His enemies His holy laws and commandments.

"And you have a plan for accomplishing their destruction?" he inquired.

"I have," answered Saul. "The noxious growth has taken most tenacious root, we hear, in Damascus, where many who had converted to the Hebrew faith from the paganism of the Gentiles have latterly converted to the blasphemous sect of the crucified carpenter. And there are among them even some of the Chosen who have been led to embrace this evil doctrine." Saul's forehead furrowed, and he lowered his voice. "The authority of the high priest embraces all those of the Chosen, even Hebrews living in other lands. And the ethnarch at Damascus, being a friend of the high priest, would not only not oppose the high priest's asserting that authority in Damascus but would assist him. Therefore, O high priest, give me a tablet of authority from you to go to Damascus and arrest and return to Jerusalem for trial certain leaders of this impious group, particularly one Ananias, who is reported to be the chief instigator of this heresy." The fire in his eyes flamed again, and he gestured with outflung clenched fist. "So shall we dig up and cast into the consuming fires the newly sprung up sprouts, so that nowhere will there remain even a vestige of the unholy vine!"

15

Ophel and the declivity of the Brook Kidron still lay in the deep shadows when Saul's train moved out through Dung Gate and began the ascent of the road to Bethany. In Saul's company were Hamor and Achbor, his staunchest supporters in defending the God of Israel, His laws, and His Temple, against the idolatrous sect of the Galilean, and several Temple guardsmen assigned to Saul by the high priest Caiaphas.

The men walked, but the Temple authorities had provided donkeys to bear the food, tents, bedding and other supplies, and Saul and members of the company, if from time to time they should become ill or greatly fatigued. Should many of the sect be apprehended at Damascus, Saul counted upon the ethnarch there to provide additional guardsmen to conduct the prisoners to Jerusalem for trial and punishment.

At the point along the road where the path turned off right toward the stoning pit, Saul glanced quickly over his shoulder. But he did not slow his pace, nor did he say anything to his companions trudging beside him. In that instant, however, the avenging rabbi saw clearly in his mind's eye the goldsmith Stephen on his knees at the bottom of the rounded depression looking heavenward and praying God to forgive those who were even then raining stones down upon his defenseless, naked body.

"We shall drive them out, O goldsmith. We shall wreak vengeance in the name of the God of Israel," said Saul, in words neither spoken aloud nor framed on his lips, "upon those evil ones whose so great sinning led you into sinning and damnation." Suddenly his countenance was grim, but still he uttered no sound. "Strengthen my arm and harden my heart against them, O Most High," he prayed soundlessly, so that none about him knew it. "Give me courage and cunning that I may deal mercilessly with those Thine enemies at Damascus."

Soon they reached the summit of the Mount of Olives, and as the sun was venturing thin yellow fingers into the gray above the eastern headlands beyond the Dead Sea, they began the descent that led steeply through stony defiles toward Jericho. Through the wearying warm day, for now summer lay heavy upon the ancient land, as the small caravan picked its way through the loose rocks in the passes, the vision came to Saul of the goldsmith Stephen, naked at the bottom of the stoning pit, bleeding and broken and struggling to get to his knees, praying to the God of Israel for those who were so horribly killing him. "O Lord Jesus, forgive them"—Saul heard the words again and again, as distinctly as he had heard them that day outside Jerusalem's walls—"for they understand not what they do."

Could Stephen have been speaking the truth? The question assailed him each time the vision recurred, as it had done many times in the days since the stoning of Stephen. Can it be that we who are so zealous in our defense of the Most High, His laws and His Temple do not understand, do not comprehend? O God in Israel, could this Galilean carpenter, this humble villager, hounded to a frightful death by the priestly authorities, could this simple youth have been indeed the mighty Messiah of God? Could he have arisen from death? And does he live now? Is he at Thy right hand? If he was the Messiah, if he *is* the living Messiah, O God, then we and not he are the blasphemers, then we and not he struggle against the Most High, then we, who with such fervor strive to defend Thee against him and those who look to him, and not he, O God in Israel, are Thy *enemies!*

"No! No! O God, no!" he exclaimed aloud once when the vision and the doubt bore down heavily upon him. "It cannot be! No! No!"

Hamor, walking a step behind, caught Saul's arm. "Rabbi, are you ill? Is it the sun's heat on you?"

"No. But the sun is warm. Perhaps I dozed an instant." He shook his head to clear it of the vision and the assailing doubt. "Let us move along. When we are past these stones the going should be better."

Saul's robe was open to his waist to give air to his steaming hairy chest; he tugged at it so that it bulged out over his rope girdle, and the hem came up high on his dust-covered legs. "Deliver me, O God, from the temptation of the Evil One! Allow me to fall not into the trap. Strengthen my arm and harden my heart against those Thine enemies who follow after the false Messiah!"

But the words this time did not escape his lips.

So they pressed relentlessly on, and when the shadows from the sun dropping behind the backbone of mountains north of Jerusalem had engulfed the Jordan valley, though it was still not nightfall, they set up their tents under trees near the river in the level region above Jericho. The next morning, while the valley was still deep in the shadows, they broke camp and started northward alongside the Jordan. Through the deeply chiseled chasm the waters of the Jordan twisted southward, like a great snake slithering through a dank jungleland of waving, tall reed grass, tufted slender papyrus plants, mazes of pink-white flowering tamarisk, and clumps of willows bending to the water on either bank, graceful poplars, and blooming plants in riotous profusion—lavender, henna, with its dye-yielding leaves and fragrant white blossoms, capers, and pomegranates flaunting scarlet flowers.

Before a week had passed they had emerged from the steaming declivity of the Jordan at the foot of the Sea of Galilee, hardly seventy miles north of the Dead Sea as a bird would fly but much farther along the meandering trail. There they turned eastward and followed the curve of the seashore until they were moving northward again through the region of Gaulanitis, along the high headlands that looked down on the sea and the river connecting it with tiny Lake Merom a long day's journeying to the north.

A few miles below the lake, where the waters of the Jordan came level with the surface of the Great Sea before beginning their precipitous descent to the Sea of Galilee, Saul and his men turned to move northeastwardly across Bashan and the Hauran wasteland between snow-topped Mount Hermon and the forbidding basalt region of the Argob. A little way north of that stony outcropping, in an oasis paradise on the edge of the great Syrian desert, Damascus with its idolatrous band of the crucified carpenter's fugitive followers awaited, unmindful of Saul and the fury with which he was planning so soon to burst upon them.

As Saul drew nearer the ancient city set down in the watered and luxuriant plain, his resolution was strengthened to visit upon these enemies of the true religion the vengeance of the scorned and insulted Lord God of Israel.

"Give me no respite, O God, until I have sought them out and bound them and delivered them to the high priest in Jerusalem for judgment and grievous punishment," Saul prayed, as he labored through blinding sun and swirling dust and heat and sudden storm toward the gates of the old city. "Do Thou strengthen my arm and harden my heart, O God, that I may be the instrument through which Thy vengeance is visited upon them, even vengeance for the deserved death of the misguided apostate Stephen the goldsmith, led of the false Messiah and his nearer followers to blaspheme Thee, Thy laws, and Thy holy Temple, O Most High God."

Saul's prayers, though offered in great earnestness, were said likewise in silence as the weary caravan plodded through shifting sand and loose stones under a pitiless sun that burned them to a leathery hard-brown leanness and parched their dust-clogged throats.

But on an afternoon as the topmost stones of the walls and the higher edifices of Damascus came into view beyond the

sweltering sands and the sun was beating upon them with un-
abated severity, the rabbi suddenly had spoken aloud. They
had been crossing a wasteland overlaid with rounded stones
varying in size from small pebbles to great boulders that threw
back into their faces the desert's scorching heat. Their frayed
sandals and the feet of the little donkeys smote against the
stones, and the dust from stones thus dislodged rose about
them to cling to their begrimed dampened mantles and sweating bodies. As Saul trudged past one of the larger boulders he
found himself on the rim of a stone-ringed small depression.
Startled, he peered through the narrow aperture, between the
corners of the mantle thrown over his head as a covering
against the sun, at an inert white object like a naked man
huddled, head down, on his knees.

"O God in Israel!" Saul had exclaimed. "Stephen!"

Achbor and Hamor, who were at that moment behind with
the plodding donkeys, had not heard. But one of the guardsmen, walking near Saul, had heard the exclamation but had
not caught the goldsmith's name.

"Rabbi, did you call?" the man asked. "Are you weary?
Would you like to pause to catch your breath?"

"I am in no distress," answered Saul, throwing back the pro-
tective covering from his face. "I must have been half-dream-
ing. Let us lose no time. If we push on until our camping at
nightfall, we should enter Damascus by midday tomorrow."
He turned again to look at the sunken place in the desert's
stony floor. From the center of it, a large irregular mass of
white quartz, polished and glistening, threw back to him the
searing rays of the sun.

They made camp in the evening at a cluster of smoke-
smudged boulders where, it appeared, many a Syrian camel
train had paused for a night, and early the next morning, before the sun had begun to lambaste the desert and its travelers,
they struck their tents and headed eastward toward the city's
walls now risen high on the inviting green plain.

The little caravan had plodded but a few miles across the
intervening waste of sand and stones, however, before the sun

had climbed high to hurl once more into their faces, shafts of blazing light and searing heat. From above, the heat smote them; it arose about their trudging feet and enfolded their wearied, parched frames like a seamless Galilean homespun robe. But ahead, the walls and taller buildings of Damascus loomed higher, and the cool luxuriant greenness of the orchards and vineyards and restful groves beside the watercourses outside the city beckoned to the flagging caravan.

Saul likewise urged his men and beasts onward toward the inviting oasis. "Soon, if we falter not but continue to press forward," said he, "we will have put behind us this heated sand and these loose stones and will be refreshing ourselves beneath the trees. Then, when we have drunk of cooling draughts and eaten our fill and slept out the night soundly, we can set our hands to accomplishing the task that has brought us on this tiresome long journey."

The stones . . . the task . . . the long journey. . . .

"Continue my feet upon the way, O God of Israel, in these last miles before Damascus. Permit neither my legs nor my courage to weaken; gird up Thou my loins and strengthen my arm to the completion of the task Thou has set me upon. Let me be not overcome by the heat or by the loose stones underfoot that make the going difficult, that slow the journeying and give opportunity for the nurturing of doubt concerning even the rightness of the mission."

But was it not plain that it was no apparition, that the thing at the bottom of the declivity among the boulders was but a large irregular block of quartz reflecting the dazzling brightness of the sun?

"Spur me onward to the task, O God. Cast away all doubt concerning its rightness and its efficacy. Remove from my mind's eye every conjuring of the apostate Stephen on his knees in the stoning pit. Cleanse Thou my mind and my heart of every vague wondering about the crucified carpenter of Galilee. Make strong my arm, harden Thou my heart against all those who in naming His name blaspheme the Most High and traduce His prophets, His laws, and His holy Temple."

The caravan had not paused for its leader to offer up his prayers; Saul had prayed as he had plodded a straight course under the pitiless sun. Nor had any word escaped his parched lips; his prayer was rather a meditation and a soul-searching, a seeking in utmost sincerity to establish communication with his God. Leaning on his staff, with which from time to time he flicked from his path a loose small stone, his shoulders hunched forward and back arched to the sun's onslaught, his eyes on the hot sands a pace ahead of his tortured feet, the rabbi from Tarsus pushed resolutely eastward. So deep in reverie did he appear to have lost himself that those walking near him did not venture to converse with him. They seemed determined, like Saul, to conserve their words as well as their remaining energies for the accomplishing of the final few miles to the gate into Damascus.

So the others in the group from Jerusalem, like Saul, intent on the way ahead, had not been aware of the sudden heavy stillness about them as the stifling sodden air enfolded them, nor were they prepared for the rage of wind that a moment later burst upon them from out of the west at their backs. As the burdened animals sank wearily to the sands and the men flattened themselves upon it, their heads wrapped in their mantles, the storm roared over them and the very heavens seemed locked in furious battle, as though the angry winds, cooled by the eternal snows crowning Mount Hermon, had determined to destroy the sun's dominion over the desert.

But as quickly as the winds had roared down upon the little caravan they were gone, and above the settling sands the sun shone triumphant again. Saul and his men arose and shook out their mantles, straightened the packs on the donkeys' backs and tightened the holding straps, and resumed the journey.

"See us through the gate into Damascus and the task that must be accomplished, O God in Israel. Keep us safe from all harm that we may do Thy will, that without faltering we may uphold the Name of the Most High, that in His Name we may encounter and overcome quickly those leaders in Damascus of the fellowship of the false Messiah. And blot out forever from our vision the apparition of the misguided apostate Stephen on his knees in the pit——"

The rabbi paused abruptly in his unspoken prayer in a sudden, determined effort to drive from his mind every haunting thought of a day and a drama in a stony field beyond Dung Gate.

Now Saul raised his eyes from the sands a few steps ahead of his plodding feet and looked toward the walls and roofs of Damascus and trees and green and flowering shrubs so invitingly near. A few hundred paces, perhaps a mile, of further trudging, and they would be free of the sands and the shifting small stones and would arrive at the edge of the oasis. He pulled wider the opening in his head covering, for already the sun was high overhead and out of his eyes, and studied the city's walls and towers and beckoning trees. His eyes were intently eastward, blinking to sweep away the gathering film of dust, and eager, so that he had no occasion to notice, coming from the direction of Mount Hermon behind them and moving fast, the deep blue ball of a storm cloud high in the shimmering brightness. Saul grasped his staff with a firmer grip and bent his back to the burning sun and the last mile before the oasis of Damascus, unmindful of the approaching cloud above and a sudden unearthly calm in the stifling heat blanketing the desert floor.

Before the sun is an hour beyond its zenith, we shall be moving alongside the stream in the shade of trees to the singing of birds, with the perfume of flowers in our dust-begrimed nostrils, O God in Israel. The goal is in sight; the way ahead is clear; soon now I shall be about the task I was sent upon by the direction of our One God to wreak vengeance in His Name upon the blaspheming, idolatrous leaders of the wicked fellowship of the impious Galilean——

With a fearful mighty blast the dark cloud exploded and an awesome spear of white light smote the scorching sands. The desert, reeling, flung men and beasts from their feet.

Saul, numbed and sightless, lay in a twisted heap, with his face turned upward to the blazing sun. A moment he lay thus dazed, and then as his senses returned, though not his sight, he heard the voice, resonant and strong: "Saul, Saul, why do you persecute me?"

"Who are you?"

"I am Jesus, whom you are persecuting."

It was the same voice, and it was firm and possessed of authority, though gentle. But when prostrate Saul, seeing with blinded eyes the effulgent vision confronting him, spoke again, it was a new Saul, questioning: "What, Lord, will you have me to do?"

"Arise, Saul, and go into the city," the voice directed. "There it will be told you what to do."

Saul stared unblinking and lifted bronzed arms imploringly to the receding vision. Then with unseeing eyes streaming, he stretched himself on the sands, shoulders shaking, his face pressed hard into his cupped palms.

"Forgive me, O God in Israel. Forgive me, O Lord Messiah. I did not know. O Master, I did not know. Forgive, O Master." He lay on the hot sands, sobbing, pleading. "O, I did not know. I did not know."

He felt hands on his arms, beneath his shoulders, lifting him to his feet.

"Rabbi, are you ill? Can you stand?" Achbor's voice was solicitous. "Did the lightning bolt—O Rabbi, are you blind?"

"I cannot see," answered Saul, as they held him on unsteady feet, "but, I thank the Most High and my Lord Messiah, I am no longer blind."

"But we do not understand, Rabbi Saul." Hamor's forehead was furrowed in consternation. "You appeared to be talking with someone, but there was none other here. Could it be that the bolt, or too much sun——"

"There was Another here." Saul's voice was calm, assured. "He appeared to me, and I saw Him and heard Him clearly."

"But who, Rabbi Saul?" Hamor was shaking his head and his countenance was grave. "Could it not have been that, in this torturing heat of the sun full upon us, a hallucination——"

"It was no hallucination." Saul answered with authority. "It was neither the lightning bolt nor the heat. He appeared in person to me, He whom I have been so grievously persecuting, Jesus the crucified carpenter of Galilee, the living Messiah of God!" He lifted unseeing eyes toward the blazing heavens. "O, God, I thank Thee, I thank Thee." Tears rolled unrestrained down his dust-begrimed face. "Forgive me, Stephen my brother; forgive me, forgive me, O Jesus my Lord Messiah." He stood silent and unmoving a long moment. Then he lowered his eyes and lifted a corner of his mantle to wipe the sweat from his face. "Let us go on into the city," he said, dropping the mantle and reaching forth for his companion's arm. "A heavy task awaits me."

†

DAMASCUS

16

Three days Rabbi Saul had been lying on a thin mat in an upper chamber of the inn of one Judas on the Street Called Straight. Blinded and helpless, he had been led there by Achbor and Hamor and given over to the care of the innkeeper, a Judaean whom Saul had known during his sojourn at Jerusalem as a pupil of Rabban Gamaliel.

Ever since the moment of Saul's cataclysmic experience on the desert, his seared eyeballs had burned like fire; in his fevered illness he had fancied them glowing, rounded bits of charcoal in his tortured sockets. He had refused all proffered food and drink; not a crumb of bread or a drop of water had crossed his parched lips. Spent, sick, suffering, he had lain on his mat, grieving and disconsolate, abandoned to guilt and shame and loneliness and utter darkness.

For although the pain in his burnt and blinded eyes was intense, it was hardly comparable with the agony that was torturing his soul. Saul lay prostrate, his palms pressed to the cold stones of the floor beside his narrow mat, and prayed that the burden of his terrible guilt be lifted from him; he turned to lie on his back and stare unseeing through burning eyeballs into the blackness and to plead with intense words that failed even to escape his lips for the forgiveness of the God of Israel and His Messiah, Jesus of Galilee, the crucified and risen carpenter, Son of the Most High.

"Forgive me, O God in Israel! Forgive, O my Lord Messiah! Forgive! Forgive! Cleanse me of my great and terrible guilt, my most heinous sinning. Show me the way to atonement, O

Most High God. I thank Thee that Thou hast turned me about in the way, that in the desert Thou didst reveal Thyself, O my Lord Messiah. Come again to me and show me what Thou wouldst have me to do. O my Lord Messiah, show me Thy way for me!"

But during the long hours of his vigil, in his pain of body and agony of spirit, Saul had been given no assurance that his sins had been forgiven; indeed, in great travail he wondered if his prayers had arisen even beyond the blackness of his chamber and the despair of his soul. He wondered sorrowfully if his newly found Lord Messiah would ever reappear to him to give comfort and counsel.

"In the desert, O my Lord Messiah, You instructed me to continue on into Damascus where it would be told me what I should do. O come again, Lord Jesus. Abandon me not, O my Lord Messiah! Show me Thy way for my life that it may be redeemed from its so great error. And do Thou give strength to my feet to walk in that way and arm my hands to accomplish the task Thou wilt give me to do!"

But no more was the vision of the desert vouchsafed to Saul of Tarsus. In moments of fitful slumber or profound meditation, when he lost his identity with the world of place and time, in such moments other visions evolved to torture him anew: he saw vividly the welt-crossed and gashed and bleeding backs of devout, humble Israelites in Ophel and along the burdened lower slopes of Mount Zion, who had been snatched by his Temple guardsmen from their wretched homes and punished fearfully in the name of the Most High; he heard the swish and slap of the leather, lead-tipped whips as they cut into the flesh of God-fearing Hebrews, whose only offense had been their faith in the Lord Messiah (though the charge invariably had been that they had been delinquent in obeying all the intricate laws and observing all the traditions and practices of the Hebrew faith). And once Saul had cried out at the sudden appearance, as clearly as though his sight had been restored and he were looking through renewed eyes, of a man at the bottom of a stony pit, a man looking upward and with a rapturous smile on his bloody face praying to the God of Israel to forgive those even then hurling stones down upon him.

"O God, forgive me! O Stephen my brother, forgive! Forgive my dastardly sinning, O Most High God! O my Lord Jesus, forgive me!"

And then, after long hours of suffering and of agonized praying for deliverance from the guilt of his so heinous sinning and for direction along the road he should henceforth travel, Saul once again heard the voice, though he was not granted the reappearance of the vision.

He knew not whether the time was day or night, for day and night alike were darkness now to the man of Tarsus; nor would he ever be able to say with assurance whether the voice came to him as he slept or during one of those intervals when he was lost in ponderous thought. But he recognized the voice, and never afterward would Saul doubt that the Lord Messiah Himself had spoken to him.

"Saul my brother," the voice had said, "Ananias will come and lay his hands on you and your sight will be restored."

As the voice finished speaking, a second vision appeared to Saul. As clearly as though he were looking with eyes made whole upon a person in the flesh, the sightless rabbi beheld a gaunt, bearded old man with a thin, long, grizzled beard approaching, hand outstretched to anoint his seared and unseeing eyes. Then, as it came up to touch him, the vision faded.

"I thank you, O my Lord Messiah. I thank you."

Saul pulled his knees under him, pushed himself upward to a crouching position, and got to his feet. Groping his way in the blackness, he found the low stool near his mat and sat down to await the coming of Ananias.

Soon there was a rapping on the chamber door, and Saul called out to the visitor to enter.

"Peace be unto you, Ananias my brother," he said, when the older man stepped inside. "And I beg your forgiveness."

"With you be peace, Saul my brother," the visitor returned the greeting. "But how is it that you know my name?"

"Jesus my Lord Messiah told me that you were coming," answered Saul. "And in a vision I saw you advancing to lay your hands upon my eyes to restore my sight, as the Lord Jesus had told me you would do. But tell me, why do you come to me and how did you learn that I was here?"

"The same that spoke to you, Saul, our Lord Messiah, commanded me to arise and go into the Street Called Straight and inquire at the house of Judas for a man of Tarsus named Saul and when I had found him to lay my hands upon him so that he might regain his sight. He told me further that you had seen me in your praying, and when I protested that Saul of Tarsus had done great evil to the saints at Jerusalem and was bound toward Damascus to work further havoc among us of the Way, our Lord Messiah assured me that you had become our brother and a chosen instrument in His hands to carry His name before Gentiles and kings as well as the sons of Israel. So, brother Saul, I have hearkened to the words of our Lord Messiah."

As he strode toward Saul, Ananias withdrew from his robe a small cruse, and when he had poured a trickle of oil from it upon a white square of cloth, he bent over the blind rabbi and began gently to wipe his eyes. "Brother Saul, the Lord Jesus, who appeared unto you on the road by which you were approaching Damascus, has thus sent me that you might regain your sight and be filled with the Holy Spirit. Therefore, my new brother in the Way"—the old man's ministering hands were gentle and his words comforting—"rise and stand upon your feet, and in the name of the Most High and His Messiah, the Lord Jesus His Son, do thou receive sight!"

Saul felt the hands of the old man at his armpits lifting him, and he felt a surge of recovered strength in his feet and legs and throughout his burnt frame, and tears of joy welled in his eyes and ran down his bronzed cheeks. And as they did, it seemed to the man of Tarsus that they bore away in their flooding a thickened, scalelike incrustation, and suddenly, as though he were looking through an open window from a chamber that had been sealed off and in utter darkness, he saw clearly.

The man standing smiling before him was in every detail of appearance the Ananias he had seen in the vision, even to the manner of his dress and the trim and thickness of his beard.

"O I thank you, my brother!" Saul stood erect and unmoving in the wonder of the moment, though tears rolled along his cheeks to drip into his beard. "O Ananias, my gracious, loving brother!"

He stood looking upon the older man a long moment, and then he dropped upon his face on the mat. "O God in Israel, I thank Thee! Lord Jesus, I thank Thee!" He clenched his fists until they went white at the knuckles, and he pressed his face into the mat and tears poured unrestrained from his opened eyes, and his shoulders and his whole gnarled and sun-blackened frame shook in an excess of emotion. "O God! O my Lord Messiah! O Jesus my Lord!"

Old Ananias bent down to lay his long fingers lightly upon Saul's shaking shoulder. "The Lord bless you, Saul, our new brother. The Lord cause His face to shine upon you. The Lord look down upon you and give you peace. May you work mighty wonders in His name, O my brother." Now the thin fingers were clutching Saul's arm. "Arise, Saul, in the strength of new life and receive baptism into the fellowship of our blessed brother, Jesus the Lord Messiah."

So saying, the venerable Ananias, leader of the Way in Damascus, took water from the pitcher on the shelf and baptized Saul, the Roman citizen from Tarsus, lately the proud Pharisee and intractable Sanhedrinist, into the simple fellowship of the crucified young carpenter of Nazareth.

17

When Saul had eaten and slept long and found his strength renewed, he arose from his mat and bathed himself carefully in accordance with the ceremonial laws of Israel, and in company with Ananias he visited the synagogue frequented by many of the brothers of the Way in Damascus.

Having been invited to discourse before the congregants, Saul arose and, wrapping himself in a prayer shawl provided by one of the officers of the synagogue, revealed in straightforward manner how in Jerusalem he had been given documents of authority by the high priest Caiaphas—which he held up for the worshipers to see and invited them to examine—that ordered him to journey to Damascus and seize the leaders of the sect of the crucified Jesus of Nazareth.

"So in frightful error and so great sinning, though I was convinced that I was defending our God of Israel against His enemies, I set out for your city breathing threatening and slaughter against those who professed allegiance to Him who I believed was the blaspheming, false Messiah of God. But at the very gates of Damascus, in the sudden blinding flash of a summer storm, He came to me. I saw Him, and I heard Him speaking to me."

Dramatically, though in simple narration, he related the shattering experiences of that so recent day on the desert that had turned the course of his life in an exactly opposite direction. "So now I come to you not as your judge and tormentor and executioner, as I was of that good man Stephen the goldsmith, but as your brother, though a grievously sinful one, in our Lord Messiah. And praise and thanks be to the God of Israel, Yahweh Most High, for His immeasurable grace and mercy. I am no longer the enemy of our Lord Messiah, but on the contrary, and from henceforth and upon whatever paths He may command me to set my feet, I will be His in utter devotion."

Some beards wagged in obvious approval when Saul concluded his discourse and resumed his place among the congregants; some worshipers scowled darkly or shook their heads, refusing to believe that this once implacable enemy of the Way could now have become an adherent. And others of the fellowship of the Galilean among the worshipers, despite the assurance of Ananias that their heretofore fierce enemy had indeed been converted, wondered but openly expressed no opinion.

"This Saul from Tarsus is a clever one who has already done us great mischief," one man whispered to his neighbor. "He may even now by this ruse be attempting to learn who among this company of worshipers are of the fellowship in order that he may bind them and deliver them over to the vengeance of the high priest Caiaphas and his Temple adherents. It is best, therefore, as I weigh the situation, that we hold our peace until he has departed."

Saul was not long in quitting Damascus. The beauty of this paradise of the East was too engrossing, her charms and pleasures too diverting, for one whose life lately had been in such violent upheaval to remain long within her ancient walls. He felt that he should seek out some quiet and unhurried region, where in solitude and much prayer and meditation and searching of his soul, he might be able to discover what course his new master, the Lord Messiah, had willed for him. Despite Saul's earnest pleading for guidance, the Lord Messiah had come no more to the rabbi from Tarsus. Prostrated on his mat in his chamber at the inn of Judas on the Street Called Straight, trudging along the cobblestone streets of the old city, or praying in the synagogue raised to Yahweh Most High, Saul had waited in vain for the reassuring presence before him of the Lord Messiah.

Yet Saul felt in his soul that unless the Messiah returned to instruct and command him in the way he should henceforth travel, he would be lost. Until the appearance of Jesus to him outside Damascus, the rabbi steadfastly, and in utter confidence that he was pursuing a God-appointed course, had been charting his way by the law of Israel and teaching the necessity of upholding that law in its every jot and tittle, and his indignation had been intensified against those who, like those who belonged in the fellowship of the crucified Galilean, appeared to him to be flouting that law.

But already deep within Saul a doubt had lodged and was fast developing, a doubt of the efficacy of the law to bring salvation because of the inability of any man completely to uphold the law in its innumerable minutiae. What man, what faithful and God-fearing Israelite, what Pharisee even knew all the turnings and twistings of Israel's law, what master teacher of the law, such as Rabban Gamaliel even, could reveal all its provisions and explain all their various interpretations? And what man, though he should be able to reveal the law in its entirety and faithfully interpret it, could possibly obey in letter and spirit its every command and every injunction? How then could man be saved by the law? And was not the law a burden impossible of being borne by sinning man?

The Galilean, he had been hearing at Jerusalem in the days when he had been the Lord Messiah's most inveterate enemy, had brought a new law of life, a simple law that did not flout the cumbersome law of Israel or set it at nought but swept away the dross accumulated through the centuries, refined it in its essence, and brought its innumerable provisions into one supreme commandment—that man should love God with his whole being and his neighbor as himself.

O my Lord Messiah, is that indeed Thy law? Is it that plain, that utterly simple? And to what boundaries does it extend, O Lord? To the Chosen only, Thy brothers and Thy sisters, sons of King David Thy father? To the Greeks, the desert-burnt Syrians, the Egyptians? Even the proud Romans, O Galilean?

He had sought earnestly for direction, for enlightenment,

for communication. On his face on the mat in the stillness of
his chamber, his arms flung out, his palms pressing hard
against the cold stones of the floor, the rabbi, learned in the
law, the pupil of the great Rabban Gamaliel, the Sanhedrinist,
the scholar trained in the university at Tarsus, the experienced
logician, prostrated himself in supplication to the untutored
young man of scorned little Nazareth, the penniless wandering preacher, the crucified carpenter. The proud Pharisee
humbled himself before the lowly Galilean. He humbled himself and pleaded for the Lord Messiah to return.

But the tall, erect form he had seen in the center of the
blinding flash, the questioning firm voice he had heard in the
violence of the storm, had returned neither to instruct nor re-
assure Saul. Had the rabbi really seen the form and heard the
voice? Or had they been but an hallucination conjured out of
weariness after a long journey in sand and dust and heat and a
conscience that had given him no rest since the death of Stephen, a shape and sound induced into seeming reality in the
sudden violent explosion of the storm about them?

Even to entertain the doubt but for an instant was for Saul
vehemently to protest its veracity.

*It was no dream, no imagining, no conjuring of a sunstruck,
remorseful brain. He appeared to me, He talked with me, He
commissioned me, though He has not yet revealed to me the
nature of the commission. "Arise, go into the city and it shall be
told thee what thou must do." It was no phantom that spoke to
me, but the transfigured personality, the spiritual made visible,
made audible. It was He, the Lord Messiah. I know it! He
chose me, the chiefest of His enemies, for Himself! O come,
Lord Jesus. Deliver to me the commission for my life. Fulfill
now Thy promise to me.*

But the Lord Messiah, the realization came suddenly to
Saul, had not promised that in Damascus he would be told
what to do. And surely the instructions of Ananias did not fulfill the promise made by the Messiah. That promise, he did
not doubt, was yet to be fulfilled and would be: ". . . It shall
be told thee what thou must do."

But not by the Lord Messiah in another bodily appearance. Not in Damascus, even in the comparative solitude of this chamber in the inn of Judas. Only after much prayer and deep concentration, soul-examining meditation, pleading for illumination and deeper understanding. What is the nature of the Messiah? What of sin, and the law? What of redemption and salvation? What is it to be the Son of the Most High? Why should redemption come out of lowly Nazareth? Why should it be brought by an unlearned carpenter? Can it be indeed that He is the Son of God, the Messiah long expected? Can it be? "I am Jesus whom thou persecutest." But He appeared to me. He . . . to me. It was no conjuring, no hallucination. I know this. I know. I know. And He will yet teach me what I must know. What I must know of Him.

And where shall I seek Him out and find Him? Where but in the burning heat of the desert at noonday, where but under the cold, sparkling stars of the desert at midnight? Once in the early days of the Chosen, our father Moses, the lawgiver in the desert, had sought enlightenment of Yahweh, and after much prayer and heavy study he had come down from Mount Sinai in Arabia with the tablets of the law. Another day in that grim wasteland, our father Elijah in his dark hour had met God. And even the Lord Messiah, so they told it in Jerusalem, at the beginning of his ministry had slipped away into the Wilderness to pray and meditate and have fellowship with the Most High. Where better to lose oneself from the world than in the desert land of Arabia southward from Damascus?

Rabbi Saul gave thanks to the God of Israel that his father had required him to learn a trade that would always and in almost every land and clime provide a means of livelihood. In the desert there would be tribesmen roving the wild lands and caravans crossing it, and they would shelter themselves in tents, and there would be tent cloth to be woven and tents to be made. And there would be employment to be found, and much time.

So on a morning early, the rabbi Saul arose and breakfasted, and when he had paid Judas what he owed him for food and lodging, he went down to the square before the eastern gate in the city's wall. And soon he joined himself to the caravan of a great merchant just then leaving Damascus on a journey deep into Arabia.

✝

CAESAREA

18

Until the day before Procurator Pontius Pilate left Jerusalem at the ending of the Passover season to return to Caesarea, his wife Claudia had not ventured far from the frowning Palace of the Herods.

She had had no friends to visit or to entertain and no place of interest to inspect; of all the structures in Jerusalem, only one was of architectural value and appealing and that was the great stone pile of the Temple and its colonnaded porches on Mount Moriah. She considered disguising herself as she had done on that memorable day when with Chloe she had stood and listened to the simple but eloquent words of the strange young rabbi from Galilee, but she knew that the Court of the Gentiles would be filled with surging throngs polluting the warm air with the stench of sweating bodies and breaths foul with garlic.

But on the morning of the day before they were to start on the return journey one of the chambermaids, an Israelite girl who had been cleaning her bedchamber, approached her when no one else was in the room. "Please forgive my effrontery in addressing you, Mistress Claudia," said the maid. "But from Chloe I have learned of your interest in Jesus of Nazareth, our Lord Messiah of Israel. Indeed, she told me how you had sought in a letter to the procurator during the trial of the Messiah to save Him from crucifixion." She was keeping her eyes on the door. "Once, said she, the two of you in disguise went to the Temple and heard the Messiah teach. So I thought that tonight"—she lowered her voice—"you might like to go with me to the meeting of the fellowship of the Messiah at the house of Mary of Cyprus. It is nearby, just a little way south on Zion Hill."

"But would not they be afraid that I was spying upon them?" Claudia asked her. "They would know that I was not one of them, wouldn't they, even though they didn't know that I was the procurator's wife?"

"No, Mistress Claudia, they would not be afraid of you. They would know that I would be fetching no one who would harm them."

"Then you are one of them?"

"Yes. I have been of the fellowship since the days before He was crucified."

"But they would know that I'm Roman."

"Perhaps they would, though they might likewise, some of them, think you Greek. But that matters not. Many Roman women, even of the equestrian class, are being converted to the religion of the Jews. They would likely take you for one of the converts interested in the teachings of the Messiah."

"Should I go with you," Claudia asked, "would I see any of your Messiah's original followers, members of his first small group they called, I believe, the apostles?"

The maid's eyes lighted. "Indeed, Mistress Claudia, most likely you would. All of them except Judas the traitor are still living, they say, and they are probably in Jerusalem for the Passover season. They will surely gather for the common breaking of bread at Mary's house tonight, including"—her eyes were flaming and her tone was one of adulation—"Simon of Capernaum, whom they call the first of the Messiah's apostles, and the Zebedee brothers who were likewise among the dearest of His friends. Their being there is one reason why I am so anxious to go myself."

She had agreed to go with the maid. Pilate, she knew, would remain late, perhaps all night, at the Tower of Antonia arranging for the return of the troops to Caesarea and perhaps the final collection and tabulation of taxes for the period ending with the close of Passover season. She would have returned to the Palace of the Herods before nightfall, and if by chance she hadn't and Pilate had come back before she had been able to slip inside the Palace gates and remove her disguise, what of it? He would not dare censure her, or even question her about it.

She went. None challenged her right to be there; though no one recognized her as the wife of Pilate, she was welcomed as a Roman matron interested in converting to the religion of the One-God of Israel and His Son, the Lord Messiah. With unfeigned reverence she sat on a mat in Mary's courtyard and listened avidly as Simon the fisherman and others of the carpenter's original small band recounted, with fire in their eyes and sometimes with welling tears, His unforgettable discourses to them as on many a day and night they tramped the towering hills and dry wadies or sailed the now calm, now boisterous, waters of their little sea.

Afterward, Claudia even spoke for a moment with Simon of the crucified carpenter whose high hopes for a better world had been destroyed with His body, on that fearfully hot and suddenly stormy afternoon three years ago, through the evil machinations of Israel's High Priest Caiaphas supported by the bumbling procurator Pontius Pilate.

"But His body was not destroyed, nor His hopes," Simon had declared, shaking his round head. "He was crucified indeed and dead when His body was taken down. But He returned to life, and now lives at the right hand of His Father, our One-God of Israel. And His hopes live too; they are not dashed. To us, frail though we be, He has left the task of seeing His hopes one day realized." Peter's eyes were bright with conviction; not one evidence of doubt filmed them. "And, praise be to Israel's God and His Messiah, they will be."

As Claudia turned away, she heard Mary of Cyprus say something to the rugged fisherman about a young rabbi who a few days before had come to her house seeking his long-time friend, her cousin Bar Nabas, then on a business journey to Cyprus. When he learned from her that Bar Nabas was a member of the fellowship of a crucified carpenter that believed this

carpenter was the long-awaited Messiah of Israel, Mary related, he had gone away greatly disgruntled. Fleetingly she
wondered if the rabbi of whom Mary was speaking might be
the one Longinus had told her about the other night as they sat
on the terrace.

When the worshipers began to knot together to partake of
the ceremonial evening meal already set out, Claudia quietly
slipped through the gate opening from the courtyard onto the
cobbled way, for she knew that no Jew, according to the religious laws of the Hebrew people, could break bread with a
Gentile, and especially a Roman, without defiling himself.

Weeks later, on an evening when Pilate with Tribune
Paulus and a maniple of legionaries had gone eastward to the
vicinity of the Samaritans' holy Mount Gerizim to quiet a
small uprising, Claudia related to Longinus the story of her
visit to the house of Mary of Cyprus. They were sitting
once more on the terrace before the peristylium of the procurator's palace on the slope above Caesarea's harbor and a light
breeze from off the sea gently stirred the flames in the lamps
bracketed to the columns and the flambeaux set at intervals
into the marble balustrade framing the mosaic pavement.

"They did not know who I was, of course," she said. "But I
had the feeling that it would have mattered little to them if
suddenly I had been identified. I heard them talk, and I talked
with them, including that fisherman from Galilee who is said
to be the leader of the fellowship of the Galilean. They are
strong folk, Longinus, not drawn from the more privileged
class and not rich, in fact, apparently very poor, most of
them, and some even slaves, I judged. But nevertheless they
are people of great strength, all drawn together and held in an
unbreakable bond of love for their Messiah and for one another. I tell you, Longinus, it was amazing. And there was not
one among them who was not absolutely sure in his mind
that the crucified Nazarene not only willed his return to life
but that he continues to live to protect and redeem those of
his own growing fellowship."

"And *you* likewise believe it?"

"I don't know, Longinus. I don't know what I believe. After living at the court of Tiberius, in the sophisticated, dissolute atmosphere of equestrian Rome, where no one of intelligence, of course, believes in our Roman gods, and then out here where I've had some exposure, at least, to the Hebrews' one-god religion, I hardly know what I believe, if anything. And then in the last few years to have had this experience with the Galilean and particularly with those who believe that he is a god, well. . . ." She paused, shrugged. "Longinus, they are amazing to me, these people. They aren't the sort I have known, surely not the type one sees in our circles in Rome and even here in Caesarea."

"That's a certainty," Longinus agreed. "And if you should find some in Rome they would be slaves, no doubt."

"Yes, and some of them I saw the other day at the Cyprian woman's house in Jerusalem were slaves, and most of them were very poor. Many likely hadn't eaten that day until they came together for their common meal that evening. But happy, and strong, and filled with hope! I'd like to possess the strength, assurance, the peace they have despite their poverty, the faith —whatever you may call it—they have and proclaim." She paused again, but Longinus said nothing. "All they seem to require in order to possess it, it appears, is what they call their belief in the Galilean carpenter as the Messiah of the Jews."

"And you, my dear, *almost* have it, too, for whether you are willing to admit it or not, even to yourself, you really believe this man must have had—"

"Must *have*, you mean."

"Yes. See, you prove what I'm saying. Must *have* supernatural powers and must therefore be of a divine nature, what we call—without knowing just what we mean by the term—a god."

She shook her head slowly. "I don't know, Longinus, I honestly don't *know*. It may be only that I have admiration, that I *had* admiration, for the man I heard teaching so marvelously that day in the Court of the Gentiles and sympathy for him when I learned how shamefully he was being treated by the high priest Caiaphas and Pilate, and maybe, too, I was anxious to believe those stories of his returning to life and"—she looked directly into his eyes and her expression was quizzical —"particularly your story about it. After all, you saw him alive *and* dead."

"Yes, and I can never forget, *I* killed him. Where you interceded with Pilate for him, I crucified him."

"No, Longinus! Pilate crucified him, Pilate and Caiaphas. Yours, I tell you again, was an act of mercy. I'm sure he knows it was."

"He *knows* it was, you say. Then he is alive, although I saw him dead?"

"Yes!" she said positively. But then she tossed her head. "Oh, I don't know, Longinus. I simply *can't* know. I wish I could. I'd be happier if I could, I know that. If I could be like those simple folk I visited the other day, I could be completely happy. They were. They were because they *knew*. They had no doubts, no reservations. Yet many there had never heard him talk, had never seen him. But they knew—from some assurance deep down inside them, I suppose."

He caught her hand, held it in close grasp. "At any rate, Claudia, don't worry about him. We are the ones to be fearful, Pilate and I. And what of the procurator? Is he still having frightful dreams about him?"

"Yes. From my bedchamber I sometimes hear him in his nightmares screaming out excuses—blaming the high priest, cursing the Jews."

"Do you ever hear him referring to the Galilean?"

"Never. I'm sure he wants it thought that he forgot the Galilean before he was back in Caesarea from that Passover festival."

"He'll never forget him. I surely can't."

"*Bona Dea,* no. Nor I. But we don't fear him. Pilate does. He lives in fear. He cannot lie down at night free of the vision of that man hanging on a cross; I'm sure of it, Longinus. And he'll never cease to tremble at the thought of the Galilean. He's aging, Longinus, and that's the reason; it's not the burden of the procuratorship, for until three years ago he enjoyed the office, he doted on it. But no longer. He lives close to terror, I do believe. The Galilean rides his back, night and day. He will never unburden himself of that innocent good man's death."

"That may explain why his hatred of the Jews seems to be growing more intense all the time and why his anger leads him into taking foolish and irresponsible action against these people he was sent out to govern. Maybe that's why he's over in the region of Mount Gerizim right now—storming and raging against the Samaritans."

"Yes," she agreed. "And that may be why he's hastening— and may all the gods and goddesses speed him in it—his removal from the procuratorship and our return to Rome!"

†

ANTIOCH

19

Tribune Lucius Cassius Longinus stood on the dock at Antioch and waited for his baggage to be brought down from the vessel. When the last case and leather-strap-secured bag was deposited beside him, he handed the sweating Nubian a coin.

"Move all these inside"—he motioned toward the adjacent warehouse—"secure them together with a cord and store them until I come for them tomorrow, or perhaps later. Then I'll give you double this. But if anything goes amiss with them, I'll search you out and have the skin flayed from your back. Do you understand?"

"Yes, master," the slave assured him, grinning, though he appeared uncertain that the tribune was serious. "They'll be secure until you come for them."

Longinus smiled, nodded. Then he picked up one of the smaller bags and started across the wharf area toward the cobbled way that led eastward to the Street of the Colonnades. When he came to the junction with that broad main way, he turned left and walked northward past innumerable statues of men and gods until soon he came even with a narrow street running eastward toward the city's Jewish district. Immediately he was reminded of the rabbi of Tarsus who three years before had turned aside here to go in search of a Tarsian friend who had emigrated to Antioch. "I wonder where the rabbi is now," he said to himself. "Perhaps still in Jerusalem raging against the sect of the Galilean. Or even"—the thought came suddenly—"here in Antioch thundering his invectives." Longinus knew that a strong fellowship of the crucified carpenter had taken root and grown in Antioch, composed in the main, he had learned, of believers in the Galilean who had fled from Jerusalem because of the persecution directed by the still malevolent and determined high priest Caiaphas and his father-in-law, old Annas.

But quickly Longinus dismissed from mind the rabbi whom he had not seen since the visit he and Tribune Paulus had made to Jerusalem for the Passover festival in company with Procurator Pontius Pilate and his wife. His thoughts returned to consideration of the problem of why Legate Vitellius had summoned him, so secretively and so precipitately, to Antioch. He had been pondering the question, in fact, almost continuously since the arrival of the legate's courier at Caesarea hardly a week ago.

The courier had been able to add nothing to the information contained in the brief letter from Vitellius. The legate had limited the message to an order to report to him in Antioch as quickly as possible, aboard the first vessel leaving Caesarea for Seleucia, and to be prepared for a long assignment away from Caesarea.

Why? he kept asking himself. What is the legate planning? Is he seeking information he considers of prime importance? Concerning Pilate, perhaps?

But Longinus knew that he had been keeping the legate informed of Pilate's actions and of the feelings of the Jews and the other subject peoples in Judaea and Samaria toward the procurator and his administration. He had sent Vitellius information in coded messages and by trusted emissaries, and in the three years since he had been given his original instructions by the legate, he had met him on several occasions in various cities of the province and reported in detail on Pilate's steadily deteriorating rule. He had even sent Vitellius, by a thoroughly reliable courier, a clear and comprehensive report of Pilate's most recent inexcusable blunder, the slaying of scores of Samaritans engaged in a religious ceremonial that Pilate professed to believe was actually an assembling to make plans for a revolt against Rome.

Longinus, before reporting to Vitellius, had investigated the incident carefully. He had even made the day's journey south-eastward to Mount Gerizim, the holy mountain of the Samaritans, where the slaughter had taken place, and had talked with many persons in an effort to obtain an accurate report to transmit to the legate. A certain impostor, according to the gist of the stories related to him, had told the Samaritans that he knew the spot on the summit of Mount Gerizim where sacred vessels related to the worship of the Samaritans had been concealed since the days of Moses the lawgiver. If they would assemble at the mountain, he had promised, he would lead them to the place of concealment. So a day was appointed and a great host gathered. The men had brought their weapons with them as a protection against robbers or in event an altercation concerning disposition of the sacred vessels might develop, so Longinus was told, and with no thought of using them against the Roman authority.

But Pontius Pilate had been informed of the assembling of the Samaritans and hastily had dispatched legionaries to Mount Gerizim to scatter the assembled revolutionaries, as he held them to be. The result was that many Samaritans were slain and that the leaders who escaped the swords of the legionaries were afterward executed. The Samaritans throughout their homeland, which embraced Caesarea and the country roundabout the port city, were enraged at the ruthless and indefensible attack upon their countrymen; and about the time Longinus was getting his report off by courier to Vitellius, the Samaritans were preparing to send to Antioch a delegation of their leading people to protest, with all the power and feeling they could command, the unjustifiable severity of the procurator.

Could it be that the message he had sent to Legate Vitellius had been delayed and that the legate was perhaps chagrined because the protesting Samaritans had arrived at Antioch before he had received any Roman report of Pilate's bungling? Surely Vitellius could not believe by any stretch of imagining that Longinus had been seeking of late to protect the procurator, to keep from the prelate's notice, Pilate's growing ineptness and dereliction. Surely he was not suspecting that something had developed at Caesarea to cause the tribune to be no longer interested in obtaining the consent of Emperor Tiberius to the recalling to Rome of Pontius Pilate.

The scowling Tiberius was looking down upon him now; he had reached the plaza, in the center of which stood the statue of the emperor. Tiberius still had his head; Longinus wondered how much longer it would remain atop the high column.

This time the tribune did not continue across the cobbled great circle, but instead turned left and walked toward the Orontes. Crossing the stream, he stepped upon the island at its southeastern corner. Entering the gates at the Tetrapylon, he walked along the wide esplanade straight northward to the palace.

Once he was admitted to the legate's chamber, Longinus was not kept long in suspense. Vitellius greeted him at the door, motioned him to a chair. "I appreciate your haste in coming to Antioch, tribune," he declared. "You must have left immediately upon the arrival of my courier."

"I was fortunate, sir, in being able to get a northbound coastal vessel the day after he reached Caesarea," Longinus revealed, "and we had good winds."

"And did you come prepared for a long assignment abroad, as I suggested?"

"I did so. I stored my baggage at the wharf."

"Very good, tribune." The legate leaned forward, crossed his forearms on his desk. "I shall speak straight to the point, Longinus. I know you have been wondering what I have in mind for you to do for me, and I am sorry that I could not inform you in the message I sent. But the very nature of the situation made that obviously impossible. Perhaps you have suspected that the assignment I have for you involves Pontius Pilate. It does. I appreciate your report of his inexcusable conduct in ordering the slaughter of the Samaritans at Mount Gerizim. It was factual, complete, objective. And it was supported by a delegation of Samaritan leaders who came here to petition me to have Pilate deposed."

The legate sat back in his heavy chair, cleared his throat. "Longinus, that is what I am going to do. I can delay no longer the action I should have taken many months ago. The procurator is bringing disrepute upon the government of the empire, upon me his commander in Syria, upon the emperor." He knotted his right hand into a fist and beat it gently on the desk to emphasize his words. "I have decided to depose Pontius Pilate from the post of procurator in Judaea and Samaria and order him to Rome for trial, and I am sending Marcellus to occupy the post until a new procurator is named by Tiberius and sent out to take over its duties. But, Longinus"—Vitellius leaned forward and his eyes narrowed and he lowered his voice, though no one else was in the chamber and the door to the corridor was closed—"no one knows this except you and me, and I am taking no action until you have had time to complete your assignment. That is why it was necessary for you to get here quickly; that is why it is urgent that you get started on this new mission for me."

He paused, and his earnest, searching eyes were fastened upon the tribune's puzzled countenance. "Longinus, I am sending you to Rome to see Prefect Marco, and perhaps, if the prefect thinks it advisable, the emperor. You leave in the morning. I am holding up the departure of a swift government trireme that put into Seleucia two days ago and was to leave today and have arranged passage for you. It should speed you to the capital. And now"—he opened his fist to permit his forefinger to tap the desk in cadence with his measured words —"it will be your considerable task, perhaps difficult, perhaps easily accomplished, to convince Prefect Marco that I had no other course. He may wish you to accompany him to discuss the matter with the emperor. But whether you are taken before Tiberius or not, much will depend upon the manner in which you present the situation to the prefect. May the gods give you good counsel, Longinus."

He paused a moment and his expression was soberly reflective. "I realize, tribune, that I am taking drastic action and upon my own initiative—without first counseling with the prefect. He may resent it, and the emperor may resent it even more. He could conceivably be so angered that he will order Pilate to continue in office, and will depose me. But that is the risk I must take. As legate in Syria, I can no longer tolerate Pilate's continuing in the office of procurator."

Vitellius put his hands, palms down, on the desk, and his stern expression relaxed. "Of course, Longinus, you understand, and so will Marco and Tiberius, I trust, that I am not actually deposing Pilate. I am suspending him as procurator and ordering him to Rome for trial. That is all. And, as I suggested, *he* may be restored to office and *I* may be summoned to the capital to stand trial instead. Much will depend upon the way you develop my case, as I have just said, and to provide you factual support I have had figures prepared for you to present to Marco. They will show in detail how the empire's affairs are suffering, how the revenues continue to shrink, how the costs of administering the government in Judaea and Samaria continue to advance as unrest and the threat of actual rebellion become more evident week after week. Well, tribune"
—he sat back, smiled broadly—"now you know why I summoned you to Antioch. Have I made everything clear? Do you have any questions?"

"Very clear, sir, as far as my assignment is concerned. But your deposing of Pilate will not be known in Rome, I hope, until I have had opportunity to reveal it on your behalf to the prefect and he has had time to communicate it to the emperor."

"Oh, indeed, tribune. You will likely be in Rome before I take action. Certainly you will be far enough along on the voyage so that the news of Pilate's being deposed cannot possibly outrun you to the capital. If the Samaritans do not renew their petitioning—demanding is a better word for it—for Pilate's early removal, I may wait several weeks before I send Marcellus to Caesarea and order Pilate to take ship for Rome. So the prefect will first hear of my action from you, Longinus. But I wish him to know, when you do tell him, that it is not tentative, that it has already been done, and that whether he or the emperor approves or not—though certainly you will not put it that bluntly—the procurator has been removed from office and is being sent to Rome for trial on the charges set out against him. And now, tribune, is that entirely clear?"

"Entirely, sir. But there is one other thing." He hesitated. But when the legate nodded, he continued. "Claudia, sir. Will she accompany Pilate when he goes to Rome?"

"I presume so," Vitellius answered. "As his wife, she would be expected to go with him. And surely it will provide her an excellent opportunity of getting back to Rome. Too, if the emperor supports me in deposing Pilate and banishes him to some distant province, he will allow his stepdaughter the divorce she has long been wanting, wouldn't you think?" His eyes searched the tribune's face. "She's still intent on getting a divorce, isn't she?"

"Yes, sir," the tribune agreed, "more determined than ever, I'm certain. But I was thinking that he might send Claudia into exile along with her husband. To make certain that she doesn't live in Rome," he added in explanation.

Vitellius shook his head. "Tiberius wouldn't be that vindictive—or fearful—surely, tribune." He smiled wryly, hunched his shoulders in an expressive shrug. "But you will know just how to handle that situation also, Longinus; I'd wager on it."

When Longinus, smiling, offered no comment, the legate arose and stepped over to an ornately carved cabinet against the paneled wall behind his desk. Opening the double doors, he searched among the parchment title strips attached by cords to the papyrus rolls stacked neatly in their cylindrical containers. After a moment he discovered the one he was seeking.

"Here it is." Vitellius pulled the parchment container from the pyramid on the shelf and came back to his desk. "The report on Pilate." He held out the cylinder for Longinus to read the title: *Pontius Pilate. Procurator. Judaea and Samaria.* Then he pulled from the cylinder the papyrus roll, with a similar title on the attached strip, and pushed the dark red container to one side of the desk. Holding the roll at arm's length so that Longinus could see the writing, he began to unroll the volume with his right hand as he rolled it up with his left. "I won't take time, tribune, for you even to scan it, but you can see that the record is extensive and the information in considerable detail. Surely after seeing this evidence the prefect and the emperor will approve my action in ordering Pilate to stand trial, unless they decide, despite all this proof of his malfeasance, to send him back to Palestine as procurator."

Quickly he rolled the extended papyrus into a neat cylinder and returned it to the container, which he handed to Longinus. "Tribune, I want you to study this report carefully, so that you are thoroughly familiar with it before you sail tomorrow. I shall expect you to be able to enlighten the prefect, or the emperor if he summons you to Capreae, on anything in it that might not immediately be clear to either of them." He held up his hand, palm toward the tribune. "But don't begin reading it now. After you have refreshed yourself from your journey and we have had a short siesta, you may find a few moments before dinner to peruse it, and perhaps some further time after we have eaten. You are our guest here at the palace, tribune, until you go aboard ship tomorrow. I shall send a soldier with servants to the dock to have your baggage put aboard the trireme."

Vitellius clapped his hands together sharply, and in that instant one of the wall panels opened and a servant appeared. "Show the tribune to his apartment," the legate commanded. "See that he is not disturbed until the time arrives to summon him to the triclinium for dinner." He turned to face Longinus. "Is there anything you would like to have brought to your chamber, tribune? Something to eat, or perhaps some wine?"

"Thank you, no, sir. I ate just before leaving the ship. A bath, a short nap, and I'll be refreshed from the voyage. But I'll find some time to examine the report concerning Pilate's administration of the government. Perhaps later this evening I may have some questions to ask about it."

The tribune did have. After they had finished their dinner, they moved from the triclinium to sit in the peristylium, which looked out upon the nearby bending of the Orontes, and discussed the report Longinus would carry to Rome. The tribune wished to be able to explain any phase of the report that Marco or the emperor might question. When finally the two had reviewed it to the tribune's satisfaction, accomplished after examination of the document in detail, Vitellius asked Longinus if he wished any further information concerning the trip he was about to begin.

"There are two things, sir," he answered. "The first is concerning my leave to undertake this mission, my leave from the Palestine assignment. How long am I to be permitted to accomplish this task and return to Caesarea? Or will I be returning?"

"You will be given no definite time limit in which to see Marco—and the emperor, if that is considered necessary by Marco," the legate replied. "I hope that you will be able, however, to see the prefect shortly after you arrive in Rome, because by that time I shall already have suspended Pilate and ordered him to report to the prefect for trial. I surely do not want Pilate to appear before him before you have had the opportunity of apprising him of what I am doing and presenting this report in substantiation of my action."

"I shall make every effort to see him at once, sir, within hours after my arrival, if he is in the capital. And if he's out at Capreae, I'll follow him there."

Vitellius nodded. "Very good. As for your return to Caesarea, I shall not include that in your orders. It will be the duty of the prefect to give you your further assignment. Perhaps he will not wish to return you to Palestine. And it will not be necessary for you to return to report to me. What is to be done will have been already accomplished before you could get back to Antioch. Unless, tribune"—the legate's eyes narrowed and a trace of smile lifted the corners of his mouth—"you wish for me to include in your orders a return to Caesarea."

"Oh, no, sir. I'd be happy to be assigned elsewhere." Longinus grinned.

"I thought you would be. What was the other question, tribune?"

"Perhaps I should not ask, sir. But I wondered if Tribune Paulus under the new Procurator Marcellus would continue to command the legionaries at Caesarea."

"I cannot say at this time, Longinus. I shall leave the naming of the commanding officer of the military at Caesarea to Marcellus. That should be his prerogative. And I suspect that he will wish to have one of his present subordinates. In event he does, of course, Tribune Paulus will be returned to Rome for a new assignment by the prefect, unless he should insist upon remaining in Palestine, even if in a less important assignment. Do you think he might insist on staying in this province?" He was still smiling.

"I shouldn't think Paulus would," Longinus replied. "I'm sure he will welcome an opportunity to get back to Rome, too."

Longinus retired to his chamber and went to bed early. He was aboard the *Actium*, one of the faster triremes of the imperial navy, when it cast off from the naval docks and started the journey down the Orontes at midmorning the next day. By noon it was entering the canal that joined the river with the harbor at Seleucia.

✝

ROME

20

Good fortune sailed with Longinus and strong winds bore the trireme *Actium* swiftly westward. When the winds slackened, the slave oarsmen tugged more vigorously at the oars, so that the vessel was able to maintain a steady speed all the way into the harbor at Ostia.

The trireme's forward progress was not even slowed when one of the rowers in the top bank of oars, a sullen Thracian who had been acting obstinately all the way out from Caesarea, died under the lash. Longinus had happened along the bench to which the oarsman was chained just as they were unlocking the cuffs to free the fellow's ankles. The tribune watched as two husky slaves, at the command of the hortator, dragged the body from the rower's bench and heaved it into the sea. Almost by the time it plunged beneath the waves, the iron cuffs were being locked about the ankles of a stout slave just brought up from the noisome hold. Fleetingly Longinus remembered another dead body being released from a cruel imprisonment that had held it pinioned by iron spikes through feet and hands to a Roman cross. And thinking of the Galilean, he thought also of Claudia. Was she still a follower, though in secret, of the crucified carpenter? Would she continue to be one once she took up again her life in Rome? And what of Pilate? In his ever-mounting difficulties in Palestine had he forgotten the Galilean he had sacrificed to the vengeful fear of the high priest and his henchmen? Or, as Claudia had revealed, was the procurator still troubled either by his conscience or his fear that perhaps the strange youth from Galilee actually had returned to life, as his devoted followers were so insistently declaring?

But soon Longinus was heavily concerned with thoughts of the mission upon which he was being sent to Rome by Legate Vitellius, for presently the *Actium* was sailing past Syracuse. Soon the trireme had cleared the narrow Strait of Messana and set its course northwestwardly toward Puteoli. And when, after another day of smooth sailing, the *Actium* sighted, over its starboard bow, a jutting precipitous promontory running outward from the coast and pointing toward a mountainous island thrust up from the blue waters of the bay, Longinus felt a great lifting of spirits.

"Surrentum and Capreae! Beautiful, fruitful Campania, the garden, the orchard, the vineyard of Italia!" Hillsides that ran steeply into the sea, green with grape and olive and studded with marble palaces, Campania the playground of Rome's aristocrats. Had not Varro been envisioning Campania when he wrote that memorable question: "You have wandered over many lands; have you ever seen any better cultivated than Italia? Is not Italia as stocked with fruit trees as to seem one great orchard?"

Tribune Longinus was home again, home from the barren and isolated land of the Jews, the land of the strange and stubborn worshipers of Yahweh the one-god. He stood at the starboard rail enjoying once more the changing panorama as the *Actium* moved northward across the bay, on whose irregular rim sat Pompeii and Herculaneum and near them the smoking, sometimes deeply grumbling volcanic cone Vesuvius. The trireme was passing westward of Capreae now, and Longinus wondered if he should ask the master of the vessel to put into the harbor at Puteoli and set him ashore there. More than likely Prefect Marco had come down from Rome either to confer with the emperor, who most certainly was in residence on Capreae, or to enjoy the sunshine and sea air in his own palace at nearby Baiae, across the harbor from Puteoli. Ordinarily the larger corn and grain merchant ships from Egypt unloaded their cargoes on the docks at Puteoli, from which they were transported overland to Rome and other regions of Italia. But on inquiring of the master of the *Actium,* Longinus learned that no stop had been scheduled between Seleucia and Rome. And he himself had been ordered by Legate Vitellius to Rome. His continuing to the capital might require his immediate return to Puteoli, but the delay in seeing Prefect Marco would perhaps be only two or three days. Because of the importance of his mission, he reasoned, he might be able to use the cursus publicus. This official government post would be carrying correspondence between Rome and the prefect at Baiae and the emperor on Capreae, and it often accomplished the journey southward on the Appian Way within a day and a half.

A gentle breeze was blowing from the land, and as the trireme drew opposite the tiny spit that provided a natural sea wall for the harbor at Puteoli, the stench from the sulphur pools would have told Longinus where he was even though he had not been on deck. And at night, too, added to the stench would have been the revealing glare of the furnaces of manufactories engaged in providing Rome and other regions of Italia with pottery, iron, and glass products. Campania was not only the garden and orchard of the empire, but the center of much of its manufacturing and industry.

And also, Longinus knew by report and observation, this strip of coast around the bay from Surrentum to Baiae and Misenum and Puteoli, this green and glittering narrow region between the upthrust mountains and the blue sea, not only brought down from Rome aging equestrians with agues and stiffened joints to bathe in its mineral springs in search of renewed physical vigor, but it also attracted countless others seeking respite from all restraints in unhampered gambling and immorality. Suddenly, the tribune was reminded of the voyage that day three years ago up the Orontes River in the *Memphis* past the Grove of Daphne and the Antiochenes' lascivious revelings in the name of worship. He wondered what had been the fate of the strange, intense young rabbi from Tarsus who had accompanied Paulus and him to Caesarea and from there to the Passover festival at Jerusalem. Saul would be as ill at ease in some of the palaces clinging to the slopes at Baiae, he reflected, as he would be in the Temple of Apollo.

Nor did the *Actium* pause at the docks when the next day the vessel sailed into Ostia. The swift trireme crossed the harbor and entered the mouth of the yellow silt-heavy Tiber to ascend the stream and in spite of the strong current overtake slowly moving barges bearing corn and grain and building stones into the capital. Steadily it moved up the channel, propelled by the lifting and falling oars of the sweating slaves chained to their benches and a gentle breeze coming in from the Great Sea, and by midafternoon the trireme, with Tribune Longinus again at the rail on the starboard bow, was drawing opposite the city wall that came down southwestward from the Ostian Gate to the bank of the river, where it turned straight northward to follow the stream to its bending at the lower end of the emporium.

Presently the vessel was rounding the bend in the Tiber and coming alongside the emporium's docks, which were alive with slaves dragging boxes and bales of merchandise into the warehouses from ships unloading at the wharves there or transporting to them goods destined for ports around the rim of the Great Sea. But Longinus gave hardly a glance toward the ferment on the emporium's docks or, across from it on the western bank of the river, the restful calm and greenness of the Gardens of Caesar or, behind the Gardens, the cluttered mass of Janiculum Hill, a quarter taken over almost entirely by Jews, most of them immigrants to the capital from Eastern lands.

Past the emporium, the river ran a straight course twice the length of the huge shipping and trading district, before it turned left to swing in a gentle curve that went westward, and then north and eastward and north again, like the meandering of a slithering giant snake. But in the center of the first twisting of the river's channel, the *Actium* turned sharply, the rowers feathered their oars, and at the precise moment braked them to bring the vessel gently alongside a dock that pushed out into the muddy stream a little way south of the Aemilian bridge.

Longinus quickly went ashore, and when he had found porters to see to the unloading of his baggage and storing it in one of the adjacent warehouses until he could send servants from his father's mansion for it, he walked along the cobbled way that led from the Old Forum to the Pons Aemilius. As he passed the cattle market on his right he was reminded of Puteoli. But even yesterday's smell of sulfur was less offensive than the rank and fusty smell from the Roman market stalls crammed with hogs and cattle, squealing and bleating and bawling their distress. Longinus thought of the precincts of the Temple in Jerusalem during Passover seasons when Jewish pilgrims returned to their holy city and offered their sacrifices. He hurried on, and after a short walk turned left and strode rapidly along Vicus Tuscus past shops displaying merchandise gathered from every corner of the empire. Soon he was passing on his right the stately Temple of Augustus and beyond it the tall, pillared façade of the Temple of Castor and Pollux. Across Vicus Tuscus from this temple, dominating the southern side of the Old Forum, stood the structure that, of all the magnificent marble edifices in this sea of marble, had strongest appeal to Longinus, the Basilica Julia. The noble structure, perfect in architectural design and finished in exquisite detail, was started by Julius Caesar, dead almost a century, to provide more adequate facilities for the administration of Roman justice. It was the empire's greatest courthouse, just as Roman law was the cornerstone and chief glory of Rome's domination of the civilized world.

Though he was anxious to get as quickly as he could to his father's mansion on Viminal Hill, Longinus paused on Vicus Tuscus to study for a moment this great edifice, the sight of which always gave a lift to his spirits; it made him appreciate all the more the privilege that was his in being a citizen of the empire and a native of this ancient capital, a city so old that already its history was lost in the fables of a stirring tradition.

Basilica Julia was a tall structure, as tall as the Temple of Castor and Pollux, but it was so much longer on its Forum side that it appeared lower. The basilica's most striking difference from most of the other splendid structures in Rome, however, was its series of double porticoes, arched on the exterior, that went around the four sides of the tremendous building, one above the other, with marble statues of heroic size in the centers of the arches.

As he stood looking at the basilica, Longinus recalled fleetingly that many times he had played as a child in the shadows of these great arches in the nondescript company of slaves stealing moments of relaxation while on errands for their masters, beggars vociferously seeking alms, government clerks pilfering time from their desks in the palaces on the Capitoline and Palatine Hills, and fashionable youths seeking diversion in assignations on the lower, and more especially the upper porticoes, with young women of whom their senatorial and equestrian parents did not approve.

Several times he himself had met Claudia on the porticoes of Basilica Julia. After their exchanging notes, accomplished at some peril by his personal slave, a young Thracian, and one of Claudia's slave maids, the girl would manage to evade her governess and to slip away from Tiberius' palace. Up there in the shadows of that third arch, on a late afternoon after they had both had dinner while her maid waited on the portico below—Longinus smiled as his eyes sought out the spot—they had talked for a moment and then, when no one else was on that side of the portico, had sprung together in a fervid embrace that was not broken until they heard footsteps approaching their corner. Then quickly she and her maid had slipped back up Palatine Hill to the emperor's sprawling palace, and he had turned again toward his father's house, vowing with all the fervor of youth aflame that one day he would marry her and, as commander of Rome's mighty legions, carry her to some far land and glorious conquest, from which he would return in triumph to the resounding plaudits of all Rome as the two rode in a gilded chariot the length of Sacra Via.

Longinus shrugged and, turning, stepped into Forum Romanum, vibrant and grandiose center of the mighty empire. Within a few paces on his left, as he walked through a forest of statues, was the actual, visible, considered center of the Roman Empire, the Millenarium Aureum (Golden Milestone), a tall stone shaft covered over with gilded bronze. On this shaft, Emperor Augustus had ordered inscribed the names of the great roads leading into Rome from the ports and chief cities and coming together here in the Forum. But nearer the tribune, almost at his left hand as he strode across the rectangular, solid blocks of travertine, with which the Forum Romanum is paved, was an even more notable landmark called the Rostra, the raised stands for the orators, so named because Julius Caesar had the peaks of captured war vessels set upon the platforms as ornamentation. In the days of the republic, some historians now believe—Longinus remembered as he passed the Rostra—it may have stood nearer the other end of the Old Forum. And somewhere nearby, within a few paces of the stones he was now treading, had been raised the great funeral pyre, with garments, golden ornaments and jewelry, tables, benches, and weapons heaped upon it, on which the body of Caesar was cremated after Mark Antony had shouted his execration upon Cassius and Brutus.

He paused a moment; from the platform a man was haranguing a motley group before him. But it appeared that he was making little impression upon his hearers. They were most of them loungers who had no dinners to go home to and had received no invitations to other homes; they were knotted before the Rostra because they could think of nothing more interesting or rewarding to do. Longinus listened a moment. The orator indeed was no Cicero. And orators in this modern day, his elders kept telling Longinus, even eloquent ones, did not excite the interest that good speakers commanded in the days of the republic and even of Augustus.

Longinus' eyes strayed above the gesticulating speaker to climb the marble-studded slope of the Capitoline. From the flat of the Forum's level pavement, statues, columns, pilasters, façades, singly and in groups, went up the slope in a jungle of stone and bronze to the summit, which was topped on the left by the most recent of the several temples to the sky-god that have occupied the site since ancient times. Between it and the smaller but loftier Temple of Juno, but lower on the ascending hillside, stood the broad several-storied Tabularium, the records office of the empire.

With the appreciation of an equestrian Roman long away from the capital, Longinus studied thoughtfully the grandiose architecture and ornamentation of this vibrant heartland of the eight-hundred-year-old city. Into this tiny level at the foot of five of Rome's seven hills, in ancient times hardly large enough for the pasturing of a few sheep and goats, the years and many men had transported from the farthest lands of the empire an immeasurable wealth in art and splendor beyond all dreaming. Visionaries and planners, architects and builders, artists and artisans, emperors and equestrians and freedmen and slaves, Romans, Greeks, blond men from the forests of Germania and dark men from Ethiopia and the hot countries bordering the southern shores of the Great Sea, countless known and unknown and lost and long gone beyond every vestige of remembrance have given of their genius and their brawn and their love and their lives to raise in this flattened small valley a magnificence unmatched in all the earth.

Longinus thought of the dullness and squalor, the drabness and penuriousness he had left in Palestine. Save for the Temple in Jerusalem—and Herod had borrowed from the Greeks and Romans in planning and building that immense and splendid structure, and the other manifestly Roman edifices scattered about Palestine—that entire province stretching around the eastern rim of the Great Sea all told could not boast art treasures comparable to the statues and temples gracing this one slope on the eastern side of the Capitoline.

He stood for a moment and, as a traveler beside a cool stream after a long sojourning in the desert, drank deeply of the beauty before his eyes. Resplendent temples with great columns of white Carrara or other marbles brought from Greece and other lands far and near; with the architraves atop them, and the friezes and cornices elaborately ornamented and often painted in reds and greens and blues; innumerable statues set into the friezes or upon slender pedestals between the pilasters or marching singly or in groups up the slope toward the temples on the crown, the nudes painted in flesh colors with hair darkened, and tall shafts lifting marbled figures skyward, figures of gods and goddesses and emperors and warriors and poets and legendary heroes—these the tribune gazed upon and drank in thirstily.

And all this, he knew so well, was but a part of the glory of Rome. Behind him rose the Palatine and the sprawling, immense mass of marble that was the home of the emperors and the seat of many of the functions of the empire's government; to his right was Forum Julium, built by Julius Caesar, with the great Temple of Venus Genetrix in the center of the plaza, where sometimes the Senate held its sessions. And beyond Forum Julium, and more modern, was the Forum Augustum.

Longinus roused himself from his momentary reverie. Already the shadow of Basilica Julia lay diagonally across the paving stones and was climbing high on the columns of Basilica Aemilia across the Forum. If he did not hurry homeward, he realized, dinner would be finished before he arrived; the women would have retired from the triclinium, and the men, refreshed after a walk about the peristylium, would have returned to the triclinium for the evening's drinking.

As he turned to go toward the northern wall of Basilica Aemilia, two ragged urchins came bounding around a statue's high pedestal and narrowly avoided colliding with him. The next moment he almost stepped upon an idler who with several others was crouched down at the base of the pedestal shaking dice in a cup above an improvised gaming-board scratched upon the travertine paving. The statue atop the pedestal, Longinus noticed as he happened to look up, was appropriately erected to an Italian abstraction, the Goddess of Chance.

Around the corner of Basilica Aemilia the tribune paused again. Before a grouping of white boards set against one sec-

tion of the wall facing toward the Tabularium, several loung,
ers were gathered, though it was late in the day and the
usually thronged Forum was being deserted.

"*Acta Diurnal*" he exclaimed as he edged his way through
the men ranged before the boards covered with writing and
pushed near enough to read the news notices posted on them.
"Any news of great moment today?" he inquired of a man in
a rather bedraggled toga at his elbow.

The fellow smiled glumly, shook his head. "The same old
grist," he observed. "The government making early excuses for
bread running short by reporting failure of crops in Egypt,
a fellow being prosecuted for stealing from his trading house,
rich old Marcus Aelius divorcing his young wife on the
grounds she was too"—he smiled impudently—"friendly"—he
emphasized the word—"with poor but handsome and robust
young Antonius Tullius. But, tribune"—the man had glanced
at Longinus' insignia—"you might be interested in this item
right here"—he pointed a stubby forefinger at a line midway
of one of the boards—"where it says that almost a whole century of our legionaries was ambushed and wiped out by those
light-skinned savages in Germania. I say transport a legion up
there, or more if it appears necessary to do the job, and slay
every man, woman, and child in that uncivilized region."
Frowning heavily, he turned away from the posted notices and
started across the Forum in the direction of Vicus Tuscus.

But Longinus continued to scan the news posted on Rome's
daily journal boards. Suddenly he bent low and peered intently at a notice near the bottom of one of them.

*Prefect Marco of the Praetorian Guard has journeyed down to
his palace at Baiae ostensibly to instruct his freedmen and
slaves in preparing it for occupancy during the summer season.
But has he really been summoned to Capreae by the emperor?*

*Gaius Caesar Germanicus is enjoying the sunshine, lavish food
and drink, and the companionship of lively friends at his palace at Baiae. It is rumored that although his wife did not accom-*

pany him, Caligula, while in Campania, will not necessarily be deprived of interesting female companionship.

Prince Agrippa of the House of Herod, brother-in-law of Tetrarch Herod Antipas of Galilee and chariot-racing favorite of Gaius, continues a prisoner in chains at Capreae by command of Emperor Tiberius.

Agrippa a prisoner in chains! And by command of the emperor himself. What could the spoiled wastrel brother of Herodias have done to bring down upon himself the wrath of old Tiberius?

But there were other startling items of news and gossip. He read down the board.

Antonia, the emperor's sister-in-law and grandmother of Gaius, has left her palace in Rome to visit Tiberius at Capreae. Antonia was a beloved friend of Agrippa's mother and in past years has frequently rescued Agrippa from serious financial difficulties. Could it be that she has gone to Capreae to urge the emperor to release Agrippa?

Certain senators and others familiar with the affairs of the imperial court are wondering if Prefect Marco, Gaius, and Antonia haven't arranged to join in petitioning the emperor to release the Herodian prince. Those who profess to understand the workings of the emperor's mind predict the three may succeed only in bringing down upon their heads the emperor's fierce wrath. A word to the prudent should suffice!

Longinus reread the items that had caught his attention and then scanned the other boards for possible further news of the prefect and the emperor. But he saw nothing that would afford him further enlightenment concerning the activities of those two or tidbits of capital gossip about them or any of the others mentioned in the notices he had just read.

He turned away from the *Acta Diurna* and walked straight

across the plaza northward past the eastern end of the Curia, magnificently distinguished in this forest of marbled splendor by its great columned high porch, and in the moment he was passing the edifice, there came to him fleeting memories of times when as a child he had played about this porch with other privileged children of senators while their fathers were meeting on empire business in the adjacent huge Senate chamber.

But Longinus did not stop to study the Curia or to recall childhood memories of it. His thoughts were on what he had just read on the white boards. Had Prefect Marco gone down into Campania to attempt to prevail upon the emperor to free Herod Agrippa? And were Caligula and his grandmother planning to join in petitioning Tiberius to release the Herodian? And what, the question persisted in his mind, did Agrippa do to anger the emperor so grievously that he ordered him into chains? The tribune agreed with the author of the gossip in the *Acta Diurna* notices that any persistent petitioning by them might inflame the crotchety Tiberius against them, and particularly against the prefect. Hadn't he already had one prefect, Sejanus, strangled? And Sejanus had appeared to be a man of more authority and influence in the empire than Marco.

Suppose that Marco should manage to get himself in ill favor with the emperor. Then what effect would the resulting situation have upon Marco's revelation to Tiberius that Legate Vitellius was removing Pontius Pilate from the procuratorship in Judaea and sending him to Rome for trial? And, of much greater moment, what effect would it have upon one Tribune Lucius Cassius Longinus!

But now the tribune was emerging from this second glade of marbled forestry and splendid façades into a third one, larger, newer, more resplendent than the other two, though possessed of less historical interest and tradition. He had often heard the story about the origin of Forum Augustum. When the eighteen-year-old Octavian, as heir of his great-uncle Julius Caesar, set out to avenge great Caesar's death, he made a vow

that if the war god Mars granted him success in that undertaking, he would raise to him a magnificent temple set in the
center of a splendid square in Rome. When years later Octavian became the Emperor Augustus, he made good the vow by
erecting, north of Forum Julium, this third forum, Forum
Augustum, more costly even than the others, splendorous,
superb.

Longinus' dark scowl disappeared as he stepped upon the
paving of the plaza. Around the expansive rectangle the tribune saw again the exquisite porticoes with graceful columns
chiseled from Numidian marble and other handsome marbles,
variegated and laid in pleasing symmetry of geometrical designs, that formed the pavement that covered completely the
openway, and the pavement upon which rested a maze of
statuary, bronze quadrigae, and triumphal arches.

But all these masterpieces of Octavian's architects and artists were but embellishments put there to adorn the glorious
edifice in white marble facing Longinus from the farther end
of the plaza and set midway between elegant façades swelled
into embracing gentle semicircles.

Precipitately the tribune thrust out a clenched fist in salute
to the glorious Temple of Mars Ultor, to the genius of the
men who had dreamed her and built her stone upon stone and
finished her in precious metals to resemble and rival the
Temple of Athena on the Acropolis in Athens.

"The beauty, the majesty, the mighty power that is Rome!"
He said it aloud and none paused to notice. "The strength, the
force, the sweep and surge of empire! Powerful, mighty is
Rome, ruler of the world." The tribune's eyes swept the
length of the esplanade before the temple and climbed the
marble steps that extended the width of the edifice to the summit of the huge stone pedestal on which it sat, and moved
upward along the graceful Corinthian columns to the ornate
architrave to study for a moment with new appreciation its intricate carvings and flutings and above it the heroic sculptured
figures of the frieze.

Nor did his searching out of the great temple's exterior

glories end with his concentrated examination of the statues in the triangular immense frieze. His eyes followed from each end of the architrave the rise of the gracefully molded cornice to its apex at the summit of the resplendent roof covered in great sheets of bronze. Above the highest point at the very edge of the front of the edifice the tribune's gaze moved still upward past the supporting pedestal to settle upon the towering bronze statue of Mars, muscled and naked except for a great plumed helmet on his cropped head and a sword belt about his middle with an empty scabbard hanging from it. Fiercely scowling, Mars the Avenger stood astride the magnificent temple, stilled forever in the frozen stance of challenge, his left arm held up and outward as if to balance the sword arm, with the point of his weapon realistically smeared with dark red, extended forward to lunge at an invisible enemy.

Basilica Julia behind him in the Forum Romanum symbolized Rome's rule of law, the empire's insistence upon meting out exact justice in man's dealing with man; the Temple of Mars Ultor, with the Avenger from his high place above its pinnacle, settling with terrible sword the fates of men and nations, stood as an awesome symbol of Rome's unconquerable mighty power.

How fortunate in this modern day to be a citizen of Rome, Tribune Longinus rationalized in a sudden soaring of spirits, how utterly fortunate to be a member of an ancient senatorial family and a tribune in Rome's thundering legions!

But there was no time to be dawdling here before this great temple to the god of war and reflecting upon the might of Rome, Longinus suddenly remembered, and he turned right and walked briskly beneath the columned portico into a short outer plaza that opened into the Argiletum. Through this narrow, shop-lined cobbled way, almost a duplication of Vicus Tuscus by which he had entered Forum Romanum in coming from the wharf on the Tiber, he soon reached the malodorous district of the Subura. It was in this region of squalor and incessant noise and turmoil, in which many poorly constructed tenements, six and seven stories in height each, housed thousands of Rome's poorest and most depraved residents, that, according to much recorded tradition, Julius Caesar was born almost a century and a half ago by a method of delivery that came soon to bear his name.

Jammed in among these towering and flimsy overcrowded insulae were countless shops of every description, taverns, brothels, and criminals' hideaways. Longinus usually passed through the Subura in walking from his father's mansion to any of the forums or going to the western part of the city beyond the river. But he always avoided it during evening hours. Anyone walking through these narrow alleys at such times was literally taking his life in his hands; the Subura was infested with brigands who would waylay and kill a man for the price of a drink of poor wine. The streets were unlighted and tortuous and at night filled with beasts of burden and carts bouncing and rattling over the uneven cobbles. Hardy souls venturing upon them after sunset usually were accompanied before and behind by slaves bearing flaming torches. And not infrequently such brave ones returned home without their purses and with heads bloodied. Residents living along these twisting narrow ways at nightfall securely bolted their doors and windows against intruders.

Even during daylight hours the Subura was hardly safe for strolling pedestrians unaccompanied. It abounded in pickpockets and petty thieves, escaped criminals, and runaway slaves. And a passer-by, who escaped other accident, might day or night be struck by something thrown or emptied from a cramped and filthy apartment fronting on the narrow way high above the often ill-smelling and polluted cobbles.

No other district in Rome reminded Longinus more of the narrow and twisting alleys of Jerusalem than the capital's crowded and noisome Subura. In both cities the streets were hardly wide enough for two carts going opposite ways to pass each other, but in Rome's Subura they were canyons dark and lost between buildings several times taller than those in Israel's holy city. In both Rome and Jerusalem the stench of animals and many people swarming, soiled and sweating, was similarly nauseous. But venturing through the Subura day or night was more hazardous than wandering about Ophel. And soon, Longinus realized, it would be quite dark in these cavernous passageways between the high structures.

So Longinus quickened his pace. He was anxious to get home to discover what news his father might have of the Prefect Marco and possibly of the emperor, and to learn if he should set out on the morrow himself for the region of Campania. He was anxious likewise to get through the Subura to Viminal Hill before darkness descended upon it and its motley denizens. Traveling would be safer after he began to ascend the Viminal to his father's mansion near its summit. And he would be getting back into a Rome he had left when he strode out of the Forum Augustum. He would be away again from the memory of the feel and appearance and smell of Jerusalem's Ophel district, which Rome's Subura was bringing back.

Soon he was beyond the foul region, and free and unharmed; none had challenged him in any of the narrow alleys or offered in any way to molest him, just as no one had ever ventured to harm him in Ophel or on Mount Zion or anywhere else in all Jerusalem. Perhaps in both cities his tribune's uniform had served him well. At any rate he was glad to be clear of the Subura, just as on the day he sailed from Seleucia's harbor, he was glad to be free once again of that eastern province rimming the Great Sea and away from its independent-minded and obstinate people, particularly the noisy and obstinate Hebrews.

He was at the foot of Viminal now and starting the ascent. He had never thought of it before, but the parallel between Rome and Jerusalem could be carried further. Climbing Viminal from the clutter and clamor of the Subura was comparable to mounting Zion Hill from the stench and press of Ophel, like pushing up the slope of Mount Moriah to the resplendent Temple to Yahweh and the Fortress of Antonia, where, on the pavement before the praetorium, Pontius Pilate had conducted the trial of the Galilean carpenter. And from the praetorium the soldiers had led and shoved the scourged and exhausted man westward through Damascus Gate to a frightful hill outside the city wall; there hours later he himself had plunged his lance into the cavity beneath the Galilean's heart, and down from the gaping wound had gushed the life blood. Westward from Mount Moriah and the procurator's praetorium. . . .

A sudden impulse led Longinus to pause and look westward above the rooftops toward the great Temple of Mars Ultor lying now in the shadow of a heavy cloud moving before the sun sinking low beyond the Tiber. Above the roof's comb, arms outthrust so that from Viminal Hill they seemed to form with his erect, lithe body a Roman cross, stood in aggressive motion suddenly stilled the defiant and challenging god of war.

"Mighty symbol of imperial power, the conquering power of Rome, mistress of the world," Longinus said aloud, as a great surge and lifting of spirit possessed him. Yet only a symbol, the further thought came to him, though the words were unspoken. Gods in the form of men, hah. If there are gods, they must be spirits. Like the god of the Jews, their Yahweh, they do not walk the earth in robes or togas, eat, drink, speak, smile and frown, laugh happily or hurl invectives. Yonder, Mars the Avenger—if indeed he is a god, he doesn't stand with a sword in hand, his brow dark with hate and destruction. He is, if indeed he is at all, but the spirit of war and bloodshed and victory earned in blood; he is no god walking among men in the flesh and bone and sinew of the physical. And if he does exist, or any of his fellows, he is indeed—as old Crito explained the gods—pure spirit. If there are any gods, any God. . . .

Longinus stood on the slope of Viminal Hill and gazed above the solidly massed houses of ancient Rome at the great Temple of Mars, whose roof rose to its apex above the carved heroic figures of the frieze like a rock-encircled hill ravined and pock-marked, for the glories of its architecture and the intricacies of its carvings were dimmed for the tribune by a heavy shadow cast upon it and the great statue at its summit. A cloud hovering low on the horizon beyond the Pons Aurelius screened away the horizontal rays of the sun that soon now would be dropping into the Great Sea.

But as he lifted his gaze to the god who stood with arms outflung and red-tipped sword, the sun discovered a narrow tear in the cloud and shot through it a beam that illumined the scowling Avenger from his bare feet to his helmeted head. And along the extended left arm, across the sword belt, out upon the right arm and the sword held menacingly with the red clotted on the point, the sunbeam danced.

Fascinated by the weird illumination of the great war god astride his temple, Longinus studied the pinpoint of fading sunlight as it played vagrantly along the arms, upon the bronzed, plumed helmet, across the sword belt.

But where was the sword belt? Craning to see the better, the tribune stared amazed, unbelieving. What he was seeing was no sword belt with scabbard appended, but only a be-draggled, soiled loincloth, dust-stained and blood-rusted, with one end loosened and hanging to a knee. Nor, by all the gods, was it a warrior's plumed helmet the tribune was seeing with startled, unbelieving eyes.

The headpiece Longinus saw in the strange light through the rift in the cloud was instead a circlet of laurel on the statue's brow, like countless other ones he had seen on the brows of victorious athletes, a simple ringlet of green leaves prized more highly than golden crowns. The laurel sur-mounted reddish-brown hair, not closely cropped like the hair of Roman soldiers but hanging down to the shoulders, curling at the ends.

Longinus narrowed his eyes and wrinkled his forehead to see the better. No, it was not a ringlet of laurel. Great Jupiter! The circlet he was seeing was fashioned of a shoot of green leaves, but thick among the leaves were long sharp barbs. The crown was not the laurel symbol of the winning charioteer in Circus Maximus but a long limb torn from a rhamnus bush and twisted into a circlet shoved down upon the slumped head of a young man, naked but for the loincloth.

But now the tribune was looking at the long bronzed arms, not freely outflung in the balanced stance of the gladiator, but stretched, mottled and bruised, straight out and pinioned to the arms of a cross. By all the gods! In the center of each palm he saw an iron spike protruding.

The moving weird light through the cloud's slit was centering upon the reddened tip of the sword, and Longinus strained forward to see more clearly. But no, by all the gods, the red he was seeing was not upon the point of a sword, for there was no sword; only a gash in the naked, beaten body, a gash toward one side beneath the heart and above the bedraggled loincloth, a straight, clean slit made by a lance, a wound from which blood now congealed had spurted at the lance's swift thrusting.

"No! No! By great Jupiter, no!" he protested audibly. "No! No!"

It was not I who killed you, Galilean. I was but trying to save you from prolonged agony. Pontius Pilate and the high priest crucified you. O Galilean, it was not I who sent you to the cross. I was but the instrument of their infamy. O carpenter of Nazareth, it was in kindness that I thrust my lance into your side beneath the heart. . . .

Longinus had averted his eyes from the strange vision atop the resplendent Temple of Mars Ultor. Now he ventured to look again toward the temple. The cloud had lifted, and from beneath it the dying sun shot its last rays full upon the edifice and the towering bronze statue above the roof's apex. He blinked his eyes to sharpen his vision.

Mars the Avenger, scowling fiercely, stood looking down upon Rome, his shining sword, blood-red at the tip, thrust forward in challenge.

Longinus shook his head slowly, incredulously, and turning, resumed his trudging up Viminal Hill toward his father's mansion.

BAIAE

21

By late morning of the third day after he arrived in Rome, Tribune Longinus had reached Prefect Marco's palace at Baiae. As he had hoped he might, he had been given a seat on the cursus publicus bringing government dispatches and other mail southward along the Via Appia for Emperor Tiberius and the prefect.

The prefect sobered noticeably when Longinus handed him the dispatch with the announcement that it was from Legate Vitellius. "It must be of great importance, since he sent it by you this long way," he observed. "Does it convey grave information, tribune? Do you know"—his forehead furrowed and his eyes studied the tribune—"what is in it?"

"I do, excellency. The message does bear grave information, but I would not describe it as disastrous."

"And he sent it by you so that I would be certain to get it and as quickly as possible?"

"Yes, and so that I might perhaps give you more detailed information than the dispatch itself provides."

"And also because it is urgent?"

"Yes. The legate wished you to receive it as promptly as possible. And good fortune has attended me all the way from Antioch."

Marco nodded. "Then let us closet ourselves with it." He clapped his hands together and a servant appeared quickly. "See that Tribune Longinus and I are not disturbed," he ordered. The servant bowed and was withdrawing when

Marco stopped him. He turned to Longinus. "You will, of course, lunch with me, tribune. But will you not also spend the night here? There is nothing in this"—he tapped lightly the sealed dispatch in his other hand—"that demands that you—or I—return to Rome immediately?"

"Nothing, excellency. You may think it necessary, though, after you have read the dispatch, to seek an audience with the emperor."

Marco paled perceptibly. "It must be important and urgent. But even that can wait until tomorrow, perhaps? In fact, it must, because the emperor isn't at Capreae now anyway."

Longinus nodded. "It is important, but not that urgent, I'd say."

Marco turned to the waiting servant. "Then we shall continue with our plans for the dinner, and the tribune will be our guest and will remain at least for the night." The servant bowed again. "And if we are still closeted here when the luncheon hour arrives—and likely we shall be—then have us served here. And make sure"—he waved his arm in dismissal —"that nothing interrupts us."

Marco read the legate's message through before commenting. "It's clear enough," he finally observed as he returned the dispatch to its case. "The legate's action comes at an inopportune time, but any time perhaps would be inopportune." He shrugged. "And I can see how his patience with Pilate would be exhausted. Pilate's handling of the Samaritan incident left Vitellius with no other course, I agree. But there is one thing I am not certain about, Longinus. When is Pilate arriving in Rome? The dispatch doesn't say. And Claudia, I presume, is coming with him. And she will ask for a divorce, no doubt." He smiled. "You two have discussed that eventuality, of course?"

"We have, yes. And I discussed it with the legate, too. But, excellency, that in no way influenced the legate's decision to suspend the procurator."

"Of course, Longinus."

"And Legate Vitellius assured me that he would not announce his decision to suspend Pilate until I was well on the way to you with the dispatch, and that he would not allow him to sail for Rome until you have had ample time to speak with Tiberius about it. He said he would allow full time even for poor winds."

"That is good. Then we will have a few days in which to obtain an audience with the emperor. He decided rather abruptly—probably as a result of something his astrologers told him—to return to Rome. But he is making the trip leisurely. I suspect we may be able to overtake him at Misenum, where he's spending several days at the villa of the late Lucullus." He narrowed his eyes and his forehead crinkled as he tapped the dispatch case still in his hand. "I do wonder what his reaction will be when he reads this. But there's no virtue in anticipating trouble." He pulled open a drawer of his desk and deposited the dispatch. "And now, Longinus," he said as he closed the drawer, "I have some perhaps startling developments to report to you. But I must caution you not to reveal prematurely anything I tell you."

"Of course, excellency." His eyes betrayed sudden excitement.

"Have you heard that Prince Herod Agrippa has been imprisoned by the emperor?"

"I saw a reference to it in *Acta Diurna* as I was coming through the Forum Romanum, and later my father told me something about it."

"The senator told you why?"

"Yes. That Tiberius became greatly offended when a slave reported he had heard Agrippa remark to Caligula that he hoped the day would soon come when Tiberius would be dead and Caligula would be emperor."

"That's the substance of it. Tiberius had him chained, and he's still a prisoner despite strong efforts to have him released. But evidently Agrippa's conduct did not embitter Tiberius against Agrippa's dear friend Caligula, because—and this you surely could not have heard, Longinus, since news of it has hardly reached Rome yet—well, because Tiberius has named Caligula his successor to the throne."

"Caligula!"

"Yes. Most Romans thought that his grandson Tiberius would be his choice, but for some reason—perhaps, again, his astrologers—he has named Caligula. And that, Longinus, explains why I'm having a small dinner today, at which you are to be a guest. It's in honor of the next emperor of the Roman Empire." He smiled wryly, but offered no comment.

"I shall be honored, excellency, and I thank you for inviting me."

"It is fortunate for me that you have come to Baiae," Prefect Marco added. "I have been wondering whom we might invite in Agrippa's place. You will be reclining on the couch he was to have occupied, Longinus. You see, I planned this small dinner for the friends of Agrippa—who were down here mainly to urge Tiberius to free him—in honor of the occasion of Agrippa's release, but the emperor refused to give Agrippa his freedom. So when Tiberius revealed that he was naming Caligula as his successor, I changed the reason for the dinner, though I left the guest list unchanged, with the exception that I am substituting you for Agrippa."

"Then is Agrippa still a prisoner at Capreae? The *Acta Diurna* said he was imprisoned there."

"He has been, but Tiberius ordered him sent to Rome. He promised his sister-in-law that he would review the case when he returns to the Palace there."

"Then Antonia has been here, too?"

"Yes, she came to add her pleas for the release of her dear friend's son. And she came on to her palace here from our meeting with Tiberius at Capreae. She will be with us at dinner. It will be a rather unusual group, old and young, but each one acquainted with all the others, whether on altogether friendly terms or not. And the conversation should be sophisticated and perhaps after a while acidulous." He smiled. "And although you know each of them quite well, Longinus, you may be surprised to hear from some of them what has been happening during the period you have been serving in Palestine."

"Indeed." Longinus smiled. "It promises to be interesting."

22

When Longinus entered the atrium, most of the other guests had arrived and were chatting with Prefect Marco and his wife before going with their valets into the triclinium.

Longinus, after lunching with Marco on cold meats from last night's dinner, bread, cheeses, olives, and a salad of mixed greens, with a delicious Falernian wine, had lain down for a moment's relaxation and had gone to sleep. When he awakened there was time only for a quick bath, shave, and change into fresh clothing. As he was lacing his sandals, he heard the litters arriving in the court before the atrium.

The first person to greet him as he stepped from his chamber door into the atrium was the stately Antonia, who happened to be standing near the doorway.

"Longinus!" she exclaimed, as she caught sight of the tribune. "My dear boy, I am so happy to see you. I did not know until a moment ago that you had returned from Palestine. I saw your father and mother hardly a month ago, I'm sure it was, and they said nothing about your being expected home."

"They did not know I was coming, Antonia," he told her. "In fact, I did not know myself until a day or two before I left Antioch."

"Antioch? Then you must have come on business concerned with the government of the empire, sent by Legate Vitellius. But"—her gentle patrician face brightened—"let us not speak of the empire. After spending several days at Capreae with my crotchety old brother-in-law, I'm sure that all of us"—she waved her arm in a half-circle to embrace the lively chattering guests—"will be glad to forgo talk of government affairs. But do tell me this, Longinus." She lifted a hand to place it on his forearm, so that the light from the wall lamps danced in the gem-set buckles of her white silken stola, shimmering in its graceful folds from the purple border at the neck to the purple flounce at the hemline. "When have you seen dear Claudia, and is she still enduring that stuffed toad of a husband? I do believe, Longinus, that he's a bigger dolt even than my Claudius yonder—and certainly he's a greater rascal."

"She was quite well when last I saw her before leaving Caesarea for Antioch," Longinus replied. But he offered no comment about Pilate or Claudius. Nor did Antonia, the widow of Drusus and the mother of the noble Germanicus, appear to notice. Instead, she leaned forward and lowered her voice.

"And you still love her, and she loves you; I know it. Oh, that obstinate, suspicious Tiberius!" She shook her head dubiously. "And one foot already—almost both feet—in the grave!" Antonia withdrew her heavily ringed, thin hand from his arm and patted his shoulder consolingly. "Why doesn't he let her divorce that fathead Pilate and come home and marry you!"

Smiling, the emperor's sister-in-law was turning aside from the tribune when suddenly she spied, coming from behind a spreading potted plant, a tall, hulking young man with a narrow, small head and protruding paunch. Immediately Longinus recognized him, though in the several years since he had last seen him the youth's head appeared to have thinned and lengthened as his stomach had swelled and sagged and the bald spot on his crown had pushed its perimeter considerably outward. But the tribune's instinctive feeling of repugnance in discovering the hulking figure near him, he realized, had not changed.

"Gaius!" Antonia called, and when the young man, unsmiling, approached, she laid her white hand on his right forearm, uncovered from the elbow, where it extended, heavily dark with hair, from beneath the folds of his carefully arranged toga. A thick mat of curling black hair from his upper chest to his scrawny neck, together with the small head and the swelled paunch, gave him, Longinus suddenly thought, the appearance of a garishly clothed black bear from the forests of Germania walking on his hind legs and about to growl. "Gaius, you remember Longinus"—she had glanced, evidently for the first time, at the insignia on his uniform—"Tribune Longinus, son of Senator Gaius Cassius. He is just now arrived home from Palestine on a mission for Legate Vitellius."

Caligula nodded, grunted. Antonia, unabashed at her grandson's crude manners, turned now to the tribune. "Longinus, you may not have heard that the emperor has designated Gaius his heir and successor to the throne." Beaming, she gave her attention again to the still-glum Caligula. But he did not relax his expression of uncomfortable boredom.

"Yes, on arriving here I was informed of it by the prefect." He bowed to the ungainly Gaius. "I congratulate Gaius and hope for him, when he takes the throne, a happy and successful reign."

Caligula's muttered response was intelligible this time, even though unenthusiastic. His grandmother faced him again, smiling warmly. "And when you are emperor, Gaius, we shall expect you—if she isn't granted one before then—to give your Aunt Claudia a divorce from Pontius Pilate and arrange her marriage to Longinus."

"My bastard half-aunt," he corrected his grandmother, his ludicrous face warming with a silly grin. Then suddenly he scowled darkly. "When I am emperor," he declared, "no one need expect me to do anything. By the gods, I'll do whatever at the moment I may be pleased to do. Do I make myself understood, my dear grandmother?" He pinched her cheek, but gently, and snickering, turned away to join a group knotted in the passageway opening at one side of the tablinum into the sumptuous column-girdled peristylium.

"Longinus, you must overlook my grandson's brusqueness,"

Antonia whispered. "He is not well. Only this morning he had another of his spells of falling sickness. But, mind you, my boy, soon Gaius will be emperor, and then"—she peered about covertly—"you will have your Claudia. Trust me to arrange it!"

Presently the guests were summoned into the triclinium and Marco's nomenclator, a handsome and patrician-appearing Greek slave, with much bowing and polite gesturing, began pointing out their respective places upon the three gracefully carved and upholstered sofas ranged on three sides of the resplendently polished citruswood table, the curving legs of which were each carved ornately in representation of the fore-leg of a lion.

Caligula, as the prefect's guest of honor, was assigned the principal position at the dinner, the place on the extreme right of the middle couch as the guests faced the table. The host was next to him on the third couch, with his wife on his right and Longinus next to her. Beyond Caligula, on his left, was his wife Junia and on her left was Antonia. On the first sofa were Claudius, in the center, a girl named Valeria Messalina at his right, and his niece Agrippina, Caligula's sister, at his left.

When the nine diners had settled themselves comfortably, with pillows under their elbows and their chins cradled in their palms, and their valets had removed their shoes and stepped back to help Marco's servants in the serving of food, they began to chatter in lively fashion of current happenings in Rome, in Capreae, in Baiae, and other places of the empire. Then quickly a group of young slave-boys, stripped to the waist and with hair curled and smelling of perfumes and pomades, entered the triclinium bearing silver bowls of scented water and dainty towels with which the diners washed and dried their hands in preparation for eating. This task completed, they were ready to begin feasting.

The serving began with the nodding of a splendidly cos-tumed servant signaling to Marco from the doorway into the kitchen area that the cooks were ready and the prefect's nod-ding in return that the diners likewise were prepared to receive the first course. In that instant the servant boys came gliding from the kitchen with silver dishes that they set upon the table's polished surface—salads, eggs hard-boiled, crab meats and other seafood tidbits, mushrooms, cheeses, olives— delectable foods eaten with the fingers and designed to stimulate the appetites of the diners. Other boys brought out drinks in silver cups, light wines and sweet mulsum thinned to protect against early inebriety.

"Delicious!" declared Longinus to his hostess as he tasted a bit of crab meat in a savory sauce. "This is Roman-style, and we get so little Roman-prepared food in the eastern provinces. We have much seafood, but even in Caesarea and other cities where the Roman influence is strong, the cooking is more kosher than Roman." He fingered another bit and chewed it with evident delight. "I am really going to enjoy this meal," he said, smiling.

Marco's wife laughed. "I do hope so," she said. "But it is to be only an ordinary dinner. No nightingales' tongues, no cranes from Ionia or peacocks from Samos, or cows' udders, or tunnyfish from Chalcedon. My husband is no Lucullus. His taste doesn't run to such delicacies, even if we could afford them, which we cannot."

After the appetizers came dishes of meats and fish perfectly cooked and garnished daintily with early fresh vegetables, and with them a great silver tray on which reposed a grinning-tusked wild boar, which was soon carved into a nonentity of great slabs by a slave in lavish livery, who wielded his gleaming knife in time with the tunes of a strolling flute-player.

"I see why Prince Gaius has added considerably to his girth since I last saw him," Longinus observed to the prefect's wife when minutes later he paused after having devoured a large serving of the boar meat.

She glanced past her husband. Caligula was chewing wolf-ishly, his mouth half-opened, his heavy lips smeared with grease. He picked up his wine goblet, downed the Falernian in one long gulp, and thrust the goblet forth to a slave who dashed forward to refill it. "I hope he is enjoying his dinner,"

"By great Jupiter and all the gods and goddesses!" exclaimed Caligula as he leaned across the tray and reached for one of the tiny swans. "Marco, when I am emperor of Rome"—he bit off the cygnet's pastry head and chewed it hungrily with smacking lips—"I'll either have your cook or your head!" He swallowed, with a lively plunging and lifting of his Adam's apple, and then reached for his goblet, whose contents he downed with one gulp. Then he held out the glass to one of the slaves. "Fill it with that pond water," he said, grinning. The slave ladled the snow-chilled wine into Caligula's goblet and nervously set it down before Marco's guest of honor, who promptly gulped a big swallow. He smacked his lips and wiped them with the back of a hairy hand.

"By Mother Ceres, Marco, it's better than this frail concoction you've been serving us," he declared as he lifted the goblet again. "The bird flavors it." He drank the goblet dry with two swallows and handed it back to be refilled, as he searched in the cavernous interior of the pastry swan and clutched a fat fig. "Marco, what's the name of the cook who concocted this?"

"Well, Gaius, several slaves helped to prepare the dessert," Marco answered a bit hesitantly. "It was a sharing of ideas and labor, and——"

"You don't want me to know his name, eh?" Caligula was grinning, and the eyes, deepset in his narrow skull, seemed friendly, though Marco fancied the tone of voice not entirely so. "You're afraid, Marco, that I will take him from you. Well, by Jupiter, I will, or else I'll——"

But he did not finish his threat, if threat he intended it to be, for at that moment the door to the peristylium opened and a soldier in the uniform of the Praetorian Guard came striding toward Marco. He saluted, and the prefect returned his salute.

"Please pardon my intrusion, excellency," said the guardsman, "but I was ordered to rush to you on a matter of the gravest importance. I come from Misenum to bear a message that on his way to Rome the emperor, while pausing at Misenum——"

"By all the gods!" Caligula exclaimed, interrupting. "Is the emperor dead? Speak out, soldier!"

The courier faced Marco, his countenance questioning.

"This is Gaius, soldier," Marco explained. "Continue your report."

"The emperor Tiberius, when I left Misenum—and I have come straight here as fast as my horse would bear me—was gravely ill though still alive. I know not how he is now, excellency. I was ordered to come here and apprise the prefect of the emperor's condition and notify you that the emperor's advisers urge you to rush there at the earliest possible moment."

Marco's face was grave. "But you are sure that he was still alive when you left Misenum?"

"I was told so, excellency. But very low. In fact, shortly after he fell into a fainting spell, it was thought that he was dead, and couriers were dispatched to Rome to announce his death to the Senate and the people. But shortly after they left, signs of life were discovered, and he appeared to improve." He shook his head grimly. "I was told to report, excellency, that your presence at Misenum is greatly needed and desired."

All the guests on the three couches, having suddenly lost interest in the magnificent pastry swan and its filling of delicacies, were straining to catch every word of the courier's message. Antonia sat up and was leaning around Junia, and across from her on the first couch, his mouth half-open, Claudius had lifted a thin hand to cup an ear. And Messalina and Agrippina, their chatter suddenly quieted, were listening intently. But not a person spoke until Marco turned to address his guests.

"You have heard the courier," he said. "Pray the gods that the emperor yet lives. And I beg your forgiveness in thus precipitately leaving you, but I must rush to the emperor's bed. And Gaius, no doubt, will wish to accompany me"—he looked toward Caligula for confirmation—"in order to be at Misenum" —Caligula nodded gravely—"to accept the reins of government should Tiberius, the gods forbid, fail to survive his grave illness."

"Yes, I shall go at once, Marco. But before we leave for Misenum I want couriers to be sent off to Rome with dispatches correcting the erroneous report that Tiberius died. That will forestall for a time"—Caligula smiled craftily—"any hasty and unwise action by the senate, the people, or your guardsmen."

"I shall send couriers immediately, Gaius," said Marco, "and instruct them to ride furiously. They should reach Rome not many hours behind those riding northward from Misenum with news of the emperor's death."

Caligula nodded his thanks to Marco and, rising, bowed to the prefect and then to the prefect's wife. "I thank you for honoring me," he said, "and I regret that I must now withdraw from this congenial company and this . . . this"—he pointed toward the swan now decapitated but still floating in the wine fast mixing with the melting snow—"magnificent bird." He faced Marco again and a quick smile warmed his somber expression. "I tell you again, Marco, if I am emperor on the morrow, I shall be sending for your pastry cook no later than the day after."

Marco's smile was genial, but he did not respond to the challenge. He turned instead to look along the third couch past his wife's concerned countenance to the last guest. "Tribune Longinus," he said, "I shall expect you to accompany us to Misenum. We shall be leaving as quickly as the horses and carriages can be readied for the journey." A frown clouded his face and his forehead ridged in small furrows. "In all probability we will be continuing from Misenum to Rome." He glanced again toward Caligula. "And, Gaius, may the gods grant us courage and strength for whatever the days ahead may bring."

†

MISENUM

23

It was still some two hours of midnight when Prefect Marco, with Prince Gaius and Tribune Longinus, several of the Praetorian Guardsmen who had been on duty at Baiae, torchbearers and other personal servants, arrived at the splendrous villa of the fabulous Lucullus, now dead almost a century.

Marco, Caligula, and Longinus went at once to Tiberius' apartment, which included a private atrium and a large bedchamber opening onto the magnificent peristylium and, on the outside wall, overlooking the blue waters of the bay.

A group of his guardsmen sprang to attention and saluted as the prefect and the other two entered.

"How is the emperor?" Marco inquired as the three returned the salutes.

A guardsman standing near the door to the bedchamber, which Marco saw was slightly ajar, spoke out quickly. "The emperor, excellency, is sleeping now. He appears greatly improved since early evening, when he was gravely ill."

"Are there physicians in the bedchamber with him?"

"No, excellency. He ordered them out"—the trace of a smile lingered for an instant on his stern countenance "—and told them not to return until he should call for them. He seems to have recovered his accustomed strength of will. The physicians were amazed. A few hours before, they were certain he was dead, and dispatched couriers to Rome announcing it. But now they say he will——"

"Soldier! Soldier! Come here! Get some light in this stygian hole! By all the gods, have you no ears!"

"The emperor! Excuse me, excellency!" The guardsman disappeared into the gloom of the bedchamber.

"Light some lamps!" The three heard distinctly now through the wider opening. "By great Jupiter, they would entomb me before I'm dead, would they? Well, soldier, by blessed Ceres, I tricked them!" A light flared, as the soldier succeeded in lighting one of the wall lamps, perhaps from the one that had been left burning in low flame. Then they heard Tiberius laugh. "Hah! So they sent couriers racing off to Rome to report to those senatorial vultures that the emperor was dead, eh? In order that those puffed toads in the Curia could start picking the old man's bones. Hah! Or, better said, those hook-beaked cormorants." The laugh was brittle, hollow, mirthless, sardonic. Longinus felt a cold shiver running along his spine. "But who is outside that door, soldier?" It was Tiberius again. "I heard voices questioning you about me. Speak up quickly, man, or I'll have your head!"

Marco heard his name spoken, and then the name of Gaius. The guardsman did not know the tribune.

"Well, by swift Mercury, bring them to me!" the three heard Tiberius command. "They doubtless came to watch me drawing my last breath, hah! That loutish charioteer of a grandnephew cannot wait for me to die, eh? Go, fetch them to me!"

Longinus knew that Caligula had heard; a sneer, sinister and menacing, twisted his narrow face. But he said nothing, for the guardsman, plainly paler, was at the threshold. "The emperor desires your presence in the bedchamber." He stood aside as the three men came into the chamber and stood facing the great bed.

In the moment Longinus first saw it he wondered if the bed had survived from the great wealth of grandly pretentious furniture with which, according to stories he had heard his grandfather and other elders relating, Lucullus had furnished the sprawling palatial villa. The bed was so high on its turned and elaborately carved bronze legs that it would be difficult for anyone except an agile youth to climb into it without using the footstool beside it. And in the tortoise-shell veneering of the frames, likely of hard wood, the flames from the lamps leaped and danced.

But not for long was Tribune Longinus' attention upon the bed itself. His roving eyes fastened quickly upon the gaunt old man almost swallowed by the luxuriously soft coverlets. One blanket, dyed a rich purple, with its turned-back edge embroidered in gold thread, came up along his flattened chest almost to his collarbones threatening to push through pallid skin at the base of his scrawny neck.

Tiberius Claudius Nero Caesar, nearing eighty, and for twenty-two years, five months, and three days second emperor of mighty Imperial Rome, mistress of the world, lay upon the high bed beneath the purple covering. But from his waist to the crown of his almost completely bald pate he was half-reclining in a nest of silken soft pillows.

Longinus was shocked at the deterioration of the once tall, physically powerful, brilliant general under Augustus, who, an already disillusioned old man of fifty-five, had ascended the throne in Longinus' childhood. Longinus still remembered how Tiberius had looked when he had been taken by his father on special occasions to the Forum Romanum to stand in the shadow of the Temple of Jupiter Stator at the turning of the Via Sacra; there he had watched with incredulous, staring eyes triumphal processions sweeping toward the Temple of Jupiter Capitolinus to the thunderous acclaim of countless arrogant Romans. Longinus remembered having seen Tiberius also on other occasions during the decade he ruled the empire from the great palace on Palatine Hill and even a few times in the twelve years he had governed from Capreae.

But Longinus could hardly believe the emaciated, shrunken, scrofulous figure propped on the pillows was the man he had seen only a few years ago on his island retreat off the Surrentum promontory. The once-commanding broad forehead seemed to have narrowed and shrunk to little more than a skull with yellowed parchmentlike skin drawn tautly over it, and the firm mouth of other years appeared to have retreated into the pock-marked flaccid face and pulled the once-sensual lips in with it. Longinus experienced a sudden shiver of aversion; he was seeing not the virile emperor of the mighty empire but a shrinking, drying, waxen undead corpse. Tiberius Caesar had settled upon the bed of long-gone Lucullus like a noble proud statue toppled from its pedestal and left, earth-stained and abandoned, in some ancient equestrian's forgotten summer garden.

But the old eyes had not lost their fire. And his voice, though it was weaker and more petulant, as Longinus observed when Tiberius, twisting to face them, spoke out sharply, had not lost its capacity to utter caustic comments and hurl bitter invective.

"So you have followed me here," the emperor Tiberius said, raising his head and bracing himself on his elbow, "to stand over me while I die. Well, by great Jove's thunderbolts"—he lifted his free arm and waggled a long forefinger toward them —"you can go back to Baiae or Rome or Pluto's dark realm. I'm not going to die, not now, at any rate." The flickering flames of the lamps danced in his angry eyes. But suddenly his manner and his tone changed. "Who's this third one?" he asked, pointing to Longinus. "Do I know him?"

"Sire, he is Tribune Lucius Cassius Longinus, son of your good friend Senator Gaius Cassius Longinus," Marco answered. "The tribune has been privileged to have audience with you on other occasions. And, sire, neither he nor Gaius nor I came here to see you die. On the contrary, we pray the gods to preserve you to continue your wise and beneficent government of the empire many years."

"I know your father the senator well and favorably, tribune," Tiberius replied, ignoring all the prefect's statement except his introduction of Longinus, "and I don't doubt that I have known you also. But *tribune*. I don't recall your name on the list of promotions to tribune confirmed by me." A cloud seemed to cross the old man's face, and then quickly it lifted, and he looked again toward the prefect. "Then, Marco, tell me why you did come here, and"—he looked with glaring eyes at Caligula—"you, Gaius, why did you interrupt your reveling with Baiae's painted harlots to ride here to Misenum to visit me, if not to watch and wait impatiently for me to die, like vultures watch with impatience the last feeble kicking of a lamb caught in the rocks?"

"Sire, we were enjoying dinner at the home of Prefect Marco this evening when a courier arrived with the disconcerting information that you were seriously ill," Caligula began to explain. "In fact, the courier revealed that you had fallen into a faint and that it was feared you were dead, so that couriers were dispatched to Rome to notify the senate——"

"And now in Rome they really think me dead! By all the gods, Gaius, by now they have made all the arrangements for *your* coronation!"

"No, sire, other couriers were dispatched to overtake if possible the first ones," Marco hastened to assure the agitated Tiberius, "but if they should be unable to do so, they will continue to Rome with the happy news that you had suffered but a temporary indisposition from which you have quickly recovered. When the courier from here arrived at my villa, sire, we were greatly concerned, naturally, but when we were assured by the courier that you appeared to be recovering rapidly, we were no longer fearful. But I had business of great importance, sire, to bring to your attention and on which to receive your instructions, a matter of extreme urgency. And should you be sufficiently recovered by tomorrow, sire, to consider it, I shall appreciate receiving your orders——"

"Tomorrow! By bountiful Ceres, Marco, I'm not dead or dying! It was but a fainting spell I had, and I'm recovered now, by all the gods! What is this urgent business, Marco? We'll settle it now."

"But, sire, perhaps you would wish"—Marco paused. "I should think——"

"You wish your audience with me to be private, eh? Then, Gaius, you and the tribune are excused."

"Tribune Longinus, sire, is acquainted likewise with the business, which is concerned with a situation in the province in which he has been serving, and——"

"And you wish him to remain with us. Then go, nephew, and I shall have you summoned when the matter has been concluded."

Turning with a scowl, but without a word, Caligula stalked from the chamber.

"Now, Marco, proceed with your business." He twisted about in his pillows, evidently in an attempt to sit up straight, and when Marco bent forward to assist him, he waved the prefect off. "I don't need your help," he said testily. "I need no one's help." He pushed himself upward and with shaking hand arranged a pillow at his back. "Now go ahead," he commanded.

Carefully and calmly Marco traced for Tiberius the story of Pontius Pilate's decade of administrating Rome's government of Judaea and Samaria in the faraway province of Palestine, of his failure to understand the Jewish subject peoples and of his stubborn refusal to attempt to understand them and keep them reasonably contented so that violence would be avoided and revenues would continue to pour into Rome's treasury. He reviewed, perhaps not with complete accuracy and with evident bias, Pilate's suspected conniving with the late Prefect Sejanus to divert much of the tax revenue into the personal coffers of the traitorous former prefect, and he was reporting Pilate's most recent difficulty in his slaughtering of the protesting Samaritans, when Tiberius interrupted.

"But what do you wish me to do about Pilate?" he asked. "Do you want me to depose him, bring him to Rome, and behead him or send him off into exile? And, by great Jove, Marco, what do you want done with his wife? Claudia's my stepdaughter, you may not know, my late wife Julia's bastard daughter." He paused, looked with eyes suddenly suspicious into Longinus' face. "You've served a long time at the post in Caesarea, tribune. You must know Claudia. Do you?"

"I do, sire. I knew her in Rome before she was married to Pilate and sent with him out to Palestine."

"And in Palestine you and she have"—Tiberius paused and his sardonic grin was quickly gone—"I won't ask you that.

What you and Claudia have been doing—if you have—is of no concern to me. But, nevertheless, it would please you, wouldn't it, tribune, if I should depose Pilate and permit Claudia to divorce him and return to Rome to live?"

"It would, sire. And I do believe it would likewise serve well the emperor and the empire."

"Well, yes, I thought so." Tiberius turned again to confront Marco. "Speak out, Marco, what do you want me to do with Pilate? Depose him, have him brought to me for trial, exile him, behead him? What, by the gods, prefect, do you want me to do?"

"It is my recommendation, sire, that when he arrives from Caesarea you conduct his trial and pass judgment in accordance with what you find his conduct deserves."

"When he arrives from Caesarea! Then you have already deposed him?"

"Not I, sire. Legate Vitellius. His patience was at an end. He removed Pilate from the procuratorship and ordered him to stand trial before the emperor. Doubtless he is now on his way to Rome."

Tiberius paled and then perceptibly his countenance flushed. He opened his mouth as if, Marco thought, to roar his imprecation, but closed it without speaking, swallowed, and wet his lips with his tongue. When he spoke, his voice was icily calm. "By what authority, Marco, did Vitellius take this action?"

"Sire, as legate in Syria he has authority himself over the office of procurator in Judaea and Samaria."

"Of course I know that." His tone was still even, but his eyes were catching fire. He pushed up from his pillows to a sitting position. "But Pontius Pilate was *my* appointment! I personally selected him for that post and sent him and Claudia out there. I had a reason for marrying her off to Pilate and getting her away from Rome. I knew Pilate and Sejanus were conniving to let some of the Jews' taxes stick to their fingers, but it was worth that to have Claudia safely out of Rome."

He looked toward Longinus as he doubled his thin fingers

into a fist with which he pummeled the coverlet. "And by all the thunderbolts of mighty Jove, tribune, she will stay in Palestine as long as I am emperor of Rome!" His eyes flaming now, Tiberius glared at the two men facing him, and then his anger seemed to melt away. When he resumed speaking, his manner was calm and he was smiling amiably. "You no doubt were discussing Pilate's being sent to Rome at your dinner this evening, Prefect Marco. Who enjoyed the good fortune of being your guests, prefect, in addition to Tribune Longinus and my nose-dripping grandnephew?"

"It was only a small dinner, sire, of friends, just a three-couch dinner, principally of those who earlier had gone to Capreae to petition you to release Agrippa, most of them relatives of yours—Antonia——"

"My beloved sister-in-law." He said it sarcastically. "But she did save my life once. She was the one who warned me about Sejanus. But go on, Marco."

"And Junia——"

"Gaius' wife, poor woman."

"My wife, and on the first couch Claudius, with Valeria Messalina——"

"Antonia's fool son—my nephew—and that eye-rolling, hip-swinging little cocotte, hah!" The old man's eyes gleamed. "She'll be the death of the old goat!"

"And Agrippina, sire."

"Gaius' sister. Another of my beloved relatives. And a woman, by the gods, to watch—smart, cool, calculating. Like her mother, whom I banished to Pandateria, after Sejanus informed me that she was plotting to kill me and put her son Nero on the throne. She believed I had her husband poisoned, my own nephew Germanicus, the only decent one, by sweet Ceres, in the whole dynasty of knaves and perfumed, unprincipled women." He sat silent a moment, his eyes narrowed deep in their sockets, his forehead wrinkled in tiny ridges above the brush of his eyebrows.

"Antonia who is Gaius' grandmother, the younger Agrippina's grandmother, addle-pated Claudius' mother, dear friend of Herod Agrippa's mother"—Tiberius seemed to be talking to himself, oblivious of the two men at his bedside—"and Claudia's aunt, by the gods!" He paused again, his forehead still furrowed.

"Agrippina, who is Gaius' sister, Antonia's granddaughter, Herod Agrippa's friend, Claudia's niece. And old bookworm Claudius, who is Antonia's son, Gaius' uncle, Agrippina's uncle, one generation nearer the throne than Gaius, but perhaps not realizing it or caring, Claudia's first cousin. And Claudia"—he looked now toward Marco and Longinus—"without my permission and in spite of my wishes, on her way to Rome!"

Suddenly the old man's eyes flashed and he doubled his fist and shook it in the men's faces. "And you, Longinus, are likewise deep in this conspiracy! That's what it is, by great Jupiter, a conspiracy to get the emperor put away in his tomb and Gaius on the thone in his stead, Herod Agrippa freed, and Claudia returned to Rome and married to you! I see it now! And, Marco, you have been either a party to this conspiracy or too big a fool to realize what was going on!"

"But, sire, you are——"

"Silence! I'll hear no whining denial!" Tiberius screamed at Marco. "And, by all the gods, I'll have another prefect of the Praetorian Guard strangled!" He pointed a skinny forefinger at Longinus. "And Jove hear me, I'll have your head! And, by all the gods, you'll never get Claudia! She'll die on Pandateria like her harlot mother!"

In that instance the chamber door was flung open and Caligula strode in, his face livid, the muscles on the right side of his head jerking and twitching spasmodically.

Tiberius thrust the pointing finger in his grandnephew's direction. "Why could you not wait!" he screamed, his voice high-pitched and cracking. "Now, by the divine Caesar, *you* will never be emperor. I shall change my will to have my grandson Tiberius enthroned instead. I'll see your ugly head roll! I'll watch your blood—no! no! Get back! Guard! Guard!"

"There is no guard out there, sire." Caligula's eyes did not stray from the old man's paling, frightened face as he approached the bed, and his voice was coldly calm despite the tic that continued to cause his head to jerk. "I dismissed them to go to their supper when I first left this chamber, and they will not return for another hour." He walked to the bed and calmly studied the old man, now collapsed deep into the pillows. "Do you understand, your guards are on the other side of the villa, and they can hear nothing being said here. No one is near, only the four of us. But, sire, I have been hearing everything that you have been saying. And not a word of truth have you spoken. No one has been conspiring to dethrone you."

He leaned over the great bed and, extending his arms so that they were hardly more than a foot above Tiberius' face, gingerly flexed the fingers of both hands. "You will never see my head roll from any axman's block and you will never see Prefect Marco strangled"—he squeezed his long fingers together above the frightened, wall-eyed Tiberius—"or Tribune Longinus beheaded." He glared at the prostrate old man. "But I *will* be emperor! And Longinus, if he wants her, will have Claudia, by all the great and little gods!"

Then he dropped his arms to his side and stepped back a pace from the bedside. Turning to Longinus beside him, he lightly caught the tribune's arm. "Come with me, Longinus. After the ride from Baiae we need food, and wine, despite the prefect's excellent dinner. And, Marco"—he glanced past Longinus to look the prefect full in the face and grin sardonically —"when you have finished your audience with the emperor, it is my wish that you leave him with his chamber door closed to insure him undisturbed rest, and come join us."

Caligula with Longinus took two steps toward the door, but paused, and half-turning, faced again the old man, now almost lost from sight in the thick pillows. "Good night, beloved Granduncle," he said, bowing, "and farewell." He lifted high his arm in military salute. "Great Caesar, *farewell!*"

†

ROME

24

Manacled, arms and legs, with a heavy chain and fettered by his wrist to the wrist of his centurion guard by order of Emperor Tiberius, Prince Herod Agrippa arrived in Rome after a grueling journey from Capreae. The centurion took him at once to Castra Praetoria, the great sprawling encampment of the Praetorian Guard beyond the Esquiline and Viminal Hills in the northeastern corner of the city's wall, and lodged him in its prison. Other guards were assigned to relieve the centurion, for Tiberius had commanded that Agrippa be kept under constant scrutiny.

The Herodian prince bore his confinement with resignation and in good spirits. "I appreciate the fact that as a good soldier and a member of Rome's most acclaimed military unit you must obey explicitly the orders of your superiors, especially when that superior is the god Tiberius himself," Agrippa assured the centurion. "I shall cause you no difficulty and no embarrassment because I am a dear friend of Gaius, the heir of Tiberius to the throne, and I am being held prisoner against his wishes and against the wishes of your commander, Prefect Marco. Indeed, centurion, when I am set at liberty, as most certainly I shall be, and my friend Gaius is emperor, if you deal with me fairly and in a kindly manner during this temporary imprisonment, I shall speak to him of you and seek for you his warm favor."

So it was not long until the centurion, because of growing regard for his genial prisoner and out of mounting apprehension of what his own fate might be should a freed Agrippa seek vengeance against him, began to relax his vigilance during these periods he himself was guarding Agrippa. At such times, particularly when the prisoner was having his bath, his guard, though he insisted on keeping Agrippa always in sight, frequently slipped from his own wrist the chain that bound them together.

One day as Agrippa was thus free of his guard and preparing to enter the bathhouse, a freedman employed at his Roman domus came rushing up and spoke in great excitement with Agrippa. The centurion, though he could not hear what was being said, knew by the joyous look on Agrippa's face that the freedman had fetched momentous information, and he urged the Herodian to divulge it. Agrippa seemed reluctant to tell the centurion, but when the officer pressed him, he yielded.

"Tiberius is dead," he announced. "He had a sudden fainting spell as he paused at the villa of Lucullus at Misenum, while journeying to Rome, and quickly expired."

"Tiberius dead!" The centurion showed his amazement. "But was your freedman certain? How did he learn of it?"

"The news was brought by couriers lately arrived from Misenum. Notices are already posted on the boards of *Acta Diurna*, and all Rome is rejoicing that the tyrant has expired."

"And presently, sir, Gaius will be mounting the throne?"

"Yes, centurion. He's likely on his way to Rome now from his villa at Baiae."

"Indeed." The centurion's stern expression relaxed into a beaming smile. "Come with me, excellency. Let us make haste to strike these chains from your wrists and ankles. Then you can enjoy a warm bath. And afterward, excellency, you will accompany me to my house to eat dinner with other friends I shall have in? And may the gods preserve Emperor Gaius."

But a few hours later, to Agrippa's great chagrin and discomfort, both the situation and the centurion's genialty would change completely.

The centurion's dinner had been excellent and the guests convivial; the main dishes had been eaten and the dessert of

sweet pastries and fruits finished. The diners had withdrawn
from the triclinium for a stroll about the peristylium—while
the table was being cleared, the floor swept, and the couch
covers and pillows changed—and had returned for leisurely
social drinking.

Soon the flowing wine had loosened the tongues and lessened the caution of those offering toasts. In toasting Gaius,
some had even spoken with levity of the sudden passing of
Emperor Tiberius. Even the centurion in lifting his goblet to
his honor guest had praised the gods for thus having provided,
for the noble and gracious favorite of the exemplary new emperor, escape from the tyrant who had so shamefully shackled
him.

But hardly had the spirits-emboldened host drained his glass
and called for it to be filled again when the triclinium door
opened and a soldier sent from Castra Praetoria strode up to
the couches.

"Centurion, I have been sent to inform you that, contrary to
reports, the Emperor Tiberius is not dead at Misenum. He had
a fainting spell and appeared for a time to be dead, but he
shortly recovered and is expected soon to arrive here."

"By all the gods!" the centurion exclaimed as he sat up erect
on the couch. "How had you this news, soldier? Can there be
any doubt of its accuracy?"

"It came by Praetorian Guardsmen from the emperor's personal century. It is true. The emperor only had a fainting spell.
He revived quickly and is expected in Rome, perhaps tomorrow
or the day after." The soldier saluted, turned to leave the
chamber.

"Wait!" the centurion commanded. "Did any other accompany you here?"

"One other, centurion. He waits in the atrium."

"Go, fetch him!" He stood up, steadying himself against the
table, and pointed his forefinger almost against the nose of
Prince Agrippa who occupied the seat of honor on the center
couch next to himself. "Do you think you can trick me with

this lie and thereby escape the shackles the emperor ordered for you!"

"But I did not attempt to trick you," Agrippa protested. "I told you at your urging only what my freedman reported and all Rome believed. And until the arrival of this courier you yourself, with all Rome, were rejoicing." His voice was calm, but his brittle laugh had a sinister tone. "When Gaius is emperor, he will be amazed to learn how fast the centurion can change his colors."

"The god Tiberius is still emperor of Rome," the centurion declared, taking his position on the couch again, "and the gods be praised for continuing him in his glorious reign." He heard footsteps at the doorway and, turning, signaled to the two soldiers. "Come, bind this man and return him to the prison. Procure the iron chain with which he was fettered and secure him again, wrists and ankles, and then chain him by a wrist to a guard. When I go on duty in the morning I will take him in charge and arrange for the guard's relief."

In another moment they had bound Agrippa's wrists and started with him toward the door. "Guard him with your lives, men," the centurion warned. "Remember that he is the special prisoner of our beloved emperor, the god Tiberius."

But in less than an hour after he reported for duty the next morning, the centurion was to hear more startling news. Couriers racing northward from Misenum brought official dispatches, signed by Prefect Marco himself and bearing his seal, announcing the death of Tiberius Claudius Nero Caesar, second emperor of Rome.

This time there was no doubt that the emperor was dead. A servant who had entered his bedchamber to bring his breakfast had found Tiberius sunk deep in the soft pillows. One pillow lay across his face. The body was cold and rigid; evidently Tiberius had been dead several hours. His physicians surmised that the aged ruler had suffered another fainting spell and that the heavy pillow dropping over his head had smothered him.

The same couriers brought also letters from Gaius Caesar

Germanicus, one to Governor Piso of Rome and another to the senate, revealing the death of the Emperor and proclaiming himself emperor in succession to his late beloved granduncle Tiberius, whose body he was bringing to Rome for a sumptuous state funeral. Another letter ordered that Prince Herod Agrippa be released from the prison of Castra Praetoria and allowed to live at his private residence, though he would remain officially a prisoner until the arrival in Rome of Emperor Gaius, who would make disposition of the case.

25

On his arrival in Rome from Misenum, Tribune Lucius Cassius Longinus, newly appointed aide to Emperor Gaius Caesar Germanicus, was given the assignment to escort Prince Herod Agrippa from his private residence to the great Imperial Palace on Palatine Hill.

Caligula greeted Agrippa warmly. "I would have sent orders from Misenum for your unconditional release, my dear friend, had not your patroness and my beloved grandmother Antonia insisted that to do so would show disrespect to the late emperor," he revealed. "So I agreed not to free you entirely until we had given the old reprobate a proper funeral." He clapped a heavily ringed hand on Agrippa's shoulder and snickered gleefully. "But now, by all the gods, he is gone and I am the emperor and what I will is law!" He stepped back a step and smiled crookedly upon the solemn face of his Herodian favorite. "And I will that you henceforth reign over the tetrarchy in Palestine heretofore ruled by your kinsman Herod Philip, to which later I propose to add the tetrarchy of Lysanias. Kneel, Agrippa."

As Herod Agrippa dropped to his knees, Caligula signaled to another aide, who brought to him on a silken pillow a jewel-encrusted golden crown. Caligula lifted the crown high and then, lowering it, set it upon Agrippa's head. "Now," he commanded, "arise, King Agrippa!"

Emperor Gaius grinned happily as King Agrippa stood, and the gems in the resplendent crown, glinting and shimmering in the light of the many lamps, were reflected in the younger monarch's excited eyes. "Your dear brother-in-law Antipas in Galilee is a tetrarch, but you, Agrippa, are a king," he said, with a note of sarcasm in his voice, "and may the gods my brothers preserve you to rule with firm hand."

But Caligula had still more rewards for his long-time friend. He lifted a finger to the courtier who had brought the crown, and this man inclined his head in a quick motion understood by a second man standing at the doorway; this aide entered the chamber and walked with brisk steps to the emperor and, bowing low, handed him a long golden chain.

"King Agrippa, as a token requital for the shame and pain endured by you because of the vengeful actions of the late emperor," Caligula declared, "I commanded them at Castra Praetoria to weigh carefully the iron chain with which Tiberius ordered you bound and to have made a golden chain of the exact weight. This golden chain I now present to you." He grinned happily and, leaning forward, placed the resplendent chain about King Agrippa's shoulders.

"In great humility and with warmest appreciation I accept the honors and responsibilities that your majesty has so generously bestowed upon me," Agrippa responded solemnly. "And I promise you, sire, that as the heavy iron chain did bind me physically to my soldier guard, so will this elegant and priceless chain of gold be a symbol of that profound devotion that binds me in great joy to our incomparable emperor, the god Gaius."

But the ceremony of elevating Agrippa to the throne of the Palestinian tetrarchy was hardly comparable to the dramatic performance at the Palace some days later, in which Longinus was ordered by the emperor to be a participant.

Longinus was relaxing in the peristylium of the senator's domus on Viminal Hill when a Praetorian Guardsman, dispatched by Caligula's command, arrived with a summons to come at once to the Imperial Palace. Longinus had been on duty late the evening before and was not expecting to return to his station until after the noon hour.

"Do you know, soldier, why I am being called back to the Palace?" he asked the guardsman.

"I do not, sir," the man responded. "I did hear, though, as I was leaving, that a minor official, from one of the eastern provinces, was being brought to trial before the emperor."

"Did you hear his name spoken? Or the province from which he comes?"

"No sir, I think not. If I did, I can't recall."

Pontius Pilate! Longinus wondered if the prisoner were the procurator of Judaea and Samaria. Would the legate Vitellius have deposed him and sent him to Rome this quickly?

"Did the man's wife accompany him, do you know, soldier?"

"I heard no mention, sir, of the man's wife."

The prisoner was indeed Pilate, as Longinus saw when he entered the great vaulted throne room and took his seat near the rear. Gaius, he saw, had noticed his entrance, but, busy as he was with the trial of a defendant who stood before him white-faced and trembling, he did not stop the case to recognize Longinus.

He could see Pontius Pilate only from the side and rear, but even from this restricted view Longinus was able to observe a considerable physical deterioration in the man. His hair, now but a thin rim circling his head above his ears, was fast graying, and his round and florid face—Longinus saw at a glance as Pilate turned his head in the tribune's direction—had narrowed and paled to a waxen color and the full cheeks had shrunk so that the skin fell down in folds like the wattles of a plucked goose hanging from a hook in the butcher's shop.

Claudia was not sitting with Pilate, nor did Longinus see her in the great chamber. Had she remained at Caesarea? Or had her nephew Caligula spared her the ordeal of being present at the trial?

Soon an attendant came to Longinus and revealed that the emperor wished him to approach the throne.

"I had you brought to the Palace, tribune," Caligula explained as Longinus bowed low to him, "to be a witness in the trial of Pontius Pilate, who with his wife arrived last evening from Puteoli, where the vessel from Caesarea landed them. Pilate is here awaiting my determination of his fate"—he nodded in the deposed procurator's direction—"but Claudia will remain in the adjoining chamber until the beginning of her husband's trial."

In another moment the prisoner was summoned to appear before Caligula. He came forward, fearful, and stood ashen-faced and rigidly at attention. But the youthful emperor, hardly half the prisoner's age, gave him only a cursory glance before he turned to an aide. "Bring in the prisoner's wife," he commanded.

Claudia entered, erect and unruffled, and bowed quickly to her nephew Caligula; evidently they had conversed earlier. She walked calmly to the seat pointed out to her and sat down. She had not seen Longinus, he knew; she glanced about furtively, and when after an instant she spotted him, her haggard face lighted with a relieved smile. Then she settled back in her chair to give her attention to Caligula, who was now glaring at the deposed procurator. Fleetingly Longinus wondered what Claudia's thoughts had been when she first learned that her half sister's wastrel son had become ruler of the Roman empire.

But now Caligula was speaking to the frightened man before him, and Longinus turned to listen. "Pontius Pilate, Legate Vitellius of Syria, who possesses the necessary authority to do so, has removed you from office as procurator of Judaea and Samaria and ordered you to Rome for trial before the emperor. In justification of his action he has dispatched to the emperor a comprehensive indictment"—he clapped his hands together and an aide standing near stepped forward quickly and handed him a large and ornate parchment cylinder. "Pull it out," Caligula commanded, and the aide withdrew the closely rolled papyrus document and placed it in the emperor's extended hand. Caligula began unrolling the cylindrical volume with his right hand as he rolled it up with his left.

Then quickly he rolled it back into a compact cylinder and handed it to the aide holding the cover. "Put it back," he said, and the man did so. Caligula turned again to Pontius Pilate, and a smile, ingratiating and disarming, warmed his cavernous face. "This is long and I have read it thoroughly," he said, his voice pleasant, "and the prisoner was provided a copy, were you not?"

Pilate opened his mouth to speak, but said nothing, and closing it, extended the tip of his tongue and licked his dry lips. Then he nodded. "I was, sire," he finally managed to reply.

"Yes. Then there is no need to take our time to read it again." Caligula leaned forward and his smile was still pleasant and his manner agreeable, relaxed. "Legate Vitellius charges you, Pontius Pilate, not only with misfeasance as procurator but also with malfeasance. He charges that, because of your failure to exercise properly the functions of your office, the rule of Rome in your region of Palestine has fallen into disrepute; that because of your refusal to give consideration to the traditions and customs of the Hebrew peoples, particularly their religious beliefs and practices, indeed in your delight in flouting these customs and in unnecessarily harassing them upon every possible occasion, you have allowed to develop—indeed, have fostered it—a state of revolution in Judaea and Samaria that may not be ended short of actual warfare."

He paused, still smiling as though he were commending the fallen procurator. "The legate carefully documents every charge he makes, Pontius Pilate; he names places and dates, he specifies and particularizes; he gives figures, including money collected by you in taxes as compared with funds placed in the empire's coffers; he reveals corruption in which you and the late Prefect Sejanus were joint participants. And he cites instances of a fault more heinous, to my mind, than embezzling the tax funds, and that was"—he paused and his eyes were beginning to flame now, though his smile was warm and his voice calm—"your cowardice, Pilate. He specifies instances, for example, when you refused to administer justice in the cases of certain prisoners standing before you as you now stand before me. I recall that he mentions the case of a certain Galilean mystic whom you unjustly condemned to the cross, despite even the warning of your wife, in order to please the high priest, so that he in turn would not report to the emperor certain other derelictions"—Caligula paused, for Pilate, his eyes wide and staring, seemed to sway. But the defendant recovered to brace himself and lift sagging shoulders, though he offered no denial or defense.

"But I need not go on," Caligula said. "You have read the legate's charges. I ask you now, Pilate, do you wish to attempt to refute them? Have you anyone who will witness for you? If you have, then let them present themselves before me."

"Thank you, sire." The deposed procurator bowed and, turning, searched the great chamber, empty except for the court attendants and a few idlers. For a moment his roving eyes settled on Longinus, and then they moved past the few other spectators to pause on Claudia, who sat immobile, her face a mask, expressionless. Pilate turned back to Caligula. "Sire, I see no one here whom I may ask to speak for me."

"Then will you speak for yourself?" Caligula's grin was feline, calming, his tone and manner honeyed. He appeared to be inviting the prisoner—with one simple statement of contradiction of the monstrous charges—to clear himself.

"Sire, I have suffered much trouble and pain and failure in my years in the East," he began. "I was at times dishonest in the reporting of taxes collected, though I acted upon the instructions of Prefect Sejanus, and whatever guilt attaches to those defalcations was primarily his." He paused, glanced about the chamber furtively, and then turned to face the still-grinning emperor, his expression deeply pained. "Sire, I tried to serve faithfully my sovereign, the late emperor Tiberius, who sent me out to that forsaken, gods-abandoned, most depraved of Rome's provinces. But from the moment I arrived out there I have been opposed at every turn by the Hebrew peoples, surely, O sire, the most obstinate and cantankerous, the stubbornest, most evil-possessed, intractable subject peoples in all the empire. I sought by temperate rule to govern them, but they fought me and my soldiers thinking that I was afraid of them; I was stern and unrelenting and they screamed that I was a barbarian. They have continued to be ungovernable and despicable, and long have I hoped to see the day come when I would forever be far removed from the borders of their wretched land."

Caligula chuckled and his large narrow head bobbled on the thin stem of his long neck. "By all the gods my brothers, Pilate," he observed, "this day your wish is granted!" He leveled a long forefinger at the prisoner. "You will never return to Caesarea!" His sudden guffaw died away quickly in a low snicker. And then his dark eyes, deepset in their sockets, were sharp and cold and menacing. "That then is your defense, Pontius Pilate? And now you await my judgment?"

Pilate's eyes were on the mosaic of the marble floor. He looked up, his expression fearful. "It was those ungovernable Jews, obstinate, quarrelsome, with their strange, frightful one-god——"

He looked down again, the sentence unfinished.

"Then, hear me, Pilate." The deposed procurator lifted his eyes, as though by force, to look upon the now-frowning emperor. "I find you guilty of the charges brought by the legate Vitellius and I sustain him in deposing you. And I do appoint and constitute as your successor in the post of procurator in Judaea and Samaria, in which Marcellus is now serving temporarily by appointment of Vitellius, my good friend Marullus, master of the horse. So now, Pilate"—he chuckled, as he sat back upon his resplendent throne—"you have your wish long held; you're forever freed of your Hebrew tormentors.

"But, Pilate," he added, as he leaned forward and once more

waggled his finger at the broken former administrator, "before I continue with the pronouncing of judgment upon you, I shall free you likewise from another alliance that perhaps you have been considering burdensome and tormenting; certainly it has been, I take it, to the other party. So be it known"—the pitch of his voice rose and his derisive bright eyes batted faster —"that I do grant to your wife Claudia a bill of divorcement from this moment." He glanced toward one of his aides standing near the throne. "Have the document prepared at once for my signature and seal."

Tribune Longinus was eying Claudia. She sat staring straight ahead as though she had not heard the emperor. Caligula was silent a moment, waiting. Then he leveled his sinister bright eyes again on Pilate's ashen features, and his narrow face twisted in a sardonic grin. "Pontius Pilate, I have adjudged you incompetent to administer the office of procurator and guilty of gross misconduct in embezzling taxes due to have been paid into the empire's treasury. I find you guilty likewise of the wanton and willful sacrifice of the lives of Roman soldiers sent by you unwisely and without sufficient provocation into ill-advised action against your subject peoples, as well as the needless slaughter of Judaeans and Samaritans. And I find you guilty, further, of the most reprehensible crime of which a Roman governor can be guilty, and that is, Pilate, his failure to render impartial judgment, either through fear or in hope of reward, in the case of a prisoner standing trial before him."

Longinus, glancing alternately at Pilate and Claudia, saw that the deposed procurator was desperately fearful. But Claudia, who until a moment ago had been his wife, her expression grim, seemed still hardly conscious of Caligula's verdict or aware of what his words might be portending. Her eyes seemed to be avoiding both Pilate and her nephew the emperor, even oblivious of the drama developing before them. Could Claudia, the sudden strange thought crossed Longinus' mind, be thinking of another day and another trial, a not-so-distant day when the frightened man now awaiting judgment was looking down from his Praetorium bench upon a tall hill-country young man, completely calm, completely without fear?

Suddenly, as the tribune glanced toward the shaken defendant, Pilate raised his hands waist-high and nervously twisted them together. In that instant to Longinus came the vision sharp and clear of a spineless judge attempting before a howling mob to deny responsibility for the impending tortured death of an innocent Galilean teacher and mystic.

But now Caligula arose and advanced a step toward the man on trial. He shot forth his arm and thrust out a long forefinger that darted toward the prisoner's face like a serpent striking. "Pontius Pilate, you have shamed your emperor and brought dishonor upon the empire!" he screamed, and light spittle foamed on his lips sprayed out before him. "You have disgraced our very race of Romans, and you no longer deserve to live! It is my will, therefore, Pontius Pilate, that you be led forth in chains from this chamber by a detachment of Praetorian Guardsmen along Via Ostia two miles beyond Porta Ostiensis, to the execution ground and there be shot with arrows until you are dead!" He stepped back, waved an arm. "Take him away!" He knotted his fists and pressed them against his hollow temples. "I sicken at the sight of him!"

"No! No! No, Gaius! O no, my lord emperor!" Claudia had sprung to her feet and with white arms extended imploringly toward her nephew pleaded for mercy. "I beg of you, spare his life! O sire, show mercy. Reveal the greatness of your heart, O my beloved nephew and my lord the emperor. Demonstrate your divine qualities by sparing his life, I humbly beg of you! O my lord Gaius, I do implore——"

"But it was upon your own testimony, my dear aunt," the emperor, settled again on his throne, interrupted her torrent of pleading, "as well as that of Vitellius and others in whom I place my trust that I have found this man guilty and pronounced upon him a just sentence. Surely, Claudia"—his violent anger appeared quickly to have abated—"you cannot love him longer."

"I have never loved him, O sire." Her tone had calmed, too.

"Nor has he loved me. Our marriage was contrived and forced by the conniving of the late emperor and the late prefect Sejanus. I am happy that it is now dissolved. But nevertheless I beg that you grant him mercy. Spare his life, O beloved Gaius, even though he may not deserve your clemency. Spare his life and the gods your brothers will approve and praise you."

Her numbering him with the gods pleased Caligula noticeably. His eyes warmed, and the corners of his sensual lips lifted in an inane grin. "My dear Claudia, has anyone told you —Tribune Longinus, perhaps"—he turned his head toward Longinus and snickered—"how beautiful you are when you shed that Augustan imperiousness to plead for some wretch's life? At such a moment, my dear aunt, all the gods must be admiring and all the goddesses envying you. So I must yield to your entreaties."

He looked from her to the still-fearful Pilate. "Pontius Pilate, I grant the petition of your former wife Claudia and countermand the sentence of death just pronounced upon you. I now sentence you to perpetual banishment from Rome"—he paused and beckoned an aide to approach him. He whispered for a moment with the officer and then faced the deposed procurator. "On the morrow two maniples of legionaries are departing for Gaul to be stationed in the region of Vienna Allobrogum, and it is my will that as their prisoner you be conducted there to live henceforth to the end of your life—an exile from the Rome whose name in Palestine your behavior there has so befouled. And now, guards, take him away!"

The white-faced prisoner opened his mouth as if he were about to speak, closed it, swallowed, and licked his lips. Then, bowing with a quick resigned nod, but without looking into Caligula's smoldering sinister eyes or glancing in Claudia's direction, he turned, and with a guard on each side grasping his arm, walked grimly and without a word from the great chamber.

Caligula watched them until the door closed behind the three. "He's gone! My late departed granduncle's pet civet is gone!" he sniggered. "And there'll be others, too, by Jupiter my brother!" He slapped the arm rests of the throne-chair with his hands, palms down, and the giggle burst into a guffaw. "Many others, by the gods!"

But quickly he sobered, and lifting an arm with forefinger pointing, first to Claudia and then to Longinus, he called out to them. "You two go also. But not to Gaul. You may go wherever you wish. My aunt is a free woman now, and I grant you leave, tribune, for as long as you wish from your duties with the Praetorian Guard. Go, then. Go, if you like, down to my palace at Baiae. The breezes will be balmy, the food and wine as you wish, the beds soft, and there will be none to disturb your trysting."

He stood up and with hands suddenly outflung indicated a doorway that was across the chamber from the one through which Pilate and his guards had left. "Go now. And when you've made ready for the journey, travel southward to Baiae, dear Claudia and Tribune Longinus, and may the gods and goddesses, my brothers and sisters, and especially Venus, attend you, protect you"—he giggled again—"and instruct you."

†

DAMASCUS

26

Judas the innkeeper dropped the cloth onto the tabletop he had been polishing and squinted with narrowed eyes at the man limping toward him from the gate in the courtyard wall bordering on the Street Called Straight.

He was a short fellow and he walked with a twisted staff, but his bowed legs, showing below the hem of his bedraggled brown robe, were knotted and muscular; his head covering fallen back on his shoulders revealed a rounded, bald dome burnt and blackened to the color of his frayed and broken sandals and rimmed on the sides and at the back by a narrow circlet of unkempt hair that merged into long, unrestrained earlocks and beard.

"He isn't long from the desert," Judas said to himself, as the stranger came through the doorway. "Everything about him speaks of sun and sand." And, the thought came to him, of poverty, and even, perhaps, of flight. He wondered if the fellow had money with which to pay for his lodging, if lodging he was seeking. And he had the strange feeling, too, of having seen the stranger somewhere in an earlier, and for him, a better day.

"You seem to have fetched nothing of value with you," he observed to the man when he was asked for a place to lodge for the night. "Do you have a coin to give me for your bed and fare?"

"I do have," answered the stranger. And, reaching into the fold of the battered robe, he brought forth a leathern pouch and shook it, so that the coins inside clinked together. He loosened the strings and pulled open the pouch, from which he extracted a copper coin that he handed to the innkeeper. "Is this sufficient to procure for me for the night"—he smiled and looked Judas in the eyes—"your upper room?"

"Indeed! Now I know you!" exclaimed the innkeeper. "I remember not your name, but you are the man who was led here, blind from a sunstroke in the desert, and lay sightless three days in my room on the roof. Is it not so?"

"I am the one, Judas. I am called Saul of Tarsus, but I have returned here from long sojourning in the hot lands of Arabia."

"Welcome, Saul, and to your upper chamber." He glanced at the coin in his hand. "This is quite sufficient. Doubtless you have traveled far and would like water for a bath, perhaps, and refreshment?"

"I would," answered Saul. "I would indeed. I am greatly in need of both."

He bathed first and brushed as best he could the sand still clinging to his threadbare garments and with a cloth wiped his tattered sandals. On the morrow he would visit a tailor shop and a sandalmaker's, and with coins earned at his trade of weaving goats' hair into tent cloth he would purchase himself new clothing for the work that he had envisioned during his days in the Arabian desert.

When he had thus improved his feelings and appearance, he came down from his chamber and ate the evening meal of wheaten cakes, cheese, olives, a three-finger cut of roast mutton, with a cup of goat's milk and a few swallows of wine diluted with water. Then he again climbed the outside stairs to his upper chamber and, closing the door and drawing the window shades against the fast-failing, last light of day, he dropped to his knees and lay face down on his couch.

"O great and merciful God of Israel, omnipotent and omniscient, O Jesus my Lord Messiah, Son of the Most High, one with God, Emanation in the flesh of the Divine Spirit, the Almighty and Ineffable, I thank Thee! With all my soul, O God, O Lord Messiah, I praise and thank Thee for Thy Grace and goodness to me, Thy once-enemy, Thy still sinful and unworthy but loving son!" Saul pressed his face into the covering of the couch, and hot tears of gratitude and rejoicing streamed from his still sand-seared eyes and ran down into the coverlet.

"O gracious God, O loving Jesus Lord Messiah, I do thank Thee for the light that came again to my eyes here in this chamber, but I thank Thee more, yea, a thousand times more, for the light of understanding vouchsafed me in my long wandering with the wild tribesmen, in my solitary sojourning in the region of Sinai, where Thou didst deliver to our father Moses the tables of the ancient law. I thank Thee, O Jesus Lord Messiah, for Thy delivering to me, Thy unworthy brother, Thy late enemy, in some small measure of understanding, of the tables of the new interpretation, Thy all-conquering and ennobling law of love. Help me, O Jesus my brother, to bring down, from the towering mount of Thy grace to these others my brothers, *Thy* brothers, O Lord Messiah, a clearer comprehension of this Thy law that makes understandable and effective and renders cleansing and ennobling the journeying day by day along the way laid out and marked and circumscribed by those tables of the olden law brought down from Sinai by our father the great lawgiver!"

Alone in his chamber, Saul lay long prostrate on his face, unmindful of the fading outside of the day's natural light, praying with great earnestness for the breaking upon his heart and his mind in the fullness of understanding of the spiritual light so happily and completely revealed in the living and teaching of the Galilean. "I thank Thee, O glorious Nazarene, for having lifted me out of the pit of so great error and sinning and set me upon the good way. Continue my feet upon it, strengthen my lagging steps, reveal to me the pitfalls at every turning, protect me from the snarling wild beasts of desire that would reach forth with sharp claws to snatch me from the Way and devour me. Lead me, show me, teach me, O Lord Messiah, that I may lead and show and teach Thee and Thy way to these countless lost and wandering ones Thy brothers!"

So thus praying and imploring and pondering and meditat-

ing and thus gaining a measure of communion with his Lord
Messiah, Saul after a long while arose and prepared himself
for the night's rest, much needed from the day's tiresome
journeying.

On the morrow he arose early and greatly refreshed, and
when he had completed the morning's ablutions, he walked
down the stone stairway and went into the tavern for his
frugal breakfast. Then he set forth for the tailor's and the
sandalmaker's.

From their shops the man of Tarsus would go in search of
Ananias, his new and greatly beloved brother in Jesus the Lord
Messiah.

27

On the first Sabbath after Saul's return to Damascus, he went
with Ananias to the synagogue in which, on a day following
his conversion and the restoration of his sight, he had told the
worshipers of his amazing conversion from an enemy bent
upon their destruction to a brother in the Lord Messiah.

On this Sabbath, when the reading of a selection from the
Pentateuch was completed, the chief officer of the congregation, having been told by Ananias of Saul's presence among
them, arose and announced that a rabbi was worshiping with
them who had come from a long sojourn in the region of
Mount Sinai, where with much prayer and meditation he had
been seeking a fuller communion with the God of Israel and
His Lord Messiah.

"Let him arise now and speak to us out of his heart of the
words spoken to him in those far places by the Most High,"

declared the head of the congregation, "for perchance in his solitude and much listening in Sinai he may have received from the God of Israel a message for us the sheep of His pasture."

Saul accepted a prayer shawl from one of the other officers of the congregation, and wrapping it about his burnt frame, he advanced to the front of the synagogue. But before he began to speak to his hearers of his dearest possession, the crucified but living Lord Messiah, he told them again of himself. "I come indeed from the region roundabout the mount of our father Moses, who received upon its summit the tables of the ancient law," he declared. "But when I was last in Damascus, I had come to you from our holy city Jerusalem, having left there with a tablet of authority from the high priest to bind and return to him for trial such of you as are numbered in the fellowship of our Lord Jesus the Messiah of God. But on the desert outside the walls of Damascus, I was intercepted by the Messiah Himself and by Him I was commissioned an apostle to bear to men His brothers the tidings of His redemption and great love."

"Indeed, I remember this one," whispered a tall bearded fellow to his squat, rounded neighbor. "I heard his story, an unlikely one if I am any judge, when he first told it here, and I believe it no more now than I did then."

"It could be true, Abiezer," the second man observed. "I likewise heard his story when he first told it here. He has not changed it in the telling, and it has been a long time."

"Perhaps he has told it so many times that he has come to believe it, or else he is seeking to entrap us so that he can yet bind us and carry us to Jerusalem to suffer the vengeance of old Caiaphas," the tall one persisted.

Ancient Damascus was a cosmopolitan city and the synagogue's worshipers, whom Saul was now addressing, were drawn from various nations, races, and religions. The majority naturally were orthodox Jews, worshipers of the One-God of Israel, Yahweh the Most High. But there was a scattering in the congregation of Greeks and even some Roman matrons, for whom the Roman gods and goddesses had lost their validity and to whom the Hebrews' God and their system of religion had been found satisfying both intellectually and spiritually. So these Roman women, pagans by race and nationality and tradition and upbringing, had converted to the religion of the Hebrews.

Within the congregation, and among those listening avidly to Rabbi Saul from the desert heat and wind-driven sands—he was surely no prepossessing figure physically, but he was quickly commanding in his powers of speech—was still another group, itself composed of diverse elements. These were the brethren of the Way, the fellowship of the crucified carpenter of Nazareth in Galilee, whose followers held with firmness that He was the Messiah of God, the long-promised One sent to deliver His people; these held that, though this Jesus of Nazareth had been crucified in Jerusalem after trial before the cowardly Roman procurator Pontius Pilate and had been entombed three days, He had returned to life, appeared to His apostles, among them Simon of Capernaum, now head of the fellowship, and had then ascended into heaven.

But these worshipers either by birth and long tradition or by conversion, as was the case of the Roman matrons and various others now attached to the synagogue, were all Jews in religion, who were scrupulous in their observance of the multitudinous laws and customs of the Hebrew faith; this was true even of those among the number who counted themselves followers of the crucified Galilean. And they all—orthodox, strict Jews, who gave no credence whatsoever to the strange story of Jesus of Galilee as the Messiah long-awaited, and the members of the fellowship of the Way alike—were zealous in their insistence that there was but one God in all heaven and earth and that He was their Yahweh the Most High.

On this Sabbath these worshipers, this grouping of diverse folk under the rulership of Yahweh now congregated in His house, were following avidly the discourse of Saul of Tarsus as he recalled the startling event that in the twinkling of an eye had changed him from an avowed and violent enemy of the Galilean into a follower, whose recent long sojourn in Arabia with the opportunity it provided for study and meditation and earnest prayer had transformed him into an utterly devoted advocate and worshiper.

"For as in the desert outside your walls of Damascus, the Lord Messiah came to me and changed completely the direction of my life, so in the wilds of Arabia and in the region of Petra and onward to Mount Sinai, He appeared to me likewise, though not in bodily form as He did before Damascus, and taught me of Himself." Saul paused, and his piercing dark eyes for an instant swept over the faces peering intently into his.

"In my much praying and meditating in hours awake and in my dreaming in hours upon my cot, the Lord Messiah came to me and spoke into my heart, words concerning the nature of the Messiah and of the Most High Himself, whom the Lord Jesus while upon earth rightly called His Father, for the Lord Messiah is not only He of whom the ancient prophets wrote who would deliver Israel from her enemies but He is incomprehensibly more. Indeed, our Lord Messiah who recently upon earth was the carpenter of Galilee is and was and everlastingly shall be the very Emanation of the Most High God; He is of God being God's Son, and with God one and the same, who came freely to earth to redeem men and claim them for Himself—"

"One and the same with God!" shouted the tall, bearded Jew near the entrance door. "Then, man of Tarsus, you hold that there are two Gods, Yahweh and the carpenter!"

"Hear, O Israel, the Lord God He is One!" Saul's eyes flamed and he shot forth a fist that shook with the thunder of his pronouncement. "Indeed, my brother, have you seen anywhere, have you heard at any time, of a Jew who declared there were two gods?"

"But did not we hear you this moment declare that the Galilean was one and the same with God? Then God is God and the Galilean is God." The tall fellow was persistent.

"You have said it!" Saul exclaimed. "God is indeed God and

He who was in the flesh a Galilean is God. But not *two* gods. One and the same, today and forever."

"Then, rabbi, how can two be one?" another man spoke up. "I am a follower of the Nazarene, whom I and others of the Way hold to be indeed the Lord Messiah, the One promised of old to redeem us from our sins and free us from the chains of the conqueror. But I do not hold him to be the Yahweh of the Jews and equal with him in power and glory, not *one and the same* with Yahweh the Most High." He shook his head sadly. "What is this mystery you bring us, rabbi?"

"It is indeed a mystery," Saul agreed. "God is truly inscrutable, above all and in all, and the creator and possessor of all, and who are we to know Him, to attain Him, to be in fellowship with Him as children to a father, except through our Lord Messiah who as God came to earth to personify Himself to us His children and His brothers?" Saul shook his head. "I have sought for Him in much praying all the days of my years of understanding; I sought to serve Him in breathing threatenings and slaughter against those of the Way whom I thought to be His enemies; and now in the days and the nights since He appeared to me in the person of our Lord Messiah on the way to Damascus and commissioned me as an apostle of His, though a sinful and undeserving one, I have not ceased to seek Him and to learn His ways. A little I have learned"—he paused and his eyes traveled about the synagogue to look into eyes angry or perplexed or wearied with his much speaking— "but only a speck, my brothers, as a grain of sand upon the seashore of His infinite truth."

"No, Saul of Tarsus, it is not a mystery you bring us!" exclaimed a pompous fat Hebrew on the other side of the congregation from the tall man who had first challenged the rabbi, "it is a blasphemy! You would make of our One-God, the Most High, our Yahweh of Israel, a two-headed god like Janus of the Romans!"

"Yea! Yea!" shouted another. "This man would change for us our Yahweh! He would give us two gods, and one of them a crucified, hanged Galilean carpenter, for our great and Most

High God Yahweh of Israel! Out with him! Thrust him forth
from the congregation of Israel! He is none of us!"

But there were a few here and there among the now
aroused worshipers who would have spoken a word for Saul,
saying that the congregation had misinterpreted his words in
believing him to have turned away from the true worship of
Yahweh, had they been able to make themselves heard above
the shouted accusations and invectives hurled at the Tarsian.
But there was now nothing to be gained from their interjecting
themselves into the tumult, and these persons, though they
were of the fellowship of the Way or leaned toward it, kept
their peace.

Soon the head of the congregation, seeing that the service of
worship had degenerated into a hubbub and confusion of
shoutings and recriminations, signaled to Saul to end his discourse, and when after a time he was able to quiet them
enough for himself to be heard, he dismissed them with the injunction to seek Yahweh's forgiveness for having so profaned
His holy temple.

Nor did Saul, once on the outside, dally in the precincts of
the synagogue. In the company of his beloved brother in the
Way of Jesus of Nazareth, Ananias of Damascus, Rabbi Saul
strode quickly away.

28

In Damascus, despite his experience in the synagogue on the
first Sabbath following his return from his sojourn in Arabia,
Saul continued to expound to any who would listen his beliefs concerning the nature of Yahweh the Most High and His
Lord Messiah. The rabbi from Tarsus was aflame for his Lord

who in His earthly sojourn had been Jesus the carpenter of Nazareth.

He went again and again to the synagogue. Sometimes he was able to speak at some length before his discourse was broken up in the confusion and fiery challenges of certain ones who held strictly to the teachings of orthodox Jewry. Sometimes he was even challenged by others who were of the Way but who did not hold the convictions concerning Jesus that Saul so vehemently expounded. But his advocacy of the cause and person of the Lord Messiah did not cease when he strode forth from the synagogue, often as the cries and indictments and snarlings of the unconvinced were being hurled at his departing back. He went into the marketplaces and talked to small groups and sometimes even to a seller of fish here and a mender of harness there; he revisited the tailor shop where he had purchased a robe to replace the tattered robe that had enfolded his sun-scalded frame on his return from deep in Arabia; he went again to the maker of sandals from whom he had bought new footwear and left behind the broken and worn-through sandals in which he had trudged many a hot and weary day's journeying.

With all these and with scores of others—Greeks; Roman soldiers, with whom he professed fellowship because of his Roman citizenship and his Roman name; Egyptians, dark and bronzed like himself from long encounter with the hot climates to the south; Antiochenes from the great wicked city on the Orontes; Jews, strict in their observance of the laws and customs of the sons of Abraham; Jews holding membership in the new Way but having little understanding of the nature of the Lord Messiah; and pagans professing but having little allegiance to many gods, some blatantly boastful, some gently benign, some base, licentious, and horribly evil—with these many persons Saul pleaded and argued the cause of his Lord Messiah.

Soon his name began to be known about the ancient city, for wherever he went to testify to the new understanding he had been vouchsafed of the risen Messiah, who on earth was the simple and unpretending noble youth of Nazareth, commotions and confusion and bickerings arose so that often the authorities of the city were forced to intervene to bring order again. Ananias and others of the fellowship of the Way begged Saul to be less impassioned, less arbitrary, more gently reasoning. There were among these brothers a few who had heard the Galilean along the shores of the little sea expounding his wondrous message, and his teaching had gained immensely in power and effectiveness, they explained to Saul, because of the gentle though authoritative manner of the teacher in his presentation of it.

Saul sought to amend his manner of discourse in accordance with the counseling of his Damascene brothers, and sometimes for a few minutes at the beginning of his discourse he would speak with moderation and calmness. But always the flame that burned deep within him threatened to burst through his surface composure; and often, upon the voicing of a challenging remark by one of his hearers, the fire would flare hot and he would begin again to press upon them with impassioned oratory his own views concerning the nature of the Lord Messiah and the Most High God His Father. And in the ensuing disputation and stir, tempers flared and other reports went forth to be scattered throughout Damascus that one Saul, a rabbi late of Tarsus, was a troublemaker and provoker of mischief. When the news reached the ears of the ethnarch of the city, who ruled Damascus under King Aretus of Syria, he gave orders for the arrest of the Jewish agitator and potential insurrectionist. Immediately the ethnarch's guards started an intensive search for the fiery rabbi. They posted themselves before the doors of the synagogue, they searched on more than one occasion the house of Ananias and the inn of Judas on the Street Called Straight, they prowled the shop districts and the places where foods ritually pure for Jewish consumption were sold. But the controversial rabbi had disappeared; nowhere could they discover him or a clue that might enable them to locate his hiding place.

Fortunately for Saul, a brother of the Way in Damascus who earned his living working at one of the fish stalls early visited by the ethnarch's men had learned that the authorities were seeking the rabbi and had himself been able to warn him. This man lived in a hovel built against the city wall, with an upper chamber upon the wall whose single window on that side overlooked a rude acreage covered over with brambles and lush weeds and wild plum trees thickly matted.

The brother had discovered Saul as he had quitted the stall when his day's work was finished; immediately he had taken the rabbi home with him and they had entered the house after darkness had fallen, so that none of the neighbors had known of the presence in the house of a strange man. And there Saul had remained for several days in the upper chamber on the wall's topmost bricks, hardly venturing to go near the window for fear that someone outside the wall might see and recognize him and report him to the ethnarch's men.

Meanwhile, though some thought that Saul must already have escaped the city, guards were placed at the gates and all persons leaving Damascus were carefully scrutinized; it was feared that the Jewish troublemaker, about whom exaggerated accounts that described him as a menace to the city's peace were now circulating, might by cleverly disguising himself be able to slip through a gate and escape into the desert.

Now with the gates thus guarded the search for Saul was intensified; if he remained in the city, he would surely be found, the ethnarch was assured; they would enter and carefully search every house, examine every possible hiding place.

When Saul's friend told him that the authorities were determined to discover his hiding place should he still be in Damascus and that it would be only a question of days and even perhaps of hours before the guards would be invading the room atop the wall, Saul was not frightened. "When I was struck down on the road to Damascus and saw the Messiah standing before me and besought of Him what I should do, He told me to arise and go into Damascus, that it should be told me what I should do. And when Ananias in the Messiah's name restored my sight, he told me that the Lord Messiah had assured him that I would be a chosen instrument in His hands to carry His name before Gentiles and kings. This He will preserve me to do, for not yet have I done it. So I fear no man, for who can stand against the word of the Lord Messiah?"

Yet Saul knew that in these present days he could accomplish nothing for the Lord Messiah, for with his first public appearance he would be arrested and imprisoned. It was, therefore, he reasoned, not the Messiah's will that he should remain longer in Damascus. So he would quit the ancient city and go to Jerusalem. There were persons in Jerusalem whom he was intent upon seeing, people who would talk of their experiences with Jesus the carpenter and teacher in the villages and upon the storm-whipped sea in Galilee and about the Temple in Jerusalem and in Mary's upper room on Zion Hill. He would learn more of the earthly ministry of the Nazarene, of what He did, what He said, how He lived day by day with His apostles. And foremost among the ones he would seek out when once he arrived in the capital of Israel was the rugged fisherman, the first of the fellowship, Simon of Capernaum. Likely he would come upon Simon at the evening meal in Mary's courtyard.

In Jerusalem, too, he would be likely to have a joyous reunion with that friend of his youth and once fellow pupil at the feet of Rabban Gamaliel, then reluctantly for a time his enemy, and now happily his well-loved brother in the Lord Messiah, Joseph bar Nabas. Joseph likewise should be able to recall for him many things concerning Jesus.

But how could he escape from Damascus?

Saul dared not attempt to leave the city through any of the several gates in the wall, for even in disguise, he feared, his short bowed legs would betray his identity. And of a certainty he would be killed or frightfully maimed if he jumped from the window of the upper chamber. The wall at that point was perhaps the height of five tall men and directly beneath the window—he had been able to ascertain this when at dusk he risked peering from it—a rough abutment of irregular large stones extended outward two or three paces, so that a man dropping from the window would hurtle down upon this foundation ledge.

Saul's brother in the Way, however, solved the dilemma. When he returned to his poor abode from his work at the fish market he brought, along with a large wicker basket of fishes he was to clean and prepare for the morrow's selling, several sections of rope of varying lengths that ostensibly he planned to weave into one long piece as a towline for a fishermen's net. These pieces he quickly tied together, however, and after emptying the basket, he fastened one end of the long rope to the short rope he had attached to the basket's handles.

Then when night had fallen and the city's wall on that side was lost in heavy shadow, Saul's host and brother in the Lord Messiah pushed the basket through the upper chamber's window and helped the rabbi lower himself into it. Carefully the man lowered the basket's burden to the protruding ledge of the foundation, and from there Saul stepped to the ground. While his friend pulled the basket up to the window and through it, he crouched silent and still in the obscuring shrubbery.

When he was convinced that no hostile eyes had been watching or ears hearing, Saul arose and stealthily made his way through the weeds and brambles and wild plums southward from the city's wall until he was past the oasis on which Damascus sat, and then he turned and trudged westward.

Soon his sandals were slipping and swishing through shifting deep sand, and he knew by his walking and by the little light of the stars and a sliver of moon that he was retracing the route by which three years before he had crossed eastward from below Mount Hermon toward the walls of Damascus. And when he came to a place in the desert from which, in turning to gaze eastward behind him, the walls of Damascus, faintly discernible in the dim light, appeared to be as far away as they had seemed that day when a fearsome flash and a vision and a voice had transformed him forever, Saul fell upon his face.

"O gracious Lord Messiah, I thank Thee. I thank Thee for Thy transforming love, for the love that redeems and enlivens and strengthens Thy brothers. Show me, O Most High God and Jesus Thy Son our Lord Messiah, the way I must go, I pray Thee. Show me Thy way for me!" He lay upon the cold sands and pleaded to be shown and to be led. "O beloved Brother, O redeeming Son of the Most High, I know so little of Thee; I have done so little for Thee. Show me and strengthen me, lead me and drive me. Encourage me and command me, O blessed Jesus my brother and my Lord!"

He stood up and looked about him in the thin light from the mounting moon's narrow crescent. "I thank Thee, O God and O my Lord Messiah, for that day and this place."

Saul started again westward in the direction of Mount Hermon, whose snow-capped crest he would have been able to see clearly had there been more light. But he knew nevertheless that the great mountain still towered above the desert and looked westward to the Great Sea. He knew too that God the Most High and His Lord Messiah His emanation and Himself personified still towered in infinite omnipotence and majesty above all the universe, even though men His children, created—sang the Psalmist—a little lower than Himself, in their darkness of sin and ignorance and indifference, could never see Him and few even could discern the nature of the Most High by knowing in faith and great love Himself become man, Jesus the Lord Messiah.

"Grant me to know and possess Thee, O God Most High, through knowing and possessing Thee, O Lord Messiah. And do Thou possess and lead and command me utterly!"

Saul lifted his robe high and trudged westward; if he walked steadily through the cool of the night until the sun should be high overhead, on the morrow he could attain the shade and rest of the great boulders ringed about the declivity in which he had seen a jagged white quartz stone and envisioned a broken Stephen on his knees in the stoning pit out from Jerusalem's wall. There he could pause to refresh himself and rest from the noonday heat and think again upon Stephen the goldsmith and their brother the Lord Messiah, and there he might be vouchsafed a new vision and a sustaining strength to travel the way of the Messiah unfaltering and unafraid.

†

JERUSALEM

29

As Rabbi Saul came over the crest of the Mount of Olives and started down the slope along Bethany road toward Brook Kidron at the bottom of the declivity, he paused suddenly to gaze in awe and with a swift surging of pride upon the ancient capital of his fathers.

Jerusalem the golden! Crowding the summits of her several hills and dropping in massed formations down the slopes, her mansions and her miserable hovels awaited in varying degrees of confidence and hauteur the coming of the day when the Messiah would arrive upon clouds of glory and utterly destroy the invader. Dominating the northeastern sector and high above the gorge of the Kidron, its white marble walls and golden plates gleaming in the sunlight, its expansive colonnaded porticoes enclosing the towering magnificent Holy of Holies, the very pulse and heartbeat of Israel, the Temple beckoned imperiously to the Chosen to gather in its courts to worship the One-God, Yahweh the Most High.

For some within Jerusalem's walls, the Messiah had come, and had been rejected and slain and had returned to His Father; the greater number by far were still awaiting his coming. Saul stood silently and looked down upon the houses thick-sown within the ancient great walls.

I thank Thee, O God of Israel, for permitting me once again to behold Thy Temple, Thy abiding place, O Most High, the pulsing heart of Thy Chosen People. I thank Thee that though upon my last beholding of Thy Temple I was departing from Jerusalem breathing threatenings and slaughter

against my then enemies of the Lord Messiah, I now return, O
Most High God, bearing the sorrow of my great guilt and only
great love for my Lord Messiah and His brothers my brothers.

Saul resumed his journeying down the slope toward Brook
Kidron, but when he was still some two hundred paces from
the little stream he turned aside and crossed a stubble field
strewn with stones to a rounded depression rimmed about with
rocks collected in piles.

Saul stood at the edge of the pit and looked down upon
cruel, sharp stones heaped on the bottom. On several he saw
splotches of rust and bending down to look with eyes that
saw into years passed by, he envisioned a naked, bleeding,
broken white body and with ears that heard sounds long gone
upon the winds he heard a prayer lifting. . . .

O Stephen, forgive! Forgive me, my brother! Forgive me, O
Lord Messiah, his brother, my brother. I thank thee, O gold-
smith, that thou didst pursue me across the sands, that thou
didst harass me and permit me no peace. I thank Thee, O
blessed carpenter, that Thou didst not abandon me to my hei-
nous sinning, that Thou didst trouble me sorely, that in the
heat and the blinding flash Thou didst come to me, Thy un-
worthy but now greatly loving slave and brother.

On the rim of the pit he stood a moment, and then he
turned and quickly retraced his steps out to the dust-thick
Bethany road. He trudged down the slope to cross Brook
Kidron and pass through Dung Gate; he continued along the
narrow, noisome cobbled ways of squalid Ophel through the
flattened lower end of the Valley of the Tyropoeon and began
to ascend the steep rise of Zion Hill.

The sun by now was reaching for the western wall of Jerusalem and the sprawling Palace of the Herods near Joppa Gate;
the shadows of the houses above were already engulfing those
on the slope below. The faithful of the Way in the holy city of
the Hebrews would have gathered at the home of Mary of
Cyprus for the common evening meal and service of worship
by the time he reached it, Saul reasoned, and afterward for a
while he might have an opportunity to speak with Simon of

Capernaum and even those cousins of the Messiah, the irre-
pressible Zebedee brothers, John and James, who like Simon,
earned their living as fishermen in Galilee's little sea.

Saul looked forward with eagerness to meeting Simon and
the Zebedees and perhaps others of the Messiah's apostles who
had enjoyed the privilege of His companionship and His
teaching. He would regale himself in their stories of the Jesus
of Galilee whom they had known well in His earthly flesh; Saul
himself had never seen Him except the one time on the desert outside Damascus when for a brief moment the rabbi had
seen and heard Him in his spiritual embodiment.

But Saul hoped greatly to converse with Simon and any of
the others who might have come to Jerusalem in order to learn
their views of the nature of the Messiah and compare theirs
with his own, evolved after much praying and deep study
during his sojourn in the desert of Arabia. Perhaps, too, in
these conversations the will of the Lord Messiah for the course
of his life might be made known to him, Saul reflected.

Even more than he wished to visit with the fisherman,
though, Saul wished to come upon once more his beloved
friend and now brother in the Lord Messiah Joseph bar Nabas.
Joseph, too, had known Jesus and doubtless had often heard
him teaching in the courts of the Temple. And to Joseph, Saul
would be able to reveal in utter frankness his beliefs concerning the Galilean. Joseph would understand and appreciate
Saul's views even though he might not entirely agree with
them. And it might be—Saul hardly dared to hope—that the
Lord Messiah had willed that Saul and Bar Nabas henceforth should work together toward the establishment upon
earth of the Messiah's spiritual kingdom. For already the idea
was shaping and becoming firm in Saul's mind that the kingdom of Jesus the Christ was not of this world, though many
looked with longing for his imminent return to overthrow the
Roman conqueror and set up his own temporal reign.

Saul hurried up the slope as fast as his tired legs could carry
him. Soon, he conjectured, the folk of the brotherhood would
be sitting down to eat, if they had not already begun the meal,

and he was wearied and in great need of refreshment. A good meal, a short discourse with Simon, and then his bed—dared he hope that Mary might permit him a blanket spread on the floor in the upper chamber?—and he would be fresh again from the long journey southward from Damascus. Then he could begin in earnest his further seeking to learn of Jesus the carpenter, Jesus the teacher, Jesus the man in flesh and bone and sinews of earth, Jesus born of Mary, the sweet and gentle Galilean girl. Then he could continue in earnestness and deep concentration in the fellowship of his brothers also to search out the other Jesus, the only Jesus he himself had ever known, the Jesus of the spirit, born of God, son of God, One with God, equal in power and majesty, Jesus God.

But as he neared the crest of Zion Hill and the house of Mary of Cyprus, Saul suddenly envisioned a disquieting possibility. Would the brothers and sisters of the Way receive him as a brother, accept his affirmation that the Lord Messiah, in an amazing cataclysm in the desert, had appeared to him bodily and called him to apostleship, and give ear to his revelation of *his* views concerning the nature of the Lord Messiah and His plans for the participation of men His brothers in His Kingdom? Could they believe his story? Would they believe it?

Indeed, Saul told himself, it was a preposterous tale. The last time he had gone through the gate in the wall he was now drawing near, he had gone forth from Mary's house an enemy of the Lord Messiah, an enemy of these His brothers, an enemy bent upon evil against Him and them. The last time he had gone through Dung Gate, before his entering the city moments ago, he had gone through it on his way to Damascus to bring Ananias and those others, his now beloved brothers in the Lord Messiah, to Jerusalem for punishment and perhaps for death.

Would these, his new brothers, some of whom he may have whipped until the blood poured from their backs, these brothers awaiting him at the tables in Mary's courtyard—could they be expected to accept him without reservation? Could even those apostles who had lived daily in the contagion of

Jesus' great love, could even they forgive freely and accept him as one among them?

Thou hast forgiven, Thou hast received me to be Thine apostle, O Lord Messiah. Put it into the hearts of these my brothers, Thy brothers, O Lord Jesus, to forgive and to accept me, once their enemy and Thy enemy but now Thy brother and craving to be accepted as their brother. Warm their hearts to forgive and to receive.

Now Saul stood before the gate in the wall. He raised his staff and rapped resoundingly upon the gatepost.

30

Once again Saul of Tarsus, prayer shawl draped about his wind-whipped, sun-baked frame, upon invitation of the head of the congregation, was discoursing in the Synagogue of the Asians and the Cilicians.

Since early youth it had been Saul's inviolable rule, in whatever city the arrival of the Sabbath might find him, to worship in that city's synagogue, if there were within its borders enough of the Chosen to afford a house of worship, and few and small had been those communities having none. But on this Sabbath several reasons had impelled Saul, returned after having been away from the ancient capital for more than three years, to seek out this particular house of Hebrew worship.

In the first place, it had been his customary place of worship in the company of Joseph bar Nabas, when as youths in Jerusalem they had been pupils of the greatly renowned and beloved Rabban Gamaliel, and in returning to it Saul believed he might discover himself reunited with a number of his friends of those days. Too, at this synagogue he might come upon acquaintances, recently arrived at Jerusalem from Cilicia and roundabout Tarsus, who could give him information concerning happenings in that area, even of the health of his father, if indeed his father was still living.

But the principal reason that had drawn Saul on this Sabbath, the first since his return from the long stay at Damascus and in the vast hot regions of Arabia, to the Synagogue of the Asians and the Cilicians—the reason of a truth that had brought him again to Jerusalem—was that in this place he might humbly confess his dreadful sinning against the Most High and His Messiah and boldly and happily proclaim that where once he was the ravening enemy of the crucified carpenter of Galilee he was now the devoted slave, the adoring friend, and the worshiping, loving brother of the Lord Messiah, the Son of God, the Emanation of the Most High, who on earth as the personification of God His Father was the noble youth of Nazareth done to a cruel death by the Roman procurator at the behest of the wickedly conniving high priest of Israel and his evil agents.

"And foremost in the leadership of those who were consenting to His death and to the destruction of the fellowship of those His followers," Saul was now telling the congregants, "was I, Saul of Tarsus, the blackest of the transgressors against Him the Holy One, the Son of the Most High God, though I labored in the grievously erroneous belief that I was defending our God of Israel against the traducers of His Holy Name. Now hear me, children of the Chosen and you others who with us bow down to the God of Israel, Yahweh Most High"—Saul lifted high his arm with clenched fist to give emphasis to his words—"I, Saul of Tarsus, likewise am he who hounded to his death, the frightful death of the stoning pit, the good man Stephen the goldsmith, who in this house raised to God the Most High sought to lead us into the saving knowledge of Jesus the Messiah! Though I hurled no stone upon him, men of Israel and you others, Hellenists and men of Cilicia and Cyrene and from wherever else you may come, I incited them his murderers to kill him. I, O hear me, brothers in the ancient faith and brothers in the faith of the Lord Messiah, I am his murderer!"

Saul lowered his arm and looked calmly into the intent, startled faces of his hearers. Then he closed his eyes and turned his face heavenward. "I thank Thee, O God in Israel, I thank Thee, O Lord Messiah, Son of God, One with God, that from the just deserts of the murderer, Thou in Thy infinite mercy hast saved me; I thank Thee that in the heat of the desert and the blinding bolt of the lightning, Thou didst come to me and turn me about and set my feet upon Thy way; I thank Thee, O Lord Messiah, that Thou didst so graciously appoint me, so great a sinner, to apostleship in Thy Name."

When he had finished his prayer, Saul addressed the worshipers again. "The mercy of God is infinite, without limit; the love of God, as exemplified in His coming to walk the earth in the body of His Son, is as immeasurable as the grains of sand upon the shores of all the seas," said he, his dark eyes flashing conviction. "And where is there a more perfect proof of His mercy and His love than that He should in the twinkling of one of His myriad stars transform murderous, blasphemous Saul of Tarsus into Saul an apostle, to bear to men everywhere His name and the report of His abounding love?"

He went on to tell anew the story of his conversion, heard for the first time from his lips in the Synagogue of the Asians and the Cilicians, though reports of it had been brought back from Damascus by the guards Achbor and Hamor, who had accompanied him on his mission against the fellowship of the Way in that ancient city. To that recital he added an account of his long sojourn into the Arabian lands and his communing there with the Lord Messiah whose cause he had embraced.

"In long trekkings across the desert sands in the caravans of the traders, in respites from journeyings while pausing for a time in the tented villages of the nomads, in the carved-out houses of the cliff dwellers at Petra, in the lonely desolation of Mount Seir and Mount Sinai, He revealed Himself to me, not in the ethereal body in which He appeared and spoke to me before the walls of Damascus but nevertheless in a felt and sure and understood communing. And He taught me of the nature of Himself and of the nature of Yahweh Most High, for He and His Father are One and the Same."

"How can this be?" whispered a corpulent Jew near the entrance door to his waspish, thin-bearded neighbor. "Would this rabbi have us worship two gods? I am of the fellowship of Jesus the Messiah, Bildad, and so are you, but I surely do not hold that the Messiah of Israel *is* God or the same with God. Do you so hold?"

"Indeed, no!" answered the other man. "This fellow is addled from too much sun. Or else"—a deep frown furrowed his forehead—"he is still intent upon deceiving us of the fellowship into making a rash observation such as his and then haling us before the high priest."

"I think it is the sun rather than trickery," the first one observed. "It appears that the high priest is no longer inclined to persecute us of the fellowship so long as we remain faithful in our observance of the law and the commandments, is it not so, Bildad?"

"But expression of such a view as this one has just expressed constitutes an offense against the Most High, does it not, and thus is a violation of our ancient law, do you not so hold? Indeed, is it not blasphemy, this making the Messiah equal with God?"

"Then would not this rabbi from Tarsus be himself subject to the high priest's wrath and punishment?"

The questioned one smiled cynically. "Perhaps the worthy high priest will have no ears for this one's blaspheming if by it he can ferret out and punish certain of us of the fellowship. Is it not possible?"

"I'd hesitate so to believe of the high priest, though"—he suddenly ceased speaking. "What is he saying now?" He cupped a palm to his ear, twisted his neck to hear Saul.

"——the nature likewise of Yahweh Himself, whom we of the Chosen in our pride and arrogance and ignorance have sought to shrink and diminish and shrivel into a small god of a small, even though Chosen, nation, whom we have set limits upon and hedged about, and———"

"Our Most High is no small God! Rabbi from Tarsus, you traduce us! You vilify your people!" a man near the speaker interrupted him, his countenance blazing with wrath. "Our God of Israel is great, supreme, alone! He is no small God, nor would we make Him small! Hear ye, O Israel, our God He is One!"

"You are right, my brother!" Saul agreed. "Our God, He is One, and the only One. He is in no way diminished, made small. It is only we who see Him so, only we who in our pride and ignorance make Him small, limit His power and His sovereignty and His love, who make of Him a small tribal god, who in reality is creator and ruler and Father and in our Lord Messiah brother of every man who dwells upon the earth, creator and governor and sovereign supreme of all the earth, the sun, moon, and stars!"

"Then, say you, rabbi, that our Yahweh the Most High is the God of the Gentiles, the pagan Romans, the Greeks, the Egyptians, the child-sacrificing Assyrians?" From his place against the synagogue wall another challenger shouted his defiant question. "Do not the Gentiles have their own gods, O rabbi?"

"There is no God but Yahweh," answered Saul, his tone calm. "The gods the Gentiles proclaim as their gods are nothings. Their God, though they know Him not, is Yahweh, the God of all the earth, seas, and stars. And our Lord Messiah, likewise, is the Messiah, the Saviour of all men who dwell upon the earth who through Him will seek salvation. No more can we limit Him, the One with God, to Israel than we can limit Yahweh Himself to the Chosen."

All about the sanctuary now, heads were bobbing and arms and hands gesticulating wildly and tongues protesting, and when he saw that decorum could not be restored so long as the rabbi from Tarsus kept the speaker's place, the head of the congregation motioned to Saul to hold his peace. Before the commotion had ceased completely, Saul had slipped away from the synagogue and joined Joseph bar Nabas on the outside to return with him to the house of Mary of Cyprus on Zion Hill. From the common meal and worship service of the fellowship in Mary's courtyard Saul would return with Simon to the fisherman's abode in Jerusalem, where on Simon's invitation he was lodging during his short sojourn in Israel's holy city.

31

The first of the Galilean's apostles had received Saul joyfully when Joseph bar Nabas had led him to the fisherman. Three years before Simon had heard the report of returning Achbor and Hamor concerning Saul's amazing conversion and had looked forward hopefully to the day when he might embrace the new brother and welcome him into the fellowship of the crucified and risen Jesus of Nazareth. And when the common meal and the service of worship were ended, Simon had taken Saul to his modest lodging so that they might have many hours together in which to talk of their Lord Messiah.

They had conversed at great length. Saul had questioned the fisherman of Capernaum in considerable detail concerning the physical appearance of Jesus, how He looked and talked and laughed and sang, what foods He enjoyed most and if He ate heartily or sparingly, if in His tramping the hills and lowlands, the mountains and the shores of the little sea with His disciples, He tired quickly or outlasted his companions, if in His encountering evil and injustice and inhumanity of one man to another His anger flamed, if in His dealing with the sick

and the sinful, the weak and the dispossessed, His eyes and
His voice warmed with a heavenly tenderness.

And when Simon described the Master, how He was a man
of strong body beautifully proportioned and perfectly controlled, how He manifested great joy in the companionship of
men and women and particularly of children, how His dark
eyes and His pleasingly modulated voice one moment could be
sternly reproving and the next warmly forgiving, Saul's eyes
were bright and his voice triumphant.

"It was He who came to me in the desert before the gates of
Damascus. It was indeed Jesus who in His great mercy came
to me, O Simon my brother!"

Simon likewise questioned Saul concerning the circumstances of the Messiah's appearance to him in the flash of the
lightning on the desert before Damascus. He inquired about
the tone of voice, the height and apparent weight, the color of
hair and the trim of the beard, and when Saul answered, the
fisherman asked another: "And you never saw the Master at
any time before He was crucified?"

"Never."

"When you were His enemy and raging against us His
followers did you inquire of anyone how He looked, how tall
He was, how He spoke, how commanding of tone and yet
gentle?"

"I never once inquired, Simon, and never once was He described to me."

Simon shook his head slowly, and when he spoke his voice
was calm, but his eyes beneath tangled, thick eyebrows were
bright and exultant. "It was the Master indeed, Saul, even to
the twin spikes of His beard, even to the manner of His speaking. It was thus He appeared to us in Mary's upper room after
his resurrection. You saw Him as we saw Him." Simon was
silent a moment, reflective. "He came to you as He came to us,"
he said, his voice lower, "as He appeared to us in the upper
room and at another time to the Zebedees and me when we had
climbed with Him high up the slope of Mount Hermon."
Now his eyes flamed again and he clapped his big roughened

hand in a gesture of affection upon the knotted, burnt knee of the Tarsian sitting beside him. "It was indeed the Master who came to you in the desert, O Saul. Now truly you are one of us."

But though Simon welcomed the rabbi from Tarsus into the fellowship of the Lord Messiah joyously and without reservation, the fisherman could not understand the interpretation that Saul offered to him of the nature of the Lord Messiah as it had come to him in his long prayers and meditations during his season in the wastelands and strange cities of Arabia. Nor could Simon understand in completeness Saul's interpretation of the nature of the Most High; he found it hard to accept Saul's understanding of the nature of the God of Israel Himself as the creator and sovereign ruler and loving father of all creation, even of the arrogant conqueror and all the other pagan peoples of the earth.

"But is He not peculiarly the God of the Chosen, of *His* Chosen People?" Simon asked.

"He is not peculiarly ours, though we are peculiarly His," answered Saul. "We have but one God, for He is One, but He has other children, for every creature of earth is His and every man, of whatever race, nation, color, or belief, is His child, and"—Saul's dark eyes brightened and he looked deep into the eyes of his brother of Capernaum—"I believe, Simon, equally loved by Him and of equal concern to Him, and to our Lord Messiah, who is one and the same with Him."

The fisherman solemnly shook his head. "Saul, I cannot understand these words."

"But did you not say, O Simon, that Jesus told you His apostles that 'I and my Father are One'? Were not those His words?"

"Yes, but I did not understand that the Master meant that He and the Most High were the same. I thought that He meant that His teaching, and His living, His whole being, all His thoughts and actions were in harmony with those of the Most High. Nor can I understand your saying, Saul, that our God of Israel is equally concerned with all men everywhere. Do you believe that He loves you no more than He loves a pagan idolater? Do you hold that He loves me, the companion throughout His ministry of His Lord Messiah and the greatly loving though unworthy upholder of His laws, no more than He loves a child-sacrificing pagan worshiper of Moloch?"

"The Most High is utter truth, utter perfection, utter love, O Simon my brother, and He loves utterly all His creatures, all men everywhere. His servants, those who love Him, His children who obey and honor and love Him give Him great pleasure; His children who know Him not, who love Him not, who bow not the knee to Him, these children cause Him great pain. But He loves them all and each to the uttermost. All are His children, all to Him are of infinite concern."

Saul's flashing sharp eyes had warmed to tenderness and his voice bespoke a growing humility. "I have not long known our beloved Lord Messiah, Simon, and only after much meditating and continued supplication for understanding have I begun to learn but a little of Him. But since that day on the desert when He came to me and commissioned me to an apostleship He has been revealing Himself to me and teaching me likewise the nature of the Most High, Yahweh of Israel, and all the earth, the sun, moon, and stars."

Simon's broad, browned forehead, tanned by the wind and sun during many a fishing season's hard labors on the waters and shores of the little sea, furrowed in tiny ridges, and he shook his grizzled head in perplexity. "I am a simple man, Saul, a man of the earth and the sea and unlearned in the law and the lore of books, a man of boats and nets and fishes. Whereas, you, Saul, my brother, you are a rabbi of the great city of Tarsus and learned in the law and the prophets, a man of quick mind and ready tongue and swift perception. I lived with the Master in close fellowship day upon day; I walked the roads and climbed and descended the mountain slopes and crossed with Him dry wadies and raging swollen streams; I sailed in His company many a day and night on our little sea in calm times and troubled." He studied the rabbi's face intently and his own countenance was without guile. "I thought I knew the

Master, Saul; I know I loved Him and love Him now with all my soul, though it is true that I both denied Him and in His great trouble deserted Him. But Him whom you reveal, O Saul, I have not known. Your words are strange to me and hard of comprehension." His eyes warmed with a fraternal appreciation, however, and he grasped the rabbi's arm in a gesture of affection. "But I doubt not, O Saul, that you are one of us in our love of the Master and devotion to His Kingdom, and I doubt not that the Master Himself called you into the fellowship and is instructing you in the nature of Himself and of our Most High Yahweh, God of the Chosen."

Nor did James the Lord's brother comprehend the strange sayings of Saul concerning the nature of Yahweh Most High or the Lord Messiah. James indeed had not become a follower of Jesus until after the Nazarene's crucifixion and resurrection. In the days of the older brother's ministry the other members of the family of Joseph the carpenter were hard-pressed to recognize Jesus as the long-awaited Messiah of the downtrodden nation of Israel. Saul's widening of the love and concern of the God of Israel to include the pagan peoples of the earth and in particular the invading and conquering Romans was a strange and heretical doctrine, for had not the long and tragic story of the land of Israel been a recountal of God's instructions to His Chosen, time after time after time, to rise up and slay utterly, to the last man, woman, and child, their pagan enemies, *His* enemies? And how now does this man from Tarsus, who professes to be a good Jew and zealous for Israel and Israel's Most High and likewise a convert to the faith of Jesus the Lord Messiah, stand up and declare that our God is likewise the God and Father, the deeply concerned and infinitely loving God and Father, of pagan enemies of His Own children, of idolaters, worshipers of cruel, child-sacrifice-demanding Moloch, corrupt and licentious Astarte?

But Saul persisted in recounting to all and any who would pause to listen the amazing story of how he, the chiefest of the enemies of Jesus of Nazareth, murderer of the Messiah's brave and good man the goldsmith Stephen, on the journey to

Damascus—in the instant of a thunderbolt's descent—had been transformed into the Messiah's devoted slave and brother. And he went on to relate how in the following days in his sojourn in Arabia the Messiah had taught him through the communion of their spirits the natures of the Lord Messiah and the Most High God, whose natures were in actuality the same since God and His Messiah were one and the same, equal in power and glory, equal in Their love and concern for all men everywhere, Their children and Their brothers.

Saul talked in the marketplaces along the slope of Zion Hill in the vicinity of the bridge that crossed high above the Valley of the Tyropoeon to connect Zion with Mount Moriah and the Temple; he harangued any of those down in fetid Ophel who would stop to listen; he went into the great Court of the Gentiles, where hardly more than three years before, he and the guards provided by Caiaphas had seized members of the fellowship of the Galilean and dragged them away to be beaten unmercifully and left to die because of their faith in the crucified Jesus and their adherence to Him. Freely he confessed his great sinning and guilt and boldly he proclaimed his new allegiance, and in the clearest reasoning he could command he strove to make comprehensible to his hearers the oneness in power and glory and in love for all mankind of God the Most High and Jesus the Lord Messiah.

He addressed the faithful of the fellowship when again they assembled in the courtyard of Mary of Cyprus, and on the following Sabbath he appeared again in the Synagogue of the Asians and the Cilicians and resumed the discussion that on the previous Sabbath had provoked confusion and dissension.

On this occasion, Saul's speaking soon caused a tumult to break forth among the worshipers, more violent than the one of the previous Sabbath, and though the head of the congregation was able to restore order and to quiet the more loudly protesting worshipers by calling upon Saul to cease his discoursing, the report of the disorder reached the ears of the Roman commander in the Tower of Antonia, who sent two soldiers to bring Saul before him.

32

"Tribune Lucius Aemilius Paulus!"

"By all the gods, Aemilius Paulus! Eastern cousin, surely you can't be the one. How does it happen that you are here?"

Saul nodded his head toward the soldiers. "They fetched me to you," he replied, smiling.

"Yes, I know. But I sent them to fetch one reported to me to be an agitator, one who was violently traducing the religion of the Jews in defending the cause of the crucified Galilean, and promoting a disturbance at the Synagogue of the Asians and the Cilicians."

"I was not traducing the religion of the Jews, tribune. That is my religion; I was born in it and I will die in it. Nor was I promoting any disturbance. But I was discoursing upon Jesus of Nazareth the Lord Messiah and how He and the Most High Yahweh are one and the same."

The tribune's expression revealed incredulity. "But when I last saw you—in Jerusalem at the Passover festival three years ago, was it not?—you were vehement in your denunciation of the Galilean and his followers."

"Indeed, tribune, I was. But since then I have received enlightenment. The Lord Messiah came to me and set me on a straight path. It was of this that I was speaking in the synagogue when I was challenged by the enemies of the Lord Messiah."

"By great Jupiter, it's amazing," the tribune observed. "That day when you came aboard the *Memphis* at Tarsus, when we paused at Antioch, at Caesarea and later here in Jerusalem, I would never for a moment have thought that you would ever become a member of the fellowship of that crucified carpenter-rabbi." He smiled, shook his head. "It must be a good story, cousin. Would you tell it to me?"

"I'll be happy to tell it. I tell it every time I get the opportunity, even though"—he smiled and his dark eyes warmed—"sometimes the telling provokes a tumult that results in my arrest."

The tribune dismissed the soldiers who had brought Saul to him. When they had gone from the chamber he turned back to Saul. "Now, eastern cousin, proceed."

Saul told his story. He related not only what had happened to him in the more than three years since he had last seen Paulus in Jerusalem, but he told also how his religious beliefs had been enlarged and matured to comprehend, at least to his own satisfaction, something of the nature of Yahweh and His Lord Messiah, so that now he had come to understand that the two, who in reality were one and the same, held dominion over the Chosen People and likewise over all the earth, the sun, moon, and stars, as well as over all peoples of every race, color, and nationality.

"Then, Paulus, your Yahweh is the God also of the Gentiles, the God of Rome and Greece, of Egypt and Arabia, of us pagans and barbarians as you Jews hold us to be, *our* God?"

"Yes, tribune, as best I am able to comprehend the nature of Yahweh and His Lord Messiah, after much prayer and sincere efforts at communion with Him—and my comprehension is but a spark from an anvil as compared with His burning sun—He is the God and Father of all mankind, concerned for and loving all His children, whether they be Jew or Gentile, white or black, Judaean or Roman."

For a long moment Paulus was silent, thoughtful. "Then, Paulus, if this be true, then you and I indeed are cousins in the race and nationality of man, are we not?"

"Brothers," Saul corrected him. "Brothers in the great family of Yahweh, Father of all."

"You have indeed changed mightily, Paulus." A genial

smile lighted the tribune's face. "I wonder what Longinus would say were he here to observe your manner and listen to the recounting of your story."

"Where, indeed, is Tribune Longinus? I have heard nothing concerning him, tribune, since our journey here from Caesarea for the Passover festival three years ago."

"He has already arrived at Rome or he is on the Great Sea nearing the capital," Paulus revealed. "The Legate Vitellius summoned him to Antioch, where he gave him messages for the emperor and Prefect Marco, and from there he went to Seleucia and caught a vessel for Rome."

"His mission must have been important," Saul suggested.

"It was. It was concerned with the legate's deposing Pilate and——"

"Pilate deposed!" Saul's astonishment was not feigned.

"You hadn't heard?"

"No. But I've been a long time in the desert wastelands and the distant cities. And none here has told me."

"Perhaps few have heard, outside the Roman constabulary. He and Claudia sailed for Rome but a week ago. Likely Longinus was there already. Legate Vitellius sent Longinus ahead to notify Emperor Tiberius and Prefect Marco that he was deposing the procurator."

"But why, tribune? Why was Pilate deposed? Because he sent the Galilean to His death? Could it be that the Lord Messiah——"

Tribune Paulus shook his head. "No, it was not that." He paused. "I don't think that had anything to do with it. Unless remorse and fear contributed to the instability that led him into making so many mistakes in administering the government in Judaea and Samaria. By the gods, cousin, I do wonder if the crucifixion of that Galilean has been preying on his mind. I suspect Longinus thinks so. In fact, I have an idea that Longinus has never been able to forget that he himself had a part in the man's death." His expression was serious. But then he smiled quickly. "That, though, has nothing to do with why I had you brought here. Perhaps you have wondered why."

"Yes, tribune. And also why you are in Jerusalem. When I was last in Caesarea you had just been sent to command the constabulary there." His eyes brightened. "Are you the new procurator?"

Paulus laughed. "No. For the moment I'm commander in Jerusalem. I was transferred here when Vitellius sent Marcellus to succeed Pilate as procurator. Marcellus properly named one of his subordinates to command the legionaries at Caesarea, and Vitellius sent me here to serve until a permanent commander should be chosen. That choice has now been made, and the legate has ordered me to report to him at Antioch. I suspect—and hope very much—that I'll be sent back to Rome for reassignment."

He was serious again. "Paulus, you must leave Jerusalem. Your presence here will continue to provoke discord. You must realize this. And surely you'll be able to accomplish nothing. Why did you come to Jerusalem anyway? It is not the season of the Passover."

"I came here to confess my guilt in the place where I had so greatly sinned," Saul replied, "and to speak a good word for my Lord Messiah against whom my sinning was most heinous. And likewise to visit with Simon and others of the Lord Messiah's apostles and to learn of Him what they might teach me."

"This then you have done, and nothing more can be accomplished in staying longer in Jerusalem haranguing your strong-willed Jews beyond the creating of further tumult." He pointed a finger at the rabbi. "And, eastern cousin, Vitellius finally lost patience with Pontius Pilate because he kept Judaea and Samaria in a continuous ferment—or permitted them to be. I would be reluctant to have to report to him when I go to Antioch that another commotion has broken out in Judaea and that you are at the center of it." He lowered the pointing finger. "So now, Paulus, there is no longer a reason for you to remain here. You have made your confession, raised your voice in behalf of the Galilean you formerly detested, and you have seen certain of his followers. But there's a better reason for your quitting Jerusalem. If you remain here, Paulus, you will most surely be killed. Cannot you understand that?"

Saul shook his head. "No, tribune. If it is the will of my Lord Messiah that I remain in Jerusalem to testify for Him, then He will protect me against all harm. This He has promised me. But I am coming to feel that it is not His will that I remain longer in Jerusalem at this time. Where then, tribune, do you wish me to go?"

"I am leaving shortly to return to Caesarea and there I'll take ship for Seleucia to report to the legate at Antioch. Go, then, eastern cousin, for the moment back to the abode of the Galilean fisherman—what's his name?"

"Simon of Capernaum."

"Yes. Go to his house and stay there quietly until I send for you again," Paulus instructed him. "Then we will journey together to Caesarea, and you can take the vessel with me, perhaps to Antioch or——"

"Tarsus," Saul spoke up. "I have been thinking of returning to my home city to bear to my father and the others in Cilicia the message of the Lord Messiah." He smiled. "I think, tribune, that the Lord Messiah will instruct me to sail with you to Seleucia and continue on to Tarsus. I am confident that you have shown what the Lord Messiah wills for me; it is His doing that you sent for me. He has, I believe, provided the light, and the way. It must be, tribune, that He has." Saul's dark eyes were flaming. "I am beginning to see it. It must be."

Saul walked down from Tribune Paulus' chamber, high in one of the four great corner towers of the Antonia, and out past the Praetorium, the great paved central court in which Pontius Pilate had conducted the trial of Jesus of Nazareth, to the Gate Tedi, through which the multitude traveling between the Tower of Antonia and the Temple moved. He stepped through the gateway and descended the staircase to the double-cloistered portico that extended along the north wall of the Temple enclosure for a thousand feet. At the eastern end of the Court of the Women he turned right and walked out into the Court of the Gentiles and before the ornate latticework of

the Chel, he prostrated himself on the mosaic stone flooring of
the great court.

"O gracious Lord Messiah, present Thyself once again to
me if it be Thy holy will and show me the way Thou wouldst
have me to go. I am confused and know not the way, O Most
High God, O loving Lord Messiah. As Thou didst on the way
to Damascus, appear to me and give me Thy instructions and
Thy blessing, O my Lord Messiah, Emanation of the Most
High and with Him one and the same, world without end."
He pressed his face against the stones, as upon many another
occasion and in other places he had done, and he prayed with
all earnestness that the Lord Messiah would come and show
him beyond all doubting the course he should take, the road
upon which he should set his restless feet.

But the Lord made no visible appearance to Saul; he saw
only Jews hurrying past, their sandals clattering upon the
stones, and foreigners from every land and of every race, their
legs bronzed and burnt by the sun and dust-covered from
much sojourning; only these he saw out of the corners of his
eyes as he lay on the stones and prayed for His Lord Messiah's
coming.

As thus he prayed, however, as thus he besought divine
guidance, a quietness and a peace took hold upon the rabbi
from Tarsus, and though he saw not the etherealized figure
of Jesus of Nazareth as he had seen Him that day on the hot
sands outside the walls of Damascus, and though he heard no
voice and no sound save the chattering voices and the dis-
cordant noises of the throngs surging through the great
court, presently Saul knew that the Lord Messiah indeed had
come to him and spoken in soundless words though clearly
understood a message of direction and encouragement and
assurance.

Saul lay quiet in an ecstasy of knowing, and he heard clearly
and distinctly, though none about him heard any sound except the raucous, mingled sounds of the multitude's commotion; he lay prone on the stones and listened and with the at-

tuned ears of a discerning spirit he heard his Lord Messiah speaking.

"Arise, Saul, and be about your task. The way you will know as you journey upon it. Did not I tell you in Damascus through the lips of our brother Ananias that you would be an instru‧ ment in my hands to carry my name before Gentiles and kings as well as the sons of the Chosen of my Father?"

Saul got to his feet. He strode along the eastern front of the resplendent Temple, past the Beautiful Gate, and at the southern end of the Chel he turned and crossed diagonally the great sweep of the Court of the Gentiles to the Gate Shalleketh that opened upon the bridge to Zion Hill, which spanned the deep gorge of the Tyropoeon.

The rabbi walked on light legs. The way he should travel would be disclosed to him as he journeyed upon it. As he walked he would be permitted the viewing of the way only as far as its disappearing over the next hill. He would go by faith and faith would sustain him.

And already, as he stepped out upon the bridge, he could discern the road ahead, the earth way and the sea way, down to Caesarea and onward to Tarsus.

33 TARSUS

33

"O my Lord Messiah, Thou didst promise to show me Thy way and lead me upon it. Thou didst promise me abundant employment in Thy vineyard, Thou didst assure me that Thou wouldst make of me an instrument in Thy hands to carry Thy name to the Gentile nations and to the Chosen, Thy brothers in Israel. Thou didst bring me to Tarsus, O my Lord Messiah, I doubt it not, and I came hither thinking to work wonders in Thy name; I came with alacrity of step and a flame in my heart.

"But the days, O my Lord, and the months and the years have come and gone, and despite my striving I have accomplished so little for Thee. I have stood up in the synagogues and told Thy story, I have walked about the marketplaces and repeated it; in Tarsus and the region roundabout Cilicia I have proclaimed to those who would hear Thy redemption and Thy love. But I have had so little success, so great failure. I have failed utterly, O Jesus my brother, even with him my father, who has now gone forth to the great judgment knowing Thee not, believing Thee an enemy of the Most High, a destroyer of the law, a disturber of the peace of the Chosen Thy brothers."

Saul opened his eyes upon the rounded wheel of stone before him, and for a full minute he stood motionless, dark eyes solemn and drawn back into their sockets, countenance grim. "O gracious Lord Messiah"—he closed them again, head bowed—"if because of a proud heart and arrogance of spirit, if because I thought that by eloquence of tongue and employment of an agile mind I could win new brothers to Thy way, if by vanity and pride I have been unable to reveal to these Thy brothers Thy loving great heart, then forgive, O Lord Messiah. Forgive me, and have patience yet to place my unworthy, faltering feet now upon the way that I may accomplish through Thy direction and Thy loving care great things for Thee, that I may henceforth bring into Thy Kingdom an abundance of souls redeemed in Thy name. O gracious, loving brother, my Lord Messiah, set Thou my feet to the dust and grime and sweat and pain of the rigorous course and give them the strength and the stamina to tread steadfastly upon it."

For a long moment, he studied the stone sealing the mouth of the sepulcher cut into the face of the cliff. In the darkness of the tomb, beside the bodies of his mother and wife and little son, lay the body of his father, still the proud, still the unbending Pharisee, the adamant son of the Chosen. Saul had tried with all the skills and power of persuasion he could command to bring to his parent the warmth and the light of the Lord Messiah, but if ever the father had wavered so much as a hair on his head he had never admitted it to the son. Saul had remained, so long as the elder Pharisee lived, a rebel against the God of Israel, an idolater, a worshiper of false gods, a tearer-down of the law, a disappointment and a disgrace to the house of his father.

O remember him, my Lord Messiah; Thou who understandest all things, who knoweth the secrets of every heart, remember him when Thou comest into Thy Kingdom.

Saul turned about from facing the tomb and looked downward upon Tarsus and the yellow Cydnus that twisted through the city like a slithering great snake suddenly frightened into precipitate flight. In the channel of the stream and tied up at the docks that stretched along both banks, innumerable vessels of many nations and classes and tonnages were busy at their tasks. Some were sailing up the Cydnus from the impounded great lagoon that provided Tarsus a commodious and safe inland harbor; others were moving outward into the stream from the wharfs and setting their sails and oars for the

Great Sea southward of the lagoon. And swarms of slaves who from this eminence appeared like scurrying ants were loading and unloading other vessels idling beside the docks. Tarsus was a city in ferment. The business carried on unceasingly beside the Cydnus demonstrated the stir and movement of commerce in the Cilician capital, and no one not directly engaged in it was more responsive to its surge and flow than Rabbi Saul, himself a man of action as well as contemplation and reflection. Often he slipped down to the Cydnus docks to watch the ships and the sailors and the slave stevedores at their tasks, the oarsmen chained at their rowing posts like oxen, tethered to the long timbers that they pulled in never-ending exhausting circles to turn the grinding stones of the mills, and the moiling half-naked slaves struggling with bundled and crated and boxed merchandise from the ships to the wharves and warehouses alongside or from the warehouses and wharves into the ships' holds for shipment to ports around the rim of the Great Sea.

Many times on such visits Saul had seized opportunities to speak to these unfortunate and weary and heavily burdened slaves, and to any of their overseers who might listen, of the redemption and freedom from the terrors of sin freely offered them by the Lord Messiah, who in His earthly sojourn had Himself been tired and hungry and hounded and scourged and crucified. Some had come joyfully in faith to accept the gift of the Lord Messiah freely bestowed, and when Saul was gone from them, though they remained in their chains, their rejoicing hearts leaped free in a new if mystical releasing and in a freedom more real than any they had known in the days before their bondage.

But in the years since his return to Tarsus, Saul had been restive and impatient in his striving to bring more souls into the fold of the Lord Messiah. As other men coveted gold and precious gems and sweet-smelling ointment and fine raiment and positions of eminence, Saul coveted souls added to the Messiah's Kingdom. He counted no day well lived that had not seen at least one soul, be it a Gentile or one of the Chosen People, free or bound, highly placed or meanly born, added to the fellowship of the crucified Galilean. Yet, despite his striving and his earnest pleading and his zeal, Saul was convinced that his labors had resulted in small accomplishment. Sometimes when he paused from his efforts in an attempt to measure them and saw them as paltry in comparison with the need of all men for the redemption and saving grace of the Lord Messiah, he was sick at heart. At such times his faith weakened and his hope dimmed, and he even fancied his love for his Messiah and men his brothers wavering.

"O my Lord Messiah, abandon me not to pessimism and the slow loss of zeal, help me to be diligent in the building of Thy Kingdom," Saul would pray when these moods of depression were heavy upon him. "Inspire me, O God Most High, to do an acceptable work for Thee, and place my feet in the right path that I may quickly be about it."

He stood with his back to the tomb, the final resting place of his youthful hopes and dreams; that it was the last earthly repository, though not the eternal ending, his Pharisee upbringing and his bright new hope in the Lord Messiah told him. He stood and looked down upon Tarsus, no mean city, his proud great city, and a deep burning desire, a compelling sense of urgency, possessed him to see his city within the fold of the Messiah, redeemed and faithful.

In Jerusalem, the fisherman Simon had told him how on one occasion Jesus had been coming with His apostles over the crown of the Mount of Olives when, of a sudden, the holy city, the golden plates and the marbled walls of the Temple glinting in the sunlight, emerged below them. "O Jerusalem, Jerusalem, thou that killest the prophets, and stonest them which are sent unto thee, how often would I have gathered thy children together, even as a hen gathereth her chickens under her wing, and ye would not!" Thus had Jesus spoken, as solemnly He looked upon the city that had rejected Him and would send Him to a cruel death; and thus felt Saul of his city

Tarsus as he stood on the hillside above it, looking downward
to the River Cydnus sweeping its yellow flood southward toward the Great Sea.

Tarsus, like Jerusalem, was rejecting the Lord Messiah and
those who in His name were offering His redemption and
His salvation. Saul had been laboring in his city almost four
years, but hardly discernible, if discernible at all, had been
the impact of his preachments. Few of his brothers of the
Chosen had even listened to him; some, rejecting his claims
for the carpenter of Galilee, had threatened to do him violence
as an idolater, a destroyer of the law, and a disturber of
the peace of ancient Israel. Few, too, were the Gentiles of
Tarsus, Cilicians, Greeks from the nearer islands westward, a
scattering of Romans colonized in the region, and here and
there a bronzed Syrian from the lands eastward from Antioch
who had been led of Saul to accept the redemption and salvation of the Most High God through the gift of His Lord
Messiah.

*How few, how few, O Lord Messiah. How few among the
countless unnumbered hosts of the Gentiles. Yet Thou hast
promised that I would be an instrument in Thy hands to carry
Thy name unto the Gentile nations. And how far their lands
reach, O Lord of the world. The Gentile nations stretch westward to the end of the Great Sea on its northern shores and
along its southern; they stretch back from the sea into the deep
forests northward and southward beyond the burning sands of
the desert; they extend onward to other seas and other shores.
And the souls outside the fold of Thy redemption and Thy salvation, O blessed Messiah, are as the stars of the night; they are
as but a pinch of sand between one's fingers to all the sands of
all the shores and all the deserts. O Lord Messiah, I covet for
Thee the souls of these Thy brothers who know Thee not.
When, O gracious Lord, when is it to be Thy will that I
should set out upon the way toward accomplishing among the
great hosts of Thy Gentile brothers wonders of redemption
and cleansing and salvation in Thy name?*

Saul turned back to look for a solemn moment upon the

great round stone that sealed away inviolate the bodies of his beloved ones to await the great day of awakening. Then he faced about quickly and began resolutely to descend the slope by the way that led downward into the city.

He was halfway to the level of the riverside when he first saw the Roman trireme. It was coming around a twisting in the stream and moving swiftly up the channel toward the wharf area, its sails filled and proud, its three rows of oars on each side flashing rhythmically in the bold sunlight.

Saul hastened his steps. If he could get down to the vessel by the time it tied up at the dock and its passengers began to disembark, he might gain news of great happenings in Rome or Athens or Alexandria or Antioch; he might even come upon a friend of other days and another place.

34

Hardly had Saul reached dockside near the now tied-up trireme when he spotted a familiar figure among the passengers coming ashore.

"Tribune Paulus!"

In that instant the tribune saw him. "Cilician cousin!" He thrust out his arm in salute and strode quickly over to the rabbi. "I was hoping that I might see you, Cousin Paulus, but I had little notion I would. Surely you had no knowledge that I was arriving?"

"No, tribune. It just happened that I was descending the slope yonder"—he pointed—"when I saw this vessel coming up the river. I thought that if I should meet it I might see someone I knew and perhaps learn of what is happening in other parts of the empire. My first hope has come to pass"—the rabbi smiled warmly and his dark eyes lighted—"and no doubt you bring interesting tidings." He saw that the tribune had set down on the cobblestones a small bag he had carried from the vessel. "Will the trireme not be sailing out again before to-morrow?"

"It sails early tomorrow. That will give me the chance to enjoy a night ashore before we start on the long voyage for Rome."

"Rome? Then you must be returning to the capital from a mission out here. Have you perhaps been to Palestine—Anti-och maybe, or Caesarea?"

"To Palestine, yes. But only as far as Ptolemais."

Saul's surprise was evident. "But why Ptolemais, tribune? Why not Caesarea, or Jerusalem?"

"It's a strange story, hardly believable. But you would un-derstand, and appreciate it, no doubt." He grinned. "I was sent out from Rome with a detachment of legionaries to escort the statue of the god Gaius to Jerusalem."

"The emperor's statue in Jerusalem?" Saul was aghast. "Where in Jerusalem, tribune?"

"In the Temple; in the most sacred place there. I believe you call it the Holy of Holies."

"But did not the emperor know that Augustus and Tiberius never permitted violation of our laws and traditions related to our worship of the Most High and did not——"

"But we did not get to Jerusalem with the statue," Tribune Paulus interrupted, seeing Saul's amazement and revulsion. "It went no farther than Ptolemais."

"May God be praised for keeping His holy Temple invio-late. But tell me, tribune, how did the Most High accomplish it?"

"I don't know by what means it was accomplished, Cousin Paulus, unless it was through the courage and sheer despera-tion of the Jews of that region." He picked up his bag. "But it's a long story. Let me tell you about it as we walk along while I seek an inn for the night."

"You need seek no inn, tribune. You must go with me and lodge at my house."

"You would receive a Roman, a Gentile?"

"Since the Lord Messiah came and revealed Himself to me, tribune, all men are my brothers. And you"—Saul's dark eyes were dancing—"are likewise my cousin. Haven't you yourself so declared?"

"But your wife, Paulus? Would not my lodging with you be an added burden to her and——"

"I have no wife, tribune, no child, no parents, no near relative save a sister in Jerusalem. I have for family only the Lord Messiah. He is for me wife, children, parents, my all. But He is sufficient." He reached for the tribune's light bag. "Come, let us be on our way. I am anxious to hear the story of the emperor's statue."

It was indeed an amazing account of an incredible young man invested with supreme power to govern a vast empire Tribune Paulus gave as they walked along the streets of Tarsus. "You must not think that I am an insurrectionist, Cousin Paulus," he said, as he began his account. "I am not. I am an officer in the Roman army and I obey orders. The emperor sent me to Ptolemais with his statue. I obeyed the orders I received. But"—he glanced about to see if any ears might be listening—"that does not mean that I countenance the emperor's actions."

"Many stories have come to Tarsus of his profligacies, but we've had no words concerning his fearful insulting of Yahweh and His Chosen People."

"I have run ahead of them," Paulus said. "But soon, no doubt, you will be hearing them. The Jews were greatly aroused. They would have let themselves be killed before they would have permitted that statue to be set up in the Temple."

He proceeded to tell Saul what had taken place at Ptolemais. The emperor, he revealed, had become obsessed with the notion that he was a divine being, equal in authority and majesty to Jupiter himself, and had begun setting up likenesses of himself in various cities of the empire. He had determined, therefore, to have one placed at Jerusalem. Where could it find a more honorable place in the capital of Jewry than in the sacred Temple itself? So Gaius had sent orders to Proconsul Publius Petronius to bring his troops to meet at Ptolemais the vessel on which the statue was being escorted by Tribune Paulus. But when the report of the emperor's plans had come to the ears of the Jews, they had swarmed to Ptolemais literally by the thousands, and after protesting with vehement eloquence to the proconsul they had thrown themselves on their faces in the path of the legionaries and the wheeled conveyance on which it was to be borne and had sworn they would die before they would permit its transportation to Jerusalem.

Petronius had then relented and sent the Jews home with the promise that he would not move the offending likeness of Gaius to their holy city, and he had written a letter to the emperor, which Paulus was carrying back to Rome, explaining his reasons for not carrying out the emperor's orders.

"The proconsul acted wisely," Saul observed. "The last one of the Jews would have died before they would have permitted the violation of the Temple. But the emperor must have lost his reason. Surely no sane man would act thus."

"Indeed, Cousin Paulus, none would. He is mad. And if this madness persists and remains unbridled, may the gods protect the empire. But"—he glanced about, for they had entered a narrow way where the pedestrians were beginning to jostle one another—"let us wait until there are no other ears to hear us before we discuss him further."

After a few minutes of walking they reached Saul's house and refreshed themselves; then the tribune resumed the telling of the interrupted story of the emperor's incredible four years in the seat of the Caesars.

Gaius had shown respect and even subservience to the senators at the beginning of his reign, Paulus declared, but almost immediately, upon realizing that the supreme power of empire had fallen to him, his attitude toward them had changed; soon they were falling to their knees before him to kiss his feet. Early he turned to the observance of Egyptian customs and ways, Paulus further reported, and perhaps in emulation of his great-grandfather Mark Antony, considered making Alexandria the capital of the empire. Early, too, he had given himself to gross immoralities. Ugly rumors had begun to circulate, said Paulus, that Caligula was living in incest with his sisters, and certainly none doubted that he was having illicit relationships with other men's wives.

"He even went to the wedding of Gaius Piso and Livia Orestilla"—Paulus grinned broadly—"and was so impressed with the beauty and charm of the bride that he took her home with him to the Palace and married her himself. But after living with her a few days he discarded her. Not long after that he took the beautiful Lollia Paulina from her husband, married her, and soon divorced her. His next wife, the one he still has—or had when I left Rome—was Caesonia, whom he likewise took away from her husband by whom she was then pregnant. And certainly Caesonia's no beauty."

"Four wives already." Saul shook his head ruefully. "The man indeed is mad."

"But he has done stranger things—and surely more potentially disastrous to the empire—than that," the tribune went on. "Some of his antics are just that—antics, such as his summoning the senate into session at the Curia to hear him sing and recite his poetry (if poetry you can call it) and dance and do monologues, or such as making his horse Incitatus a Roman senator. But these things only show him to be a buffoon. The tragedy for the empire in his being on the throne"—the smile was gone and his countenance now was pained—"is his utterly reckless spending. Tiberius left a heavy surplus in the treasury; it's gone now. Soon, if this mad extravagance is not quickly abated, the government will be bankrupt. Taxes already are unbearable; he has taxed everything, Paulus; he has even placed a tax upon the earnings of prostitutes. He has rich men charged with high crimes and then executes them and seizes their estates. Spend, spend, spend. By the gods, Cousin Paulus, the empire cannot much longer survive him! Do you know, he can't spend it fast enough, so he literally throws it away. Sometimes he climbs to the high porticoes of Rome's public buildings, such as Basilica Julia, and throws down great quantities of coins to see the people below scrambling for them. But his greatest extravagances are revealed in his orgies of building things. Have you heard about the bridge he built across the bay down at Baiae?"

Saul shook his head. "No, though I have heard that he seems to care nothing for the proper administration of the empire's government, that he is concerned only with satisfying his personal appetites. What of this bridge at Baiae, tribune?"

"It was constructed, of course, on boats, since the water was too deep to permit the building of permanently secured supports. And it required so many of these vessels that there were not enough left to provide Rome an adequate grain supply." The tribune shrugged. "I could go on recounting his crimes against Rome and her citizens, but there's no need. And I beg of you, if you yet have any affection for the house of Aemilius, Paulus, to say nothing to anyone of what I have been telling you concerning the emperor. If one word should get to him"— he drew his stiffly extended fingers across his throat—"my head would roll and doubtless my father's also. Caligula would then have an excuse for confiscating the senator's entire fortune"—he frowned darkly, observed further—"not that he would need any. He might do that any time, of course, without any provocation whatsoever."

Tribune Paulus and Rabbi Saul sat late into the evening, talking of what had been happening since they first met. That had been in Tarsus, too; when Tiberius was still emperor and Pontius Pilate procurator of Judaea. And not long after Pilate's banishment—Paulus continued his narration of some of the more dramatic happenings that had followed Caligula's becoming emperor—Herod Antipas and Herodias his wife had arrived in Rome from Tiberias, the Galilean capital. The ambitious and unprincipled Herodias, sister of Herod Agrippa, had been irritated at Caligula's elevation of her spendthrift brother to the kingship, even though his kingdom was small and not affluent. But she had been even more annoyed with her husband. She had scolded Antipas for his apparent lack of ambition, his willingness to sit by, calm and unprotesting, remaining only a tetrarch, while his indolent brother-in-law was given the high honor of kingship. She had pleaded and urged and threatened until Antipas had agreed to go with her to Rome and to petition Caligula to make him king. They took a boatload of costly gifts to present to the impressionable ruler.

But Herod Agrippa, who had come out to Palestine, heard of the plans of his sister and brother-in-law, and he sent a letter to the emperor charging that Antipas had raised arms for seventy thousand soldiers and that he was planning a revolt against the Roman rule in Galilee. The messenger reached Gaius before Antipas and Herodias arrived, and when they did appear before the emperor he was furious. He threatened to have Antipas executed but decided instead to exile him. But since Herodias was his friend Agrippa's sister, he offered to allow her to live in Rome as a guest in the Palace. Herodias gratefully refused his clemency and went with her husband into exile. Gaius extended Agrippa's realm to include the region that had been ruled by Antipas.

"What has happened to them?" Saul inquired. "I heard that they were exiled, and that Pilate had been exiled too. You told me in Jerusalem, you remember, that the legate had deposed the procurator."

"I have heard nothing of them or of Pilate. All three seem to have dropped out of sight completely. Claudia, Pilate's former wife, is still living in Rome with Tribune Longinus, whom she married after Pilate was banished—at least she was when I sailed eastward. Had you heard that she and Longinus were married?"

"No. Nor had I heard anything of Longinus. I have wondered if evil fate had overtaken him. He, too, with Tiberius, Pilate, and Herod Antipas—though Tiberius probably knew little of it—was involved in the crucifixion of the Galilean, and appeared concerned about it. Is Longinus a courtier in Rome at the emperor's court? Surely Longinus doesn't fawn on Gaius."

"Longinus is still in the army and is often sent upon missions for the emperor. But to him Caligula is just as obnoxious as he is to me—and to virtually all the Roman army, I'd say, as well as the senate and the people, generally."

"What of Claudia? Does she yet remember the Galilean for whom she interceded with Pilate?"

"I'm sure she does and that Longinus does too. I have heard that she communicates with the Galilean's followers in Rome and that sometimes in disguise she even goes across the Tiber to Janiculum Hill to meet with them. She must be careful, of course. Caligula would be furious if he learned that his aunt had been associating with such folk. He might even have her killed." He paused, his countenance sober. "The emperor, Paulus, is capable of unbelievable crimes. It is generally believed that he even forced his grandmother Antonia, a noble woman if there ever was one, to kill herself."

"It is amazing that someone hasn't assassinated the emperor, or attempted to," Saul observed. "Of course, I am not advocating this, nor would I countenance it. That is the prerogative of none but God."

"It is indeed strange that he hasn't already been killed," Paulus agreed. "I half expect to hear any day that someone has thrust him through with a sword or succeeded in getting his wine goblet poisoned."

The next morning Saul walked with Tribune Paulus down to the Cydnus docks. They stood and talked as the last bales of merchandise were being put aboard.

"Come with me to Rome, Cilician cousin," Paulus said. "You could bring to those Jews of the Galilean's fellowship the amazing story of how you changed from being his fierce enemy to his enthusiastic apostle. They would believe such a story from none but you. And you would be welcome in my father's house."

"I thank you, tribune. I have long wanted to set foot in Rome. But the Lord Messiah has not yet directed my travels westward. Perhaps someday He will. I must wait and seek to do His work here until He sends me into another part of His vineyard." Saul laid his hand affectionately upon the arm of the tall Roman. "May the Most High and His Lord Messiah attend you, tribune, and may we one day meet again."

Tribune Paulus raised his arm in a salute of farewell. "And may they attend you, Cilician cousin, and all the gods preserve you."

He lowered his arm and bent to pick up the handbag. A moment later he waved from the deck of the trireme as the vessel, completely loosed now from its moorings and propelled by the oars of the striving rowers, eased away from the wharf and, turning, pushed out into the channel and headed downstream toward the Great Sea.

†

35

ROME

35

The trireme on which Tribune Paulus had sailed westward tied up in late afternoon at the docks below Pons Aemilius. Paulus disembarked quickly and sent a Greek fellow lounging on the wharf to the domus of Senator Aemilius Paulus with instructions to have two slaves sent down to the docks to transport his baggage to the mansion on Esquiline Hill. Paulus scribbled a note for the man to take; he would be given a coin when he delivered the message.

Paulus was unwilling to chance provoking Caligula's ire by going to his father's house before reporting to the emperor. Should he be told that the tribune had not come at once to the Palace, the emperor might be infuriated. So Paulus walked quickly eastward, past the Forum Boarium, the always foul-smelling cattle market from which the workmen were streaming toward their tenements in the Subura, and along Clivus Victoriae until he came to a narrow way that turned off some two hundred paces from the northwestern gates of the huge Circus Maximus, and then he started to climb Palatine Hill. Soon he identified himself at the Palace gate and entered the gardens; in another few minutes he had been admitted to the huge sprawling Palace itself, and upon his insistence that he was bringing a message of vital importance to the emperor, he was escorted to Gaius' apartments.

There he was told that the emperor was then being honored by his devoted friend King Agrippa at a dinner being held in the great dining hall of the late emperor Tiberius in the western wing of the Palace. Did the tribune feel that the message he bore from Proconsul Publius Petronius was of such gravity that they should risk the emperor's anger by interrupting his evening's dining, which by now had probably deteriorated into gorging and heavy drinking and ribald jesting?

"Should he learn that this report from Proconsul Publius Petronius had been withheld from him even for one night," Tribune Paulus observed, "I would not wish to be that man who had caused it to be withheld."

He was taken immediately to the great triclinium. Outside the door the aide paused. "Perhaps, tribune," he said, "it would be wise for you to stand inside and await an opportune time to have your arrival announced to the emperor."

"Yes, I agree." He smiled appreciatively. "I wouldn't venture to interrupt while he was speaking."

On the inside of the great chamber he whispered to a servant at the door, and then the two stood quietly against the wall in the shadow of one of the marble columns. But though they would hardly be noticed by the guests, Paulus and the liveried Palace servant had excellent views of the diners themselves, and the tribune immediately spotted Caligula. His balding head, small on the slender stalk of his neck, shone in the light of the lamps around the walls and on the columns. He was half-sitting, half-reclining on his couch in the place of honor, the third place on the central couch, listening intently, it appeared, to King Agrippa, who had arisen from the host's position next to the emperor on the adjacent third couch, and was addressing the sovereign. He was talking when Paulus slipped into the chamber. The tribune sought to catch the thread of Agrippa's discourse.

"———not out of any expectation of gain that in the days of the late emperor Tiberius, and contrary to his commands, I was devoted to you, O my lord the emperor, or in the days since you have ascended to the throne of the world that my devotion has continued and strengthened. The gifts you have already bestowed upon me, O sire, have been great and beyond the hopes of even a craving man, for though they may be less than you have power to bestow, yet are they greater than even

I could envision and far greater than I deserve. So, sire, I wish no gifts other than your continued friendship and affection."

Caligula got to his feet, somewhat unsteadily, Paulus observed. With stiffened forearm he braced his hulking frame against the table before him.

"I insist, my friend; I insist, I insist"—he waved the other arm protestingly above the table, and staggered, but quickly steadied himself. "Too modest, Agrippa. I want you to accept of my bounty." He picked up his wine glass and downed the wine with one gulp, set it down and wiped his lips with the back of his hand. "Why have friends if you cannot give them gifts?" He paused, and a frown creased his forehead; Paulus could see the emperor's face as he turned to confront King Agrippa.

"Agrippa, will you offend me your friend by refusing to allow me this pleasure?" Quickly the frown was gone and a crooked smile lighted the narrow face as he rocked on his heels but quickly caught his balance by clutching again at the table. "Name it, Agrippa! Anything you wish, my friend! Anything!" His heavy paunch swayed on his thin legs and he sat down heavily on his couch, as Agrippa arose.

"O sire, emperor of the earth and my undeserved beloved friend, surely I would willingly do nothing to offend you or even to cause you a moment's grief or disappointment. So I shall name a gift that would make me happy indeed and would also please greatly an immense multitude of your subjects; granting me this request would please me doubly because it would demonstrate to your people your regard for me" —Agrippa paused momentarily—"and render the Divinity helpful to you in your designs."

"Then speak your wish," Caligula commanded, as he raised high his right arm, though he continued to recline on his side, his head cradled in his left palm with the arm upright and elbow thrust into a cushion. "What would you have me give you, Agrippa, or do for you? By all the gods, my friend, you have but to name it!"

What would Agrippa ask for, Tribune Paulus wondered.

Would he petition Caligula to restore the ancient kingdom of Israel as it was in the days of Agrippa's grandfather, old Herod the Great? That manifestly would please the Jews. And surely it would show them that Agrippa had tremendous influence over the emperor if Gaius should grant such a startling request. And the Jews no doubt would think that restoring the old kingdom would please the Jews' Yahweh. Paulus craned his neck to catch Agrippa's reply, for the king was rising again to speak.

"Then, O sire, if you insist on showing your humble subject further generosity in thus granting his wish for his people, I pray you that you no longer insist upon the setting up of your statue in the Temple at Jerusalem."

"By great Jupiter!" But the exclamation did not escape Paulus' lips. What would Caligula do? Would his face go purple and would he explode in a veritable tirade of cursing Agrippa, the Jews, his fellow guests at Agrippa's dinner, and the Temple hierarchy in Jerusalem? And what would he do indeed when he had read the message brought by the tribune from Publius Petronius? Shouldn't he present that message now, before Caligula's anger had for the moment driven him to the irresponsibility of madness?

Paulus was about to send a Palace servant to the emperor's couch with an announcement of his arrival from the mission to Palestine. But he said nothing, for Caligula was about to answer Agrippa. He pushed cumbersomely to his feet, turned to address his host, and a heavy scowl clouded his narrow cavernous face.

"It is indeed a singular request, my dear friend King Agrippa," he said, and his lips lifted into a sardonic grin. "But I would grant it were it possible. But I assume, Agrippa, that the statue already rests in the Jews' holy place. Weeks ago I sent Tribune Paulus, the son of my beloved friend the senator"—Caligula pointed toward another triclinium of couches about a table heavily laden with food and wine, and it was then that Paulus discovered his father seated among the guests —"with legionaries to escort the statue to Ptolemais, from

which Publius Petronius with other legionaries of his own
command was to transport it to Jerusalem and establish it in
the Jews' Temple."

Once more Paulus was about to send the servant forward to
inform the emperor of his arrival with the letter from the
proconsul, but again he held the man back, for Agrippa had
begun to speak. "But, O Sire, it is possible that the proconsul
was delayed in his task of setting up the emperor's likeness. If
so, would you then write Petronius and order him to halt the
transporting of it to Jerusalem. In the event that it has already
been put within the precincts of the Temple, could you not instruct the proconsul to have it removed to some other place?
And I have in mind such a place, O sire, a most advantageous
position from which countless thousands would be able to see
and admire it and venerate that one for whom it was designed
to be a likeness."

For a tense moment, an uneasy long moment during which
every eye was upon the glum-faced scowling youth who held
in his ungainly big hands the life as well as the fortune of
every person in that great hall, Caligula uttered not one word.
Then he turned to a servant who stood near his couch. "Go,
bring me a secretary with parchment and pens," he commanded petulantly. He turned to Agrippa. "For none other
would I do this, King Agrippa, for none other in all the empire. And I wouldn't do it even for you, my friend"—he was
smiling, but Paulus could see that the smile had no warmth—
"had I not given you my solemn promise to grant you anything you desired." He sat down.

"Write this letter," Caligula commanded the secretary, who
had just entered with the servant who had gone to summon
him, "to the Proconsul Publius Petronius at Antioch, and say
that the emperor thus declares. . . ." Then, as his dictating
and the scratching of the pen on the parchment were almost
the only sounds in the great triclinium, Caligula thanked
Petronius for having set up the statue in the Temple of the
Jews at Jerusalem, as well as for having accomplished other
tasks that the emperor had assigned him. If the statue had

been set up, the proconsul was to allow it to stand; but if it was not yet placed in the Temple, he was to trouble himself no further about it. He added that he was writing him thus "as a favor to Agrippa, a man whom I honor so very greatly that I am not able to contradict what he would have, or what he desires me to do for him."

He confronted Herod Agrippa. "You have heard, King Agrippa, what I have written the proconsul. I can do no more." He turned again to the secretary. "Dispatch this to Antioch on the first vessel leaving for Syria."

Tribune Paulus dared wait no longer, though he was fearful that the message from Petronius would infuriate the emperor. He leaned over and whispered to the servant beside him. "Go tell the emperor that Tribune Paulus has arrived with an urgent message for him from Proconsul Petronius."

The servant went forward quietly, and whispered to another standing behind Caligula's couch; this one bent down and spoke into the ear of the emperor; Caligula turned around quickly to face the door at which the tribune waited. When he saw Paulus he motioned to him to advance. "Tribune Paulus," he said, as the tribune approached, "welcome back to Rome." Then he glanced toward the couch on which the tribune's father was reclining. "Senator, your son has just now returned from Palestine." The elder Paulus, sitting up and seeing his son, smiled broadly and from across the triclinium raised his arm in greeting. Caligula turned back to Paulus. "You bring a message from Publius Petronius?"

"I do, sire." From the fold of his toga he took a waxed tablet, which he handed to Caligula. "It was handed to me by the proconsul as I was preparing to leave Ptolemais."

Caligula frowned. "Ptolemais? Then he came back to Ptolemais from Jerusalem after he set up the statue in the Temple there?"

"No, sire. The proconsul——"

"——wrote me a report of his plans for transporting it to Jerusalem. But it would have been better to have reported *after* he had completed his mission in accordance with my orders."

He pulled the end of the thread wrapped around the folded tablet and secured at the knot with a round bit of wax stamped with the proconsul's signet ring. "But the letter itself will reveal what he did." He opened the folded sheets. "Here, Tribune Paulus, read it to me." He handed the tablet back to Paulus. "It will contain nothing that the ears of Agrippa's guests should not hear."

The proconsul had marched his legionaries to Ptolemais, the letter reported, but the assembled Jews had sworn that they would die before they would permit the statue of a man, even though he was the emperor himself, to be conducted to Jerusalem and set up in their holy house of worship to the One-God of Israel, Yahweh. They had thrown themselves faces down upon the earth before the conveyance on which the statue was to be taken to Jerusalem and in the path of the legionaries and had declared they would be trampled into the dust before they would permit the profaning of the house of their One-God. . . .

"Profaning! Profaning!" shouted Caligula, his face livid. "My statue, they say, would be a profanation of their tribal god's temple! My statue! The likeness of the ruler of the empire, the sovereign of the world, the brother of Jupiter!" Caligula picked up his wine glass, emptied it, hurled it across the chamber to shatter to bits on the mosaic paving of the great chamber; the lights from the lamps sparkled in the small broken pieces. Paulus had paused in his reading at the emperor's violent outburst. Caligula pointed a long finger at him and shouted. "Read on! Read on! I would hear the remainder of this treasonable insolence!"

Paulus read rapidly. He wanted to get away as quickly as he could from the presence of the now thoroughly maddened ruler of the empire. Caligula's sunken cheeks were livid now and his deepset eyes flamed as though they would fly from their sockets. His mouth opened and he licked his lips from time to time, but no words escaped them as he listened to the proconsul's narration of what had occurred at Ptolemais and as he sought to defend the course he had taken in refusing to

massacre the unarmed Jewish multitude. He sat inwardly raging but saying nothing as Paulus concluded the reading with
the proconsul's revelation that he had agreed not to transport
the offending statue to Jerusalem, but had ordered it placed
aboard ship for return to Rome; he himself had started with
his troops on the return journey to Syria.

When he finished reading, Paulus handed the tablet to the
emperor. Caligula accepted it, and then with a thundering
oath, he hurled it to the floor at his feet. "By all the gods great
and small!" he shouted, "he shall transport my statue to the
capital city of your miserable Jews, O Agrippa, and there in
the holiest place of that Temple he shall raise it high! He shall
not flout my orders! And when he has done this, if it requires
the blood of all the Jews in that miserable gods-forsaken province, I shall have his head! By great Jupiter my brother, this I
swear! I'll command him to kill himself!"

Caligula had sprung with alacrity to his feet. The heat of
his anger, the vehemence of his outburst, seemed momentarily
to have sobered him. And as he got up on his thin legs,
Tribune Paulus started to withdraw. But now Caligula thrust
out his long hairy arm toward him and screamed his denunciation. "And you, Paulus! You were a party to this detestable
cowardice, this blatant treason! You offered no protest! You
sought not, when Petronius fell frightened and cowering before a motley throng of sniveling Jews, to take upon yourself
the responsibility of carrying out the emperor's orders so wan-
tonly flouted by this Petronius! You, Paulus, were willing likewise to see your emperor's orders disobeyed and himself, the
ruler of the world, insulted and humiliated by a herd of Jewish cattle sniveling and whining that their puny god would be
profaned by sharing his Temple with a likeness of the god
Gaius!"

"But, sire, my orders from the emperor himself were only to
see that the statue arrived safely at Ptolemais and was given
into the hands of the proconsul. These orders I obeyed, O
sire. I could do nothing more. At Ptolemais the proconsul
was my superior; I had no authority to countermand his——"

"Silence! You, an officer of the Roman army, stood by un-protesting while your emperor was being insulted and humili-ated before a multitude of provincials. Whether Petronius was your superior or under your command in the circumstances made no difference, Paulus. You should not have stood along-side him and permitted him to commit this treasonable act against the emperor, against the empire!" His eyes were blaz-ing, furious; as he denounced the tribune, flecks of foam sailed out from his lips ahead of his raging words. But of a sudden he was calm, and a reassuring smile lifted the corners of his lips, and he spoke in even tones and soothingly. "You *were* an officer in the Roman army, Paulus. You are an officer no longer. Before this time tomorrow"—his tone was rising now—"you will be dead!" He turned to the servant behind him. "Who is the Palace officer of the day?"

"Sire, the tribune Chaerea."

"Bring him here!" Caligula calmly reached for his wine glass, which had replaced the one he had shattered, and slowly sipped the wine. The great dining chamber was utterly still except for the sounds of the hastening servant's footsteps. The emperor selected a fat fig from the bowl of fruit in front of him, burst it open, and studiously ignoring the tribune standing stiffly erect at his back, nibbled at the reddish meat. But suddenly he looked up, for across the hall there was a subdued sound of movement.

An elderly tall man, with frightened wide eyes, his face as white as the elegant, soft toga of Milesian wool draped about him by his valet with such skill that each fold settled with precision into its place as he arose, was confronting the arro-gant youth hardly half his age. "O sire, my son sought as best he could to carry out the orders given him by our beloved em-peror. But, sire, he could not control the reasoning of the proconsul, nor could he have——"

"Mind your words, senator! Would you say your emperor was a liar!"

"O, no, sire! No, indeed. I was just attempting to ex-plain——"

"Silence! You have already said the emperor lied in declaring that your traitorous son could not control the proconsul's reasoning." He waggled a long forefinger at the ashen-faced Senator Paulus. "You are but one of a kind with him. The empire no longer has need of you, senator. Your estate will serve the city and the empire far better than you would were I to spare your useless life, which I shall not do! Tomorrow the headsman will wait upon you as he will likewise wait upon your son!" Caligula twisted about on his couch to face the entrance door, for the servant was returning with an erect, powerfully framed young man in the uniform of a tribune.

"Chaerea, come forward!" Caligula commanded. The officer advanced to the couch on which the emperor was again half-reclining, brought his heels together smartly, jerked his arm upward in salute. "Take this one"—he nodded with his small narrow head on its long neck in Paulus' general direction—"and this other one, his father"—he bobbed his head toward the still-standing senator—"and imprison them in the Palace dungeon. On the morrow, choose a quaternion of Praetorian Guardsmen and conduct the two beyond Porta Capena to the execution ground and there behead them! They have been found guilty by the emperor of treason and other high crimes against the emperor and the empire! Go!"

"Hold, Tribune Chaerea!"

A woman's voice had shouted the command. Caligula whirled around, furious. But he said not a word when he saw that the woman on her feet at one of the triclinia near Senator Paulus was Claudia, his mother's half-sister. He simply stared at her for an instant, and then his angry features relaxed into a ludicrous, sinister grin. "Wait a moment, Chaerea," he said calmly as he turned back to that officer. "It appears that the Lady Claudia is about to give the emperor the benefit of her great experience in administering the affairs of the empire. And so, Claudia"—he addressed her now and his manner was mockingly deferential—"what were the words of wisdom you were about to offer us?"

"O sire, O Gaius my beloved nephew," she said, as she stood

straight and steady of eye, "I beg of you, hear me. These men are excellent men, of the highest nobility of Roman citizenship. They are no traitors, O Gaius; on the contrary, they are patriots loving and serving the empire and its great and noble young emperor. I myself have known them both, father and son, as long as I can remember. And I have had occasion to know well the quality of the tribune's service in Palestine and his devotion to the empire and its emperor. He was there during much of the time I lived in Caesarea as wife of the procurator Pilate. My husband of those years honored him and gave him positions of responsibility, whose duties he performed with skill and faithfulness. My present husband, Tribune Longinus, will likewise tell you this, O Sire." Her glance dropped for a moment to Longinus, whom Paulus had just seen for the first time since his entering the triclinium, and then she continued her plea to her nephew, who seemed more amused than impressed. "And Senator Paulus, O Gaius, I have held in veneration since my earliest days of recollection. He was likewise a friend of my late mother, daughter of the god Augustus——"

"And your late father?" Caligula interrupted, grinning sardonically. "Did he also know and venerate the senator?"

"I never knew my father," Claudia answered him, eyes level and fearless.

"And did your mother know him"—his smile was a leer, cold, malevolent—"which of her great company of lovers, I mean, was your father?"

But Claudia remained calm, maintained her dignity, though Longinus, Paulus saw, was being consumed inwardly by his hatred of this dangerous and at times utterly mad buffoon to whom now fearful Rome had committed the supreme power.

"I was but an infant when my mother died," she replied, "and consequently I never had the privilege of knowing her. I know of her friendship for the senator from the senator himself, whom I know, O sire, to be a most excellent Roman, an honor to the empire, and an honor to the emperor. And I know also, O my beloved nephew, that the Proconsul Publius

Petronius is a loyal Roman and an ornament to the empire. And, sire, because of my long living in Palestine I can appreciate the gravity of the situation the proconsul faced at Ptolemais. I know the temperament of the Jewish people, I know the strength of their devotion to their one-god Yahweh——"

"And I know, my dear *half*-aunt"—Caligula paused in his interruption to give emphasis to his scornful tone as well as slighting words—"that *you* likewise are devoted to the puny small one-god of that obstinate and most despicable people of all the empire's provincials—hear me, King Agrippa. Reports have come to me that you have been observed slipping over to Janiculum Hill to participate in cannibalistic orgies of that bloodthirsty sect of the Jews that continues to profess allegiance to the Galilean revolutionary whom your first husband—and the gods know I hold him in no esteem—perhaps was justified in sending to the cross."

He whipped out his arm from beneath his toga and waggled his finger toward Claudia, and his voice rose to an impassioned falsetto. "Do you deny it, O Claudia? Do you deny that you go to secret orgies of this infamous sect and with its members eat human flesh and drink human blood in accordance with certain of its rites? Do you"—his head was beginning to shake as though it had become loosened from the long, reddened column of his neck—"deny the truthfulness of this report that certain of my agents have brought me? Answer me, half-aunt!"

"I do deny it, O sire, positively. I deny that I go to any orgies on Janiculum Hill or anywhere else." She was still calm, unruffled. "I deny likewise that the sect of the Jews of which you speak engages in any orgies. They are a religious people who worship Yahweh of Israel and seek to obey His laws. The flesh and blood of which you have heard they partake is really but bread and wine eaten and drunk by them in commemoration of the Galilean crucified upon the orders of my former husband. Nor are they revolutionaries, Gaius my nephew; they are not interested in political matters."

"Did I say they were revolutionaries?" Caligula shouted.

"Did I say *you* were a revolutionary? By great Jupiter my brother, Claudia, you deny when none accuses."

"Sire, you spoke of the Galilean as a revolutionary——"

"And was he not?" He paused, but only momentarily. "And are not these who call themselves followers of the fellow, are not they revolutionaries?" He shrugged his gaunt shoulders, grinned craftily. "My dear Claudia, I know something about this nefarious sect. They are looking to the return to life of this Galilean, when they will revolt against Rome and set themselves up a new empire." He pointed his finger at her. "Isn't that true, my beloved half-aunt?"

"As best as I understand them, they are looking for his return to establish a spiritual empire when all men as brothers will——"

"Swine swill! What sort of empire would that be!" His smile was gone and he glared at Claudia. "I'm not stupid enough to believe such nonsense. If that's what they say, it's only a scheme they have for covering up their real designs against the empire, yes"—his countenance was lurid and his voice had gone high again—"and by all the gods great and small, against the emperor!" He struck his fist on the table with such force that the dishes danced.

Then he pointed toward her again and waggled his long finger. "And you, Claudia, are one of them, are you not?" His voice was low now, but his tone insistent. "You are a follower, too, of this crucified fellow, this revolutionary against Rome, and as you are one of that credulous but potentially dangerous sect, you give your allegiance to this coming kingdom"—he leaned back and snickered contemptuously, and then he sat up quickly and his scowl was fearful—"rather than to Rome, and to this crucified fellow instead of your emperor!"

"O sire, as I understand this Galilean and his fellowship, there need be no conflict between his kingdom and Rome or between him and the Caesar."

"As you *understand* him? Then you hold that he still lives, hah! And shortly may begin his attempt to overthrow Rome and himself sit upon the throne of the Caesars, upon *my* throne."

"O sire"—Longinus, who had been reclining beside Claudia, sprang to his feet—"perhaps I can help Claudia make clear the difference——"

"Indeed, Tribune Longinus, you can try to help her to continue to evade my question. But she has already answered in attempting not to. And you, tribune. You were stationed many years in the East. Doubtless you have become infected in the same manner as has your wife. You knew this Galilean, did you not?"

"I am the one who killed him, sire. I drove my spear into his side to end his agony."

"I have heard that. And you believe him some sort of god who will return to earth and take over the rule of the empire after he has destroyed Rome and slain the Caesar and his armies?"

"He said, sire, that his kingdom was not an earthly one and that he——"

"More swill!" He stood up, and leaning across the table, stabbed a long forefinger in the tribune's direction. "Are you one of those of the sect who look forward to his overthrowing the emperor and usurping the throne? Answer, Longinus!"

"Sire, I am a Roman citizen, a tribune in the empire's army, a soldier at the command of my emperor."

Caligula's low laugh was insolent, contemptuous. "Hah! Nobly said, brave tribune. And likewise"—his voice was low now and almost a hiss, and his narrow face was contorted with his wrath and his returned madness—"a traitor waiting the opportune moment to betray the empire, the army, and the emperor." His angry eyes held for a moment on the solemn face of the tribune, and then he twisted on his couch to confront Paulus behind him. "And you, are you not likewise one of them? In your tour of duty in that insufferable land, were you not infected with that same Oriental mischief and madness?"

But he did not wait for the tribune's reply. Instead, he turned back to scream his rage at Longinus and Claudia, still standing at their places. "By the infernal Pluto, I see it now! The plot is clear, the conspiracy revealed. By Ceres my sister, you would have betrayed the empire and me, but you betray yourselves instead." He stabbed his finger toward Claudia. "My dear half-aunt, you and your husband—who was your paramour all the years you were Pilate's wife and even before you went out to Palestine—I understand it now. You connived to get Pilate disgraced and exiled and thereby to smooth your way to the crown, Longinus, by being the husband of the royal granddaughter of the god Augustus——"

"But, sire, Longinus and I are innocent of even such a thought as——"

"Silence, Claudia! I will hear no more of your chattering. You would gain the throne for your *tribune*"—he spat out the word with contempt—"and you would deliver your native land and all its subject peoples to a despicable religion paying obeisance to a crucified revolutionary. You would have done this, but I have circumvented you, dear, *dear* half-aunt, and your conniving tribune and his conspiring friend Paulus and the great senator his father"—he turned about to punch a finger toward Paulus and his father, who in response to Chaerea's signal had slipped around the edge of the triclinium to join his condemned son. "And now your damnable conspiracy is laid bare before me and these my friend Agrippa's guests."

He reached for his wine glass, gulped the sparkling liquid, set it down, wiped his lips, belched loudly. Then he stood up and faced the gathering. "Claudia and Longinus, I find you guilty of conspiring among yourselves and with Tribune Paulus, and others, against the Roman state and its emperor. I find you guilty of conspiring to introduce into Rome the worship of a false and despicable Oriental revolutionary, whom you, in your effort to gather to your support the naïve of our citizenship, represent as a god. For these heinous crimes against the peace and dignity of the empire and the person of the emperor, I do order that your individual and joint properties, personal, estates, and whatever, be confiscated, sold, and the proceeds therefrom be given into the treasury of the state. And I do further order"—his smile was genial, friendly, and his voice calm, almost gentle—"that the two of you be escorted by the tribune Chaerea to the Palace dungeon, in the company of Tribune Paulus and his father, Senator Paulus, and there be confined until tomorrow, when he will take you under sufficient guard to the execution ground beyond Porta Capena and there behead you. And in recognition of our blood relationship, my dear half-aunt"—Caligula's tone and manner were mocking—"I decree that you will be the first to step to the block." He turned his back upon them and confronted Chaerea. "Take them away, Chaerea! I am sick of the sight of them!"

Chaerea with a quick motion of his hand signaled the two to approach him. Claudia, her head high, stepped out from the couch ahead of her husband, and the two crossed the chamber without a glance in the emperor's direction. Caligula, a contemptuous smirk twisting his hollow cheeks, watched until the five had grouped and started toward the door. He was reaching for his wine glass, when suddenly he whirled about. "Wait, Chaerea! Hold them a moment. I have a better plan. It just occurs to me that it would be a great waste to behead these four on the morrow when if we hold them in the Palace prison another four days, we can likely be entertained pleasantly by them in the arena. So save them, therefore, Chaerea, for the games, and we shall observe how bravely the three men fight the lions and how gracefully my dear half-aunt is eaten by them." He held his head back and laughed raucously. Then suddenly he was fiercely scowling. "Go, Chaerea! Take them away!"

When the door to the corridor had closed behind the tribune and his prisoners, Caligula turned to face his long-ignored host. "Friend Agrippa, may the gods protect us from our relatives! You too can appreciate the peril one always faces as long as he has the misfortune of being afflicted with relatives!"

"Yes, O sire, I can understand and appreciate the apprehension one in a position of authority must have because of the jealousy of relatives."

But Caligula was paying no heed to the king's reply. His

eyes were roving along the couches on which Agrippa's guests were reclining in varying stages of inebriety. Suddenly they focused on a group at one of the triclinia toward the right center of the chamber. He laughed merrily, in unfeigned amusement, and pointed. "Don't be frightened, dear Agrippina, beloved sister," he called out. "Surely I had no thought of you as a disloyal relative. Nor of you, Uncle Claudius." He bowed ceremoniously, spoke in a tone banteringly deferential. "Nor even of you, beautiful *young* Aunt Valeria Messalina. Indeed, how could you bring grief upon any *man?*" But of a sudden his merry mood had vanished; his face clouded. "Unless, Agrippina, you wish to challenge my treatment of your Aunt Claudia?"

"My *half*-aunt, O Gaius." She shrugged. "She doubtless got what she deserved; likely she was plotting against you, along with the men. I care not a fig what happens to her; she's utterly of no concern to me, dear brother."

"And you, Claudius? Do you protest the judgment of the emperor in these cases?"

Claudius pushed slowly to his feet, swayed on his thin legs, and clutched at the table to steady himself; his toga falling in folds over his rounded paunch emphasized rather than concealed it. His white hair framing a guileless, friendly face, with long, pointed narrow nose, thin-lipped straight slit of a mouth, and bulbous, uncleft chin, indicated an age considerably older than his actual fifty years. His shuffling gait on shrunken, bony legs, his head wobbling as he moved awkwardly along, gave him the appearance of being intoxicated rather than a victim of infantile illnesses. A worse handicap was his tendency to stutter when excited and laugh uproariously when amused; this caused many to consider him a feeble-minded, harmless dolt who was interested only in gorging on rich foods and wines, trying to write dull treatises on strange subjects, and keeping company too frequently with women too young.

"Must you make a speech in protest, Uncle Claudius? And cannot you sit to do it? You may fall into your wine rather than have it fall into you." He had been frowning, but now he snickered in appreciation of his witticism.

But Claudius remained upon his spindly legs. "O sire, my revered nephew, lord of the world"—he sought to hold his head stiffly erect as he eyed Caligula—"I have not arisen to protest, but rather to declare that I am happy to leave all matters of a political nature to the profound wisdom and good judgment of the emperor. And is not conspiracy against the emperor and empire political? But, sire"—he raised his hand, palm forward, as in admonition, and his head began uncontrollably to wobble—"I do p-p-petition the emperor to administer all such matters himself and leave me free to enjoy f-f-fine food, my good F-F-Falernian, and my beautiful and loving w-w-wife."

"And you, Messalina, do you reprove me?"

"On the contrary, sire," answered Claudius' youthful wife, "I approve." She smiled coyly. "It means that in Rome there will be one beautiful woman less." Messalina lowered her head coquettishly and studied Caligula from beneath her long, black eyelashes. But he did not respond, for Agrippa beside him had arisen and proposed a toast to the god Gaius, ornament and glory of the empire, lord of the world.

And in the Palace dungeon, far below the great triclinium of the late Tiberius Claudius Nero Caesar, already the fast-being-forgotten sometime god Tiberius, once ornament and glory of the empire and lord of the world, Tribune Chaerea was turning the key to lock the door between the long corridor and the prisoners' runway upon which the cells in the women's quarters opened. A moment ago he had jailed the two tribunes and Senator Paulus in the nearby men's section of the darksome prison.

"Have no fears, Claudia. But remember"—he held a warning finger across his lips—"not even the smallest hint to anyone about what I've just told the four of you." He smiled reassuringly and patted her arm through the grating. "You can depend upon the Praetorian."

36

Every detail of the fourth and last day's program in the amphitheater on the slope of Palatine Hill, adjoining the Imperial Palace, had been planned with fiendish delight by Emperor Gaius, whose days of madness now were being relieved infrequently by moments of rationality.

The first three days had been given over to theatrical entertainments in which the emperor himself had appeared in various roles to the thundered applause of thousands of citizens and slaves alike, who reasoned that their approval would bring down upon them another shower of golden coins and a largess of food supplies from a treasury already all but depleted by Caligula's prodigal and senseless spending. The three days had been successful; they had offered Rome famous actors and actresses in refinements of the ancient and modern dramas.

But this last day, Caligula had decreed as a day of bloodletting to be long remembered by Romans inured to the sights of seas of blood being spilled. It would offer a refinement in blood offering, a meticulosity and a generosity in the offering of sacrifice.

It would be a day of sacrifice to the god Augustus, and one to make even the god Moloch jealous. It would begin with the sacrifice of a bullock; it would build popular excitement with the sacrifice of two former tribunes in the Roman army and a senator, who until a week ago was one of the empire's wealthiest and most powerful patricians; it would come, at the afternoon's lengthening shadows across the amphitheater, to a screaming, thundering climax with the sacrificing to the god Augustus of the god's own granddaughter!

Throughout the forenoon's gladiatorial games, Gaius watched with little interest the slaughter of men and animals; he was relishing already, like a child anticipating the presentation of a promised present, the enactment of the day's final drama. The lions, he knew, would perform their roles well; they had been starved for a full week. He wondered how the three men would face the ravenous beasts, whether barehanded they would battle as long as strength remained or if they would huddle supinely to await death from ripping claws and tearing fangs. But visions of the men in their death throes little excited the deranged emperor. It was when he conjured, on the sanded floor of the arena, the white nakedness of his suddenly vehemently hated aunt, her smeared clothing shredded, her proud body mangled and gore-splotched and jerking and twitching in the last spasms of a horrible death, that concentric circles in bright yellow rolled outward from his fastened eyeballs to explode into long flaring fingers of flame.

For the tortured execution of his aunt, Caligula had arranged for a further and unusual refinement in cruelty and sadism. After an intermission in early afternoon, during which he would return to the Imperial Palace for a short period of refreshment, Caligula would retrace his way along the subterranean passageway connecting the Palace and the amphitheater, and signal the resumption of the games. Then Claudia, to a great fanfare of trumpets, would be escorted to the royal box, from which she would be invited to watch the lions as they attacked, killed, and fed upon the senator, his son Paulus, and Longinus, her own husband. When this spectacle had been accomplished and the arena sands freshened for the next event, Claudia would herself be led into the arena and left there to confront another group of snarling, hunger-crazed lions.

Never had Rome witnessed a more thrilling spectacle, Caligula told himself proudly, than her populace would see as the closing, triumphal, unrehearsed act of the four-day entertainment. He himself was impatient for the intermission time to arrive and be ended.

At length it did arrive. The emperor with his retinue arose to leave the amphitheater, and immediately a great horde of other spectators began to push toward the exits. Caligula with several bodyguards entered the passageway to the Palace, and closely behind them came King Agrippa.

But as they reached an intersecting, narrow passageway, Caligula remembered that it led to an apartment some paces away, in which a group of singing and dancing boys recently brought from one of the provinces was being quartered. He wished to see them, though but for a moment, for he was anxious to return as quickly as he could to the amphitheater. So in the press of his guards and swarming courtiers, he slipped from them and stole along the corridor.

Caligula would not see the pampered boys. Nor would he sit again in the imperial box. A moment later Gaius Caesar Germanicus, emperor of Rome and lord of the world, lay threshing on the stones of the corridor in a widening circle of his own blood. As he had rounded a corner in the passageway, he had come suddenly and alone upon Tribune Cassius Chaerea. And before Herod Agrippa, hastening behind and finding him cut down, could carry the gore-soaked emperor into his apartment in the Imperial Palace, Caligula was dead. There, another of the conspirators sent not long afterward by Chaerea, one Lupus, also of the Praetorian Guard, found the widowed Caesonia, with her small daughter Drusilla at her side, moaning over her slain husband. Quickly Lupus slit Caesonia's throat. Then he caught up the screaming child by the feet and crushed her skull against one of the marble columns of the bedchamber.

Early in the confusion of the assassination Chaerea had sent a conspirator to release Claudia and the three men. And Gaius was hardly dead before others of the Praetorian Guardsmen, determined to maintain the Roman army's ascendancy over the senate, proclaimed Caligula's uncle Claudius the new emperor. They had come upon him cowering in a secluded chamber in the Palace and, believing him the one Roman most likely to prove amenable to their demands, they

had pulled him out—not to assassinate him as he at first feared
—but to place him upon the now-vacant throne. In this they
were supported by the conniving Agrippa, who with his usual
diplomacy jockeyed between Camp Praetoria and the senate
to win Claudius' accession without bloodshed.

Before this momentous day and the night following it were
ended, the conspirators had also discovered the new emperor's
wife, Valeria Messalina, young but already experienced in
amours, in the bedchamber of yet another tribune of the guard
—the story would be repeated for many a year—and had
borne her promptly and triumphantly to her husband as
Rome's new empress.

37

Proconsul Publius Petronius laughed humorlessly when the
message arrived from Emperor Gaius commanding him to kill
himself because he had not obeyed the emperor's order to set
up the statue of Gaius in the Temple in Jerusalem. Twenty-
seven days earlier the report had arrived of the assassination
of the madman and the enthronement of Claudius. A storm
had driven the vessel bringing the message to the proconsul
far off its course and delayed for weeks its arrival in Syria.

Soon other reports were coming to Petronius and to Roman
governors in the various provinces of the far-spread empire of
the rapidly improving state of the government. Claudius was
quickly beginning to demonstrate that he was neither the
buffoon nor the pedant that many Romans had considered him
—as purposely, no doubt, he had led them to believe in order
to escape the attention of his insanely jealous nephew.

One of the first official acts of Claudius was his enlargement of Herod Agrippa's kingdom to embrace all that region in Palestine that half a century before had been governed by Agrippa's grandfather, dissolute but able old Herod the Great, including not only the tetrarchy that had been ruled by Herod Antipas and Herodias but also Judaea and Samaria that had been governed by Pontius Pilate. And at Agrippa's prompting, Claudius by decree had reaffirmed and restored to the Jews throughout the empire their right to worship undisturbed their Yahweh and to enjoy all the other privileges that had been assured them by Emperor Augustus.

In further making effective his decree, Claudius addressed a message to the Jews at Jerusalem announcing that he was returning to their custody the Temple vestments; for years they had been kept by the procurator in the Tower of Antonia and let out by him only when they were required in the Temple worship. In the ancient stronghold of the Chosen the news of the emperor's action was received joyfully by those of the fellowship of Jesus the Lord Messiah as well as by those orthodox Hebrews who still looked for the coming of their long-promised Messiah.

But the new emperor's redress of wrongs, some of them of long duration, was not confined to the Jewish population. He was diligent in righting old wrongs both at home and among the citizens and the subject peoples on the extended perimeter of the empire. He returned to provincial lands many of the works of art belonging to them that Gaius had confiscated and carried to Rome; he freed from prison numerous persons incarcerated because of fancied crimes against the majesty of Gaius; he returned to their homes many persons unjustly exiled and to their owners much property seized and confiscated by Gaius, including that of Senator Paulus, which, though legally confiscated, had not been appropriated by Gaius before he fell before the swords of Chaerea and his fellow Praetorians.

The new emperor's good works went beyond the righting of old wrongs, however. He busied himself with the accomplishing of reforms in every phase of the administration of govern-

ment. Immense public-work projects—among which were such
mammoth operations as the building of a great harbor at
Ostia with warehouses, docks, and other facilities to accommodate a tremendously increased volume of shipping; the finish-
ing of aqueducts begun by Caligula and the construction of
others; the draining of Lake Fucinus, which would employ
thirty thousand men over an eleven-year period; and countless
smaller construction works—gave work and encouragement to
thousands, who under Caligula had fallen upon evil days. Im-
provements were made in the procedures of the various courts;
Claudius himself sat on the bench long hours in the adjudi-
cation of lawsuits and the trial of men charged with the commission of all manners of crimes. The emperor labored earnestly and in good conscience to equate the administration of
Roman law with justice. The man who had been considered,
even by his mother Antonia, an other-world bookworm and a
shuffling, stammering bumpkin, studied day and long into the
night to improve the empire and to knit together its far-
stretching provinces by speeding communication and transportation from its imperial hub outward to every part of its rim
and from the rim back to Rome. His purposes in so doing
were many; one principal purpose was to join the capital and
even the most remote provincial cities more closely and fra-
ternally in the frame of empire. And after a time even the
more distant provinces were enjoying a prosperity they had little known since the days of the god Augustus.

Claudius had been raised to the throne literally on the
shoulders of the officers and men of the Praetorian Guard. So
the first thing he did as Caesar was to give fifteen thousand
sesterces to each member of the guard. This interest in the
military continued, and soon Claudius was leading efforts to
strengthen, better equip and better train, and generally mod-
ernize and bring to a new level of efficiency Rome's mighty
legions, not only those stationed at Rome and on the Italian
peninsula but also those quartered in Germania, Gaul, the
islands of Greece, Palestine, Africa, Spain, wherever Rome
held dominion.

But though Claudius worked indefatigably, he could not personally administer all the affairs of so great a complexity as the Roman empire. He was at the apex of a vast bureaucracy, and soon this bureaucracy was breeding a vast and burgeoning corruption. Freedmen and government slaves constituted the civil-service establishment that operated the government, and soon they had gained the ascendancy in power and wealth over even Rome's equestrian families. Two particularly, freedmen Narcissus and Pallas, would achieve wealth unequaled in all the empire. Narcissus, it was told about Rome, had amassed a fortune of some four hundred million sesterces; jealous Pallas, with only three hundred million, said Rome, felt himself poor. These fortunes and countless others more modest were obtained—insisted indignant Romans—through the sale of offices, extortion, the confiscation of estates of senators and other wealthy patricians and other illegal though highly remunerative schemes. Claudius, too busy himself to investigate an occasional charge that inadvertently his advisers permitted to reach his ears and too charitable to believe ill reports concerning the activities of his aides in their administration of the empire's affairs, was becoming the victim of these unconscionable opportunists.

But the emperor was becoming even more the victim of his wife's machinations.

Claudius was three times as old as the sixteen-year-old Valeria Messalina, whom he married a year after Caligula's enthronement. She was the daughter of Senator Marcus Valerius Messala Corvinus and his wife Domitia Lepida. Already Claudius had been three times married, once to a sister of the slain Prefect Sejanus, and in the affairs of the heart and the boudoir he was experienced extensively outside the bonds of matrimony. But soon all Rome was whispering, and many were proclaiming brashly, that Messalina, in the few years since she had attained the age of puberty, had employed more tutors and had herself given more instruction in the arts of Eros than even her grandfather-old husband had in a long life that had been both pedantic and considerably dissolute.

Almost from the moment of her husband's enthronement it was being told about Rome and even beyond the capital that the young empress was employing her lofty position not only to satiate her inordinate sexual appetite and to enrich her personal treasury but also—and this was far worse—to elevate to positions of honor and great enrichment her favorites and to ruin and destroy those who refused to succumb to her proffered charms or help her advance her villainous schemes.

For much of the calumny he would receive because of Messalina's evil conspiracies, Claudius himself was to blame. She had tested him and his yielding had emboldened her to go on to wilder conquests. Messalina had taken a fancy to a dancer then popular in Rome, one Mnester; she had with brazen coquetry sought to thrust herself upon him, but the dancer had resisted her. Furious, she had gone to Claudius and with a carefully contrived story had urged her husband to require Mnester to obey her commands; that the emperor did not know what those commands were did not deter him from granting her petition. Mnester was compelled to obey Messalina's commands until she wearied of giving them.

But having learned how to gain her way, the young empress used the scheme on other men—senators happily married, army officers of high or low station, muscled gladiators currently popular for their prowess in the arena, chariot race drivers. If they refused her advances, she contrived crimes with which to charge them, and invariably they were the losers; some lost vast estates, some lost their freedom, some even their lives. It was told about Rome that the wanton Messalina, carefully disguised, would steal from the Palace and on the streets seek out men more virile than her customary companions from the Palatine or Esquiline or Viminal mansions or even the noisome alleys of the Subura.

Messalina's crimes were ostensibly the crimes of Claudius. Estates were confiscated and senators and other leading Romans were slain upon the command of the emperor, who was coaxed by his young wife into believing perjured testimony and invented evidence contrived by her in her vindictive cunning and jealous rage. And Claudius, busy in the affairs of the empire, and in the boudoir with young companions provided generously by the empress herself, who was then left free of him for her own more diverting amours, continued happily ignorant of Messalina's evil machinations.

And the strange emperor, of whom little had been expected when he was thrust upon the throne by the Praetorian Guards, continued also to amaze Rome with the excellence of his leadership of the empire, which was prospering throughout its widespread provinces as it had not prospered since the days of the great Augustus. But when, some two years after his accession, he revealed plans to invade far distant Britannia and complete its subjugation, Rome whispered that the aging, crippled ruler was attempting a conquest he would certainly be unable to achieve.

But within less than a year from the time he had launched his plans, Claudius was back in the capital, completely victorious over the rebellious island province. Once again he had broken precedent; instead of bringing to Rome the captured Caractacus, king of Britannia, to have him dragged behind the imperial chariot before killing him for the entertainment of the exultantly screaming spectators enjoying the spectacle of a Roman triumph, Claudius had pardoned him.

In Gaul, Tribune Longinus, who had been assigned to a special duty in that region, and his wife Claudia learned from returning legionaries of the emperor's startling victory before it could even be acclaimed by the populace in Rome. And it was weeks later before couriers speeding eastward had borne the amazing news around the rim of the Great Sea to the cities of Greece, to Tarsus, to Antioch, and southward along the Palestine coast to Tyre, Caesarea, and Alexandria.

At Caesarea it reached the ears of King Herod Agrippa and the emperor's representative in Judaea, Tribune Lucius Aemilius Paulus.

✝

TARSUS

38

TARSUS

Rabbi Saul had eaten his usual frugal supper—a small round wheaten loaf, a bit of cheese, olives, two dried figs, and a cup of warm goat's milk. Now he sat at his window in the unlighted chamber's gloom of a fading afternoon and gazed across the darkening slit of the Cydnus to the distant range of the Taurus.

But Saul's thoughts were not upon the river, now fast clearing of moving vessels, nor on the mountains beyond, nor even of the tomb cut into the stone face of one of the nearer slopes. His musings rather were introspective and sombrous, and darkening like the mountains and the river and the many huddled houses.

O gracious Lord Messiah, my days are fast dropping away as the sun drops behind yonder range, and so little have I accomplished for Thee, so little, so little. When, O Lord Jesus, wilt Thou summon me to greater service, when wilt Thou make of me an instrument to work wonders in Thy name both among those of the Chosen and those of the Gentile brothers? When, Lord, when?

He sat in the enveloping gloom of his chamber and of his soul and reviewed the fled years since that day that, on the burning sands outside the walls of Damascus, the Lord Messiah had appeared to him in the blinding shaft of light and commissioned him to apostleship. He had given largely of his days and his nights in the intervening years, to contemplation of the Lord Messiah's nature and His purpose for him and to earnest effort to spread among men his brothers, Jew and Gentile alike, the good news of the Messiah's having come to earth, sacrificed Himself, and ascended to His Father. But Saul's harvest of souls joined to the Kingdom had been so lean, so short of the burgeoning he had envisioned.

When, O Lord, when? I pray Thee soon, lest my faith weaken with the weakening of my frame, lest my enthusiasm begin to flag with the slowing of my feet. Wilt Thou soon, O Lord, send me upon my mission, for must it not be, O Jesus Master, that Thou dost envision for me greater accomplishments in Thy name? Must it not be that for me Thou hast ordained journeyings far beyond these mountains into the lands of the Gentiles, voyages far across the waters of the Great Sea. Surely, O blessed Messiah, Thou didst not envision for my region of laboring for Thee only this small corner of Thy world, this pittance of land split by the river and lying between the mountains and the sea. Then send me forth, I pray Thee, O Lord, to Thy work. Set my feet upon the pathway, strengthen me to the task awaiting; enliven me, and give wings to my feet and a flame to my words——

A heavy belaboring on the outside door broke rudely into his prayerful meditating. He arose quickly and went to open the door. A soldier in the uniform of a Roman legionary stood at the portal.

"Peace be with you," the visitor greeted Saul, his voice pleasant.

"With you be peace," the rabbi replied as he peered intently at the man. Then his questioning expression brightened into a warm smile. "Tribune Paulus!" he exclaimed, recognizing the soldier. "Welcome! Do enter my humble house." He stood to one side and swept his arm in an arc to emphasize his invitation, and Paulus stepped inside. "Sit there, tribune"—Saul pointed to a stool near his seat at the window—"until I can light the lamp. I hadn't bestirred myself from my place there by the window until your rapping brought me to my feet."

When a moment later he had ignited the wick, and the flame had set their shadows dancing on the wall, the rabbi turned again to Paulus. "Have you eaten your evening meal, tribune? I have just finished supper, but there is still food in the house, even though it is hardly what a Roman military man is accustomed to have set on his board"—the rabbi smiled appreciatively. "It's just wheaten cakes, olives, figs, milk, a pomegranate. But of what I have, tribune, you are welcome to partake."

"I thank you, eastern cousin. Often as a soldier I would have been happy to have been privileged to share such food. But I ate my evening meal on board ship."

"Then you have just arrived in Tarsus? And are you coming from Rome, Antioch, or Caesarea this time?"

"I am on my way to Rome from Caesarea and Jerusalem."

"Then you must have news of Judaea and Samaria; perhaps you can inform me of what goes on among the brothers at Jerusalem." But suddenly his expression was apologetic. "Forgive me, tribune, for having not already asked you. But will you lodge with me here tonight? It would be a joy for me to have you under my roof, and I crave especially, too, to learn from you of the recent happenings both at Rome and in Palestine."

"I have come here hoping to lodge with you. I remember happily your hospitality when I stopped at Tarsus on my way to Rome with the dispatch from Publius Petronius. That was in the early spring"—he paused, thoughtful—"just a short time before Caligula's death. By Jupiter, eastern cousin, that was four years ago this spring past. I got to Rome in time to report to the emperor at the banquet being given him by King Herod Agrippa. And now Agrippa's dead." He shrugged. "Time flies, indeed, Paulus. We're getting old, eh?"

"Yes. But tell me, tribune, about the death of King Agrippa. We've had many reports, but they are at variance."

"I can well understand how they would be. Agrippa was both greatly beloved and thoroughly detested. The high priest and his party fawned upon him because in his outward appearance he set great store by following every jot and tittle, as you Jews would say it, of the Jewish law's requirements. But the followers of the Galilean carpenter who is so beloved by you hated Agrippa bitterly. You know that he ordered that one of the fellowship's leaders be executed, do you not?"

"Yes, the grievous news came to us. The man of whom you speak was James bar Zebedee, one of the Messiah's apostles. King Agrippa also imprisoned Simon bar Jonah, another of the group. He would have been killed too had he not suddenly been freed by an angel sent by Yahweh to deliver him, according to reports that came to members of the Messiah's fellowship here."

Tribune Paulus smiled knowingly. "Reports came to Caesarea, too. Simon was mysteriously released during the night and was slipped out of Jerusalem. He had been imprisoned, by order of Agrippa, in the dungeon of Fortress Antonia, where he was chained by his ankles and wrists to rings in the wall of his cell. But in early morning, when a new quaternion of guards came to relieve those on duty, it was discovered that he had been freed from the chains, his cell door was open, and so were the outer doors of the prison. And Simon was missing. That much is known."

"What is your explanation of his disappearance, tribune?"

"His friends of the Galilean's fellowship, I presume, spread the story that an angel of your Yahweh came down and released him." Paulus smiled wryly. "But other reports were abroad, too, that the angel who released him was a Roman soldier, one—or maybe two or three—of the guards who in secret had joined this fellowship of the crucified Galilean." He shrugged, gestured with hands outflung. "I think the angel was a man, or maybe more than one. But you may believe either version. The important thing, certainly to that fisherman, is that he escaped with his head. But there's another significant thing. If a Roman intervened—or several—to help Simon escape, it proves—as some of us already know, in fact—that this sect is fast gaining adherents who are not of your Chosen People, eastern cousin, even among, as you would doubtless express it, us pagan Gentiles. Is not that true?"

"It is true, indeed, tribune. Even here in Tarsus the Way of the Lord Messiah is beginning to embrace as true brothers many folk not of the Chosen. And it is to these Gentiles our brothers that the Lord Messiah commissioned me His apostle to carry the message of His love and His salvation. Of this I have no doubt. I only wish the more effectively to be about my commission." His eyes were wistful, his tone calm though assured. Paulus had the feeling that the rabbi, though his eyes were on the tribune's face, was looking beyond him, hardly seeing him. But quickly Saul's expression changed; his interest was in the present again. "As for King Agrippa's death, tribune —you were going to tell me about it. Conflicting stories concerning it, too, have come to us here." He paused, and Paulus nodded agreement.

"Yes, the circumstances of his death provided a certain aura of mystery that led to rumors being circulated over the province and even to regions as far away as Rome that the gods or your Yahweh, depending on the one who was relating it, had decreed the king's death out of jealousy, because he had not rebuked the people when they bowed down to him as a god."

Saul smiled wryly, but offered no observation. "What were the circumstances?" he asked. "Were you in Caesarea at the time?"

"Yes. I was seated near him when he was stricken. It was at the amphitheater. Agrippa had arranged an elaborate program of gladiatorial shows in honor of Emperor Claudius. It was the second day of the shows, and a multitude filled the great stadium. Agrippa had dressed that day in a resplendent uniform of silver that shone with such a dazzling brilliance in the sunshine that it hurt the eyes of those who looked on him. That gave his flatterers an excuse for calling out that the king was now a god and falling on their faces before him and imploring his mercy. But Agrippa did not rebuke them; he smiled broadly and appeared to be enjoying the new status accorded him by his fawning subjects. It was at that moment that Yahweh or the Roman gods—and Agrippa in Palestine professed to worship Yahweh and in Rome appeared to venerate the Roman gods—struck him down."

Saul shook his head. "I think it was neither Yahweh's

jealousy nor his vengeance. It is true that our God is a jealous God in the sense that He will countenance our worship of none other, even of those others who are but fancied and have no existence, but He is likewise a God of infinite mercy and love, as He is exemplified in His Lord Messiah. Surely the Lord Messiah would not have struck Agrippa down. He did not deal that way with any man, even the high priest, even Pontius Pilate." Suddenly his eyes were wistful again and he seemed to be addressing himself rather than the tribune. "He didn't strike down even me, and I was the chiefest of His enemies, praise His blessed, precious name!"

But his reflective mood passed quickly. "What was the manner of his death?" he asked. "Did he fall over dead in that instant?"

"No. On the contrary, Paulus, it was a slow and agonizing death. I was watching him when he had his first seizure. It was while the throng was doing obeisance to him. Momentarily he had looked above his head and discovered an owl perched on one of the ropes supporting the canopy above the royal box. The sight of the owl terrified him; he cried out that its appearance there was an omen of his imminent death. It seems that during the period when Agrippa was held prisoner by Tiberius he had one day seen an owl in a tree nearby. The owl, he had been told on that occasion by a star-gazing fellow prisoner, was an omen of good fortune foretelling his early release. But when he should again see an owl above him, said that old fellow, it would be for him a herald announcing his death within a few days. So when some days later, after Tiberius' death, he was freed from his bonds, Agrippa remembered the man's prophecies and evidently set much store by them. When at Caesarea he saw the owl, he was seized with terror and told those about him that Yahweh would shortly require of him his life because of his failure to rebuke the multitude who had given to him the worship that should have been accorded only to Divinity.

From the amphitheater, Paulus revealed, King Agrippa had been borne to the palace. There after five days of intense suffering he had died. The agony in his stomach had recalled to older residents, Paulus had been told, the ailment that many years before had taken off Agrippa's grandfather, old Herod the Great.

"Claudius proposed to name Agrippa's son king to succeed his father," the tribune continued. "But the emperor's counselors insisted that the seventeen-year-old youth, who was then living at the court in Rome, was too young and lacking in administrative experience to have the responsibilities of kingship thrust upon him. Later when he was a little more mature he could be given the kingdom. To this the emperor agreed, and it was decided that Agrippa junior would remain in Rome and a procurator would be sent out to rule Palestine as in the days of Pontius Pilate. Cuspius Fadus was sent to Caesarea as procurator."

"Has any word come to Rome or to you at Caesarea concerning Pilate's fate since he was sent into banishment? In Tarsus we received the report that he had been exiled, but we have had no word since then."

"I've heard nothing," Paulus said. "Perhaps when I get back to the capital I may get a report, particularly if Longinus and Claudia have returned from Gaul. You remember that they were married soon after Caligula granted Claudia a divorce from Pilate."

"Indeed, yes." Saul's eyes brightened. "But I've heard no word about them since you were here last. Do you know whether she remained interested in the Lord Messiah after her return to Rome? And what of Longinus? Was he still remorseful because of the role he had in the crucifixion?" Saul leaned nearer, his eyes sharply questioning. "Tribune, here at Tarsus we get reports from time to time that the fellowship of the Messiah is gaining adherents among even the powerful at Rome. Could it be that the tribune and his wife are of that number?"

"I don't know, Cousin Paulus. But I can tell you that I wouldn't be surprised to learn that they are of that group. I do know that in Rome there are Romans of the equestrian families, as well as freedmen and slaves, who worship your Yahweh. I suspect, too, that there are those from families of wealth and power who secretly belong to the Galilean's fellowship, though surely it would be indiscreet to reveal it."

They sat late into the evening talking. Before they sought their beds for the remainder of the night they were speaking to one another in utter frankness, and Saul confessed his disappointment and chagrin at having been unable during these last years at Tarsus to accomplish more for the Lord Messiah. "But I have not lost hope or faith," he assured his guest, "for the Lord Messiah declared to me that He would make me an instrument in His hands to bear unto the Gentiles His brothers and to those of the Chosen the good news of His mighty salvation." His eyes were shining with a resurgence of hope in the Lord Messiah's promise. "And one day, tribune, I shall bear this glorious gospel even unto Rome and the lands beyond! Of this I have no doubt."

"I hope so, eastern cousin. And when you are in Rome, you will be more than welcome to lodge in our domus."

"That will be pleasant, tribune, and I thank you. And even before then"—Saul's eyes warmed and his tone softened—"I trust that the report may be brought to me, either by you yourself or another, that you, along with Tribune Longinus and Lady Claudia, have entered happily into our fellowship in the Lord Messiah."

Early the next morning the two arose, and when they had breakfasted simply, Saul walked with Paulus down to the docks on the Cydnus and stood talking with him as the last of the bales and crates of merchandise were put aboard.

A moment later from his place beside the rail of the vessel Paulus raised his arm in the salute of farewell. "Until one day in Rome, eastern cousin!" he called out.

"If not before, until one good day in Rome!" Saul shouted his response.

Slowly, pondering the tribune's short visit and the reports brought by him, Saul walked the cobbled ways toward his lodging and the tasks to be resumed in his service of the Lord

Messiah, a service that of late years had seemed so small and of such little lasting effect.

But Paulus' unexpected short sojourn with him had given a new soaring to the rabbi's flagging spirits, and his own declaration to the tribune that the Lord Messiah had set him apart for a great labor among the Gentiles as well as among his own brothers of the Chosen People had served to strengthen his hope and his faith. "By the grace of the Most High God and His Son our Lord Messiah," he declared in words unspoken as he trudged along the cobbles, "I yet will bear unto our brothers of the Chosen and of the Gentiles in those regions even as far distant as mighty Rome the glorious gospel of our Lord Messiah's grace and salvation!"

Two days later Saul had returned from his work at the loom and was preparing to eat his evening meal when there was another sharp rapping on his door. He strode across the chamber and opened it. At the threshold stood a tall, muscular man whose heavy black beard fanned out across his thick chest. The man looked familiar; Saul's forehead crinkled and he squinted with his better eye.

"Praise the Most High and our Lord Messiah," said the stranger, "I have been led aright. Peace be with you, Saul my brother."

"With you be peace. I— Joseph! Joseph bar Nabas!" He sprang forward a pace and the two embraced warmly. Then they stood back and each studied the other. "Welcome, Joseph, to my humble lodging. Welcome, my brother." He caught Joseph's arm and led him into the chamber. "You have arrived in time to partake with me of the supper I was just sitting down to eat." Saul pointed toward a pitcher and basin on the shelf nearby. "Wash, Joseph, and let us eat."

Joseph had arrived that afternoon from Seleucia, he said. The vessel on which he had sailed from Antioch's port had left in early morning and the winds had been favorable. From the docks he had gone at once to the synagogue and there had been given directions how to find Saul's house. He had found it without difficulty.

"But all these years I had supposed you were at Jerusalem," Saul said.

"I was there until King Agrippa began to persecute the fellowship with such vigor," Joseph revealed, as his countenance darkened. "You have heard how he sought, with the high priest's warm support, to stamp out what he and the high priest's party considered a heresy undermining the true worship of Yahweh, how he had James bar Zebedee killed and was planning to kill Simon of Capernaum——"

"Who was conducted from the Fortress of Antonia dungeon by an angel of the Lord Messiah——"

"Then you have heard the story?"

"Yes. And of King Agrippa's strange death. But where is Simon now?"

"He divides his time between Galilee and Judaea. Lately he has been on a journey in the coastal region of Judaea and Samaria spreading the story of the Lord Messiah even among the Gentiles. At Caesarea, as I learned from brothers of the Way coming from Judaea, he was instrumental in converting a Roman centurion, one Cornelius, and his household and baptizing them into the fellowship."

They talked late into the night. Saul inquired about many brothers and sisters of the faith of the Messiah and of how the fellowship was faring. Joseph bar Nabas reported how the persecution of Agrippa had scattered many abroad so that already groups of the Messiah's followers were putting down roots in communities far removed from Jerusalem. At Antioch, for example, the fellowship had grown until it likely exceeded in numbers the group in the holy city of the Jews. How, he wanted to know of Saul, was the building of the Messiah's kingdom progressing at Tarsus and the region of Cilicia?

Saul's countenance darkened and his forehead crinkled in tiny ridges. "Not, because of my ineffectiveness, I fear, in a way pleasing to our Lord Messiah," he replied. "Though I have with industry sown the seed and cultivated the ground, I have been unable to reap a large harvest. And this despite the fact that at Damascus He told Ananias to bear to me the promise that I would be used to work in His name wonders among not only us of the Chosen but likewise among the Gentile brothers. And I yet rely upon that promise, Joseph, though thus far few wonders have I been permitted to work for Him."

"Perhaps, O Saul my beloved brother, you labor in the wrong field. Perhaps the Messiah wishes you to seek another field for your sowing."

"But I have besought of Him that He would show me the way I should go, that He would point out to me the fields wherein I should labor, and I have listened with ears attuned for His gentlest whispering. Yet I have heard nothing, Joseph. But I doubt not that He will yet send me into far lands to accomplish great things for His kingdom, and that in due season He will make known the way I should travel and direct my feet into those cities——"

"He is doing that now, O Saul my brother! Praise Yahweh Most High, praise our Lord Messiah!" Joseph's broad face was suddenly alight; his dark eyes shone in the flame of Saul's lamp. "He is giving His message through me, through me, O Saul, He is pointing out to you the way He would have you go! I doubt it not. He, O my brother Saul, has sent me to you!" Joseph's eyes were ablaze; the flame in them burned brighter than the tiny reflected flame in each of them from the dancing light of Saul's lamp.

"But how, O Joseph? How is He pointing through you the way for my feet to tread? And what is that way? Where does it lead?" Now Saul's weak, peering eyes were likewise ablaze with a new excitement, a quickened lively interest.

"I was sent to fetch you." Bar Nabas laid his big hand firmly on the shorter brother's shoulder. "Antioch is a great city. There are many Jews there, some of our Way, but many of the ancient way of our fathers and ignorant of the coming of our Lord Messiah and unredeemed. And there are likewise countless Gentiles assembled there from every nation of the earth, to whom the gladsome story of our Lord should be told." He leaned nearer, and his radiant eyes searched the eyes of the rabbi of Tarsus. "Among them who reside in Antioch and the region roundabout, O Saul, you could accomplish wonders indeed, both among those of the yet unknowing Chosen and the Gentiles unnumbered!"

On the morrow Saul arose early and went into the market-place where he arranged for the selling of his house and its furnishings and other possessions impracticable for transporting. Then he visited the synagogue and joined once more in the worship of Yahweh Most High. All the next day, until the sun had dropped low beyond the range of the Taurus, he spent in the homes of dearer ones among his brothers of the Way. The last visit he made was to the tomb, hewn from the rock high on the slope above the Cydnus, that held his loved ones.

On the third morning after the arrival of Joseph bar Nabas in Tarsus, while the sun was still above the Amanus Mountains beyond the Gulf of Issus, which thrust like a blunt thumb into eastern Cilicia, the two reunited brothers in the Way went aboard a vessel that shortly sailed down the Cydnus and on entering the Great Sea turned southeastward toward Seleucia.

✝

39 ANTIOCH

39

In population the vast city on the Orontes yielded place only to Rome and Alexandria; in carnality, in pollutions of idol-worship, in the utter corruption of a seething horde of polyglot peoples drawn together from the far ends of the earth, Antioch yielded first position to no region in all the empire.

And set down in the midst of this sea of putrescence, like a sweet-aired verdant island raised above the foul-odored waters of an evil morass, was the colony of Hebrews clustered about their synagogue. The several structures of the synagogue area formed the pulsing heart as well as soul of this community of worshipers of Yahweh, a still homogeneous body that might well have been transplanted whole from the region of Jerusalem, though many of its members were Jews born at Antioch of parents and grandparents long resident in the Syrian capital. There were even among them some of adult years who had never visited Jerusalem.

Out from the synagogue along narrow, cluttered cobbled ways in an enlarging circle pushed the homes and shops of these Antioch Jews. Some residences and working places were hidden-away hovels on noisome alleys, some were comfortably adequate, a few were situated on the better streets in affluent neighborhoods and were even pretentious.

On his arrival with Joseph bar Nabas from Tarsus, Saul found lodging with a Jewish family, and soon afterward, in a shop operated by an opulent Jew, he obtained employment at his trade of weaving goat's hair. This shop, in which the weavers much of every day except the Sabbath sat at their clacking looms, was situated down near the docks. Often on pleasant days the rabbi with other workers in that vicinity would sit in the sunshine on the wharf, and as they ate hurriedly of their frugal lunches, they would watch the stevedores, their bronzed, muscled bodies naked but for loincloths of many colors and dripping with sweat, as they tugged at boxed and baled shipments of merchandise being moved between the warehouses and incoming and departing vessels. Sometimes Saul would arrive at the wharf area when the slaves and their overseers were having a short respite from their arduous labors, and then he would speak to them of the young Galilean workingman, a poor carpenter from a scorned village, whom God had sent to live for a time on earth. This youth, who was known by the name of Jesus ben Joseph, as an Emanation of Yahweh Most High, the one and only God, had come down from heaven to live a simple, upright life of love and service and thereby show to men His brothers the nature and omnipotent love of God the Father and to provide through any man's acceptance of Him perfect redemption and salvation.

"Nor did He in his short career of service to men His brothers permit Himself to escape any of the sufferings of men. Not one of you, my brothers, be you bound or free"—Saul raised his arm to gesticulate and lifted his voice—"has experienced in his body the pain He experienced, and for your sakes. He, the Son of God, the one with God, the creator, the ruler of all men and all creation, He Who did no man ill but did all men good was scorned and rejected, betrayed, deserted, was made to suffer the pain of seeing His offered love, His offered redemption and salvation refused. Yea, my brothers, He the Lord Messiah, the Ruler of tetrarchs and kings and emperors, the Lord of the earth and the uncounted stars of the heavens, was seized and bound and spit upon and scourged almost to His death, and was then led forth to suffer the ultimate in humiliation and rejection and agony of the flesh, death on the despised cross. . . ."

Inevitably at this point in Saul's dramatic narrative every eye would be fastened upon the rabbi's earnest countenance and many mouths would be agape. And before anyone broke the spell of his presentation, he would resume the story of the Lord Messiah's triumph over His shameful death through His willing His resurrection, and of His subsequent return to a heavenly reunion with His Father. Often, if sufficient time remained, he would continue his recital to reveal his own amazing experience, how from the Lord Messiah's bitterest enemy he had become, in the thunderclap of a lightning bolt's descent, His adoring slave and redeemed brother.

Frequently someone in the group, sometimes several of them, would question the rabbi, sometimes even interrupting his discourse.

"But, rabbi, you see me and my condition," such a man might exclaim. "How say you that such a one as this God who came to earth in the form of a simple man, a man of earth rather than of might and power, but who nevertheless possesses all authority, could be concerned with the likes of me, a slave. Though once I was a person of affluence, I am now entirely dispossessed of everything, even almost of hope itself?"

"The Lord Messiah, the Emanation of the Most High, the One with God, sees neither your former affluence, O my brother, nor your present enslavement. He sees only into your innermost soul; He sees neither your vanished wealth and authority nor your lost freedom nor yet your shackling bonds. He sees you only as a child of the Father, a brother of the Lord Messiah, and His concern for you is not one whit less than His concern for the emperor himself. O brother, He yearns to see you reach out to accept of Him redemption and eternal salvation!"

And over and over a questioner would ask: "But how, O rabbi, can I so reach out and accept this redemption and salvation, I who am of the lowest of the worms of earth? How can I go to the Temple at Jerusalem and offer an acceptable sacrifice, I who am held fast by these bonds to the interminable pushing and pulling of these crates and boxes and bales of endless merchandise from ship to wharf and wharf to ship?"

"The Lord Messiah neither requires nor wishes of you an ox or a lamb or a brace of doves, O brother in bonds. He wishes only you. He wants your penitence, your trust in Him, your utter love. And that love you can give Him here, in this moment, without so much as the lifting of one finger."

One day when he was discoursing on the Lord Messiah to a group that had assembled hastily in a marketplace near the synagogue, he had thus answered a man who had so questioned him. And his words were challenged by a tall youth, square of shoulders and earnest of countenance, sharp-eyed and warmly attentive, who seemed to be engrossed in the rabbi's recital.

"So you say, rabbi. But how? How does one give Him one's trust, one's penitence, one's complete love? What is the way by which one gives himself to this Lord Messiah, this holy one of whom you speak with such eloquence and convincing power?"

Saul saw that the young man was questioning him out of the depths of his soul, out of a yearning and a great eagerness to comprehend all those things of which the rabbi had been discoursing. His heart was warmed to the youth and he felt himself drawn irresistibly to him; he desired mightily to bring him into the fellowship of the Lord Messiah, to know him as a beloved young brother in the Way. He fastened his weak eyes upon his questioner, and his tone was warm and his smile inviting.

"But I know of no prescribed way, no one way, my young friend," answered Saul, "by which one gives himself to another. It is an action that proceeds from the heart, from the inmost depths of one's being. Does not one give as one wishes to give?" He studied the youth's open and frank, inquiring countenance. "What you seek to know, is it not, is what is the sign that one has given himself to the Lord Messiah, what is the seal of the gift thus given?"

The tall young man nodded. "Perhaps, O rabbi. Is there then no sign by which the world about him can know that a man has given himself to this Jesus of whom you speak, that he is of the fellowship of the Lord Messiah? And surely there must be some ceremonial of entrance into this group, some rite of initiation."

"Our brothers and sisters of the Way wear no distinctive garb. But the world about them know that they are followers of Jesus the Christ the Lord Messiah by the lives they live. Already they are known here in Antioch by their soberness and good propriety"—the hint of a smile lightened Saul's solemn countenance—"and certain of the loosely living Antiochenes even in derision refer to them as the 'anointed ones' and 'the Christians.'" He paused, and his eyes swept the small group before him. "Though the name was coined as a term of scorn, it will survive through the ages, I verily believe, as a badge of honor." Then he turned to give attention again to the youth who had questioned him. "But is there a ceremonial, a rite of initiation, you ask. Only, my young friend, the rite of repentance, and baptism unto a new life, and faith in the Lord Messiah, and obedience unto the law of Yahweh Most High."

The young man's eyes were solemn with bewilderment. "But, O rabbi, I am not of your Chosen People. I am a Greek."

"Then for you there is the additional rite of circumcision, and in Tarsus and here in Antioch there have been many Gentiles who have submitted gladly in order to bear upon their bodies the sign——"

"The sign of Israel," the questioner interrupted Saul. "But I am a Greek, O sir, and I am proud of the body the Creator, whom you call Yahweh, gave me. Must I mutilate my body and become a Jew and an obeyer of the burdensome laws of the Jews in order to be a follower of the Lord Messiah of whom you have been speaking?" The young man's earnest eyes were searching Saul. Saul knew he had asked an honest question, one not offered as an entrapment, but a valid question demanding an honest answer. But what should he say to the question?

"I have perceived, my friend," he began, "that you were not born of the Chosen, as we Jews describe ourselves, but were a Gentile. Yet our Lord Messiah was not sent by the Father to bring redemption and salvation to us of the Chosen alone, but unto all men whom He calls His brothers, whether they be Jews or Greeks, Romans, Egyptians, Ethiopians, Asssyrians, worshipers of Yahweh or Zeus, Jupiter, Astarte, Moloch or any other in the panegyric of those worshiped." Saul knew well that he had evaded the question the young Greek was asking. And so did the Greek.

"But does this Lord Messiah insist that all these others become Jews before he accepts them as his brothers?"

"It is a hard question, my young brother," Saul admitted frankly. "And I must be returning now to my loom. But can you come to my lodging, even tonight perhaps, and let us put our minds to answering it?"

"I can indeed, rabbi."

"That is good. Then come, and break bread with me, and we shall talk, and the Lord Messiah, I know it, will give us the answer." He leveled his eyes on the youth's intent face. "What is your name, my friend?"

"I am called Titus, rabbi."

Throughout the afternoon as Saul rhythmically passed the shuttle of the woof back and forth between the threads of the warp he thought of the question asked by the Gentile Titus. He considered and he reasoned, but the steady clack-clack of his loom brought him no answer. Nor in his praying to the Lord Messiah was the answer provided.

"But does this Lord Messiah insist that all these others become Jews before he accepts them as his brothers?" O my Lord Messiah, dost Thou? Must a Greek indeed become a Jew? But how, O Lord, how? The sign upon the body of the Jewish male is but the sign of his Jewishness, is it not? It is but the sign of his race. But a Greek is not of the race of the Chosen. Then why indeed must a Greek make upon his body the sign of Jewishness? And if to enter the brotherhood of the Messiah a Greek has only to become a Jew in his faith, in his religion, if he has only to become a worshiper of Yahweh rather than of Zeus, why take upon himself the sign of a people of whom he is not? Why, O my Lord Messiah?

In the evening Titus came to Saul's house, and when they had eaten supper, they sat a long while. And to Titus the rabbi talked of the Lord Messiah, of His earthly life and His love and sacrifice for all mankind, and he related the often-repeated story of how in one moment of fire and thunder he himself had been changed from a rampaging enemy of the Lord Messiah into a devoted servant and brother.

And when Saul, looking into Titus' eyes, saw them rimming with tears of repentance and faith and exaltation and a newly found joy that could not be contained, and when he heard upon the young man's lips confession of his errors and his wanderings from the path of rectitude, and a happy declaration of his newfound faith in the Lord Messiah and Jehovah Most High of all the earth and the sun and stars, and his determination to abide happily with all men his brothers in that love, then the rabbi took water and baptized young Titus and welcomed him into the Way of the Lord Messiah.

But on this momentous night Saul the rabbi did not lift up his knife to carve upon the flesh of his Gentile brother, Titus, the sign of the Chosen.

40

The new brother Titus quickly became one of the most devoted and useful of the workers in the vineyard of the Lord Messiah at Antioch. Since he had entered the fellowship not as a Gentile converted to Judaism with the sign of the Chosen upon his flesh but simply as a Greek owning allegiance to Yahweh and the Lord Jesus and professing his love for Him, Titus was all the more effective in bringing his Gentile broth-

ers into the fold of the Messiah. And in the young man Saul
had great pride and for him an abounding love.

So when distressing tidings came to Antioch that the brothers in Jerusalem, because of the long-enduring famine in Judaea, were in dire want and a collection was taken among
those at Antioch and dispatched to Jerusalem in the hands of
Saul and Joseph bar Nabas, the two messengers took with
them their Gentile brother Titus.

Presentation of Titus to the Jerusalem brothers of the Way
provoked a controversy that for a time was heated, however,
because some of the more legalistic of the Jews insisted that,
before the Greek convert could become a true member of the
fellowship of the Lord Messiah, he would have to be circumcised and make himself fully amenable to all the obligations
and requirements of the Mosaic law. Others of the fellowship,
though they were not in agreement with these determined
legalists, were disposed to end the discord by yielding, at least
to the extent of effecting a compromise by decreeing the circumcision of Titus.

But Saul was adamant in his stand—the Judaizing of his
beloved young brother was not necessary to the Lord Messiah.
And soon he was supported in his stand by the more powerful
ones of the fellowship, including rugged Simon bar Jonah of
the Lord's original twelve disciples, John bar Zebedee, another
of the twelve and brother of the martyred James, and James
ben Joseph, the Lord's brother and leader of the Jerusalem fellowship. These agreed with Saul their Jewish brother that
Gentiles who wished to enter the way need not be circumcised
or compelled to take upon themselves the onerous burden of
upholding the Jewish law in its every minutia. The Lord Jesus
before returning to His Father had admonished His disciples to
go into all the world and preach the tidings of His redemption
and salvation, these Jerusalem leaders remembered, and were
not the Gentiles a great segment of that world? And had the
Lord even remotely suggested that the multitude of Gentiles in-
habiting the earth were first to be made Jews?

And for the task of leading the forces who would carry the

gospel to the Gentile world, who was better equipped than Saul the Jew, who had once sat at the feet of Rabban Gamaliel and had been reared among the Gentiles and was acquainted with their histories, traditions, customs, and even their religions? It would be fitting likewise that Simon the Rock, the fisherman of Galilee, the intimate friend of the Master, should labor to extend the Kingdom primarily among his fellow Jews. Simon would go to the Jews, that would be the expedient course, and Saul his brother, educated, a cosmopolite, possessed both of a wealth of knowledge and great powers of reasoning, would journey widely among the Gentile nations sowing the seeds of the Kingdom.

When Saul learned of the views of these his brothers in Jerusalem—he never could forget how once he had striven with such high dedication to destroy them—he was deeply grateful, as they were grateful for his and his companions' work of succor among them, and he was seized anew with a deep yearning to set out upon the task to which he was still confident the Lord Messiah had called him, a task that in the main remained yet unfulfilled.

But was it indeed the will of the Lord Messiah that he should turn aside from working among the Jews his brothers? Here in the ancient capital of Israel, he and Joseph bar Nabas and Titus were successfully employed in the advancement of the Messiah's Kingdom. Should he strike out into Gentile lands where dangers untold might await his coming? He was being used to reap a harvest of Hebrew souls unto the Lord Messiah. Should he abandon the harvest ripe for the reaping, a harvest of his own brothers of the ancient faith? Should he withhold the bread of salvation from the mouths of his own to offer it to a pagan horde scattered unto the four winds? If it was the Messiah's will that he should cease his labors at Jerusalem and undertake to spread the tidings among the Gentiles, why then was his preaching among the Chosen being so rewarded?

Once again Saul feared he had lost sight of the way the Lord Messiah had ordained his feet to tread; once again dark doubt began to cloud and shadow the course of his reasoning. In earnest prayer to Yahweh Most High and His Lord Messiah, Saul pleaded to be shown plainly the road he was henceforth to travel.

One day he was thus pleading as he lay stretched face downward upon the stones in a courtyard of the Temple, where he had gone regularly, after the Jewish manner, during his Jerusalem sojourn, when a vision of the Lord Messiah appeared before him. The mosaic of the pavement dissolved, the columns of the great porches swam away, the white marbled walls of the glorious Temple and the shimmering bronze of the Beautiful Gate faded into nothingness; he saw only the glory of His Lord. He lay inert, as he had lain that day on the sands outside the gate of Damascus, and listened for the voice to speak.

"'Arise, Saul, my brother, and go hence." The tone was gentle but authoritative. "Your mission is not to the Chosen; they will reject your testimony concerning me. Henceforth I shall send you unto far places as my apostle to the Gentile brothers."

Saul stood to his feet. The marble columns, the walls, the resplendent Beautiful Gate, the worshipers, the traffickers in animals and doves for the sacrifices—all were settled again plainly in their places. The effulgence of the moment was gone from his eyes. But as Saul of Tarsus crossed the great Court of the Gentiles toward the Gate Shalleketh he knew of a certainty that the glory had found lodgment forever within his inmost being.

That evening in the upper room of Mary of Cyprus, where with Joseph bar Nabas he had been lodging during the sojourn in Jerusalem, he told Joseph of the transforming experience at the Temple. "So, Joseph my brother," he observed as he ended his recital, "I must be about my commission. Tomorrow, if I can arrange it that quickly, I shall be leaving for Antioch. Will you be going with me?"

Bar Nabas nodded. "I am ready," he said.

"Ready to go with me unto the Gentiles, my brother?"

"If it is the will of our Lord Messiah, yes, Saul my brother."

Saul's eyes were shining. "May the Lord Messiah so will it

that together we begin the great task—Joseph bar Nabas, once of Cyprus, and he who was Saul of Tarsus, one Paulus, apostles of the Lord Jesus to the world of the Gentiles!"

On the morrow they set forth from Jerusalem for Antioch, and with them to serve them as their young brother in the Lord Messiah they took John Mark, son of Mary.

Days later, arrived at Antioch, the two revealed to the leaders of the fellowship there the Lord Messiah's commissioning of Saul and Joseph's impelling desire to accompany him to the undertaking of the great task. After much consideration and examination and prayer and fasting, the brethren of the Way were called together, and they laid their hands upon Joseph and Saul and ordained them to go forth unto the world of the unnumbered Gentiles.

From the harbor at Seleucia, with John Mark to attend their needs, the missionaries sailed southwestward toward Salamis on the island of Cyprus.

†

ASIA MINOR

41

The name of Jesus the Lord Messiah was not unknown among the dwellers on the island of Cyprus. Tidings of the Galilean's mission of redemption and salvation, his sacrificial death and resurrection had been brought to the Cypriotes on the lips even of certain Jerusalem Jews of the young fellowship fleeing from the fierce persecution of Rabbi Saul of Tarsus.

But in those early days following the crucifixion of the Nazarene, the small fellowship in the region of Cyprus, like the cells at Jerusalem and other places, was considered nothing more than a frail shoot growing out of the trunk of the tree of Judaism, and was regarded as an unorganized and undisciplined grouping of slaves from the copper mines and other unsophisticated poor and unfortunate folk, credulous and given to harboring strange superstitions, drawn together around the person of a now-vanished Galilean mystic. Many queer sects had sprung up out of the fertile soil of the ancient religion of the Chosen, bloomed for a while, and then shriveled and died. So, prophesied the orthodox sons of Abraham, would this new cult of the Galilean shrivel and die.

And indeed as Saul and Joseph bar Nabas, journeying westward, spoke in the synagogue at Salamis and in many others in their trudging back and forth across the mountainous spine of the island, they appeared to be accomplishing little in the adding of souls to the fellowship. In most communities visited by them the missionaries were received with indifference, in some even with a measure of suspicion and fear, though nowhere did anyone offer to do them violence.

"Is not this smaller one he who in Jerusalem some years ago sought to destroy those of the Way?" sometimes one brother in the fellowship would ask another. "And this other, is he not also an accomplice of the Temple leaders bent upon doing us ill? Is not their appearing among us but an artifice by which they would entrap us into revealing that we are of the fellowship? Let us therefore have nothing to do with these cunning deceivers."

Nor in their crossing of the island of Cyprus did they have any measurable success among the Gentile population, to whom they preached in the public squares and the marketplaces when the Chosen refused to heed their messages delivered in the synagogues.

But as the two neared the western end of the island, reports of their mission came to Sergius Paulus, the Roman proconsul, in his home in Paphos, the capital of Cyprus and seat of the government, and on their arrival in the city Paulus had them brought before him. As the emperor Tiberius had been, and as many others among the equestrians of Roman society continued to be, the proconsul was concerned about what the varying arrangements of the heavenly bodies might portend and so he maintained, at the court, astrologers to keep him informed of the meaning of the movements of the planets and stars. The chief of these and the one possessed of greatest cunning was a Jew who went by the name of Bar Jesus. This man stood at the proconsul's side as Saul and Joseph bar Nabas entered the proconsul's audience chamber.

When Sergius Paulus learned that the smaller of his two visitors was a Roman citizen with a Roman name derived from a family at the capital to whom he himself was related, he was intrigued. This interest mounted as the two visitors related to him the story of the Galilean carpenter sent by Jehovah, the Yahweh Most High of the Jews, ruler of all the earth and the heavens, to redeem the world and bring to men eternal salvation; and the astrologer Bar Jesus, fearful that in the proconsul's regard they might supplant him, began to challenge them with skillfully contrived questions and interruptions.

Saul's indignation rose, his eyes flamed. He paused in his discourse to Sergius Paulus, thrust forth his hand and waggled his forefinger sternly at the sardonically smiling Bar Jesus.

"You son of the Devil!" the impassioned Saul shouted. "You enemy of righteousness! Will you never stop twisting the clear understanding of the Lord's ways!" His wrathful words terrified the now-cringing astrologer. "You are blind to all things spiritual! You servant of the Evil One, as it was once upon me, so will the hand of the Lord be now upon you, and you will be unseeing for a season!"

With one spread palm shielding his eyes and the other arm outthrust and probing, the stricken charlatan stumbled from the chamber.

But from that day forth, Paulus the apostle to the Gentiles believed in all faith, as he took ship with Joseph bar Nabas and John Mark for Pamphylia on the southern coast of Asia Minor, that a light of understanding and a flame of love would illuminate and give warmth to the new life of Sergius Paulus, proconsul of Cyprus.

It was early summer when the three messengers sailed from the harbor at Paphos. The cooling breezes of upland Cyprus and the gentle winds over the Great Sea were refreshing, and the firm assurance that the Lord Messiah was directing the course of his labors lifted Saul's spirits; he burned within to be about more bold actions in the name of the Master.

The vessel bearing the three men came abreast of the coast of Pamphylia, and passing by Attalia it entered the mouth of the River Cestrus and moved inland some seven miles to Perga, sacred city of the god Artemis. Here the ship entered a miasmal, low region between the sea and the encircling Taurus range of mountains, and, suddenly, from the delightful climate of the island and the sea, the passengers were dropped into the humid and enervating heat of this flat country baking beneath a relentless sun.

Before they could escape northward to the invigorating elevation of the mountains and the country of the Gentile hordes beyond, Saul and Joseph bar Nabas suffered the buffeting of double misfortune. Saul was struck down by a malarial fever that regularly plagued the inhabitants of that region of Pamphylia, and John Mark, tired of the rigors of travel and perhaps fearful of the harder days and dangers beyond the Taurus, homesick for his mother and the gentler life at Jerusalem, left them and caught a vessel to Palestine.

When the severest stage of his fever abated, Saul arose from his bed, and with Joseph set forth for the hills, which, he hoped, would restore him to health. But the many days of rigorous traveling on foot, always at the mercy of sudden summer storms and wild animals and lurking brigands, were too much for the weakened Saul. When they made their way wearily into Antioch of Pisidia, he was nearing exhaustion. Before he could undertake his mission he was once more laid low by the recurring fever, and Bar Nabas sent for a physician to minister to him.

"I am Paulus, a Roman citizen of Tarsus, though likewise Saul a Jew," the sick man introduced himself when the physician entered his chamber.

"And I am called Luke," the physician responded, "a Greek of Antioch."

Soon, under the skillful ministrations of the young physician and the alleviating conditions of the region, which was high above the sweltering swamps of the Pamphylian coasts, the rabbi's health began to be restored. Luke came often to attend him and Saul found the physician an interested hearer of his story of the Lord Messiah. Already Luke was numbered among the God-fearers in Antioch of Pisidia, that company of Gentiles to whom the One-God religion of the Hebrews was deeply appealing, although many of them had not submitted to the ceremonial rites of the rigid Mosaic law.

One day when the fever had abated and Saul was growing restive to enter the synagogue to proclaim the good tidings of the risen Messiah, the physician, eyes earnest in questioning, sought to learn more of the Galilean of whom the man of Tarsus had been telling him. How did he look? Was he tall or short, of stern or gentle visage, of imperious manner or warmly fraternal? And in his daily living among his disciples how did he talk and what stories did he tell them, what sort of lessons did he teach, and what were his methods of teaching? His disciples, too, what were they like? Did they follow him out of fear or because of their great love for him? And of what did they talk of day after day as they traversed the hills and the wadies of Galilee and Judaea and Samaria?

"I have seen Him only in vision and not in the flesh," Saul hastened to reveal. "And of the band of His disciples I know little."

"Then you did not know him in the days he was ministering and teaching?"

"No. Though He did appear to me on the road to Damascus, it was in His transfigured body. And He appeared to me likewise, it must have been, that day in the Temple courts. But I knew Him not as the carpenter or the teacher going His way among the people."

Luke's eyes were flaming now. "It is an amazing story, filled with joy and a great wonderment. It should be gathered together and written down so that succeeding generations might know it in its truth and grace."

"It is indeed such a story," Saul agreed, his own eyes bright with the fever of his love for the Lord Messiah, "whose telling should encompass all the earth and unto the last generation upon it."

When his strength was sufficiently recovered, Saul went up to the synagogue and when the Jewish leaders invited him to speak, he went forward and stood before the people and in the manner of a Greek orator reviewed the history of the Chosen and how the promise of the Messiah had been fulfilled in the coming of Jesus of Galilee, His sacrifice and His resurrection.

But when Saul came to discoursing upon the crime of the Roman conqueror and the Temple leadership and the people themselves, a crime in which all mankind shared guilt because of the sinning and depravity of every soul, mutterings began, and then argumentation and recriminations. So, on the next Sabbath an overflowing throng of Jews and God-fearers greeted his appearance at the synagogue, and although many listened to him eagerly and reverently, others began to speak out in jest and ribaldry against the Lord Messiah. Then Saul and Joseph bar Nabas, with Luke the physician, who was recording the salient observations of the rabbi and the reactions of his hearers, quitted the synagogue and went into the market squares and other places of assemblage and carried the tidings of the Lord Messiah directly to the Gentiles who would pause to listen.

And many gave heed to the message, so many indeed that the ire of the leaders of the synagogue was aroused against the missionaries from Antioch of Syria. Certain of those God-fearers who had abandoned the religions of the foreign gods and attached themselves to the religion of Yahweh of the Jews were likewise indignant, for they felt that Saul and Joseph bar Nabas were seeking to destroy or grievously alter the faith they had so joyfully embraced. Thus these persons who refused to give heed to the tidings brought by the two men joined in raising a great clamor against them, and Saul and Joseph at the end of summer strode eastward toward Iconium.

As they were preparing to leave the city, however, Saul spoke with flashing eyes to some of those who had rejected the tidings they brought. "We felt it fitting, being ourselves of the Chosen and devoted sons of Abraham, to offer the Lord Messiah first to you. But you have closed your ears and hardened your hearts against the good news. And now we leave you in your impenitence and stubborn pride and go forth to bear to the Gentiles the glad tidings you yourselves have rejected."

But not all the ears that had heard had been closed to comprehension, and many of the hearts had been responsive, and so, as Saul and Joseph bar Nabas journeyed toward ancient Iconium on the frontier of Phrygia, they gave thanks that even in Antioch of Pisidia, a new and tender bud was beginning already to grow forth from the trunk of the tree of the Lord Messiah's own planting.

At Iconium, the experiences of Saul and Joseph bar Nabas were repetitions in many respects of the experiences at Antioch. They went first to the synagogue, and their preaching brought into the fold of the Lord Messiah converts both of the Chosen and of the Gentile God-fearers who had converted from their pagan gods to Israel's One-God Yahweh. But soon this success so aroused the enmity of the leaders of the synagogue as well as the civil rulers that they provoked an actual physical assault upon the Lord Messiah's messengers, and the two departed from Iconium, leaving the little brotherhood newly established there, and trudged southward to Lystra. Lystra, fortified town high above the sea, was occupied almost exclusively by the native Lycaonians and by persons attached to the Roman garrison, established there since the time of Augustus. Lystra had no Jewish community, no synagogue, and only a scattering of Jews. But though the Lycaonians had their own language and their pagan gods, they could also speak the common Greek of the unlettered folk and thus were able to comprehend the teaching of Saul and Joseph bar Nabas concerning the ministry and sacrificial death of the Lord Messiah. And many of the Lycaonians joined the Greeks and others in worshiping at the temple that had been erected to Zeus and the lesser Greek divinities.

One day in the marketplace at Lystra, as the two missionaries were preaching to a group of Greeks and Lycaonians— who worshiped the pantheon of Greek pagan divinities—Saul noticed again a cripple who had been among the listeners to his recounting of the story of Jesus the Galilean several other times. This fellow, who had to be carried from place to place because his legs would not support his walking, had been avidly following Saul's discourse concerning the Lord Messiah, and Saul perceived the building in the crippled one of a growing great faith. Singling out the man in the circle of intent listeners before him, Saul turned blazing eyes upon him and thrust forth his arm toward him.

"Arise!" he exclaimed, his forefinger waggling toward the poor fellow's amazed countenance. "Stand upon your feet!"

Without a look about him, without an instant's hesitation, the unfortunate man stood erect. Then, as a smile wreathed the face that for long years had been pain-twisted, he ventured a step—and another and another. And now happily and with no fear or even the slightest trepidation, he advanced toward Saul beaming his immense thankfulness.

But the Lycaonians did not rightly interpret the amazing thing that had been done before their eyes. The clamor arose, as quickly the awe-struck group began to disperse, that once again the gods had taken the forms of men and come down to earth to walk among mortals. The tall and handsome Joseph bar Nabas, they declared, was the supreme god Zeus and the smaller, eloquent-tongued Saul was Hermes, the attendant and messenger of Zeus. But the missionaries did not comprehend the excited words.

Later these folk and others, led by a priest from the temple of Zeus with dancing attendants leading oxen garlanded with flowers and wreaths, came to the lodging of Saul and Joseph bar Nabas. When they erected an altar at the gateway of the house and prepared to begin offering sacrifice, the missionaries realized that these folk of Lystra were according them worship due only to God Most High. They rushed from their dwelling and remonstrated sternly against this idolatry and implored the people to desist from such practices. The priest and his attendants were greatly offended and the thwarted worshipers chagrined, and this smoldering resentment was kindled into tumult. Soon after, certain Jews who had been enemies of the missionaries at Antioch and Iconium arrived at Lystra and heard Saul preaching in the marketplace.

"This fellow," they told the Lystra folk, "is an impostor and his teaching is false. His stories indeed are all lies."

Soon, these visiting Jews had fomented a riot, and in the ensuing disorder stones were hurled, one of which struck Saul to the ground; there he lay stretched out and motionless. His assailants, thinking him dead and fearing that they would be seized and punished for the crime, dragged his body through the city's gate and left it in a field outside the wall. There, after darkness had fallen, Saul was found by a young convert to the Lord Messiah's Kingdom, a half-Jew named Timothy;

his mother, Eunice, and grandmother, Lois, were of the Chosen but his dead father had been a Greek. Saul was helped tenderly to their house, where the women ministered to his needs until he had mended.

After a while, Saul, with Joseph bar Nabas, departed from Lystra toward Derbe, a day's hard walking westward, leaving behind a young fellowship loving the Lord Messiah and the youth whom Saul in his affection would henceforth speak of as his greatly beloved son Timothy.

They reached Derbe in late summer; by midwinter much had been accomplished in that region for the Lord Messiah, and happily it had been achieved peacefully. Now, they reasoned, it was time to turn back to Antioch of Syria to prepare for a journey that would carry them farther into the lands of the Gentiles.

At Derbe they were again in the foothills of the Taurus; on the other side of the mountains was Tarsus and around the rim of the Gulf of Issus lay Antioch. But already the mountain passes were filling with snow, and to return by continuing eastward would be both difficult and hazardous. Saul was no longer a young man and his small frame had been assailed further by recurring fevers, hard journeying over wild terrain, and ill treatment at the hands of sometimes jeering, angry mobs. But a more impelling reason determined that they return by the way they had come. Saul wished to salute and encourage those new brothers in the Lord Messiah whom Joseph and he had led into the Way. And especially Saul wanted to see again young Timothy and Luke the physician.

So westward they retraced their journeyings and joyfully greeted the brothers, stopping to ordain presbyters among them to lead the fledgling fellowships and to exhort them to continue steadfast and achieving in the faith of the Lord Messiah. At Antioch, Luke, thinking perhaps of a book he might write, made notes of their labors. Saul and Joseph, he wrote, "confirmed the souls of the disciples, exhorting to continuance in the faith, and that we must through many afflictions enter into the Kingdom of God."

At Antioch of Pisidia the road turned southward. One day as they were preparing to set forth toward Perga and the nearby seaport of Attalia, Saul stood a moment and gazed westward. Beyond Colosse in Phrygia and Philadelphia and Ephesus, on a straight line into the setting sun, lay Athens, and beyond that cultural capital of the world, past Achaia and the Ionian Sea, far northwestward, lay mighty Rome, mistress of the world, unconquerable by sword and spear and battering ram but defenseless against invasion and conquering by the Lord Messiah with the weapons of His love.

Send me yet, O blessed Lord Jesus, into that bastion of the Gentile hordes. Grant unto me the joy unutterable of lifting high Thy name and offering Thy redemption and Thy salvation to Thy brothers upon the Palatine and the Capitoline, on Janiculum and in the festering Subura, in the forums and the porches of the temples of the pagans, in the homes and at the games, wherever, O Lord, there may be one who will hear Thy tidings and accept Thy abundant grace.

In the spring Joseph and Saul started southward again, and soon they were ascending the steep trails of the Taurus, braving by day and night not only the hardships of the journeying but also its perils of sudden storms and roaring freshets, wild animals and fierce brigands lurking in wait to rob and slay. And on the other side of the mountains, in the coastal flatlands of Pamphylia, a more threatening peril awaited Saul—enervating summer with its chills and fevers.

So when they came down the mountain into Perga as summer was beginning, they paused only until they could obtain passage on a vessel sailing out of Attalia for Antioch of Syria.

On this ship, Saul happily discovered before it had cleared the harbor, was Tribune Paulus. He too was voyaging to Antioch. Emperor Claudius, Paulus revealed, was sending him eastward on a mission to the proconsul in Syria.

42

Before their vessel had swung around the southernmost cape of Trachaea nearest Cyprus, Tribune Paulus had related many of the happenings at Rome and elsewhere in the empire of which the two missionaries, in their long sojourn in Asia Minor, knew nothing.

Valeria Messalina was dead, and Claudius was now married to Agrippina, daughter of General Germanicus and the elder Agrippina and sister of the dead Caligula. The emperor's young wife had been thrust through with a sword by a soldier sent by one Narcissus, a crafty freedman who, as Claudius' secretary of state, exercised tremendous power. Narcissus had feared, rightly no doubt, that if Messalina were allowed to remain alive, she would by her tearful pleas have soon been able to obtain the emperor's pardon. Paulus revealed the cause of her downfall: she had gone through the formalities of a wedding ceremony—while Claudius was away from Rome—with a handsome paramour, Caius Silius; her enemies charged that she was conspiring to have the emperor assassinated and this paramour succeed him.

Claudius, despite the revelation of Messalina's innumerable adulteries and, worse, of her many unconscionable conspiracies that had procured the deaths of a host of innocent persons who had fallen out of her favor, for a while mourned his faithless wife. But very quickly, under the ministrations of his scheming niece Agrippina, his grief was assuaged and he was her mooning captive. Agrippina was his fifth wife, Claudius her third husband. She was in her early thirties, he was almost sixty. To this strange union of niece and uncle, the niece brought also her son Nero, Claudius' grandnephew.

"In Rome they declare that Agrippina is as unprincipled as her brother Caligula was but much shrewder," Paulus observed. "They are already wagering that she will inveigle Claudius into adopting her brat, Nero, that she will dispose of Claudius' son Britannicus, and after that Claudius himself, so Nero can have the throne. But she will have to wait a few years before getting rid of Claudius"—he smiled wryly—"because Nero is only about twelve, a little young to be emperor of Rome."

But Saul was more interested in the replies of the tribune to his questions concerning the spread of the fellowship of the Lord Messiah in Rome and the cities of the West, than he was in hearing about the emperor's domestic problems. Had the tidings of the Lord Messiah been carried into many cities of the empire? Had members of the Way, pushing westward from Jerusalem and Antioch and Caesarea and other regions around the eastern rim of the Great Sea, gone forth to establish new fellowships far into the distant lands of the Gentiles? And what of Rome? Had the followers of Jesus of Galilee been able, under the very noses of the emperors and their pagan and dissolute advisers, to organize a fellowship? Were they able to bring into it converts from the Jewish colony on Janiculum Hill and even the idol-worshiping Gentiles themselves?

"During the years since my assignment in Judaea, I have spent much of the time in other provinces far from Rome," Tribune Paulus answered. "And during my periods of service at home I have kept close to my duties in the army and my circle of friends who are generally not inclined to religious practices, except"—he smiled warmly and, reaching forth, laid his hand on Saul's knee—"two in whom you will be interested."

"Tribune Longinus and Claudia? Can it be, tribune, that *they* are of the Way?"

"I cannot say positively. But I have no doubt they are. It would be highly dangerous for them should it be said in equestrian circles that they are, but I have heard whispers among their friends that they consort with certain Jews and others, principally slaves and poorer freedmen, in celebrating the mysteries of their sect, oftentimes in the homes of these poorer ones. This I can say with assurance, however, eastern cousin." He looked Saul in the eyes. "They no longer seem to walk with a weight of sorrow or guilt on their shoulders."

"Praise Yahweh Most High and His Lord Messiah, may you be speaking the truth!" Saul's eyes, even the half-closed one, were bright with his uncontained new joy. "From His slayer, praise Jesus the Lord, Longinus has been transformed into His loving brother, and Claudia with him! God grant that it be so." And then suddenly Saul's radiance fled his countenance and it was solemnly questioning. "But what of the domus Aemilius, my brother? Do not its members number themselves within the fellowship?"

"My father's household still outwardly reveres the Aemilian lares and penates, though I suspect there may be in our domus a slave or two who slip out to meet with these Christians. That's what the Galilean's followers are being called by some —in derision."

Saul nodded, and then his brightening eyes searched the tribune's. "And you, Paulus? Have you sought of our Lord Messiah redemption and salvation?"

"I've always had great sympathy for him, eastern cousin. I knew even when he was being tried that he was being unfairly and unmercifully dealt with——"

"But you have not accepted Him as Lord of all creation," Saul interrupted, as sadly he shook his head. "Nor are your eyes and heart aflame with His presence. You have not sought Him in conviction of sin and in penitence, Paulus my brother. You are not yet one of His." For a moment his countenance was dark; then suddenly it was lighted. "But He calls you, He loves you. One day, if you will but allow Him, He will claim you as He has claimed Longinus and Claudia and maybe even—God will it—Pontius Pilate." Immediately

Saul's eyes were questioning. "Has any word of him come to Rome since last I saw you?"

"I've heard nothing. Nor have Longinus and Claudia—they told me when I inquired."

The tribune and the two missionaries said their farewells at the dock in Antioch. "Peace be with you," said Paulus, raising his arm in salute. He turned to Saul. "And again, Paulus, eastern cousin," he said, smiling broadly, "until one day we meet in Rome."

"Until a good day when we meet again, in Rome, with you be peace, Paulus my brother. And pray the Lord that when the day comes you will be with us in His fellowship."

Tribune Paulus went at once to the palace to report to the proconsul; Saul and Joseph bar Nabas sought out the brothers of the Way to lay before them tidings of their long journeying among the Gentiles.

They were received by the Christians, both Jews and the Gentiles, with acclaim and rejoicing when the results of their laboring were revealed. But soon a new discord arose. Pilgrims coming to the Passover at Jerusalem from Antioch of Pisidia and other cities in Asia Minor, in which the missionaries had sought to plant new brotherhoods, told of the contentions between the apostles and the synagogue adherents; they had borne prejudiced reports and fabrications concerning the teachings of Saul and Joseph bar Nabas. Soon the fellowship at Jerusalem was in a tumult, so that Simon of Capernaum was sent to Antioch to investigate.

Soon after the missionaries from Asia Minor arrived in Antioch—before they could rest and gain strength for beginning a new conquest of the Gentile world—Simon came to Antioch. Very quickly the grizzled fisherman, greatly beloved by Jesus in His earthly ministry, was convinced of the good works of Saul and Joseph, and happily he fraternized with his Antiochene fellow followers of the Lord Messiah. Without hesitation he sat down to table with his ceremonially unwashed Gentile brothers, and partook with them of their common meals. And for Saul, who had once sought with determination to injure him, Simon manifested a strengthened great affection.

But the serenity of those of the Way in Antioch was to be broken grievously with the coming of others from Jerusalem, members of that faction that continued to insist that those Gentiles who wished to enter the fellowship must first become Jews, that they must become members of the congregation of Israel and promise their full obedience to Israel's laws. At once these orthodox Jews charged Simon with violating those laws in eating with uncircumcised Gentiles. When Simon then ceased to share the meals with his uncircumcised brethren, Saul heatedly charged the fisherman to his face with disloyalty to the Galilean and his new Gentile brothers, so that Simon rejoined the uncircumcised Gentiles-become-Christians at their table.

The Judaists refused to relent, and when the controversy seemed impossible of settlement, the brothers decided to send certain ones to Jerusalem to consult with the venerable James the righteous, brother of the Lord, and the other elders of the Way there. Leading the delegation southward were Saul and Joseph bar Nabas.

When the council came together at Jerusalem, the argument was heated. Saul held firmly to his contention that a Gentile might enter the fellowship of the Lord Messiah without first entering the fold of Israel, that he did not need circumcision or to take upon himself the burden of obeying the jots and tittles of Israel's ceremonial laws. And when grizzled Simon, remembering how the Lord Messiah had wrought in Cornelius, the centurion of Caesarea, a great work, came warmly to Saul's defense, the elders concurred in Saul's firmly pressed views, and their concurrence was given voice by the beloved James.

So a letter was prepared, to be sent throughout all the regions of the growing fellowship, announcing the decision of the council of elders. It closed with the pronouncement of the right of Gentiles everywhere to enter the Way of Jesus the

Lord Messiah without first coming through the doors of Judaism: "It was the Holy Spirit's decision and ours to impose upon you no further burden beyond these essentials—abstinence from things sacrificed to idols, and bloodshed and fornication. From these you will do well to keep yourselves. Farewell."

To bear the council's letter to Antioch and to accompany Saul and Joseph bar Nabas, who, now eager to resume their journeyings among the Gentiles were returning to Antioch, the Jerusalem elders sent Judas bar Sabbas and Silas, both of whom were Jews. But Silas was a Hellenist, who was called Silvanus—just as Saul the rabbi from Tarsus was called Paulus the apostle to the Gentiles—and he was also a citizen of great Rome.

But at Antioch, when Saul and Joseph bar Nabas began to lay plans for returning with tidings of the Messiah to the lands of the Gentiles they fell into heated disagreement. They were planning to return along the route they had first traveled and had agreed on that course. Then Joseph proposed to take with them a second time his cousin John Mark. The youth, Joseph insisted, was repentant; long had he been sorrowful because he had abandoned them at Perga and turned homeward. This time he would remain steadfast, and he would be greatly helpful.

"The man deserted us in Pamphylia and went not with us to the work!" Saul shook his head and his dark forehead crinkled in small ridges. "I refuse to take him to the new work!" Nor would the rabbi relent. So they ended their controversy by agreeing that Joseph bar Nabas would depart for Cyprus, and Saul, taking with him Silas, would set forth on foot northward, through the Antioch region of Syria, and when he rounded the rim of the Gulf of Issus, he would strike westward past Tarsus, through the Cilician Gates in the Taurus, onto the plain of Cilicia into Derbe. There they would renew the spirits of the brothers of the Way and exhort them to greater endeavors for the Lord Messiah. Then they would journey on to Lystra, where, the Lord willing, they would enlist young Timothy to accompany them, and at Antioch in Pisidia they might come again upon Luke the physician and add him to Messiah's small band moving ever westward into the pagan lands of the unnumbered Gentile lost brothers.

Already the zealous soul of Rabbi Saul, like spirited horses harnessed to the chariot awaiting the starter's signal to plunge forth on the racecourse, yearned to set out upon the new conquest for souls for his Lord. But he would not begin the journey until he had seen Joseph bar Nabas down to the Orontes docks and aboard the vessel that would bear him southwestward to his native Cyprus.

On the wharf, as the last passengers were going aboard the ship, the companions of long years and many shared perils embraced. "Peace be with you, Saul my beloved brother," Joseph said fervently as he clutched to his powerful tall frame the smaller apostle, "and may Jesus our blessed Lord grant you many souls unto His fold."

"With you be peace, O Joseph my honored and beloved brother in our Lord. May He reward you likewise with a host of souls added unto His fellowship. And many times again on this earth may our paths cross, O Joseph, friend and brother."

Eyes streaming, Saul stood in his tracks and watched the vessel as it pushed out into the river's current and after a time disappeared around the bend of the stream. Then he turned to the silently watching Silas. "But it is never to be." He shook his head slowly, solemnly. "I feel in my soul, and so does Joseph, I believe, that never will we meet again until we stand together in the presence of the blessed Lord Jesus."

They returned to Saul's lodging and completed their small preparations for the new mission; then, taking only their mantles and a change of clothing, their stout staves and two small leather pouches of dried food, they set out from the city. The warming weather of spring had cleared the Syrian Gates in the Amanus Mountains of snow, and soon they reached Tarsus, where they lingered to rest awhile from the hard and hazardous journeying through the wild and rugged uplands and where, on a day of sunshine and hope, a renewed Saul climbed the slope to stand before the great stone sealing the tomb of his beloved ones.

At Derbe the arrival of the missionaries incited the brothers of the fellowship Saul and Joseph bar Nabas had established to further labors in the Lord Messiah's Kingdom. At Lystra, where Saul had been stoned and dragged away to die, they likewise found a fellowship of Christians still eager for the spreading of the tidings of Jesus the Lord. And here also, to Saul's great joy, he found young Timothy still faithful and accomplishing. When, after a short season spent in exhorting the brothers to continue steadfast and to strengthen and buttress the stronghold of the Lord in that region, Saul and Silas departed for Antioch in Pisidia, Timothy journeyed with them.

At Antioch, Saul's joy again would be full. Not only did he find the brothers of the fellowship happy to greet him on his return into the region of Pisidia but eager to report their continuing zeal in the cause of the Lord Jesus. And at Antioch he found again Luke the physician. When he and Silas set out from the city, Luke walked with them.

Saul had planned to journey straight westward until he came to the flatlands bordering the Aegaean Sea and then, by traveling northward and southward along the coastal region, to carry the tidings of the Lord's redemption and salvation into the provinces of Mysia, Lydia, and Caria. But it was early summer when he prepared to leave Antioch, and, as Luke reminded him, in the alluvial lands running out from the seashore the miasmas would soon be rising on the night mists and the fevers that had felled him at Perga, on the first mission into Pamphylia, might well lay him low again. So he listened to the counsel of the physician, which he felt was likewise the directing of the Holy Spirit, and from Antioch traveled northwestwardly through Phrygia and Mysia, avoiding the cities— Philadelphia, Thyatira, Pergamos, Sardis, even Ephesus beside the sea straight eastward from great Athens and her men of deep wisdom. But to the people of the small villages, the

camel drivers and merchants passing on the trails, the sheep-
herders and men of earth plowing their oxen, the loungers
about the watering places and around campfires of warm,
moon-bright evenings, to these countless lost and scattered
and little loved small ones of the world, even to these his Gentile brothers, Saul and his companions, with flame in their
eyes and love bursting their hearts, brought the joyous tidings
of the young Galilean, the Lord Jesus the Christ.

So after many weeks of sojourning thus among the Gentiles,
the three apostles of the Galilean came, on a warm day in the
late summer, to Alexandria Troas on the sea. When they had
bathed themselves and had eaten and rested, Saul walked
down to the harbor and stood watching as the lowering sun,
still splashing brightly the brazenly flaunted sails of the passing ships, reached for Macedonia far in the west.

Somewhere near this spot, Saul allowed his fancy to reason,
had stood almost a thousand years ago the great Homer to
dream his immortal *Iliad*. On these ancient shores men had
dreamed and fought and ships had foundered and sunk, nations had flourished and passed into oblivion, stories had been
told, legends arisen and countless dreams fashioned. And time
and the sea, inscrutable, had seen all and remembered nothing.

Upward along the shore and sitting in the edge of the sea
was the island of Samothracia, Saul knew, and on the main-
land beyond were Neapolis and Philippi and around the
swing of the sea Thessalonica, and southward from Macedonia were the province of Achaia and her great cities Athens
and Corinth. He closed his eyes against the sun and his vision
of the Hellenist cities, and he saw far beyond and northward
a long great land flung like a giant boot sideways into the sea.
Italia, and at its center mighty Rome, mistress of all the earth!
And Gentiles unnumbered as the birds of the air, as the sands
beside all the seas, lost and shut away forever from the redemption and salvation of Jesus the Christ, Son of the One-
God Yahweh of all the world and the sun and moon and stars,
Himself God, Himself loving brother of all men. Lost and

hut away forever unless to them are borne the tidings of the
Lord's marvelous salvation, His unbounded love.

O Lord Messiah, O Jesus the Christ, Thou didst commission me, upon a day long ago on the burning sands of the desert, Thou didst confirm Thy commissioning of me through the words of Ananias of Damascus, as Thy apostle to the Gentiles. Again, O blessed Jesus Lord Messiah, as I lay upon the stones in the Court of the Gentiles, Thou didst reveal that I would be sent as a light unto the pathway by which they would journey to Thee. And over there, O Lord Messiah, across the waters into the sun's setting, are Thy Gentiles thickly sown as the stars in the heavens.

But Saul turned away from the harbor and his contemplation of the far shores beyond and returned to the lodging the three men had found for their stay at Alexandria Troas. And when they had eaten and Saul had laid the burden of his heart upon the Lord Messiah and had given thanks for the protection and sustenance so abundantly vouchsafed him through all the perils of his venturing, he lay down on his mat and fell quickly asleep.

That night Saul stood again down by the seashore looking westward into the sinking sun. As he gazed out over the waters of the Aegaean Sea, envisioning the lands beyond the darkening horizon, a man came toward him, straight toward him out of Macedonia directly westward. He came from Macedonia, Saul reasoned, because he was dressed as a Macedonian in a Grecian mantle and broad hat that might serve him as protection from the sun. He was sure the man was a Macedonian when he spoke.

"Come over into Macedonia," the stranger entreated, "and help us."

Then as suddenly as he came, he was gone.

On the morrow Saul told the three companions of the vision that had come to him in the night. "I thought that the Lord Jesus wished that I go southward from Alexandria Troas through the provinces of western Asia Minor and thence to

Perga and by ship again to Antioch in Syria," he said, his eyes shining with a fire burning deep within him. "But now I know that such a mission must wait for another day. The Lord Messiah has spoken again to me; He has set me finally upon my way unto the Gentile brothers beyond the seas. Praise be His blessed Name, He has sent me this day unto the lands of the setting sun. Our course, brothers, is westward!"

That day the physician Luke added to the notes he was putting down, for the book that someday he envisioned he might write, these words:

"A vision appeared unto Paulus in the night. There stood a man of Macedonia, and prayed him, saying, 'Come over into Macedonia, and help us.' After Paulus had seen the vision, immediately we endeavored to go into Macedonia, assuredly gathering that the Lord had called us for to preach the gospel unto them."

ROME

†

43

Claudia was reading in the peristylium when the young slave entered quickly and approached her. She looked up from her scroll.

"Yes, Marcipor?"

"This morning, mistress, as I was coming past Saepta Julia I saw in one of the shops a shipment of handsome glassware from the manufactories in Phoenicia." The Greek's dark eyes were questioning. "I wondered if you might wish to——"

"There are no ears hearing us," Claudia interrupted, understanding. "What did you hear, Marcipor?"

"I came on Croesus there, mistress, the slave from Emperor Nero's kitchens, that one——"

"I know him." She dropped the scroll upon the ivory-topped small table beside her. "Did he bring news of Nero or Poppaea?"

"Of both, mistress. But mainly concerning the apostle Paulus."

She showed sudden alarm. "Not evil tidings, I hope."

"Not yet evil, perhaps, but grave. Croesus reported that Poppaea was angry with Emperor Nero because he released Paulus. She has joined with those Jews who oppose him violently and are even threatening to slay him, Croesus said."

"Yes, I don't doubt it. Vile as she is, she professes to be a convert to Judaism and she flaunts her hostility to the Christians." Her countenance indicated concern. "But, Marcipor, the gathering of the fellowship this evening to celebrate the release of Paulus and to give thanks to the Lord Jesus and

Yahweh Almighty"—she paused. "We must warn Paulus and
the others of the Way who were coming to the service."

"That's what Croesus was doing, mistress. He was on his
way here. And others are spreading the word. The meeting
will not be in the house where the apostle has been lodging; it
will be in an upper-story chamber in Tribune Paulus' insula
in the Subura. Do you wish me to accompany you there, Mistress Claudia?"

"No, Marcipor. I know where the place is. We have met
there a few times, even before Paulus' arrival in Rome. It may
be that Longinus will go with me." She smiled. "Are you going, Marcipor?"

"I would risk any danger to hear him speak again of our
Lord Jesus," he said, his eyes shining. "I may never again
have an opportunity to listen to his comforting words."

"But why, Marcipor?"

"Croesus said that Paulus was going on another mission for
the Lord, to carry the tidings farther into the West, perhaps
even to Spain. And somewhere along the journey he might
suffer misadventure, like the perils of his previous journeys,
from which he would fail to be delivered." He looked her in
the eyes and his own were steady. "And I'm a slave, mistress. I
might likewise come upon ill times."

"I pray that neither of you will fall on evil days, Marcipor,
my slave"—her eyes, too, were unwavering—"and my brother
in the Way."

Claudia walked out on the terrace and sat on the railing of
the balustrade enclosing it. This terrace adjoining the peristylium was her favorite place for relaxing. She and Longinus had
purchased the mansion from the man to whom it had been sold
by Emperor Claudius; its previous owner, a wealthy senator,
had been executed on the perjured testimony of Messalina.
On the upper slope of Viminal Hill, not far from the mansion
of Longinus' father, the mansion faced a street that ran close
to the spine of the hill; the peristylium and terrace looked off
almost directly southward. Below and a little to the right was
the massed turmoil and stench of the Subura; and straight

ahead, as Claudia sat facing that densely populated region of insulas, and beyond was Forum Romanum and looming above the forum the huge marbled spread of the Imperial Palace topping Palatine Hill.

Directly westward, as she looked off to her right, Claudia could see the bending of the Tiber and the Campus Martius and on the other side of the river the Gardens of Agrippa and Vatican Hill. And the sun, hanging above the hill, sent its oblique rays to shower with gold the resplendent roofs and marble walls of the great palace in which as a child and young woman she had lived under the treacherous upbringing of her stepfather, the emperor Tiberius.

Now the Palace had a new master and one who, she suspected and feared, would shortly become a tyrant more dissolute than even her nephew Caligula, successor of Tiberius, had been in his brief reign. Already Nero was well on the way; three years ago, he had procured the death of his own mother, Claudia's unprincipled niece Agrippina, sister of Caligula. Nero had murdered her, all Rome had said, at the insistence of Poppaea Sabina, then his beautiful but wanton mistress, now his wife. But Rome, caring little, had remembered that Agrippina, five years before her death, had murdered her husband, Claudius; she had fed the old emperor a bountiful helping of his favorite food, mushrooms, into which she had had the foresight to pour a liberal dosage of poison.

This Nero Claudius Caesar Drusus Germanicus, Claudia's grandnephew, now but a few months past his twenty-fourth birthday, ruled the empire and the world from that great pile of masonry on the Palatine. And from a small house in the region of Janiculum Hill, provided him by his long-time friend and new brother in the Way of the Lord Jesus, Tribune Lucius Aemilius Paulus, another man, with crooked short legs bowed all the more under the weight of six decades and much traveling back and forth from Jerusalem and Antioch into far-spreading lands of many races and tongues, a man, twice as old and half again as the emperor Nero, mightily sought to bring all men, his brothers, into a Kingdom ruled by another man forever young. How different, mused Claudia, her eyes intent upon the lowering sun's rays glinting upon the roofs and walls of the great palace, how vastly different in every way from Nero was this perennially young Galilean she had seen and heard speak long years ago—ages ago, it seemed to her now—far across the Great Sea in a court of the Temple in ancient Jerusalem. Today in the capital of a mighty empire two young men confronted each other, Claudia told herself, two men, worlds and a universe apart, who were more different from each other than Rome was different from Jerusalem. And which, she likewise wondered, would win in the day of confrontation. She doubted not which in the aeons of time would be victor.

As she sat thus meditating in the waning sunshine of early spring and looking toward Palatine Hill and the Imperial Palace crowning it, her thoughts were no longer upon her dissolute grandnephew; now they drifted pleasantly to the older man whom she would within a few hours be seeing and hearing, maybe for the last time, as years ago in the Temple court, for the last time, she had seen and heard that marvelous young man. Through all the succeeding years, with persistence and amazing great love, the young Galilean had pursued her across the seas and into the cities and up and down the far-spread lands of the barbarian hordes, finally to claim her forever and irrevocably in loving fellowship.

Claudia had journeyed back and forth between Rome and the various foreign posts to which Longinus had been assigned by Emperor Claudius. Sometimes, if the missions were quickly accomplished, she remained with her husband until his return to the capital. But when his duties continued to demand Longinus' presence for months and even for years, as had happened when he was sent out to Gaul and Germania and into Spain, she left him at his post and returned to Rome.

The same arrangement had been followed after Nero's accession to the throne. He had continued to send Longinus on long missions into distant provinces, and on some of these, by special permission of the emperor, she had been permitted to

accompany the tribune. She had not, however, gone with him
out to Palestine when five years ago he had missed by only a
few days encountering the Apostle Paulus at Fortress Antonia
in Jerusalem. Sitting here on the terrace, Claudia recalled the
story that she heard from Longinus, when he returned to Rome,
and from their old friend Tribune Paulus, who by chance was
home at the time from an assignment across the Adriatic in Dal-
matia. Later Paulus the apostle himself had told her and
others of the Way at Rome in greater details the events of
those significant few days at Jerusalem and Caesarea.

Paulus had returned to Jerusalem at the end of more than
six years of traveling, in which he had traveled from Alexandria Troas across the Aegaean into the Grecian lands and back
along the eastern coast of Asia Minor to Caesarea and Jerusalem again. Then he had turned northward to Antioch, from
which he had once again set forth to visit the fellowships he
had established and to spread the good tidings of the Lord
Jesus the Emanation of Yahweh Most High to other regions in
the West. He had faced in his extensive traveling, much of it
on foot, many disappointments and great perils, but he had
never lost faith in the Lord Messiah's determination to continue to provide his apostle Paulus every necessary encouragement and protection.

So, the apostle had revealed, in recalling these drama-filled
days of his evangelizing, he had come in late spring to the
ancient capital of his fathers to celebrate with his Hebrew
brothers the Feast of Pentecost, which to those of the Way of
the Lord Messiah had come to have a new significance, since
it was on that festival day that the gift of the Holy Spirit was
conferred upon the fellowship. And, as had frequently happened on other occasions, the apostle's lively presentation of
the tidings of the Lord Jesus the Galilean had provoked a controversy, and when it promised to turn into wild disorder, the
Roman authorities in the Fortress of Antonia intervened.

Paulus was arrested, and at his request he was permitted to
harangue the mob assembled before the steps leading up into
the fortress. But a still livelier tumult arose, and the apostle

was hustled into the tower. When he was importuned to confess crimes of which he was not guilty and refused, the commander of Antonia, one Claudius Lysias—he happened to be a friend with whom Longinus had served years before in the early years of the reign of Claudius—ordered that Paulus be scourged.

"When they were binding him to the stake to beat him," Longinus told Claudia on his return to Rome shortly after the incident in Jerusalem, "Paulus demanded of the centurion if he dared scourge a Roman citizen who had not had trial. The centurion reported to Claudius Lysias what the prisoner had said. Lysias, amazed, questioned Paulus. 'Are you, a Jew, a Roman citizen?' Paulus assured him he was. Lysias was incredulous. 'I paid a great sum to purchase my citizenship, since I was a provincial,' Lysias said. 'But I was born free,' declared Paulus. So Lysias ordered him freed of his bonds, but kept him in custody to protect him from the bitterly angered Judaists. And several days later Paulus was sent under guard to Caesarea. When I reached Jerusalem—I was on a mission to Lysias from the proconsul at Antioch—Lysias told me what happened. And"—Longinus, Claudia remembered, had smiled when he said it—"Lysias hadn't entirely recovered from his fright upon realizing that he had almost scourged a Roman citizen against whom no judgment had been pronounced."

But at Caesarea the apostle Paulus had suffered another misfortune. He had come before Antonius Felix, the procurator of Judaea, for trial on charges the persistently hostile Judaists had brought. He had stood before the procurator at the palace that for almost a decade Claudia had shared as wife of Pontius Pilate.

Claudia narrowed her eyes to concentrate her staring and her thoughts upon a pillared section of the great structure beyond the maze of narrow ways and crowded insulas of the Subura. "Poor Pilate," she murmured aloud. "I wonder, I wonder." She shook her head slowly. Two and a half decades ago, in the great throne chamber behind those columns, she had interceded with her crazed nephew Caligula to spare his life, and a moment later she had seen him for the last time as he was led out between two guards to lifetime banishment. And in all the years since that day she had received no word of him.

She had known this Felix, and compared with him, Pilate was a man of courage and virtue. She had known his last two wives, too. The first of these, in fact, was a cousin; like Claudia, she was a granddaughter of Mark Antony and Cleopatra. The second was Drusilla, daughter of Agrippa, whom Caligula had made king. Felix had been a freedman of the noble Antonia and a brother of Pallas, the clever but unscrupulous henchman of Claudius. He was a reprehensible character, this arbiter of Roman justice before whom Paulus had been brought. And he had kept the apostle imprisoned two years without bringing him to trial; he was hoping, many said of him, to hold Paulus until a ransom to purchase his freedom could be collected.

But then Nero had recalled Felix and had sent Porcius Festus out to Caesarea to succeed him. Festus arranged to send Paulus back to Jerusalem for trial before his Judaist accusers, since he knew nothing of the Jewish laws Paulus was charged with having broken, and Paulus, sensing what the verdict would be, had appealed to Caesar. So Festus had sent him as a prisoner to Rome. And two years ago, while Claudia was away with Longinus, Paulus had arrived after having survived a violent shipwreck off the island of Malta. Indeed, Claudia reasoned, the Lord Jesus must have been guarding the lives of the apostle and his companions in their much journeying or they would have perished in the assaults of frenzied men or ravenous animals or nature's rampaging. So Paulus believed, she knew, because she herself had heard him testify to a faith that had sustained him joyfully through trial and storm.

Quickly Claudia stood up, for now the sun was slanting long shadows toward the Tiber and down the eastern slope of the Palatine. Soon the Subura would be a dark region infested with prowling brigands eager to slash a throat for a copper coin. It would be well for Longinus and her to slip out to the fellowship's gathering while there was still a little of daylight and without the nocturnal fanfare of servants going ahead and flaming torches and sedan-chair bearers. Nero's spies, it was being whispered, were everywhere. Nor could anyone be certain what direction his inflamed imagination might take. And Poppaea's vindictiveness against the sect of Christians, particularly those few individuals from equestrian families who had joined the fellowship of the crucified Galilean, might at any moment incite her to propose for them some desperate fate.

"If she should discover that I had enlisted with slaves and shopkeepers in the Galilean's fellowship"—Claudia shrugged, left unfinished her observation. She crossed the mosaic of the terrace's paving and entered the peristylium. Any moment Longinus likely would be returning from Castra Praetoria, where he had been stationed during the week he had been home after a long assignment in Germania. They would eat lightly—perhaps some apricots or figs and grapes—for they had eaten their dinner in midafternoon, and then, dressed inconspicuously and probably disguised, would leave, maybe by separate ways, for the service in the Subura.

Tonight, Claudia sensed it in a great lightness and a lifting of spirits, Longinus would come in great joy to the end of his fleeing, across seas and lands and many years, from the vision persisting and the voice unforgettable of a bronzed Galilean impaled high, imploring His Father to forgive those who had treated Him so. Tonight his hand would lose, henceforth and forever, its fancied feel of a spear gripped firmly, a long, sharp spear blood-tipped.

44

Two flickering lamps, one bracketed near the doorway and the other on the crude table beside which the apostle Paulus was sitting, cast weaving, grotesque patterns of the worshipers on the dingy, smoked walls.

The chamber was filled when Marcipor admitted them and pointed toward the long bench against the rear wall; the others on the bench squeezed together to make places for them. Next to Claudia sat Croesus, the emperor's slave; she recognized him with a quick smile and a murmured greeting.

Across the small table from Paulus a man was unrolling a scroll.

"He has aged greatly," whispered Longinus. "Paulus, I mean."

"But it was many years ago when you saw him last," she said into his ear. "And think of the perils he has encountered and the hardships endured."

Now the man was reading from the scroll:

> *"Who hath believed our report?*
> *And to whom is the arm of the Lord revealed?*
> *For he shall grow up before him as a tender plant——"*

"From the writings of one of their ancient prophets——"
"Yes. I too spent many years out there. Remember?"
The man was rolling the scroll slowly and reading:

> *"——despised and rejected of men;*
> *A man of sorrows, and acquainted with grief:*

And we hid as it were our faces from him;
He was despised, and we esteemed him not.
Surely he hath borne our griefs, and carried our sorrows:
Yet we did esteem him stricken, smitten of God, and
    afflicted.
But he was wounded for our transgressions,
He was bruised for our iniquities:
The chastisement of our peace was upon him;
And with his stripes we are healed."

"He's bald, and his shoulders sag a little, but there's still the flame in his eyes," Longinus whispered as he faced Claudia, and his eyes were shining. But quickly he turned to study again the enraptured apostle.

The reader unrolled a further portion of the scroll and continued his melodic intoning of the prophet's words:

"Therefore will I divide him a portion with the great,
And he shall divide the spoil with the strong;
Because he hath poured out his soul unto death:
And he was numbered with the transgressors;
And he bare the sin of many,
And made intercession for the transgressors."

The reading was ended; the reader rolled the scroll into one compact cylinder. When one of the men near the table nodded to Paulus, the apostle arose. For a moment his dark eyes surveyed the assemblage as he sought in the unstable soft light of the feeble lamps to take into their embrace these beloved ones from whom shortly he would be departing. Then calmly he began to speak.

"Our brother Pethuel has read to us the prophecy of our ancient father Isaiah concerning the nature of the Messiah who would come to bring deliverance to Israel. But through the long generations since the vision of the suffering Messiah came to the great Isaiah, countless sons of the Chosen have disputed Isaiah's description of that Great One who was to de-

liver Israel. And unto this day countless sons of Abraham look
for a Messiah who will descend in lightning and blood with
flaming sword and a legion of angels and drive forth the conqueror from the ancient land."

The apostle paused, and the chamber was still until he resumed speaking; every ear was awaiting his words. "Yet, beloved in our Lord, Isaiah saw aright, though not in the fullness
of understanding that the mounting generations would bring.
For with an eye truly prophetic he envisioned the nature of the
One who would be sent to save His people, that One who
has come to suffer and to die as a recompense for our sinning
and to give us victory over evil and death as He Himself was
victor in His resurrection from the tomb." The apostle's eyes
were taking fire now, and the pitch of his voice was rising.
"Beloved, we know the glorious One foretold by Isaiah has
come among us, has lived in our day, and yet liveth. We do
know that the long-awaited Messiah of Israel was the carpenter
of Galilee, we do know that He *is* the Messiah, sent of God
Most High to redeem His people!"

Paulus paused again and his blazing eyes, even the one
over which the lid drooped and in which the vision was blurred,
searched the eyes intent upon his own, and he lifted an arm
and thrust it forth in emphatic gesture. "This Jesus the Nazarene, Him whom I so fiercely resisted, Him whose brothers I
tortured and slew in the days of my great ignorance and sinning, is indeed the Messiah of God of whom Isaiah the
prophet in the long ago spoke.

"But, beloved, He is more, vastly more. He is the Son of
God, the Emanation and Wisdom of the Most High, He, my
brothers, is God! He was in the beginning, before anything
was created. He is the Creator, the Redeemer, the Saviour who
willed His death that all men might return to Him from whom
in sin they have strayed away." Paulus thrust out both arms,
palms extended, and in his eyes the leaping flames of the lamp
danced. "He came to redeem all men of His creation—the Jew,
the Gentile, rich, poor, enslaved and free, all races, all colors of
skin, evil men and good, all of them creations of His hand, His

potential sons of heaven, His potential brothers of earth. As by
Adam's fall all men died, my brothers, so by His dying all men
may have eternal life, if they but come to Him in repentance
and faith and accept it of His hand."

For a moment the apostle's shoulders sagged, as though his
impassioned words had drained him of strength; but quickly
he straightened them again and, dropping his hand to rest it
on the table, smiled warmly into their questioning countenances.

"Is what I have said unto you, beloved of the fellowship,
difficult of comprehension? Behold, I show you a mystery.
How can it be that the Word of God, the Logos, my brothers,
the Creator of all things, omniscient and omnipotent, the Lord
of earth and sun and moon and stars, how could He, why
would He, take upon Himself the body of a man and come
among us, live with us, teach us, and finally, brothers, give
Himself in tortured death to redeem us, to restore us, to save
us utterly and forever, for Himself and to Himself? Why, O
beloved, why?"

Paulus ceased speaking. With the palm of his hand he
wiped the beading perspiration from his cheeks, his broad
high forehead, past the crown of his balding dome. Then he
braced his hand on the tabletop, leaned forward, and his flaming eyes burned into the intent faces looking into his.

"Never can we comprehend this mystery, beloved, until we
comprehend the nature of God, and we can know God only
in knowing His Emanation on earth, Jesus the Christos. But
since God is love, the more we love and the more we transform
love into works, the more Godlike we become and the nearer
we approach to an understanding of the mystery of God's
boundless love as exemplified in His sending His Son into the
world. For we are saved by our faith in the Son and not
through our obedience to the law and our good works. But being saved by faith and filled with love of God and men our
brothers, we are constrained to abound in good works."

Paulus was propounding now the essence of his own faith
born out of the travail of his soul, purged in the fires of hard-

ship and distress and pain, and strengthened to a profound assurance. He leaned toward them as though he would enfold them in the security of his love for them, and his impassioned tones began to soften and his words to flow and sing.

"God, O my brothers, is all and in all, and His Son our Saviour is One with Him, omnipotent and omniscient, and God is love. Without God, without His Son, we are but poor creatures of the earth, lost and undone; without love, we are of no moment, we are nothing. Once, not so long ago, I wrote of this in a letter sent to those of the Way of Corinth. Perhaps as I take leave of you on a further mission for the Lord Jesus, brothers, I can recall it as my valedictory and benediction. I would that you keep it always in your hearts."

Paulus looked toward the ceiling, begrimed with the smoke of many lamps, and closed his eyes. The light glistened in the beads of perspiration on his bald head. He was silent a moment and then calmly, melodiously, he began.

"Though I speak with the tongues of men and of angels, and have not love, I am become as sounding brass, or a tinkling cymbal. And though I have the gift of prophecy, and understand all mysteries, and all knowledge; and though I have all faith, so that I could remove mountains, and have not love, I am nothing. And though I bestow all my goods to feed the poor, and though I give my body to be burned, and have not love, it profiteth me nothing."

The apostle opened his eyes upon his assembled brothers and sisters of the Way. Down the cheeks of several he saw tears rolling unrestrained; some sat staring and entranced; others, their countenances solemn and eyes unblinking, appeared translated to another place and time. He paused a moment, and then continued:

"Love suffereth long, and is kind; love envieth not; love vaunteth not itself, is not puffed up, doth not behave itself unseemly, seeketh not her own, is not easily provoked, thinketh no evil; rejoiceth not in iniquity, but rejoiceth in the truth; beareth all things, believeth all things, hopeth all things, endureth all things. Love never faileth; but whether there be prophecies, they shall fail; whether there be tongues, they shall cease; whether there be knowledge, it shall vanish away.

"For we know in part, and we prophesy in part. But when that which is perfect is come, then that which is in part shall be done away. When I was a child, I spake as a child: but when I became a man, I put away childish things. For now we see through a glass, darkly; but then face to face: now I know in part; but then I shall know even as I am known.

"And now, beloved"—his voice lifted, resonant and triumphant—"abideth faith, hope, and love, these three, but the greatest of these is love."

Paulus sat down, and not a soul stirred. Then Claudia, eyes moist, turned to face Longinus. Tears were overflowing from his eyes; in tears rolling down his cheeks she saw reflected the flickering flame of the lamp on the wall. And in her eyes her husband saw questioning, and hope long unfulfilled. Smiling, he nodded. They slipped from their places and approached the apostle. Looking up, he saw them.

"Praise God! Longinus!" Paulus sprang to meet the tribune, embraced him happily. "Claudia, you have brought him to our Lord Jesus!"

Longinus shook his head. "No, Aemilius Paulus. She has long besought me to come, but now I come of my own accord. A long time I have been trying to escape Him, but since that day on the Hill of the Skull He has pursued me day and night that I too might accept of Him pardon and cleansing and salvation." He glanced toward the radiant Claudia, then turned back to Paulus. "He forgave me, Paulus, even as I was crucifying Him, and never has He ceased to call me to Himself. Now I come humbly to Him, confessing my evildoing and imploring Him to remember me as on that long ago day He remembered that one we crucified on the cross beside His."

So there was great rejoicing, and fervent thanks were offered to Yahweh Most High as Tribune Lucius Cassius Longinus was baptized by the apostle Julius Aemilius Paulus into the fellowship of the Galilean carpenter, Jesus ben Joseph of

Nazareth, the Messiah of Israel, Jesus the Christos, Lord of heaven and earth, the sun, moon, and stars. And among those standing near him as he entered into the Way were Fulvia, wife of one of Rome's most powerful senators; Croesus, a slave at the emperor's palace; his wife Claudia, granddaughter of the god Augustus; and his own slave Marcipor. They were the first four to give to their new brother the right hand of fellowship.

In the ecstasy of their coming together in worship the time had passed swiftly. Soon in many a palatial domus the overseers would be inspecting the apartments of the slaves, and here and there on Esquiline and Viminal Hills and in other regions in which the equestrian families lived, some poor slave returning late would be severely beaten.

So Paulus arose again. "The hour grows late, beloved in our Lord. For many of us even our days in this world may be moving quickly to their ending. For me the remaining days likely are few. It may be that our Lord will Himself come soon. No man knoweth when his hour will strike. But what does it matter to those in the Lord whether we live or die?" He swept with eyes warmed with his love for them the worshipers raptly listening. "Whatever may come, whatever is in store, be you strong in the Lord, and in the power of His might. Put on the whole armor of God, that you may be able to stand against the wiles of the devil. For we wrestle not against flesh and blood, but against principalities, against powers, against the rulers of the darkness of this world, against spiritual wickedness in high places. Take unto you the whole armor of God, that you may be able to stand in the evil day."

When he had exhorted them a short moment longer, he nodded to one of the elders who went into an adjacent small chamber. This man returned carrying a tray with several small loaves of dark bread and a pitcher with a goblet, which he set upon the table before Paulus. The apostle picked up one of the loaves and began to break it into small pieces. As he broke the bread he recalled again that Simon of Capernaum had told him that on the night before He was crucified Jesus

had assembled His twelve apostles in the upper room of Mary
of Cyprus and with them had eaten of the Passover. It would
be His last meal with them, Jesus told the twelve, and He
asked them to come together from time to time henceforth to
partake of bread and wine in memory of Him. The broken
bread, the Master had said, would be the symbol of His crucified body and the wine the symbol of His blood spilled for
the redemption of the world. And this intimate service of commemoration and adoration should be continued until He himself returned to earth.

"For I have delivered of the Lord that which also I delivered
unto you. That the Lord Jesus, the same night in which He
was betrayed, took bread." Paulus lifted before the worshipers
another loaf. "And when He had given thanks, He broke it"
—the apostle broke the loaf—"and said, 'Take, eat; this is
My body, which is broken for you: this do in remembrance
of Me.'"

He lifted the tray with the broken loaves, and quietly, reverently, but with eyes shining and countenances radiant, the
worshipers came to the table and ate solemnly of the bread. As
Longinus and Claudia moved forward with Marcipor and partook of the ceremonial food, Paulus' eyes were aflame, and
though he said no word to them, he felt that his heart might
burst with joy.

When each of the worshipers had eaten of the broken loaves,
the apostle raised high the goblet, which he had filled with
wine from the pitcher.

"After the same manner also He took the cup, when He
had supped, saying, 'This cup is the new testament in My
blood; this do you, as oft as you drink it, in remembrance of
Me. For as often as you eat this bread, and drink this cup, you
do show the Lord's death till He come.'"

Once again they came solemnly but with eyes ablaze to the
table to sip, each one, from the goblet, and when they had returned to their places and dropped to their knees, Paulus raised
his arms above the bowed heads.

"Now unto Him who is able to do abundantly all that we

ask or think, according to the power that worketh in us, unto Him be glory in the fellowship through Jesus the Christos, throughout all ages, world without end. Amen."

With souls aglow they descended the stairway to the ground level, and at the faltering flame beside the doorway they lighted torches to guide their ways through the Subura's twisting alleys and protect them from its perils.

Marcipor, with a torch held high, walked two paces ahead of Longinus and Claudia; Croesus, with another, two paces behind. When the four came to a broader way joining Viminal and Palatine Hills and Croesus did not turn off to return to the Palace, Claudia protested that he might be missed in the counting of slaves and be punished.

"I think not. But if I am. . . ." In the torches' light she saw him shrug. "And it will take only minutes longer to see our new brother and his wife to their domus."

They were nearing the door when Claudia broke the reverie. "Longinus, beloved, my happiness is full; I have prayed so long that this hour would come." But a shadow dulled the radiance. "Tonight, though, I have been thinking, too, of another——"

"Pilate?"

"Yes. I wonder if he is still living, and where. I wonder if he also has found forgiveness and peace in our Lord Jesus. Truly, Longinus, I hope so."

"Poor fellow. I hope so, too, my dearest."

In the atrium a centurion from Castra Praetoria was awaiting their return. He had brought a dispatch that had been sent by Emperor Nero to the commander of the Praetorian Guard. Quickly Longinus read it. He thanked the centurion and dismissed him. When that officer was gone from the atrium, Longinus turned to the staring Claudia. "The commander of one of our legions in Gaul has died," he said. "The emperor has named me to succeed him, and I must be leaving as quickly as arrangements can be made." He saw the shadow clouding her countenance, and smiled wryly. "And you are assigned by Nero to accompany me." He handed her the orders.

"If you must go," she said, "I'm glad that I am going with you. But it's strange that Nero's *sending* me. Heretofore I've always had to request permission to accompany you. Unless" —she was suddenly thoughtful, musing—"yes, that's it. It's Poppaea's doings. She wants me sent away from Rome."

She glanced a moment at the dispatch, and her forehead crinkled in tiny furrows. "The legion's headquarters, it says, are in the vicinity of Vienna Allobrogum. Longinus, wasn't that the place to which Caligula banished Pilate?"

VIENNA
ALLOBROGUM

45

During the first year after their arrival in Gaul, Longinus and Claudia sought to discover the fate that had befallen Pontius Pilate. But despite their inquiries, they were able to learn nothing. Natives in the region of Vienna Allobrogum and veterans of long years of service in the armies of the empire professed never to have heard of the man.

But one day an old centurion whose scarred face gave testimony to his long battling in many lands came to Longinus. "I am Musonius, sir," he introduced himself after he had saluted. "Twenty-seven years I have been a soldier of the emperors, as far back as Tiberius, in posts in numerous provinces of the empire. It has been told to me that you have been inquiring of Pontius Pilate, Tiberius' procurator in——"

"Indeed, centurion, I have. What do you know of him?"

"I was a raw recruit, sir, hardly finished my first training, when Gaius became emperor and banished Pilate. I was one of the soldiers in the maniple that brought him here."

"Then it may be that you know what happened to him, where he is now, if he's living."

Musonius shook his head. "No, tribune. I was sent back to Rome less than a year after I came out. I've never seen Pilate since, or heard a word concerning him. But I would say, sir, if you asked me what I thought, that he has been dead many a year. He was in poor condition then and, sir, that has been"—he paused and his heavily tanned forehead wrinkled in little ridges—"more than twenty-five years, I'd say." He waited for Longinus to ask another question, but when the tribune said nothing, he tapped his forehead with a blunt forefinger. "He was worried, sir, frightened, sometimes out of his mind, I thought. It seemed to me that every time I saw him he was washing his hands. I remember I wondered why."

But there was no dearth of information from Rome. Soldiers coming from the capital as replacements, units of raw recruits being sent out for seasoning in rebellious provinces, sometimes a veteran friend of long years, and even now and then a soldier recognized by Claudia as a brother in the Way, brought reports that grew more alarming as the tribune's assignment in Gaul lengthened. Nero in his profligacy was already rivaling Caligula. Caligula had come to the throne at twenty-five and was dead four years later; his nephew Nero was now twenty-five; by the time he was twenty-nine, he would have achieved a record in infamy outstripping his notorious uncle's.

His physical appearance, Romans coming from the capital further revealed, already had become as repulsive as that of Caligula in his last days. Skinny legs supported perilously a tremendous paunch and slender, unmuscled arms and a leering, fat face; his skin was mottled and splotched with pimples and his yellowish hair curled down upon malevolent weak eyes. Like Caligula, too, the emperor fancied himself not only a capable patron and critic of the arts, but also a genius in performing them. He considered himself a poet, an actor, a musician, and a champion athlete in the various games.

One of his skills he was bent upon employing, so the report came out to Gaul, was that of designing a new Rome, architecturally magnificent, and building it on the sites of countless structures he would pull down. He was determined to erect for himself a tremendous new palace on Palatine Hill. But with that elevation filled with structures already, and with the Circus Maximus at the foot of the slope on the southwest and Forum Romanum on the northwest, in what direction could he expand? Surely he would not pull down the Circus and the Forum. The only other direction expansion might take would be toward the Subura and the other slums across Palatine from Circus Maximus.

But Longinus and Claudia were more concerned with her grandnephew's flaunted utter criminality. Hardly had they established themselves in the new post when they were horrified to learn that her dissolute young kinsman had followed the slaying of his mother with the murder of his first wife, the virtuous young Octavia, daughter of Claudius. Soon after Nero had divorced her and married Poppaea, he had banished Octavia to the barren island of Pandateria off the Campanian coast —to which Augustus had exiled his daughter Julia, Claudia's mother—and now, Claudia was told, he had sent men there to kill her. And these wretches had brought the girl's head to the exultant Poppaea.

Fortunately, Longinus had been too involved in his own affairs to meditate upon Nero's evil conduct and the steadily deteriorating position of the empire. The Gauls were a fractious people, difficult to rule peaceably, and small rebellions were often breaking out, particularly in the mountainous regions of Cisalpine Gaul. Longinus frequently was forced to send heavily armed detachments of legionaries on forays into the lairs of these fiercely hostile factions. Sometimes the soldiers were unable to punish the revolutionaries, however, because they could not discover their mountain hideaways.

One day after such a failure the centurion of a returning maniple was reporting to Longinus. The Romans had marched a long way eastward into the mountains inhabited by the Helvetian tribesmen, he said, and several times had been close on the heels of the insurrectionists. "But always they managed to evade us," the centurion revealed unhappily. "The only person we saw, except for women and children and tottering old men, was a hermit who declared he was a Roman. And I think he was. He looked it, and he spoke our language, though it appeared to us that he hadn't spoken it in many years."

"A Roman? Why was he there? And did he tell you his name?"

The young centurion smiled at the commander's avalanche of questioning.

"He said he was a Roman, sir. And he didn't say what his

name was or why he happened to be there. We found him sitting outside a cave in the side of a steep mountain high above a great lake. He was a strange one, tribune. I believe he went up there to hide. He must have done something of which he has been ashamed a long time, maybe deserted from one of our legions up here years ago. Something has been troubling him greatly." He paused, smiled wryly. "I believe the old fellow was out of his mind, and I'll tell you why, tribune. He was dirty and his clothes were torn and threadbare, and he had a long beard; unkempt and bedraggled. But, sir, his hands—I noticed them particularly. They were clean, and pink like a child's, and crinkled, as if they had been in water a long time. And, tribune, he kept saying something about some Galilean —senseless talk, I took it to be. We tried to bring him back with us, but he refused to come."

46

He was sitting on a stone beside the cave's mouth when they found him.

The centurion, leaving his men two hundred paces below and behind the jutting shoulder of the cliff, guided Longinus and Claudia along the steeply ascending path to the ledge high above the forest-encircled green waters of the lake.

He saw them approaching, they knew, but he made no effort to escape either into the cave or along the other end of the ledge. Instead, he watched them indifferently as the three eased their way past the narrowest place on the ledge where stepping on a loose pebble might plunge them into the water far below.

When he turned toward them, Claudia and Longinus knew of a certainty that at last they had come upon the one for whom they had been searching. And they suspected, what in a moment they would discover, that passing years and a fearful inner turmoil had wrecked beyond earthly repairing the powerful frame and haughty spirit of the long vanished procurator of Judaea and Samaria in the days of Tiberius.

Claudia spoke first. "It has been so long since we have seen one another, Pilate. How are you?"

He arose, stood stiffly erect, and bowed. "You should have come earlier, Claudia. The trial is ended and the verdict rendered; I fear the Galilean is dead." Pilate confronted Longinus, and his countenance, in spite of his bald head pushing out from a narrow rim of completely white hair above a bedraggled and soiled long white beard, was solemn. "Centurion Longinus, is not the Galilean dead? Has the body been removed from the cross?" Before Longinus could determine how to answer, Pilate was speaking again. "You must forgive me, wife, for so ignoring your message to me during the course of the trial; hereafter I shall give any letter you write full consideration. And you likewise, Centurion Longinus, must forgive me for assigning you, out of spite and jealousy, such a disagreeable task." His shoulders had sagged, but he straightened them and held out his bony and bloodless hands. "But, see, I am guiltless. I washed my hands of his blood. Do you see one speck of blood on either hand? The bloody hands are those of Caiaphas and Annas." He rubbed his hands together in the motions of washing them. "See, they are clean. But he follows me, that young Galilean, he tries to look at my hands to see if they have been fouled with his blood. I cannot hide from him. Why, Claudia, will he not cease to follow me and torment me and charge me with killing him? Why, wife, why? Why!"

"He does not follow you, Pilate, to condemn you and torture you. He has followed you, as He has followed Longinus and me, to claim you for Himself, to rescue you from your long suffering, to cleanse your soul and renew your mind and bring it clarity, to save you, O Pilate, to a new life and a new peace and joy."

"She speaks the truth, procurator. He followed me in my every turning, just as He has been following you, until in joy I surrendered to Him and accepted His redemption and salvation."

"But these hands, centurion"—he held them out and examined them carefully and rubbed them together—"they are innocent of his blood, and clean. I washed them of his blood even at his trial. Your hands, centurion, *your* hands, not mine, are guilty; you killed him! Yet he forever follows *me*, wherever I go, even up here away from the haunts of men, he follows me and torments me!"

Pilate was beginning to tremble now as he stood before the mouth of the cave, only a foot or two from the edge of the precipice.

"Come with us, procurator. We have brought clothing for you, and food, and the men will shave your beard. Return with us and live again in a Roman military post."

"Yes, Pilate, return with us and accept of the Lord Jesus out of His abundant grace healing of body and mind and tortured spirit, and one day soon we shall petition the emperor in Rome to lift the sentence of banishment. Then you may return to the capital and live out your days among friends. Trust us, Pilate. Come with us to Vienna Allobrogum——"

"Vienna Allobrogum! By all the gods, wife, what foul trap are you making for me! Does the god Caligula wait at Vienna Allobrogum with his axman to behead me? Did your evil nephew send you and the centurion to catch me in your net and bring me squirming and kicking to him? By great Jupiter, Claudia, I won't go with you. Be gone, all of you! I'd rather remain here and face the Galilean than stand again before your bestial nephew Caligula."

"But, Pilate, Caligula has been dead many years. You need fear him no longer. Let us help you to find peace and"—she stepped forward to take his arm and lead him across the ledge.

"No! Get back!" he shouted. "I'd rather take chances with that Galilean———" He started to back away from her reaching hand———

"O Jesus, Lord! O mercy, Lord Jesus. O, O!" She jammed fists to ears, but they could not shut out for her the horror of Pilate's screaming as his gaunt frame, the long white beard streaming, plummeted downward.

The centurion's soldiers recovered Pilate's body and carried it to Vienna Allobrogum, where it was buried on a grass-covered slope within the garrison's grounds. Claudia and Longinus, standing beside the grave, prayed to the Lord Jesus to receive the troubled soul of Pilate into the peace of the eternal brotherhood.

And before the red earth had settled, a courier arrived with a dispatch from the emperor ordering Tribune Longinus with Claudia his wife to return at once to Rome.

†

ROME

47

Longinus and Claudia were about to set out for the capital when a sudden uprising among the Raetian tribesmen delayed their departure. Longinus instructed the returning courier to report that Claudia and he would start for Rome as soon as the insurrection was put down.

But the resistance was fierce and was being fought out over a large territory, and it was weeks before Roman rule was firmly reestablished and the tribune and his wife could begin their travel southward. The journey was tiring, too, and the summer weather, as they came down Via Flaminia from the Apennines into the sweltering coastal region, was enervating. So after a long day of steady riding they were glad to stop for the night at an inn from which by next midday they could be relaxing in their own house on Viminal Hill.

Hardly had they stepped into the public room when Claudia noticed a man with a long apron serving several coarse-looking men sitting at a table across the room. She nudged Longinus and nodded her head in the waiter's direction. "Gnaeus Arrianus, isn't he?"

"I do believe so." Longinus was about to hail him, but the man had seen them and with a finger across his lips signaled them to remain silent. In a moment he came over to them.

"I can explain," he said in a low voice, "but not here. Are you stopping for the night?" They nodded. "Then in a few minutes I'll come to your chamber."

"But Arrianus working in a place like this!" Longinus shook his head in perplexity when, a few minutes later, they entered the room they had engaged. "A rich senator's son with an apron around his waist serving working people and travelers."

"Perhaps since his entering the Way he has decided that this is the manner in which he can best serve the Lord Jesus."

But Arrianus himself ended their questioning. "I know you both wonder why I am working here," he said, after he had greeted them warmly. "I'm fortunate. The proprietor, once my father's slave, is of our fellowship. I've got food, a bed, clothes of a sort"—he smiled grimly—"and what's better, my life. Many a senator since the fire would be happy to exchange places with me."

"Since the fire?" Longinus was puzzled, Arrianus saw, and so was Claudia.

"Do you mean that you have not heard about the great fire?" Arrianus was incredulous. "Surely you know that in midsummer two-thirds of Rome was destroyed and thousands upon thousands of Rome's residents killed, and that the city now lies in ruins——"

"No! No! Oh, no, Arrianus!" Claudia clutched Longinus' arm; her face was ashen and her frame seemed suddenly to sway and tremble like the trunk of a tree being uprooted by flooding waters. He led her to the short bench against the wall, helped her down upon it. Then he confronted Arrianus again.

"Did my father perish?" His countenance revealed fearful apprehension.

The other man nodded. "Yes. But not in the fire, though it destroyed the domus, Longinus. And likewise my father's home and him with it, and mine"—he caught the tribune's arm—"and yours, Longinus, and"—he put an arm awkwardly about his friend's shoulders—"virtually every mansion on Viminal and Esquiline, all the Palatine palaces, including Nero's new domus Transitoria; in fact, the whole city, except for the structures on Capitoline and in the forums, was destroyed or ruined everywhere east of the Tiber. Rome is utterly devastated. I have nothing—not a possession escaped—but even at that I am more fortunate than most Romans. I have my life—thus far, at any rate."

"But my father, Arrianus, how then did he die? From shock and grief?"

He led the tribune to the bench and pushed him down gently to sit beside Claudia.

"No, Longinus, but he died bravely—as bravely as the proudest Roman who ever fell in battle. He leaves you a great legacy, even though, I suspect, not a denarius in money, or houses or works of art"—he gestured with hands outflung—"or anything. Yet you should be happy that——"

"But how *did* he die, Arrianus?"

"He died"—Arrianus' eyes were bright and his voice firm—"fearlessly and triumphantly as a good soldier of the Lord Jesus under the sword of Nero's executioner."

For a long moment no one broke the strained silence. Longinus sat dry-eyed, staring gray-faced and grim at the wall on the other side of the chamber. Claudia's head sagged heavily in the hollow of his shoulder. After a while, as though he were awakening to reality from a frightful dream, Longinus spoke. "I didn't know that my father was of the Way. For his being in the fellowship I thank the Lord Jesus. He could have left us nothing of more consummate worth than knowing that."

"Yes," Arrianus agreed. "He told Paulus that it was the example of you and Claudia—his children, he called you—that led him to seek His redemption and salvation. I myself heard him say it on the night he was baptized. He declared——"

"Then Paulus returned to Rome from his journeying on which he had planned to start about the time we were leaving for Gaul?" A sudden apprehension seemed to chill him. "Has anything caused him hurt? Where is he now?"

"Tell us, Arrianus." Claudia sat upright and her expression showed her deep concern. "Has any tragedy befallen the apostle?"

Arrianus was hesitant. "He's still alive, or was when last I heard some days ago. But I fear for him. You see, I don't often venture into Rome and what tidings I get come from those of the Way who happen into the tavern. And they are few." He shook his head sadly. "Nero, they say—and that iniquitous

Poppaea supports him in it—has threatened to destroy completely the fellowship of our Lord."

"Poppaea?" Claudia's grieving countenance was questioning. "I wonder, Longinus, if she prevailed on Nero to order us back to Rome in order that she might procure our deaths."

But Longinus offered no opinion. He sat grimly shaking his head. "He will never succeed," he said. "Nero will never uproot the seed of the Lord's good tidings, never! They will spread out from Jerusalem and Antioch and Rome and the fellowships in Asia Minor and Greece until one day, Arrianus —we shall not live to see it, or the next generation or the next —but one day the fellowship will spread into every corner of the earth. Old Paulus has sown the seed, and in many a far land it will sprout and grow and produce harvest. Mark that well, my friend." A moment he was silent. Nor did either of the two speak. "But my father, Arrianus—was he tortured before he was beheaded?"

"No, they tortured only slaves and the Jewish members of the Way." He stared ahead, suddenly silent. Longinus suspected that Arrianus was envisioning scenes that forever would haunt him. "Nero is a monster," he resumed. "Beside him, Claudia, your nephew Caligula was a gamboling lamb. Nero likewise is insane. None but a madman could find enjoyment in what he did: he ordered that oil be poured on living persons after they were nailed to crosses—then they were set ablaze, and while they were burning in horrible agony he went racing in his chariot between the rows of human torches to the screamed plaudits of thousands of our Roman jackals."

"Nero did that?" Longinus' voice trembled. "He is really a monster like that?"

"You have no comprehension of the man's depravity."

"How long, O Lord Jesus, how long, how long?" He dropped his eyes to the floor and braced himself with hands on knees. Then suddenly he looked up again. "These victims of the emperor, Arrianus, how did they fall into his evil clutches? Why did he turn upon the Christians?"

"The story got abroad in Rome that Nero had started the

great fire in order to level the Subura and other regions in which he hoped to raise tremendous new structures. It was reported that he actually started the fire in the area of the Circus Maximus. Others said that he hired arsonists to do it. At any rate, when the talk grew ominous, the story goes, he sought some group on which to place the blame, and the fellowship was chosen. So they began to arrest those of the Way whom the emperor's spies betrayed. That's how your father fell into the trap and——"

"Father refused to cast his pinch of incense upon the emperor's altar?"

"Yes. And many others. So when anyone refused, they knew him to be of the Way of the Lord Jesus. Your father had not been long in the fellowship, but he was firm in his refusal to bend his knee to any man. And so were"—he paused, looked toward Claudia—"your Marcipor and Nero's own slave Croesus, our brothers."

"And they were——"

Arrianus completed Longinus' question. "They were two of the flaming torches that lighted the way for Nero's racing chariot."

"O Yahweh Most High, O Jesus Lord." The words, though, were more meditation. Longinus sat, head bowed; they said nothing, for his thoughts were theirs. After a while he spoke. "Arrianus, where did my father die? Were you there?"

"No, Longinus. But I know the place. It is outside the gate on Via Ostia, past the pyramid tomb of Gaius Cestius about a mile, and then a short way off to the right, where there's a shallow depression; persons standing on the rim could look down upon the revolting crime."

"Did you hear where they put his body away?"

Arrianus shook his head. "That was never told me."

Claudia spoke now; she had seemed in a deep reverie. "Have you heard anything of Tribune Paulus? Has he, too, suffered for our Lord?"

Arrianus shook his head. "Not a word, Claudia. The Aemilian clan's ancient domus was destroyed. Paulus may have been killed in the falling of buildings during the fire. I've heard no report that he was arrested. It is possible that he, like you two, was away in some distant province and, like you, may return one day not even knowing of the great fire."

"May the Lord have willed it. But a moment ago you said that Paulus the apostle was *still* alive when you last heard of him. Are you fearful that something dreadful may befall him? Where was he then?"

"Yes, unless the Lord stays the hand of Nero, he and old Peter the Rock may be dead before this week is finished. To-night, Claudia—I am loath to add to the distress I have so heavily laid upon you already—they lie chained in the lower hole of old Tullianum Prison."

"In Tullianum! May the Lord Jesus protect them!" exclaimed Longinus. "But we did not know that Simon—we called him Simon in Judaea and Galilee, Simon the fisherman of Ca-pernaum—had come to Rome. Has he been laboring here long?"

"Yes, he came, I believe, shortly after you two went out to Gaul on this last duty. And he had accomplished much toward advancing and strengthening the fellowship. The old apostle has given us in Rome strong leadership." He shook his head hopelessly. "But I fear his labors, too, are over."

"Are they under sentence of death?"

"So I have been told, Longinus. And their time on this earth could end any day."

"Longinus"—Claudia's eyes were bright with suddenly found purpose—"we must go to them—this night!"

"But where would we go, my dear? No visitor goes into the hole of Tullianum—ever."

"And were you to present yourselves there, in all prob-ability you would be dropped into that hole—as prisoners," Arrianus observed. "And in Rome, Claudia, where would you stay, where would you lodge this night even? And were you able to visit Paulus and Peter, how could you serve them?"

"We could tell them of our love for them in our Lord Jesus, and of our devotion. And we might bid them to have courage and hold steadfastly to their faith."

"But they know of our love for them," Arrianus said. "And does not their faith, even in the hole of Tullianum, far exceed ours? No, Claudia, nothing can be gained for you and Longinus or for Paulus and Peter the Rock by your attempting to visit them. There is no help for them now, I greatly fear, except the help of our Lord Jesus. Pray to Him to give them courage and strength to endure faithful to the end."

"Yes, Claudia, Arrianus speaks sensibly. We could accomplish nothing tonight by attempting to visit them. Instead, we will lodge here and we shall pray earnestly that the will of the Lord be accomplished in them to the end. Then, early in the morning, we shall set out for Rome."

48

Longinus and Claudia stepped down from their carriage at the gate where Via Flaminia ended. He sent the carriage and the two vehicles with the baggage around the northern sector of the wall to Castra Praetoria. It would be safer to walk down broad Via Lata to Tullianum Prison.

As they strode southward they were appalled and sickened at the desolation. Gnaeus Arrianus had failed to describe it adequately. The great fire had razed Rome as Rome had in years past razed many an enemy stronghold. And although the fire damage appeared to have been small along the park sections on both sides of the Tiber in the northern half of the city, they could see, as they walked past Campius Martius, that the gardens and temples and statues had by now been trampled and torn and chalked with obscenities by the hordes of homeless persons driven there to find shelter in thousands of tents set up as temporary abodes.

But eastward and southward from Via Lata, Rome—it appeared to Longinus and Claudia as they ventured to look toward Viminal Hill—was utterly destroyed. Here and there a domus on Esquiline or Viminal or Quirinal had survived to flaunt its walls above the rubble, but a closer look disclosed that it, too, was ruined and fit only to be torn away.

That they could not see from Via Lata even a trace of what had been their own home or the great domus of Longinus' father, they realized, when they had summoned courage to look in that direction. They discovered even more destruction as they went through what had been the region of expensive shops, just north of Capitoline Hill. And as they came around the foot of the Capitoline and looked southward toward the ancient Palatine, where she had spent her youth in the sprawling marble palace crowning that eminence, Claudia paused momentarily. She could hardly believe what she was clearly seeing. The Palatine was a maze of rubble. Workmen—hundreds, it appeared—were scurrying over the ravaged mound like ants streaming across an ant hill.

The closely massed many-storied insulas of the Subura were gone, too. From blackened and shattered Viminal southward to Aventine Hill and the bending of the Tiber at the city's wall, there was nothing but rubble and empty space. Yet, miraculously, Forum Romanum, Rome's timeless heartbeat, and the Capitoline, studded with government edifices, had escaped destruction and apparently even major damage.

They had reached the place on Via Lata where a narrow way leading from it turned left into Forum Julium. Tribune Longinus, glancing eastward toward Viminal Hill and his shattered mansion, saw the rays of the morning sun playing upon the bronze god of war standing astride the apex of the magnificent Temple of Mars Ultor in Forum Augustum.

Vividly there came the remembrance of the day on which the sunshine coming through a slit in the clouds had transformed in his imagination the outthrust arms of the war god into the pinioned arms of a man of peace impaled high on a cross.

Now Rome lies blackened and shattered, but Mars Ultor still stands astride his temple, Longinus thought to himself. And in the foulest hole in all Rome lie chained, and soon to be slain, the two greatest emissaries on earth of the man of peace.

Longinus shook off the apparition as he had shaken off the other that day long ago. "We must be hurrying," he said to Claudia, wondering why he had said it, for he knew that the guards would not let them into Tullianum to see the prisoners.

But when they reached the prison, he would ask them; he was a tribune in the Roman army and he had certain authority. Or did he? Perhaps at Tullianum he would soon know. So with Claudia he strode down Via Lata toward Tullianum on the side of Capitoline Hill.

They were too late arriving.

As they came even with the prison, Longinus and Claudia saw the two files of soldiers, with two prisoners walking side by side between them, moving slowly down the slope into the flat of Forum Romanum. Immediately they recognized the prisoners, though each had changed in the years since they had last seen each other. Chains about their wrists and ankles impeded their walking, it was true, but age had slowed them also. Saul the rabbi of Tarsus, opinionated, intense, fiery, determined defender of the ancient law of Israel; and Simon the big fisherman of Capernaum, bluff, vacillating, frank, quick of words and action. These two men had now become Paulus the apostle to the Gentile world, intense, man of fire, proponent of the higher law of love, and Peter the Rock, calm now and patient, strong, faithful; two men of hope eternal, of faith unshakable, of love unconquerable.

Two old men, observed Longinus, though no word escaped his lips: one short and bandy-legged and bald, his narrow frame of silver hair rimming the great dome enclosing a brain of immense import, pushing forward on manacled legs that have tramped the roads of many lands to bring freedom to men his brothers and lifting pinioned hands that have held pens to write soaring, brave words of deathless beauty; the other one tall, muscled even now, grizzled, following and leading, and greatly loving. Two old men raising and yet to raise over long ages a world to a young carpenter on a cross.

O loving Jesus Lord, walk with them this day. Sustain them, O Lord; strengthen their courage; embolden them to walk fearlessly these last difficult ways; O God of infinite mercy, dull the edge of their pain.

The procession was passing between the Golden Milestone and the Rostra to enter Vicus Jugarius where it joined Forum Romanum at the western end of Basilica Julia. Already, certain idlers about the Forum were beginning to fall in alongside and behind the two quaternions conducting the condemned men to their executions.

"If we join them, we may be able to signal Paulus without anyone's noticing it," Longinus suggested. "Then he will know that there are still some in Rome who are indeed his brothers to the death."

So he and Claudia pushed ahead and quickly came abreast of the marching quaternions flanking the prisoners, each commanded by a centurion. Longinus recognized none of the soldiers, and none appeared to recognize him or Claudia. They had gone down Vicus Jugarius as far as an intersecting cobbled way that went westward to the river when the procession halted.

"They must be separating here. This will be each one's final farewell to the other."

He had judged rightly. Hardly had the columns paused before the two brothers of the Way fell together in affectionate embrace. Longinus and Claudia, straining to hear what they might say, edged nearer. They missed some of Peter's words.

". . . strong in the faith of our Lord Messiah, O Saul my brother. Many souls from among the Gentiles you have sent ahead, and from your bringing to them the tidings of Jesus our Lord, many others will enter into the Kingdom." He bent down and with his arm shackled to the soldier beside him laid the manacles over those on the shackled wrist of Paulus. "Brother Saul, thus are we bound forever in the bonds that hold us in the eternal fellowship of our Lord Messiah."

"O Simon, my well-loved brother and beloved on earth of our Master, I delight in any bonds that fasten us to our Lord. Be strong, Simon, as you have been a strength to countless of your brothers. Go, brother and father, into His Kingdom awaiting you."

"Go you likewise, O Saul, into the presence of our Lord Jesus, and be not envious of me that I go to Him in the manner that He gave Himself for us." He turned to the centurion. "Soldier, let us be gone."

"Then he is going to the cross. Will you go with Simon or Paulus, Claudia?"

"I could never bear another crucifixion."

"Nor could I. We will follow in the group going with Paulus."

But as the quaternions separated, she watched with tearful eyes the going of old Simon, whom in the long ago in ancient Jerusalem she sometimes had seen in the courts of the Temple, even in the company of a young Galilean of smiling countenance and compelling, melodious words. Nor could she resist inquiring of a rough fellow beside her where the soldiers were taking the taller man and what they were going to do with him.

"They are crossing the river on Sublicius Bridge," he said, "to lead him up to Vatican Hill to crucify him. And I heard it said that he asked the soldiers to crucify him head down. I suppose he thought it would be quicker that way."

Soon the procession was beyond the pyramid tomb of Gaius Cestius on Via Ostia, and a little later it turned off right onto a less frequently traveled road and went across a stony field to stop before a small depression ringed about with stones piled high.

In the bottom of the depression a heavy wooden block had been set. As Paulus walked with the soldiers into the shallow place, those who had followed him from the city ranged themselves around it. The apostle's eyes circled the rim, and Longinus and Claudia, looking with tearful eyes upon him, knew that he had recognized them. But only his radiant, quick smile told them.

Now Paulus stepped to the block. Raising his tired shoulders, he stood erect, turned his face toward the heavens, closed his eyes.

Longinus, watching entranced, saw his lips moving, sought to distinguish his words.

". . . forgive, O Father . . . Stephen . . . brother . . . O Lord Jesus, forgive——"

Paulus opened his eyes. The centurion advanced with a black cloth.

"Must I, centurion?"

"It is the law of Rome."

Paulus smiled grimly, nodded. Quickly the centurion bound his eyes. Then gently he guided the old man's hand to the block. From the quaternion one of the soldiers stepped forward and unsheathed a heavy long sword.

With both hands Paulus was feeling for the block. He bent forward, laid his head on it, stretched out his neck. The sun glistened on the rounded dome of his bald pate.

"I thank Thee, Yahweh Most High; I thank Thee, gracious Lord Jesus; I thank Thee"—the apostle's voice was firm and unafraid, sonorous, triumphant, joyous.

The soldier raised the long sword.

"O Holy Spirit. Lord Jesus, receive my. . . ."

But already, with a muffled sob, Claudia had turned her back to the pit to cling to the solemn-faced tribune.

They were nearing the Ostian Gate before she spoke. "Oh, Longinus, what is there for us now? We have no home, not a sesterce, not even food—only vindictive enemies, hate, tragedy."

He squeezed her arm in his against his side. "We have, on the contrary, everything, my dearest. Tomorrow we'll go to Viminal Hill and see if we should lay plans for starting our new domus. Soon we'll have it. But now, at this moment, we have life, and ourselves, and hope, and love, and surely after today we must always have an enduring faith." Now he grinned wryly, and pinched her cheek. "And as soon as we can get to Castra Praetoria, I'll wager you my mansion on Viminal, we'll have a good dinner and a soft bed." He shrugged. "And I'm in dire need of both."